# Allegheny Front

### A Laurel Kile Novel

*Relax. Read. Repeat.*

ALLEGHENY FRONT
By Laurel Kile
Published by TouchPoint Press
Brookland, AR 72417
www.touchpointpress.com

Copyright © 2021 Laurel Kile
All rights reserved.

ISBN-13: 978-1-952816-45-1

This is a work of fiction. Names, places, characters, and events are fictitious. Any similarities to actual events and persons, living or dead, are purely coincidental. Any trademarks, service marks, product names, or named features are assumed to be the property of their respective owners and are used only for reference. If any of these terms are used, no endorsement is implied. Except for review purposes, the reproduction of this book, in whole or part, electronically or mechanically, constitutes a copyright violation. Address permissions and review inquiries to media@touchpointpress.com.

Editor: Analieze Cervantes
Cover Design: Colbie Myles
Cover images:
Adobe Stock, Couple sitting in front of a mountain looking at the horizon in the holiday by last19;
Old log cabin in the forest.by Creaturart

Connect with the author:
https://laurelkile.com/

@laurelkileauthor   @laurelkileauthor

First Edition

Printed in the United States of America.

To my husband and two amazing daughters, you are my world.

# Chapter 1

### Saturday, June 20, 2015

THE MOMENT THE WHEELS OF THE Cessna touched down, Jeremy threw off his seatbelt and shot to his feet. As he reached for his ruck sack, the jet's brakes engaged, slowing its momentum, but not his. His lanky body shot forward and slammed into the seat facing him.

"Just bloody brilliant," he sulked as he looked around the empty cabin.

A metallic voice came over the speaker. "Sir, please remain seated until the plane comes to a complete stop."

"Yes, ma'am." He sank into the leather seat and drummed his fingers on the armrest. When he boarded the private jet in Heathrow, he'd envisioned it as an escape pod. Now it felt like a holding cell. On the other side of the sealed door lay freedom: bright, green, paparazzi-free liberty. Just when he thought he couldn't stand another second, he heard the uncivilized pfft of the cabin's pressurized seal being broken.

The pilot's voice echoed through the cabin. "Mr. Fulton, you may now exit the craft."

He sprang from his seat like a thoroughbred from the starting gate. "Yes ma'am, thank you." He hefted his bag onto his back and bolted down the small staircase.

He shielded his eyes from the bright afternoon sun and spied a tall woman with gray hair standing at the edge of the runway. Jeremy walked toward her and extended his hand. "You must be Journey. It's nice to meet, y—"

The greeting was cut short as the woman wrapped him in a rib-bruising hug. "Jeremy Fulton, Mr. BBC Star," she gushed. "It is nice to finally put a name with a face."

Jeremy wiggled out of the python-strong embrace. "Nice to meet you too." He rubbed his aching side. "And thank you for the use of your airstrip."

She waved her hand dismissively. "Oh, it was no trouble, dear. I'm glad Phillip's mom asked."

Phil, his agent, was one of the few people he trusted. When Jeremy decided he needed an extended holiday, Phil had taken care of the travel details.

Jeremy motioned to the airstrip. "So, Phil grew up close to here?"

Journey nodded proudly. "Philip's great-great-grandparents bought land right beside my great-grandparents close to two hundred years ago. The farms got passed down through the generations. Both families are very lucky to have been able to keep things afloat."

Jeremy looked around at the antebellum mansion, black rail fences and expertly manicured fields. He thought, *if this is staying afloat, I'd love to see what thriving looks like.*

Journey continued, "I don't watch a lot of TV myself, mostly *PBS* and the news. So, I hope you'll forgive me for not recognizing you."

Jeremy rubbed his freshly shaved scalp. "To be honest, it's refreshing."

"I imagine the life of a celebrity can get claustrophobic."

"It can be a bit much." He tried to sound nonchalant. In fact, claustrophobic was an understatement. When he took his first big role, he knew his life would change. However, nothing could have prepared him for the rubbish that came with fame. The intrusive fans, the lack of privacy, and the parasites who had the gall to call themselves journalists had robbed him of any sense of identity. It was why he desperately needed this escape into anonymity.

Laugh lines creased Journey's mouth as she smiled. "Well, rest assured nobody knows you're here except me and the horses."

He pointed to a chestnut mare grazing in the adjacent field. "You sure they can keep a secret? That lass there looks like she could spread a good bit of gossip."

"That's Fancy. She spreads a lot of stuff, but it's not gossip, if you know what I mean." She laughed at her own joke. "Phillip said you'd be using a fake name while in the States?"

He stroked his newly grown beard. "Aye, I'll be Tim Jones. It's an alias one of my characters used. The show runner came up with it because it sounded so generic. I hope it's a common name in the States, too."

"It's quite common," she reassured him.

"Good to know."

Journey's eyes widened. "Oh, and your car arrived yesterday."

His face lit up like a child on Christmas morning. "It's here?"

Journey laughed at his reaction. "It's a real beauty. Hope you don't mind, but I had a look at it. There's a bunch of camping stuff in the trunk, too."

He smiled. "Phil thought of everything."

Journey looked at her watch. "Well, I hate to cut this short, but I have a new stallion arriving for breeding this evening, and I have to make sure everything is ready. The car is sitting beside the smaller barn at the top of the hill. Keys are on the dash, and the doors are unlocked."

Jeremy kissed the hippy woman on each cheek. "I can't thank you enough."

She got a motherly glint in her eye. "Thank me by taking the next week to relax."

Without another word, he turned on his heel and ran in the barn's direction. When he crested the small knoll, he stopped in his tracks and uttered, "Mother of all things Holy." In the shade of the two-story, black barn sat a candy-apple red, 1967 Shelby Mustang.

He sprinted to the car and made several tight laps, marveling at the epitome of American ingenuity. He ran his fingers along the white racing stripes that extended the length of the pony car. "Hello, pretty lady," he purred.

The inside was as impressive as the outside. The shiny black bucket seats, the three-spoke chrome steering wheel, four on the floor shift; it was as beautiful as the Monet hanging in his study. He lowered himself into the driver's seat and opened the glove box. Inside he found the old-fashioned map he'd requested. The paper felt soft between his fingers, like a twenty Euro note that had been forgotten in a trousers pocket.

He unfolded the map across the steering wheel, closed his eyes, and let his finger fall on a random spot. It landed on a small dot with the word Riverside written next to it. "Brilliant," he whispered.

He put the map and his wallet in the glove box, then pulled a brass pendant from his pocket. The words: *Not All Those Who Wander Are Lost,* were engraved into the metal. He set the pendant on the dashboard and turned the key. The V8 engine sounded like a dragon under the hood. He was ready to wander and sincerely hoped to get lost.

THOUGH IT TOOK A BIT OF GETTING used to driving on the wrong side of the road, Jeremy soon felt like he was an extension of the car's steel and muscle. As the miles passed, he shed the stresses of his day-to-day life like a reptile molting dead skin. The drive was so relaxing he hardly noticed the robotic voice of his GPS declare, "You have reached your destination."

*This is a town?* Jeremy thought as he looked around the narrow valley. Along the road were a post office, a country store, and eight white wooden houses. He checked the Garmin again. His car's avatar was sitting right beside the name Riverside. He raised his eyes and saw a hand-painted sign that read *Riverside Grocery.* He shrugged then made a sharp left turn into the gravel lot. After parking the Mustang between two massive pickup trucks, he grabbed his wallet from the glove box and walked toward the store's sagging wooden deck.

A gray-haired man with leathery skin leaned against the peeling wooden railing. He took a long toke on his cigarette and gave a friendly nod. "Pretty car you got there."

Jeremy looked from the man to the car then back to the man. "Thanks, sir. It's my mate's. He let me borrow it for the week." He was not sure why he lied. The car was his. Phil found it through a private dealer, wired the cash, and had it waiting on him with a trunk full of camping gear. For some odd reason, he felt the need to hide the fact.

The cigarette smoking man's voice rumbled like a diesel engine. "Hope I can find me a friend like that one day."

Jeremy nodded a cordial reply and climbed the stairs. Through the mesh of the screen door, he could see three men sitting in lawn chairs behind the counter.

He pulled the handle, and the door's spring whined, alerting those within that a customer had arrived. The white-haired gentlemen behind the counter rose from his seat. The other two men, a gentleman with wool-like hair spread thinly across his leather-brown scalp and a thin man with a heavily lined face and mischievous blue eyes, stayed seated. All three looked at him with surprise, and then suspicion.

From the men's reactions, Jeremy knew he had to proceed with respect and caution. Trying to buddy up to the men and pretend he was no different from them would be condescending. He was an outsider, a foreigner, and to pretend differently would be insulting. He stepped over the threshold and cleared his throat. "Hello, gentlemen."

For several, uncomfortable seconds nobody spoke. Finally, the man behind the register said, "I'm Kenny. What can I do for you?"

He smiled sincerely. "Hello, Kenny, I'm Tim."

The thin man got an impish grin on his face. "You sound foreign."

Jeremy nodded. "Yes sir, in fact, I am."

Kenny asked, "Whatcha' doing in this neck of the woods?"

"I'm here on holiday."

"Okay?" Kenny said, hinting that he expected more of an explanation.

"Well, I..." He'd stopped at the country store to pick up a few supplies and get advice on a place to camp, but the coolness coming from the man behind the counter made him uncertain. He decided to steer the conversation away from himself. "This is a gorgeous valley." He motioned to the outside. "It's nice to see natural beauty preserved. Places like this are disappearing back home."

Kenny nodded. "Not a prettier place in all the US."

Jeremy smiled. "I'd have to agree with you, there."

The rotund man asked, "Where's back home?"

"Scotland, sir."

Kenny knitted his eyebrows in suspicion. "What brings you to Riverside?"

Jeremy chose his words carefully. "I needed a rest, and I thought the mountains of western Virginia would be a great place to escape for a while."

The thin man leveled him with a steely glare. "This is West Virginia, son, a whole different state."

Jeremy gulped; it was easy to read on the face of the men he'd made a mighty faux pa. "Yes, yes. I mean the beautiful mountains of West Virginia."

"What made you pick here?" the skinny man asked, still eyeing him.

"Would you believe I closed my eyes and picked a random spot on the map?"

Kenny snorted a chuckle. "And you ended up in Riverside?"

Suddenly a gravelly voice boomed behind him. "You say your name is Tim?"

Jeremy swore under his breath. Less than five minutes, and his cover was blown. He turned to see the cigarette smoking man standing in the doorway. He made his voice overly friendly. "Yes, Tim. Why do you ask?"

"Is that short for Timothy?"

Jeremy's dread turned to confusion. He cocked his head to the side. "It is."

A proud smile spread across the man's face. "I've got a grandson named Timothy, born two days ago!" Before anybody could utter another word, the man pulled out his smartphone and began showing pictures of a baby boy wrapped in a hospital-issued, red and blue blanket.

Jeremy felt a lump in his throat. "He's one handsome young man."

With the bragging grandfather gauntlet being thrown, the men seemed to temporarily forget the foreigner's slipups. Each man pulled out his phone and shared pictures and stories of their own grandchildren. Tales about t-ball games, softball practices, and princess tea parties flowed forth.

Jeremy showed genuine interest, and the frosty edge to the men's words began to thaw. Before too long, tales of grandchildren morphed into unadulterated, old-man gossip.

After a round of fountain root beer, Kenny pulled a plastic chair from behind the counter. "Have a seat, son." He motioned for Jeremy to sit. "Sorry about the chilly reception. Not all outsiders are as friendly as yourself. Many city dwellers come to rural West Virginia to get away from the rat race, but they aren't that nice once they get here."

"They treat us like we are some sideshow." The rounder man changed his voice to a high-pitched mocking tone, "Look at the poor hillbillies and their backward ways. Aren't they cute?"

"Better that than thinking they can educate us poor dumb rednecks with their culture," the thin man added. "I'd love to culture them in the hayfield for just one afternoon."

"Believe it or not," Jeremy said, "my grandad was a coal miner in Fife. It's part of the reason I chose this part of the country to get lost in. The landscape is different, but I was hoping the people would be the same." He looked at the faces of the men. "Happy to say I was right."

Jeremy whiled away the entire afternoon with the men. They shared gossip, personal stories, and precious insider secrets, such as the fishing holes where the biggest bass could be found. He knew what a precious gift he had received. They'd awarded him their trust, and it was more valuable than any of the gold statues sitting in his office.

When it was finally time for him to be on his way, Jeremy purchased several bottles of water, a few granola bars, and two sandwiches. He tipped the bill of his baseball cap. "Gentlemen, so long, and thanks for all the fishing advice."

As he headed for the door Kenny called to him, "Tim."

He spun around. "Yes, sir?"

"Might as well leave all of your electronic stuff in your car. There's no signal beyond this part."

"Thanks, Kenny."

"Good luck, son," the smoking man called.

Jeremy nodded in appreciation. "I'll stop by on my way out to tell you how I fared."

Over the whining of the screen door, he heard Kenny laugh. "Of course, that silly Scot is going to stop by on his way home. He's leaving that shiny car in my parking lot."

Before throwing his phone in the trunk, Jeremy checked the radar. Tropical Storm Barry was projected to make landfall within twenty-four hours, and the effects would be felt as far west as Kentucky. "Not going to let that dampen my mood." He laughed at his own pun and repacked his bag so that his rain gear was easily accessible. He patted the Shelby's hood. "See you in a week, pretty lady. Kenny will check on you several times a day, I am sure of it." He checked the door locks one last time and started on his way.

After a short hike, he found the spot the men had told him about. It was just as described. The steep valley walls opened up, creating the perfect camping spot.

With the use of some colorful Scottish swear words, he pitched his single person tent. *Time to try out that fishing advice.* He grabbed his gear and hiked downstream until he found the fishing hole the men had told him about.

He baited his hook and aimed his cast at the green patch of water hidden under the roots of a leaning oak. The lure struck a low-hanging branch and spun several times. He cut the line, got a new hook and new bait. This time, the cast landed a yard from where he stood. Casts three through six landed on the opposite bank, in the tree limbs, two yards from him, and finally somewhere two yards behind him.

Resisting the urge to throw the damn pole in the river, he stomped to his campsite and munched on dry granola. Once his stomach was filled and his temper calmed, he sat where the river met the stones and allowed cool water to flow between his toes. Constellations crept across the night sky, and lightning bugs flitted along the valley. When Jeremy finally lay his head on his pillow that night, he felt a peace he hadn't felt in a very long time.

# Chapter 2

### Sunday, June 21, 2015

KATE WENT THROUGH THE CHECKLIST in her head. Red suitcase? Check. Purse? Check. Phone charger? Tennis shoes? Toothpaste? Check, check, crap! She threw her head back and swore in frustration. "Wouldn't be me if I didn't forget something!" she grumbled as she skulked to the master bathroom.

She flipped on the light and gaped at the disheveled woman looking back from the mirror. Her mousy brown hair was tangled in a frizzy halo, and the makeup she'd been too lazy to remove the night before had smeared, making her look like a tired, frowning clown.

Her shoulders slumped. *This is pathetic, even for me.* She wet a piece of toilet paper and wiped the smeared mascara from under her eyes. Then she threw her hair into a tight ponytail and applied a liberal amount of tinted moisturizer, hoping it would plump out the pillow marks on her cheek.

She studied her reflection. "I guess that's a little better," she said as she riffled through the side cabinet and found a capless tube of toothpaste. She plucked a congealed glob of goop off the opening and threw the tube into her bag.

After two more trips to the bedroom for forgotten items, a quick rummage through the pantry, and a frantic search for her keys, Kate climbed behind the wheel of her little red Chevy. She set her road trip playlist, and by the time John Denver was crooning *Country Roads*, she was merging onto Route Seven with only Riverside, West Virginia on her mind.

When the last guitar strum faded, she hit the 'speak' button on her steering wheel and clearly spoke, "Call Penelope."

After two rings a polished female voice answered. "Hello, Katherine Thorn, how are we today?"

Kate mirrored the tone. "I am well, and yourself, Penelope Kesner?"

The voice of the woman on the other end changed. "Crappy; I swear I work with a bunch of fourteen-year-olds!"

Kate laughed. "Nope, that would be me."

"Yes, but the people you work with act like that because they actually *are* fourteen, not fifty. It's Sunday morning, and I just got a phone call from a millionaire client throwing a complete temper tantrum because he may have to pay income tax for the first time in twenty years. His former CPA always found loopholes, and I clearly don't know how to do my job."

"Sounds like fun."

"Fun as a barrel of entitled, pompous monkeys." Penny exhaled. "I need to decompress. I'm so glad we picked this week to head home."

Kate smiled and repeated the word *home*. When she and Penny became friends at West Virginia University in the mid-nineties, she felt like she had gained the sister she'd always wanted. Later in the semester when they visited Nan, Penny's grandmother, Kate bonded instantly with the kind and spunky matriarch.

Three years later, their bond was strengthened when Kate's father passed away and the Thorn family farm was sold at auction. When the final gavel fell, Nan was at her side. She held Kate's hand and whispered in her ear, "My house will always be your home."

Penny's voice interrupted her thoughts. "Are you on your way yet?"

"Just pulled onto Route Seven, heading west."

"So much for getting an early start."

"It's summer vacation," Kate protested. "Nine a.m. *is* an early start."

"Teachers!" Penny scoffed.

"Accountants," Kate returned the tone. "So, what is the plan for the week?"

"I talked to Nan this morning, and she visited the farmer's market yesterday. She bought strawberries, peaches, and apples. The mulberry tree is full, so she picked a few quarts of those too. She wants to start canning first thing tomorrow morning."

"I am sure she does. I know how proud it makes Nan that her pies and jellies get top dollar at the church auction. We mustn't disappoint the bidders. Plus, I checked the weather. Looks like it will be a perfect time to stay inside canning. It's supposed to be drizzly and yucky."

"Nan will find plenty of things for us to do."

"I don't doubt that."

Penny's voice took on a cautious tone. "So, how did things go last evening?"

Kate gripped the steering wheel so tight her knuckles turned white. "Exactly the way I told you it would."

Penny tread gently. "Are you all right with—"

Kate cut her off, "I'm hitting a dead spot. I'll try to call when I get to Petersburg. Once I hit Seneca, I barely get a signal."

Penny didn't push it. "Sounds good. If something happens and you don't get a chance to call, I'll talk to you at Nan's tonight."

"See you tonight," Kate replied and clicked the end call button.

Penny's question had taken the wind out of her sails. Last night had gone as predicted. The short relationship with Stewart, if it could be called a relationship, had run its course. Kate had taken the initiative to say what they both knew. It ended with an awkward hug and empty promises to keep in touch. She returned to her condo, blended margaritas, and binge-watched X-Files until she fell asleep on the couch.

Kate shook her head, as if the motion could shake off the unhappy thoughts. This wasn't a time to be thinking about Stewart or drudge up the memories of every disastrous relationship she had over the past four years. This weekend was about leaving all of that behind. She was going home; she was going to Nan's house.

WITH EACH HAIRPIN TURN AND majestic overlook, Kate could feel the stresses of her day-to-day life melt away. By the time she saw the peacock blue mailbox with the name Kesner written in gold, she'd forgotten everything she was trying to forget. She made a sharp left turn down a gravel driveway and parked beside a little white farmhouse.

An elegant woman walked onto the covered porch. Though Nan was in her early seventies, she looked a decade younger. Her alabaster skin showed only fine laugh lines. Her once strawberry-blonde hair was now a beautiful golden silver. However, the most enchanting thing about Nan was her radiant smile. It was a smile that said *Welcome home.*

Before Kate could put the car in park, Nan was standing barefoot in the gravel driveway, her arms wide. Kate turned off the car, jumped from the driver's seat, and ran to Nan. The older woman pulled her tight and whispered in her ear, "I'm so glad you are home."

Kate kissed her gently on the cheek. "It's good to be home," she murmured. Then she pulled back and sniffed the air. "Is that... fresh baked bread?"

"Still have your superhuman sense of smell, I see. Hungry?"

As if scripted, Kate's stomach growled. She laughed. "For your bread, anytime."

Kate followed Nan into the kitchen. Even though the gray clouds made the outside look cheery as a mortuary, the white-painted cabinetry, cobalt blue curtains, and blue willow backsplash made the traditional country kitchen look bright and inviting.

On the counter beside the stove sat three loaves of freshly made bread. Before Kate could even ask, Nan cut her a thick slice and was loading it with mulberry jam. "So, catch me up on the exciting life of a Northern Virginia teacher."

They moved to the table. "I don't know how exciting it is, but I definitely have some stories for you."

Nan's tone became cautious. "And how have you been doing, with... well, you know."

Kate smiled reassuringly. "You mean with my bi-polar?"

Nan swallowed and nodded. Even though Nan and Penny had stood beside her in her darkest days, through the mania, the mood swings, the abusive words, and the stay at an inpatient facility, it was still hard for Nan to talk about mental illness.

"Doctor Lee says I am doing great. The magic cocktail of meds is doing its job, and I have been really stable."

"Are you happy?"

"Happy is a relative term." Kate shrugged. "I'm balanced. I'm content. I'm healthy."

"Contentment is sometimes better than happiness." Nan smiled. "The Voice is still at bay?"

Kate nodded. 'The Voice' was the name they had given the inner dialogue of self-doubt and self-loathing that taunted her when she was depressed. "It's still there, sometimes. I just know it for what it is, and I know how to handle it." Kate shrugged. "I've made peace with the fact that anxiety and depression will always be a part of who I am. I just refuse to let them take the driver's seat again."

"You're such a strong woman, Kat bird."

"Well, I surround myself with strong women." Kate winked at her.

Nan blushed at the compliment. "Well, how are things going with Stewart?"

Kate gritted her teeth, she had dreaded admitting to Nan that once again, she'd failed at a relationship. She straightened her spine. "We had dinner last evening, and we both agreed it was best if we were friends, just friends."

Nan nodded. "I didn't see you two having a future anyway."

That was not the reply Kate expected, she cocked her head to the side. "You didn't?"

"I could tell by the way you talked about him, he was just a bookmark, a place holder. There was no spark and no future." Nan tapped the side of her head. "Old women have a sixth sense about these things."

"You are certainly wise." Kate was eager to remove her love life from the spotlight. "Pen says you have all the fruits ready to begin canning right away."

"Got everything ready to go. I was thinking we'd do pie filling in the morning and jam in the afternoon. If it doesn't rain all day, I'd like to make it to the cemetery and plant some annuals on Arlin's grave." Sadness tugged at the corner of her eyes. "I wish you could have met him."

Kate took Nan's hand. Unfortunately, she never had the pleasure of meeting Penny's grandfather. He'd passed away when Penny was still in high school. Like many men in West Virginia from the 1930s through 1970s, Arlin had provided for his family by working in the coal mines. And like many men who worked in the mines, he had paid a hearty price for his livelihood. He was only fifty-six when he succumbed to black lung disease.

Kate asked, "What flowers are you thinking of planting?"

"Well, Arlin loved impatiens, probably because they fit his stubborn personality so well." Nan gave a puckish smile. "But the deer ate them off the ground last year, so this year I'll stick with marigolds and geraniums. Deer don't like the taste." She carried the dirty dishes to the sink and began filling it with hot water. "Kate," she called over her shoulder. "You may want to grab your stuff from your car before the storm hits."

Kate looked out the window. The gray dreary clouds from before had morphed into angry thunderheads. "Good idea," she said. "Looks like it's about ready to let loose."

She ran to her car, and with the ferocity of a game show contestant grabbing groceries from the shelves, pulled bags from her trunk. As she gathered the last bag, the thunderclouds burst and released a tirade of water, soaking her to her underwear. "Just my luck," she grumbled as she did the soggy pants dance back to the porch.

Nan stood waiting, a dry towel in hand. "It's really coming down out there. I hope Penny doesn't get caught in this stuff."

Kate rang water from her shirttail. "She's a West Virginia girl. We know how to drive in anything."

Nan exchanged Kate's sopping towel for a dry one. "You're right. Old women worry; it's what we are good at."

"You are not old, you're… you're…" She searched for the word. "Wizened."

"Wizened?" Nan laughed. "Well, these wizened bones are feeling a bit arthritic. Once you get dried off, would you mind making a few trips to the basement to get the canning stuff?"

Hours flew by as Nan and Kate sorted jars, lids, rings, and gossip. Around five o'clock the muffled sound of a slamming car door pulled them from their tales. Nan shot from her seat and sprinted to the back porch. Before she could reach for the handle, a flash of gray and orange streaked through the door. Nan halted the blur in a strong hug. "I'm so glad you are home. I was getting worried."

Penny returned the embrace. "It's ridiculous out there. I had to pull over twice because I could hardly see three feet in front of me."

Nan smoothed Penny's kissed by fire, red ringlets. "Well, you're safe and sound, that's all that matters."

By now Kate had made it to the back door. She stood, hands-on-hips. "'Bout time you showed up."

Penny brushed droplets of water off the jacket of her gray pants suit. "Some of us have to work on the weekend." Her tone held all the attitude of a know-it-all fifteen-year-old.

"Well, if you knew how to handle your clients' money more expertly, maybe you wouldn't have to." Kate could not keep up the charade. With the last quip, she burst out into laughter and stepped forward to wrap her best friend in a hug.

When Penny pulled back, she stuck her nose in the air and sniffed. "Is that homemade bread?" Without waiting for a reply, she followed her nose to the kitchen. By the time Kate caught up, Penny had grabbed a knife from the butcher block and was cutting herself a generous slice. "How was the rest of your drive?" she asked between mouthfuls.

"Not bad, sounds like yours sucked."

"It's been raining since I hit the state line." Penny pushed the rest of the bread into her mouth then continued, "When I was pulling into the driveway, the radio said we are under a flash flood watch."

Nan rolled her eyes at Penny's lack of manners. "I just hope the brook doesn't wash away all the gravel and leave huge puddles in the driveway. I'll never understand why your grandfather insisted on building the house in this tight little valley instead of on top of the hill where it's flat."

Penny tapped her finger to her chin and looked pensive. "If I remember the story, he did it because you insisted. You said that little brook was the most beautiful place on the farm."

"Pish posh! When did your grandfather tell you this?"

Penny smirked. "You tell me that story every spring when we are planting the annuals in your flowerbed."

Nan smiled mischievously. "I never remember telling a story like that." She turned to Kate. "Do you ever remember a story like that?"

Kate tried to look innocent as she shook her head.

Nan cleared her throat. "Well, before you can tell any more tall tales, why don't we start dinner?"

Half an hour later, Nan placed a smoked venison ham, fresh zucchini, and a chilled Moscato on the table.

As Penny was pouring drinks, Nan asked, "So how are my great-grand babies? More importantly, when are they coming to see me?"

Penny feigned offense. "Are you saying Kate's and my presence is not enough?"

"No, I'm saying that I love them more."

Penny rolled her eyes, then began filling them in on the adventures of her brood. Her husband, Lenard, was a contractor with the federal government. His job frequently required him to travel for weeks at a time, leaving Penny to manage their two high maintenance children. Lauren, their oldest, was the star goalie on her travel hockey team. Their youngest, Spencer, was on the autism spectrum. When Penny wasn't shuttling Lauren to or from practices and games, she was running Spencer to therapy or one of the science clubs where he'd found like-minded peers.

Though it would have overwhelmed an ordinary woman, Penny was Supermom: able to quell Spencer's meltdowns with a single word, plan an entire hockey tournament on a twenty-minute lunch break, and balance the books for gazillionaires in two hours flat. She could do it all. Kate often envisioned a bright gold W embroidered under her business jacket.

However, tonight, something was amiss. Exhaustion tugged at her superhero smile and there was a heaviness in her posture. And Penny wasn't the only one who was acting off. Nan's usual ease was gone. Instead of dinner being the sacred, uninterruptible time it had always been, she left the table several times to turn on the TV or call a neighbor.

Between Penny's palpable exhaustion and Nan's uncharacteristic fidgeting, Kate felt an uneasiness that was foreign to her within these walls.

AFTER THE DINNER DISHES WERE CLEAR and the second bottle of wine was opened, the house phone rang. Nan excused herself and disappeared for several minutes. When she returned, she sat at the table and rested her head in her hands. "The low water bridge is underwater. That hasn't happened in thirty years."

Penny looked anxious. "That was before we moved to this house, wasn't it? What happened then?"

"The farms in the lower part of the valley took on a lot of water. Crops got ruined. Several farmers had to buy feed. With the price for beef down this year, having to buy feed could keep farmers from making much of a profit."

Kate sank back in her chair. She'd grown up on a small farm in a neighboring county and knew how damaging flooded crops could be to a farmer's bottom line. She softly touched Nan's hand. "I know when the flood hit in 1985, Dad got aid from the Department of Agriculture. I'm sure those programs still exist." She chose not to mention how bureaucracy and paperwork had made actually getting the aid an arduous task.

"We'll be fine." Nan put her hand over Kate's. "We're a bunch of tough old buzzards, us Riverside folk." She forced a smile. "Besides, you two didn't come to hear an old woman lament about farming troubles. You came to help an old woman make jams and pie filling." She glanced at her watch. "Speaking of which, we've got a busy day ahead of us. I'm going to head for bed."

Kate said, "Sounds good. I'll lock everything up when I head upstairs."

"Sweetie, you've been living in Northern Virginia for too long. You're in Riverside, we don't lock our doors." Nan stood and kissed each girl on the forehead. "Love you, ladies. See you in the morning."

"Love you," they replied in unison.

Kate heard Nan's door click shut, then took a long sip of wine and looked at Penny. "Do you think Nan's okay?"

"She's fine," Penny said, though it sounded like she was trying to convince herself as well.

Sensing an opening, Kate pressed, "Are you okay?"

Penny made a dismissive motion. "We've seen the water get high before; it'll recede. It always does."

"I wasn't talking about the flooding; I was talking about you. You look... well... worn thin."

Penny gave a soft smile. "I guess I am. Worn thin, I mean."

"Is everything all right? At home? At work?"

"Nah, I'm tired. I need rest. When I'm at home, it's *run here for a meeting, run there for a game, make sure you are on time for therapy, did Lauren do her homework, when's the last time Spencer took a shower*? It wears on you." She exhaled. "Don't get me wrong, I love Lenard, I love my kids, I like my job. It's just..." She took a long sip of wine and laughed. "Do you remember when we were in college, we imagined the job, the husband, the kids, the vacations?"

"Yeah," Kate said sadly, thinking about her own unfulfilled dreams.

"Nobody tells you about the bitching clients, the ten p.m. practices, the sleepovers with stinky, messy, bottomless pit, preteen boys."

Kate opened her mouth to reply but was cut short when Penny's phone buzzed.

The light from Penny's cell phone screen reflected in her eyes as she smiled. "Speaking of the little boogers, Lauren wants to FaceTime." She put her hand on Kate's. "Gotta take this. If not, they'll be in bed soon."

Penny scurried off, leaving Kate alone at the dining room table. She could hear Lauren's excited chatter and Penny's amused replies. Her feelings of concern became tainted with hues of envy.

She carried the dirty dishes to the sink and made her way to the bedroom she had called her own for over a decade. After changing into comfy pajamas, she curled up under a heavy quilt and allowed the pattering of raindrops on the tin roof to lull her to sleep.

## Chapter 3

### Sunday, June 21, 2015

SUNDAY MORNING, SOFT SUNLIGHT COAXED Jeremy from a restful sleep. He unzipped the U-shaped flap of his tent and stepped into the crisp morning air. A low cloud hung between the valley peaks like an ill-fitting lid. It made the open space feel more compact. Not closed off or claustrophobic, but like a sheltered, safe sanctuary. A cool breeze cut through his t-shirt and nipped at his hairless scalp. He ducked back into his tent and returned donning a thin windbreaker and baseball hat.

He washed his face in the cold creek water and weighed his options for the morning. He could try his luck at the super-secret fishing hole the men had shared with him. He could spend the morning relaxing by the water's edge. He could hike back to Kenny's store and while away the day listening to the old men gossip.

"What to do, what to do?" He whispered as he glanced around the valley. Then his eyes settled on a limestone outcropping cutting through the trees, and he made up his mind. He returned to his tent, stuffed a water bottle into each of his jacket pockets, and started toward the stone formation.

After hours of using small saplings and exposed roots to help him climb, he finally reached the base of the limestone crag and ascended to the overlook. His head swiveled to the left and right as his eyes fought to take in every ounce of vibrant beauty. Not only could he see for miles in every direction, he saw miles and miles of unmolested, lush mountain terrain. To the North, the narrow stream zigzagged through steep valley walls. To the South, the creek joined a wider, more powerful river; Kenny's store sat in a narrow strip of land between them.

As he balanced on the limestone peak, he felt a peacefulness, like a greater power ordained for him to be at that exact spot at that very moment in time. He retrieved the sandwich he'd purchased at Kenny's from his pocket and ate breakfast while sitting on top of the world.

After eating, he explored the forest surrounding the outcropping. He found ghost-white flowers hiding under decaying leaves, stood in a fern-filled clearing where ethereal sunbeams shone through the forest canopy like rays directly from Heaven, and explored a small cave. He felt like he had won the golden ticket, except instead of touring a factory of sugar creations, he stood in the center of Mother Nature's glorious creation.

As he watched bees flit back and forth between rhododendron blooms, the smell of ozone mixed with the mustiness of decaying leaves. He looked to the sky. Black thunderheads were bullying away the thin wispy clouds of the morning. A sudden wind barreled through the forest, making pines bend in half.

Jeremy ran back to the small cave he'd discovered that morning. The moment he was safe inside, the dark clouds released a tirade of water. As he stood at the mouth of the cave watching raindrops explode when they met the ground, his stomach began to feel queasy.

After an hour of sitting in the cave, the queasiness turned to painful stomach cramps. He thought maybe getting out of the stale cave and into the open air would help, but the moment he stood upright, the walls of the cave spun, and the floor tilted. He dropped to his knees and vomited. Shards of limestone dug into his knees and palms, but he hardly noticed.

He spent the following hours in a vicious cycle: stumble to the mouth of the cave to retch and heave then crawl back inside to sweat, shiver, and wallow in self-pity. He berated himself. *What kind of git eats a day-old sandwich bought in a dodgy shack of a store?*

His sister had always called him a hapless nitwit. She would say, "You're so helpless, you couldn't wipe your own arse without your agent there to help you."

He laughed wryly. At least he had proven that statement false. Over the past six hours, thanks to the rapid expulsion of poisons from his digestive system, this was a task he had rightfully mastered. Unfortunately, it was mastered using scratchy leaves.

His own self-deprecating voice returned. *Let's hope they weren't poison ivy leaves.*

"Oh, shut up!" he said out loud. There were enough problems without adding the paranoia of an itchy bum.

Hours crept by, and the sky grew darker. Finally, he crawled to the back of the cave, curled into a little ball, and fell into a fitful sleep.

WHEN HE AWOKE MONDAY MORNING, Jeremy's mouth tasted like a garbage heap, his muscles ached, and his abdomen felt like he'd been repeatedly punched. With great effort, he pushed himself into a seated position and pulled his knees to his chest. Something dug into the skin of his thigh. He reached into his front pocket and found the metal pendant his father had given him.

A memory hijacked his thoughts: the sun was fighting to shine through the clouds covering the Scottish November sky. He was wearing blue jeans and a Ramones t-shirt. Across the table, his father, Arthur, sat wearing the traditional black shirt and white color of Presbyterian Clergy.

"Why didn't you change into something more casual, dad?" Jeremy asked.

Arthur rubbed his stomach. "Why, does this color make me look fat?"

Jeremy rolled his eyes. "Okay, fine. Don't change, but will you at least tell me why it was urgent that I come over this afternoon? I have a red-eye tonight to Toronto."

"Well, I was hoping you'd make it to this morning's service."

Jeremy shuffled uncomfortably in his chair. "I was planning on it—"

Arthur held up his hand. "I shouldn't have mentioned it." He cleared his throat. "I asked you to come over because I have something for you. It's nothing big, but…" He pulled a small wooden box from his pocket.

"You don't have to—"

"Just open it," Arthur said.

Though Arthur had a smile on his face, there was an electricity in the air that made Jeremy nervous. He slowly opened the box. On a small satin pillow sat an oblong piece of burnished brass engraved with his favorite quote from *The Fellowship of the Ring*: *Not All Those Who Wander Are Lost*. He furrowed his brow in confusion. "Thanks, Dad?"

Arthur plucked the brass piece from the pillow, held it to his lips, then placed it firmly in Jeremy's hand. He looked intensely into his eyes. "No matter where you wander, your Father is always with you."

*Your Father is always with you.* It was a constant theme in Arthur's sermons, but Jeremy knew that something much deeper hid behind those words today. "I know that, Dad."

Tears brimmed in the older man's eyes. "I pray that you do."

They sat like that, palm on palm, for a long time as Arthur spoke. It was the first time Jeremy had heard his father say the hideous words: cancer, oncologist, prognosis… time.

Memories fast-forwarded. Now he was on a large balcony of a historic church in Glasgow watching mourners stand in line for hours to shuffle past his father's casket and pay their respects. The previous day, his sister had insisted he should not set foot in the sanctuary, fearful that his presence would cause a stampede, or hysteria, or some other ridiculous byproduct of celebrity. "Dad's funeral is not to become some fan panel," she had asserted.

Though he resented her, to save others grief, he had let her have her way. Later, in a private service, those who were allowed to be on the floor with the casket relayed the beautiful sentiments he could not hear firsthand.

A pain in his palm snapped him back to the present. He opened his fingers and saw white lines where the metal had dug into his flesh. He thought he'd be too dehydrated for tears, but when he brought his hands to his face, his cheeks were wet. *This is not how life is supposed to be! I did everything I was supposed to do. I stayed humble; I didn't lavish in excess; I didn't get into drugs, go to rehab, father illegitimate children. I did everything right!*

The protective barrier of anger evaporated, and despair covered him like a shroud. He was sick and afraid, but it wasn't just the food poisoning or isolation of the woods that made him feel so hopeless. It was the thought of who would, or more aptly would not, be there to welcome him home once he got off the mountain. His mum and dad were gone. He and his sister could hardly stand the sight of one another. His ex-wife had eloquently expressed her desire to never be in his presence again. Millions adored him, but he could not name one person who truly loved him.

Despair pierced him at his core, and from the wound escaped the hurt and pain he'd buried for years. Guttural wails ripped from his throat as he held his knees to his chest and sobbed. Then a seductive thought came to his mind. *What if this is it? What if I never get up?* He sat up straight and wiped the tears from his face. For the first time in a very long time, he felt in control of his destiny. His voice was steady and peaceful as he announced to the emptiness of the cave, "This is how it ends; it ends on my terms!"

Then a whisper sounded in his ears. It was so soft, it could have been mistaken for the wind, but the wind could not have spoken in his father's voice. It whispered only three words, "Get up, son!"

Jeremy looked around, frantically searching for the source of the voice, but the cave was empty. Sure that dehydration and exhaustion had muddled his brain, he rested his forehead on his knees and berated himself for his overactive imagination.

Then Arthur's voice sounded again, this time louder and sterner. "Get up, son!"

Jeremy looked to his left and to his right. He was alone, yet somebody had spoken, spoken to him in the one voice he so desperately longed to hear. He repeated his father's words. "Get up, son."

His muscles protested, his head pounded, and the ground tilted under his feet, but he refused to fail. He took a shaky step, then another, then another, until he reached the mouth of the cave.

When he stepped onto the ledge, his knees buckled, but not from weakness. The peaceful valley he'd explored the day before, was gone. While he'd battled food poisoning, Mother Nature had waged a war of her own. The storm had unleashed torrents of rain which poured down the steep mountainsides. The banks of the little stream could only handle so much. Eventually, the creek pushed back, forcing the runoff up the steep slopes. Now, there was nothing peaceful or tranquil about the angry, mud-stained cauldron that churned below.

Jeremy didn't know how long he watched the waters devour the valley, but suddenly he heard his father's voice a third time. "Go, son!"

He took one last look at the flooded valley below, then turned his gaze to the crest of the mountain. It was so far away, but it was the only logical direction. He took a deep breath then launched himself on the seemingly impossible trek. As he took one ragged step after another, his muscles burned, and his head swam, but the memory of his father's voice forced him to keep moving.

He'd made it halfway to the top of the mountain when his will gave out. He leaned against a scarred oak tree and looked bitterly toward the heavens. And that is when he saw it: smoke. His mind was sluggish, but he knew with all the rain, there was no way a forest fire could be burning. The only way for smoke to be in the air was if people were close by.

Adrenaline rushed through his veins, giving him the strength to move forward. After an hour of brutal climbing, he crested the summit. Below sat a small village. Thirteen identical log cabins circled a large brown building, like spindles from the axle of a wagon wheel. Wispy gray smoke rolled from one of the cabin's chimneys. If he'd had the energy, he would've jumped for joy. Instead, he smiled brightly and took a step toward his salvation.

Suddenly, the mud under his boot shifted, throwing him completely off-kilter. He flailed his arms in a desperate effort to regain balance, but dehydration and exhaustion made his body slow and clumsy. He hit the ground with a loud smack and groaned, "Nothing can be easy, can it?"

He pushed himself into a seated position, which was the fatal mistake. The mud under his body convulsed. He was thrust forward and downward, like a water park thrill ride. The momentum turned his body one hundred and eighty degrees and sent his feet flying over his head. There was a sickening snap, and excruciating pain shot from his right arm. Stars filled his vision, then everything faded to black.

Finally, his body was still. He felt nothing, no pain, no sensation, nothing at all. He wondered, *is this what it feels like to die?* There was no bright light. His mum and dad weren't there waiting to welcome him. Tears filled his eyes as he slipped into despair.

Then the voice of an angel said the most peculiar thing: "Holy shit!"

## Chapter 4

MONDAY MORNING, KATE WAS YANKED from her deep sleep. Now, instead of rhythmic raindrops pattering on the tin roof, angry bullets of precipitation battered the metal. She looked at the digital clock beside the bed and groaned, *6:02 a.m. Too freaking early*! She put a pillow over her head to block the angry sound of water against metal, but the pounding still vibrated in her ears. She burrowed under the quilts but was quickly roused by a knock on the door.

"Kate, Penny, I need you girls to get up." Nan called from the hallway. There was an edge to her voice that Kate had never heard before. She rushed to the door and threw it open.

Penny appeared in the doorway of her room. "Nan, what's wrong?"

Nan held up her hand. "There isn't time for chit chat. The flood watch has been upgraded to a flood warning. Part of the valley is already flooding. Looking at the radar, it doesn't look good for Riverside." Her voice broke on the last word.

Penny asked, "What does that mean?"

Nan swallowed hard. "The residents of Riverside need to head for higher ground. Sam Carr and a couple of farmers with trucks are taking people to Slate, that old lumber camp a few miles above here. It's almost finished being renovated into a resort, so it's livable. We'll wait out the storm there. We have about twenty minutes before Sam returns. We need to pack non-perishable foods, bottles of water, and cooking supplies. It may be a few days, so take several changes of clothes. Bridges between here and the mountain are almost flooded, so move quickly."

BY EIGHT O-CLOCK, KATE, NAN, AND Penny were standing in the nearly finished Slate Wilderness Resort near the top of Mongold Mountain. The state division of tourism had almost finished transforming the century-old logging camp into a new-wave wilderness resort. Luckily, renovations on the cookie-cutter log cabins had just been completed. Each villa had electricity, running water, a small kitchenette, and either one large or two smaller bedrooms. Emergency generators were available in case the camp lost electricity.

A large brown building sat in the middle of the circle of cabins. When Slate had been a functioning lumber camp in the early 1900s, it was where the foreman lived. Now the cabin was a conference area.

Though the resort had creature comforts, the lack of technology, TV, Wi-Fi and the absence of any cell phone signal was what designated Slate as a "wilderness" resort. The state had invested large sums of money transforming the camp into the epitome of the newest vacationing fad: getting back to nature without actually interacting with nature.

When the last evacuee from Riverside had safely arrived, everybody met for a quick meeting in the Foreman's cabin. Residents sat around the perimeter of the room in folding chairs, while Sam Carr, the neighbor who had given them a ride to Slate, stood in the middle of the circle.

Sam cleared his throat, and when the room quieted, he shared what little information he had: A storm cell had stalled over the valley and dumped six inches of rain in twelve hours. The bridge at the base of the mountain was under water, and as tributaries dumbed into the Greenbrier, the river would continue to rise.

Penny shot to her feet, "So everything is flooded, and we are stuck up here? What if there's an emergency?"

Nan put her hand on Penny's shoulder. "Chris brought his CB radio with him, so if there is an absolute emergency, we can get in touch with the State Police."

Penny looked Sam up and down, "But you have no idea how long we will be stuck here." Her tone was frantic.

Sam shook his head. "Right now, we're not a priority, and we need to be thankful that we are not a priority."

A panicked mummer took hold of the room. Sam raised his voice. "Listen, I know we are all scared, but we will get through this together. That's what we do in West Virginia! We are strong. We take care of each other, and now won't be the exception. And let's remember the most important thing." He paused for dramatic effect. "We're safe, dry, and out of harm's way. That's what matters. I'll let you know the details as we find them. If you have any concerns, I'll be in cabin twelve with Sy. I think we could all stand a bit of rest. If you need help getting to your cabin Chris, CJ, or I can help."

Before Sam could escape, a man with gray hair and a scraggly beard stood. "Do you think you could find some firewood? That electric heat just doesn't warm the room, and it's barely seventy degrees today. My arthritis just cannot handle the cold."

"Sure, I'll have one of the younger members of camp get on that."

Kate looked around the room and realized that other than Penny, she was the youngest member of the camp.

AFTER KATE FOUND DRY WOOD AND started a fire in Sy's fireplace, she checked to see if any of the less mobile residents needed anything. What they all needed was the one thing she couldn't provide: a guarantee it would be all right. She did her best to listen and comfort, but in the end, she felt woefully inadequate.

After visiting the last cabin, she was emotionally spent, and her stomach growled like a disgruntled bear. She looked at her watch; it was after four. The only thing she'd had all day was a cup of black coffee. She grabbed a Kashi bar from her purse and snuck outside the circle of cabins.

When the electric company strung the lines to bring power to Slate, they had cut a right-of-way through the woods. Though Kate detested seeing the mark it had left on the beautiful forest, it provided easy access to the top of the ridge. On the other side of the mountain sat Snowbird Rock, a beautiful limestone formation where she and Penny would go hiking when they were in college.

A movement at the top of the clearing caught her eye. Something large was limping along the horizon. It didn't look like a deer or a bear. It looked like a man. She wondered, *why would anybody be hiking in the woods during a flood?*

She decided to make her way to the top of the mountain and find out but was stopped dead in her tracks. Terror replaced curiosity as she watched the man's footing slip and his arms flail. His body hit the ground, hard. When he tried to push himself into a seated position, it was too much for the waterlogged earth. The mud under his body shifted, tossing him down the side of the mountain. He tumbled end over end, like a rag doll in a clothes dryer. Finally, his body came to a halt two hundred yards from her.

Kate swallowed the vomit rising in her throat and approached the corpse. She was surprised to see all his limbs were still attached; however, one arm was bent at a very unnatural angle. Blood was soaking through the leg of his shorts, and blood flowed from a huge gash on his forehead.

She studied the man's face, then jumped back in shock. She knew that face! Even under all the cuts, bruises, blood and dirt, she'd recognize it anywhere. She saw that face in her dreams, on her television, and in all her favorite movies. Jeremy Fulton, her celebrity crush, was lying dead at her feet.

She exhaled sharply. "Holy shit!"

## Chapter 5

KATE SQUEEZED HER EYES SHUT. "This is a dream." She scolded herself, "It's just a dream, dreamt in the head of a silly girl. It's a nightmare, nothing more. When I open my eyes, I'll wake up under a heavy quilt at Nan's house. The flood, the evacuation, the corpse at my feet, when I open my eyes they will fade away."

She didn't realize she'd said the words out loud until she bit the side of her cheek and tasted blood. She opened her eyes then squeezed them shut again. The hellish vision was real. She really was standing on the side of a mountain with a dead man at her feet.

Her skin broke out in a prickling sweat and the trees of the forest began to spin. Kate dropped to her knees and forced herself to take several deep, steadying breaths. She opened her eyes and looked at the dead man's face.

Blood streamed from a gash on his forehead, and a deep bruise was forming below his left eye. The bruises and swelling made it harder to recognize the actor, but Kate knew without a doubt this was the corpse of Jeremy Fulton.

She cursed under her breath and searched her mind on how to proceed. On TV, someone covered the body with a sheet or towel, but she had neither. As she scanned the area for anything she could use as a makeshift death shroud, a movement at the man's abdomen caught her eye.

She leaned closer. The man's chest rose and fell in a shallow, yet steady rhythm. She gently lay her head upon his sternum. A weak ta-dum, ta-dum sounded in her ear.

She touched his cheek. "It's all right. I'm right here," she whispered. "I'm going to call for help, but I won't leave you."

Kate stood upright. The cabins of Slate were more than two hundred yards away. She mustered all of her breath and screamed, "HEY! CAN YOU HEAR ME? I NEED HELP!" She held her breath and prayed for a reply, but none came. She yelled again, "CAN ANYBODY HEAR ME? IT'S KATE, I NEED YOUR HELP!"

She listened for a moment then knelt by Jeremy's side. "Okay sweetie, it's just me," she said softly. "You're going to be fine, but I need you to listen to me carefully. I need to look at your injuries."

Kate examined the gash on his forehead. Blood gushed from the wound and pooled on the ground by his temple. She remembered in the spring when her niece fell off the swing set and hit her head on a rock. The amount of blood terrified Kate, but her brother reassured her head wounds usually look deceptively gruesome. It was true then; she hoped it was true now.

Next, Kate shifted her attention to the man's bleeding leg. When she lifted the hem of his shorts, she saw an angry gash dividing the flesh. The sight of fat and muscle beneath the skin made her stomach turn. She swallowed back the bile then untied the flannel from around her waist and applied pressure to the wound.

After what seemed like an eternity, Kate heard footsteps behind her. She turned, and a flood of relief washed over her. "Penny, thank God you're here!"

Penny put her hands on her knees and took deep, gasping breaths. "I heard you screaming, what's going on?" Her eyes moved to the body on the ground. "Oh my God is he... is he alive?"

"Yes, but he's hurt. He needs help."

"What happened?"

"He fell down the side of the mountain."

Penny knelt beside her. "What do we do?"

"I'll stay here and keep talking to him. You go back to camp and get Doc."

"That's a good idea, you've always been good under—"

"Penny!" Kate used her teacher voice. "Go get her, now!"

"Sorry, going now." Penny got to her feet and ran toward camp.

Kate turned her attention back to the injured man. She whispered in his ear, "I know you're scared, but I won't leave your side. You're going to be just fine, I promise."

His eyelids fluttered, and he opened his eyes. Kate wracked her mind for something to say, but before she could formulate any words, his eyes closed, and his breathing became labored.

"Hey!" she screamed as she moved so that her face was an inch from his. "Stay with me!" She wiped the blood from his brow. "Look at me. Make those big, blue, dreamy eyes focus on me, okay sweetie? Help is on the way, but you have to stay with me." Panic flooded her voice. "Look at my eyes, look at my face! Hell, if you are like most men, look at my boobs! I'll get naked and dance the mambo if you like. Whatever you want to look at, look at it, just stay with me."

Forever seemed to pass, but eventually, Kate heard the sloshing of boots. She turned and saw four men marching toward her. First in the line was Sam, then Chris Billings, and Mike Davis. Bringing up the rear was CJ McDonald, who held a backboard above his head. CJ was a volunteer EMT and luckily had the foresight to drive the ambulance to Slate during the evacuation.

Following the men was Dr. Iris Kile, the general practitioner who lived in Riverside. Once the patient was in sight, she sprinted ahead of the men. "What happened?" she said as she knelt beside Kate.

Kate fumbled over her words, "I had to get out of camp. I took a walk and saw him at the top of the ridge. He fell like a rag doll, end over end."

Doc moved the chest piece over the man's torso. She said patiently, "Take a deep breath and start over."

Kate took several deep breaths then described the events of the last forty-five minutes, beginning with her decision to take a walk and ending with the rescuers arriving. By the time she finished, the men had caught up to Doc. Kate stood back while they strapped Jeremy onto the backboard and secured his head. When he was stabilized, Doc removed Kate's shirt from the wound on his thigh and made a face of disgust. "That is ugly. Lots of blood, lots of stitches."

Kate asked in a shaky voice, "Will he bleed to death?"

"Just a flesh wound; no major veins or arteries seem to be hit, but he's losing blood." She called over her shoulder, "Chris, hand me that vinyl strap right inside my bag."

With agile fingers, Doc tied a tourniquet around Jeremy's upper thigh. Then she leaned close to his ear and spoke. "My name is Doctor Iris Kile. You've been in an accident, but your breathing and heart rate are both strong." She gave the good news first. "However, your arm is badly broken, and you've quite a nasty gash on both your head and leg. We'll take you back to our camp, and I can get a better look at you there. You're in good hands."

## Chapter 6

KATE WALKED BESIDE THE BACKBOARD as the men carried Jeremy toward camp. In her peripheral vision, she saw CJ ask Doc, "What are your thoughts?"

"His heart rate is steady, strong pulse in all of his limbs, and his abdomen feels normal."

"But what are *your* thoughts?"

She sighed in frustration. "No way to know more without imaging."

"And I left my spare CT scanner back at the house."

Doc shot him a reproachful glance.

He was serious again. "There's no way to get him to a hospital. Chris told me on the hike up here that the bridge at the base of the mountain is under water."

She pinched the bridge of her nose. "What about Pegasus? Could Chris radio the state police and order an air evacuation?"

CJ shook his head. "Even if there is a helicopter available, there is no place to land it. They would never risk it."

"So, we are all he's got."

CJ's voice was sincere. "Then he's got a lot."

When they finally broke through the circle of cabins, Doc barked like a general, "Take him to the Foreman's Cabin."

Kate stopped short. "No! Don't take him there."

Doc wheeled around. "Why not? The electricity is on, and there's running water."

Kate stood her ground. "The Foreman's cabin is where everyone gathers. Every nosy Nelly will be chewing at the bit to get a look at him if we take him there."

Doc pinched the bridge of her nose. "You're right. He will be a spectacle in the Foreman's Cabin, but where else can we take him?"

"My cabin," Kate said matter-of-factly. "It's the cabin closest to us. That way we won't be parading him through the center of the circle and advertise his arrival."

Doc nodded. "Cabin one it is."

At Doc's direction, the men carried the patient to cabin number one and lay him on the dining room table. She began taking vitals and checking reflexes, stopping periodically to scribble notes on her clipboard. When the exam was finished, she leaned close to Jeremy's ear and said, "Sir, I am Doctor Iris Kile. We brought you back to our camp, where I can better treat your injuries. Can you speak?"

Jeremy's lips moved, but no sound came from his mouth.

Doc put her hand on his uninjured arm. "Can you nod and let me know you can hear me?"

His head moved in a slight up and down motion.

"Good, I need to ask you a few medical questions." She grabbed her clipboard again. "Are you allergic to opioids, like morphine?"

His head moved slightly from side to side.

"Have you ever had an addiction to any opioids like oxycodone or heroin?"

He slowly shook his head.

"Are you allergic to any antibiotics, like penicillin?"

He shook his head.

"Are you allergic to any medicines, food, anything?"

He shook his head.

Doc turned to CJ. "Check his neck and wrists to see if we missed any medic alert jewelry, then start an I.V. and push fluids. With those open wounds, I'll give a few rounds of antibiotics with the pain meds. If I don't get morphine in him before I set his arm, it will not be pretty."

CJ inserted the I.V., and Doc grabbed a clear vial of liquid and a syringe from her bag. She pushed the liquid into the I.V., and the man's body went limp.

Kate inhaled sharply and reached for his hand, but Doc caught her wrist. "I had to knock him out to set his arm."

Kate blinked back the tears she didn't realize had rushed to her eyes. "How do you have an I.V. and morphine with you?"

Doc bristled. "The I.V. is from the ambulance. When we evacuated, I grabbed some essential medical supplies from the clinic. I didn't know what I'd face once we got here."

Kate laughed nervously. "You must have been a Girl Scout; always be prepared."

"Actually 4-H," Doc answered curtly. "Now, if you'd give me a bit of room?"

Kate retreated to the corner and watched the experts set bones and stitch wounds.

When Doc finished, she wiped her brow. "It's the best I can do."

Sam put a reassuring hand on her shoulder. "You did great, Iris. Even if he needs surgery later, thanks to you, he'll be around to have it."

She gave an appreciative nod, and for a moment, everybody was silent.

Then CJ said, "Should we leave him here, or should we move him?"

Doc looked at the table and studied the setup. "This table is high, and it doesn't have protective rails."

Mike spoke up, "We don't have any open beds. I don't know where we can put him."

Sam said, "You could give him my room."

"Where would you sleep?" Mike asked. "Besides, aren't you rooming with Sy? I'm not sure he can take care of himself, much less an injured man."

CJ said, "There is a small couch in cabin thirteen."

"He's too tall," Doc said. "And besides, do you really think leaving him to the mercies of Hazel Phelps is a good idea?"

Before anybody else could offer suggestions, Kate blurted, "Put him in my bed."

Sam and Mike looked at her like she had sprouted a second head.

"No, seriously!" Kate looked at Doc. "It's a king-size bed. I can push it up against the wall. That gives him a lot of room, and we can put a barrier to keep him from falling from the other side. Plus, he shouldn't be jostled about, and my bed's less than ten feet from here."

Sam asked, "Where will you and Penny stay?"

"Nan has a king bed, and she's bunking by herself. Penny can sleep with her." She locked eyes with Sam. "I promised him I wouldn't leave his side, and I won't. I'll sleep on the floor tonight. We can rethink sleeping arrangements tomorrow."

Doc nodded. "Kate has the best plan. I don't want to move him any farther than necessary." She turned to look at the men. "But before we move him to bed, we need to take care of his clothes. He's covered in mud, and maybe vomit and stool. We'll get his soiled clothes off and get him cleaned up as best we can. If he wakes up a bit, we may be able to get clean clothes on him." She turned back to Kate. "Probably best if you step out of the room while I undress him."

Kate felt red creep up her neck. "Um, yeah, sounds good, I'll get out of your way." She backed out of the room and onto the wooden porch. Before the door closed, she took one last look at the unconscious man.

Then a thought struck her so suddenly it made her stumble. *Jeremy Fulton is laying on my kitchen table... naked.*

## Chapter 7

KATE RIGHTED HER CENTER OF GRAVITY, but the thought still bounced around in her head. *Jeremy Fulton is naked on my kitchen table!* She sprinted to Penny's cabin and pounded on the door. She knocked until her knuckles stung, but nobody answered. Frustrated, she headed toward the Foreman's cabin.

Before Kate made it to the entrance, she could hear voices inside buzzing like an angry beehive. She took a deep breath and reached for the door, but before her fingers wrapped around the brass knob, the door burst open. Planted in front of her was a seventy-year-old woman with bubble gum pink lipstick and a purple velour tracksuit.

"Kate!" Hazel's pink acrylic nails wrapped around her wrist. "We were just talking about you!"

She yanked Kate into the room, and with acute hive precision, the residents surrounded her. Questions flew from every direction: "What's his name?" "Why's he in your cabin?" "How long did you have to do CPR?" "Did you see the bear that attacked him?"

Though she was tempted to turn and run, Kate knew it would be futile. Little old ladies could be agile when in pursuit of hot gossip, and the gossip she possessed was better than any liniment on the market. So, she stood rooted in her spot and did her best to remain patient as she answered questions about the mysterious stranger: "Yes, I saw him fall." "No, there wasn't a bear." "Yes, he was breathing." "No, his brains weren't oozing out of his ears."

She answered questions and dispelled rumors until her throat was dry. Finally, after every resident felt like they had their appropriately allotted time for cross-examination, people began to trickle back to their cabins. By nine o'clock Kate found herself in an empty room.

She turned off the lights and walked onto the front porch. The sun was setting behind the mountains. Magenta streaks ran across the sky, reminding Kate of a phrase her mom used to say. *Red in the morning, sailors take warning. Red at night, sailor's delight.* Her shoulders slumped as the weight of the day bore down upon her. There was no delight this night, be it from sailors, farmers, or teachers.

A voice broke through her thoughts. "How's it going?"

Kate spun around. Penny was walking toward her, a mason jar of clear liquid in her hand.

"Don't scare me like that!" Kate reprimanded.

"But you're so cute when you're startled." Penny smiled. "So, really, how's it going?"

Kate plopped down on the bottom porch step. "It's going."

Penny held out the mason jar. "Want some?"

"What is it?"

"Mr. Coots brought his peach moonshine. With the rush, he only brought the essentials. Apple and mulberry got left behind."

Kate grabbed the jar, took a gigantic swig, and immediately began coughing. "That used to be smoother when we were in college."

"Not sure if it's that, or if our palate has gotten soft." Penny mused. "To be twenty-one again."

Kate looked at her intently and saw the deep worry lines creasing her friend's forehead. She asked gently, "Have you been able to get hold of Lenard or the kids?"

Penny shook her head. "He's in Nicaragua until Sunday, so I wouldn't have heard from him anyway. We have no cell signal here and no Wi-Fi, so I can't reach the kids either."

Kate tried to sound reassuring, "Lenard's mom is with the kids. I'm sure they are okay."

Penny sat beside Kate and covered her face with her hands. "I know they are. I just wish I could talk to them. I don't know if the flooding has made the news, but if it has, I'm sure Spencer is a mess. Lauren too, but Spencer especially." Penny wiped tears from her cheeks. "You know how he is when things don't go like planned."

Kate did know. As a teacher she had intimate experience with how kids on the autism spectrum handled anxiety. She scooted closer to Penny and put an arm around her shoulder. "I bet the media hasn't even mentioned it. Nobody cares about what happens in the sticks of West Virginia. I'm guessing that your kids think we're sitting at Nan's watching Hallmark movies and ignoring their texts because we're lazy."

Penny tried to smile. "I talked to Chris. He said the next time he talks to the State Police on the CB he'll see if he can get word to my mother-in-law to let her know we're safe."

"Well, that's good, but I bet you haven't even considered the worst of your problems."

Penny moaned, "Oh no, what?"

"Your kids are spending extended time with your mother-in-law! You'll have to do so much work to deprogram them when you get home." Kate pretended to be pensive. "Do you think Tammie let them have two scoops of ice cream for breakfast this morning, or do you think she was a stickler and restricted them to one?"

Penny forced a laugh. "I'm much more worried about the crap that I'll have to find a place for in my house."

"Speaking of houses, sorry I volunteered you out of our cabin. I figured you wouldn't mind sharing a king-size bed with Nan."

Penny took another sip. "Nah, it's not a big deal, but when Sam talked to her about it, she was kinda weird."

"Everything about this entire ordeal is weird."

"That's the understatement of the year. I don't understand why when Chris talks to the state police, he'll only share what he finds out with Sam and Nan. It makes me wonder if they're hiding something."

"I don't think that's it. Maybe they want to keep the rumor mill at a minimum. The last thing we need is more anxiety, especially with so many elderly and fragile residents. Doc's good, but I don't think she could handle a full cardiac arrest."

"Maybe, but the secrecy doesn't sit well with me."

Kate didn't know how to respond, so she used one of her best teacher strategies: diversion. "I didn't know Mike Billings moved back to town, when did that happen?"

Penny transferred seamlessly. "About a year ago, when Mike Sr. passed away, he came back to take over the farm."

"I'm sure his mom is happy to have him home. Looks like he found a wife too. She… um… doesn't sound like she is from this area."

"You are out of the loop, aren't you? It was quite a scandal." Penny leaned closer. "Mike went onto that farmers.com dating site and this girl, Elle replied. They talked for a while and really seemed to like each other. Well, when he traveled to 'rural' New York to meet her in person, he found out she wasn't a farm girl. She didn't even live in the country. She was from the Bronx."

"You're kidding me!"

Penny made a crossing motion across her chest. "I swear it's true. Elle said she was tired of city life and wanted to restart in a small town with a good man."

Kate laughed. "How did Mike react?"

"He was mad that she'd lied, but by that point, he said he was in love with her. They got married by a judge in New York and returned as man and wife."

Kate passed the jar back to Penny. "I guess it's going well."

"Seems to be. Mike's mom, April, was pissed he'd gotten married to a girl she hadn't met, in a ceremony she wasn't invited to, but she got over it."

"Elle enjoys living without all the comforts of the city?"

"She says she loves it. She gets up early and feeds the cows and brings baby lambs into the kitchen when it's cold outside. She'd even asked Nan if she could stop by this weekend and learn how to can."

Kate took the mason jar from Penny and knocked back a swig. "I'm happy for him. He's an authentically nice guy."

Penny looked at her sideways. "I remember when you two had a thing for each other."

"Yeah, but we live in two completely different worlds." She took a smaller sip. "Part of me wishes I could have been happy moving back to rural West Virginia, being a farmer's wife. But we both knew that's not who I am."

It was Penny's turn to change the subject. "How's the mysterious stranger?"

"I think he'll be fine. He's got a badly broken arm and several places that needed stitches, but Doc seemed hopeful." Kate handed the jar back to Penny. She found it odd that she wrestled with whether she should tell her best friend about recognizing Jeremy. Penny was the one person whom she had trusted with every secret, every ambition, and every dream.

Luckily, she didn't have to wrestle with the idea very long. Penny looked at her watch then shot to her feet. "Crap! I've got to check on Aunt Millie. If she doesn't take her medicine, cardiac arrest may not be something we can just joke about." She drained the rest of the moonshine from the glass without coughing.

"Have fun with that." Kate laughed. "I'm off to get a hot shower before I sleep on the hardwood floors."

"Joke's on you, there's no hot water."

"That doesn't make sense."

Penny smirked. "According to Sam, when they ordered the hot water heaters, whatever bozo was in charge ordered the wrong size. The new ones were supposed to arrive tomorrow, and unless they have an arc, that won't happen."

KATE TIPTOED THROUGH THE FRONT DOOR of cabin one. Though the prospect of a hot shower was off the table, she figured she should at least wash off the mud splattered on her arms. As she began filling the sink with freezing cold water, a movement in the mirror's reflection grabbed her attention. She whirled around.

"Kate," the shape whispered.

Kate let out a yelp.

The object moved closer. "Kate, it's me."

She realized the voice belonged to Nan. "You scared me half to death!"

Nan whispered, "Sorry, Kat-bird."

Kate said, more calmly, "What are you doing here?"

"Doc wanted somebody to sit with the patient."

"How's he doing?"

"He's been unconscious most of the time."

That wasn't the reply she'd hoped for. "He hasn't been awake at all?"

"Doc knocked him out to set his arm. He woke up just long enough for the men to get him into clean clothes. He was very foggy, but he could give one-word answers."

Kate breathed a sigh of relief. He'd been awake; he'd talked. He'd gotten clothes on. She was split on how she felt about the last fact. She peered into the bedroom; a metal folding chair was sitting beside the bed. "How long have you been sitting in there?"

Nan shrugged. "I relieved Chris about an hour ago."

"That couldn't have been comfortable."

"I read for a while, walked around for a while. Wasn't that bad." She pointed to the bedroom. "And Doc dropped off a sleeping bag and several blankets for you."

Kate smiled. "Thanks, Nan, I can take it from here."

Once Nan had gone, Kate unrolled the sleeping bag and climbed inside. Physical exhaustion, paired with eighty proof moonshine, made falling asleep on the hardwood floor easy. Unfortunately, hours later, she awoke with a stabbing pain in her lower back. She sat up and winced as her sciatic shot shards of pain down her leg. She shifted and rolled, but no matter the position, she couldn't get comfortable. *Perhaps volunteering to spend the night on a hardwood floor wasn't the swiftest idea*, she thought.

She looked around the room and weighed her options. She could stay on the floor and be in pain, she could go to Penny's cabin and make it three in a king bed, or... Kate looked at the sleeping man taking up only a third of the king-size bed.

She reasoned, *He's under the covers. If I'm on top of the covers, that isn't creepy. Besides, it's not like I have the energy to try anything funny; I just want a comfortable place to sleep. I'll be up before he is awake tomorrow. He'll never know.* She climbed on top of the covers and pulled the sleeping bag over her. *Plus, this is a safety issue. Doc said that it would be terrible if he rolled out of bed. I'm only worried about his safety.*

Kate rationalized her actions until she fell into a deep sleep that could only come from being exhausted and comfortable.

## Chapter 8

"WHERE AM I, AND WHO the bloody hell are you?"

Kate rolled over and blinked groggily at the offending voice's owner. Slowly, the blurry form beside her took shape.

In a lightning strike of clarity, she remembered where she was and who HE was. She leaped from the bed. "Don't panic! I can explain." Words spewed from her mouth. "You fell down the side of a mountain. I found you. You were hurt. All the beds in camp are taken. They put you in my bed. I was exhausted. I tried to sleep on the floor, but my back... I didn't touch you. I promise I'm not a creep. You were under the covers the entire time, and I was on top. I promise!"

He squeezed his eyes shut. "I've got a bugger of a headache, and I didn't understand a word of that."

Kate had to find the right words, the words that would effectively communicate that she wasn't some psychotic stalker who crawled into bed with random celebrities. She took a deep breath. "Yesterday, I took a walk and saw you standing at the top of Mongold Mountain. I think you were trying to make your way to me, but you fell. You tumbled down the side of the mountain. I thought you were dead. I mean you obviously aren't or else we wouldn't be here, would we?" She swore under her breath, this wasn't the eloquent explanation she'd desired. She tried again, slower and more deliberate. "After I found you, some of our men carried you back to camp. We patched you up the best we could. There aren't any open beds, so they put you in mine. I promise you, I tried to sleep on the floor, but my back was killing me. I was on top of the covers the entire time. I give you my word, there was no funny business."

He held up his hand. "Let me get this straight, I fell down the side of a mountain?"

"Yes."

"And your friends brought me back to their camp and took care of me?"

"Yes."

"And they put me in your bed?"

Kate breathed a sigh of relief, he was understanding. "Yes, there aren't any open beds in camp, and since I'm one of the youngest residents and could handle sleeping on the floor, they gave you mine."

"But you couldn't sleep on the floor, so you crawled in bed with me?"

Kate lowered her head. "Yes, and I'm sorry."

He narrowed his gaze. "You said when you first saw me, I was on top of a mountain? Do you have any idea how I got there?"

Kate looked up. "No, I'm sorry. I only know what happened from the moment you fell onward."

He nodded slowly. "So, after I fell, you found me. Then, the men from your group brought me back here and patched me up?"

She nodded.

An uncomfortable silence fell over the room. When he finally spoke, his voice was cautious. "You don't know me from Adam, but you took care of me?"

Kate cocked her head in confusion. "You were hurt, and you needed care."

"But I'm a stranger."

"You're a human being who needed help."

He stared at the knotty pine ceiling. "Wow, that's incredible."

"It's what any decent person would do."

"Ah, there's the difference. Not a lot of decent people in my world."

Kate could hear the sadness in his voice. In America, show business was a cutthroat profession. Perhaps it was the same across the pond. She leaned closer. "You are in West Virginia now. Stranger or not, we take care of people."

He looked at her, and her heart skipped a few beats. "Well, this stranger is most thankful, miss… I'm sorry. I didn't even ask the name of the woman who opened her home to me and gave me her bed."

"Katherine, but most people call me Kate. This isn't my home, it's just a cabin where I'm staying temporarily. But yes, I gave you my bed. And I swear on all things Holy, I didn't intend to be in it with you!"

He chuckled. "Listen, I believe you. I don't think you are a creep. Quite the contrary, sounds like you were my savior." He inhaled deeply. "By the way, my name is Tim."

"Tim?" Her voice betrayed her surprise.

He tensed. "Yes, Tim. Does that name surprise you?"

She recovered quickly. "No, my friend's wife had a baby a few days ago. They named him Tim. I guess it's just a name that's on my mind."

"On your mind," he repeated. "I wish I had things on my mind, like how the bloody hell I got to the top of a mountain. The past forty-eight hours are a blur."

"They're a bit of a blur for me too." Kate frowned. "Unfortunately, I remember every detail."

"You're on holiday. Shouldn't your memories be happy ones?"

"I'm not on holiday." She gave a wry laugh. "I was supposed to be. I came to visit Nan in Riverside, but we got evacuated when the flood came. I'm trapped on this mountain top with forty elderly evacuees. There will be many memories, but not happy ones."

## Chapter 9

JEREMY WAS PRETTY SURE THE WOMAN who had just leaped from his bed was not a Misery-esque stalker. She seemed genuinely embarrassed about how they had awoken. When she spoke about seeing him fall, he could hear the sincere concern in her voice.

But there were still many questions which needed answered. Like, where the bloody hell was he? What events led to his falling? And most importantly, was his anonymity still intact? The last thing he wanted was for this to end up on the front page of *The Sun*.

The frizzy-haired woman with the tired eyes had said she was visiting family in Riverside. Riverside, the name replayed in his head, like the opening chord to a forgotten song. He closed his eyes and forced himself into murky memories. Blurry images began to take shape: a private jet, a bright red Mustang, a barely standing shack of a store in Riverside, the spot he'd randomly picked on the map. Though a bass drum pounded in his brain, he focused harder. He'd camped by the stream and gone hiking. It had rained. Angry sheets of water blew into the cave where he sat huddled sick with food poisoning. The valley flooded, so he'd hiked to the top of the mountain to find civilization. That's when he fell. He remembered! Time wasn't lost!

With a burst of energy, he pushed himself into a seated position, which was a very bad idea. The sudden movement awoke every pain receptor in his body. His right arm shot bolts of white-hot pain to his brain, his ribs felt like he'd been kicked by Pele, and the pounding in his head thudded harder. For the first time, he realized his lips were swollen and scabbed.

Panic gripped his chest. "What happened to me?"

Kate moved to his bedside and put her hand gently on his non-injured shoulder. "You fell down the side of a mountain."

"But what's wrong with me?" He sounded like a frightened child.

She chewed her bottom lip. "I don't know the full extent of your injuries. I do know your arm is broken. Doctor Kile said both the radius and ulna snapped. She set the break last night after she gave you pain meds in your I.V."

"Doctor who?"

"Dr. Iris Kile. She's the general practitioner who lives in Riverside. Luckily, she brought some supplies with her. She came to where you fell and patched you up a bit then worked on you more once we got here."

It was all too much. His heart thudded against his sternum, and his breathing became erratic. The more erratic his breathing, the greater the pain in his ribs. He circled through the vicious cycle several times before he felt a soft hand on his cheek.

Kate's face was now inches from his. "Tim, look at me." Her voice was deliberate yet kind. "I know this is a lot to take in, and you must be scared. But it's all right, I am right here. Breathe, steady breaths… in… out… in… out… Good, like that."

His breathing leveled out and his pain lessened. "Am I going to be okay?"

"Doc wouldn't share much information, but I was in the room when they were patching you up. She said that your arm may require surgery, but that it's your worst injury. Your vitals are all strong, and she didn't believe there was any spinal or organ damage. Would you like for me to get Doc? She can answer your questions better than I can."

He nodded, because he didn't trust his own voice.

# Chapter 10

JEREMY HEARD THE DOOR CLICK SHUT, and he was alone, in pain, and scared. The ticking of the clock on the wall became like a rhythmic wrecking ball in his head, the pain shooting from his right arm was excruciating, and the air became thick as glue. Just as he thought his mind would collapse upon itself, there was a knock at the door. He fought to keep his voice calm. "Come in."

A silver-haired woman wearing a faded Jimmy Buffett t-shirt walked into the bedroom. "Hello, I am Doctor Iris Kile. How's the patient?"

The doctor smiled at him with compassion and no pity. It put him at ease. "I am buggered up pretty good."

"I'd say that's a fair assessment." Doc set her bag at the end of the bed. "How's the pain?"

"Pretty intense."

"Last night you told me you weren't allergic to any medicines."

"I talked to you last night?" His heart raced. He was not allowed the luxury of conversations where he wasn't in control or had no memory of what he'd said.

"Well, you didn't actually talk. More like I asked questions, and you nodded or shook your head."

"Oh." He relaxed a little. "Yes, that's correct. I'm not allergic to anything that I know of."

"How about addictions? Have you ever been addicted to opioids?"

"Why on Earth would you ask that?" His voice rose in indignation. How dare she make assumptions that just because he was famous, he had to be a druggie or sycophant?

Doc shrugged apologetically. "Unfortunately, in West Virginia, we're in an opioid crisis. Oxycodone and morphine are too easy..." She trailed off. "I won't get into the politics of it. But I've seen too many lives torn apart to not ask."

She seemed to age just saying the words, and Jeremy felt like an arse for his reaction. "No," he whispered. "Thankfully, I've never been victim to addiction."

Doc nodded. "And the pain, any areas of significance?"

"My arm and my ribs."

Doc made a note on the chart then looked back to him. "Can I look at your injuries?"

Jeremy nodded, and then immediately regretted his reply. The doctor's fingers felt like blunted hammers as she palpitated his abdomen. When she examined his arm, it felt like his bones were being splintered in a vice.

Doc finished her exam. "I'm sorry about that. With no imaging tools, the only way for me to evaluate is by touch."

"What did your evaluation by touch reveal?" he asked through clenched teeth.

"That there is nothing life-threatening or permanently debilitating."

Though pain still coursed through his body, the knowledge that he wasn't permanently broken helped him relax. "That's good, right?"

Doc sat down her clipboard. "The break on your arm is nasty. Both the radius and ulna snapped. You may need to have surgery or physical therapy when you get home. Good news is, there doesn't seem to be any internal or spinal injuries. Long-term prognosis is great."

He touched his brow. "When will my head stop pounding?"

"Concussions can be tricky. You'll probably have a headache for a couple of days. For pain management, we can go the route of a strong NSAID, or we can try an oral opiate. You don't have any issues with opioids, so I'd suggest the morphine."

"If you think that's best."

"I do. Could you wait until I ask you a few questions, or do you want it immediately?"

"I can wait, now that you have stopped banging on my injured body," he tried to joke.

Doc smiled apologetically and grabbed her clipboard. "I'll try to be quick. Name?"

"Jeremy Fulton."

Doc raised an eyebrow. "Kate said your name was Tim?"

He lowered his gaze. "I lied. I told her my name was Tim because I don't want to be recognized. I'm on the telly in the UK. The main reason I camped in the woods was that I wanted to go somewhere nobody would recognize me."

"I see."

He looked back at Doc, his eyes pleading. "Do you think anybody here recognized me?"

Doc sat in the folding chair. "I think you're safe. Riverside is a small farming community. Most residents probably don't even know what the BBC is."

He let out a breath he didn't realize he'd been holding.

Doc continued, "Tim, on the other hand, is the talk of the town. Don't be surprised if people pop in to check out the mysterious stranger. You're an enigma wrapped in a mystery in a town full of gossipy old men and women."

He didn't really care to have visitors, but it sounded like a moot point. "When do you think they will start showing up?"

Doc smirked. "If they know what is good for them, not until your doctor says it's okay."

Jeremy smiled. He had a feeling that this wasn't a woman that many dared to cross.

"I, however, need to know if there is anything in your medical history I should know about?"

"Not that I can think of."

"You were really dehydrated when you rolled into camp, any reason why?"

Jeremy looked slightly embarrassed. "I had a dickey tummy?"

Doc's eyes grew wide. "You had what?"

He chuckled. "I had food poisoning."

Doc laughed out loud. "Oh," she composed herself. "Did you have vomiting and diarrhea?"

Jeremy lowered his eyes in embarrassment. "Both."

"Do you have any idea what may have caused the food poisoning?"

"A chicken sandwich I got from that little store beside the river."

"Kenny's store?"

"Aye."

"That explains it," Doc mumbled. "Family history? Any immediate relatives with diabetes, autoimmune, or heart-related issues?"

"My mum died of a heart attack at seventy-two. No history of heart disease or diabetes, just out of the blue. My dad passed three months ago from cancer."

"I am very sorry for your losses," she continued in a professional yet sympathetic manner. "Do you have questions for me?"

"Nah, I'm just feeling a bit off my trolley, but I don't think you can help much with that."

"How about this? I'll go to my cabin and get your meds. I can send Kate back in if you like."

Jeremy was surprised at how good Kate returning sounded. His frizzy-haired bedmate had a comforting way about her that lessened his anxiety. "I like that idea."

## Chapter 11

BEFORE DOC COULD PULL THE FRONT door closed behind her, Kate sprung from the corner of the porch and grabbed her arm. Words shot from her mouth like bullets from a machine gun. "Listen, I understand doctor-patient confidentiality, but is he going to be okay?"

"Heavens, Kate, you scared me."

"Sorry about that, but is he going to be okay?" Her words were just as fast.

Doc quietly closed the front door. "It will take some time to heal, but he'll be fine."

Kate released Doc's arm. "Is he still freaking out?"

"He seems much calmer."

Kate's shoulders relaxed. "I'm glad to hear that. He was slightly panicked when I left him."

"Wouldn't you be? Waking up in a strange environment, your body battered and in pain? Honestly, I'm surprised at how well he's keeping it together." She paused, "I do think he shouldn't be alone. Too much time in his own head could be disastrous."

Kate needed no other prodding. She reached for the doorknob.

"One more thing." Doc made sure she had Kate's attention. "I've been doctoring stubborn farmers for over twenty years. I don't pretend to understand it, but some men have trouble admitting their own frailty. Bringing their pain and anxiety into the light can rob them of their bravado, and sometimes that's all they have left."

Kate took a moment to process Doc's words. "I understand."

"I thought you would. I'll be back in a few minutes with food and more meds."

WHEN KATE ENTERED THE ROOM, Jeremy lifted his head and smiled at her. "Hello stranger."

Kate felt her knees go all wobbly. Now that they weren't in triage mode, or she wasn't desperate to convince him she wasn't a creep, she was able to truly see him. He looked more like the man who had been the object of her desires for the past two decades. His tired but sultry blue eyes, sleepy smile, and sexy as hell accent made it hard to suppress the blithering teenage fangirl lurking just beneath the surface. She lowered her head to hide the scarlet creeping into her cheeks and scurried to the folding chair beside his bed.

Suddenly, the toe of her boot caught the edge of the bearskin rug, sending her flailing. Her hands grasped desperately for anything to stop her from falling, but they found nothing. With a thud, she landed on her hands and knees.

Jeremy gasped, "Blimey, you okay?"

Though Kate's knees stung, her sprained dignity was excruciating. For a moment she considered lying flat on her stomach and slithering quietly out the door. However, she reasoned being seen scooting out the door on your stomach would be more embarrassing than the actual fall. She pushed herself onto her feet, plopped down in the metal folding chair, and covered her face with her hands. "I'm fine."

Jeremy cleared his throat to keep from laughing. "Good, because there's a one catastrophe per cabin limit, and I've claimed that position."

Kate said nothing.

"Because, if you remember, I slipped on mud and fell down the side of the mountain, which takes a whole new set of skills."

She raised her head and gave a small laugh. "I think it takes way more talent to trip on flat ground than it does to slip on mud."

"Ah, that's where you're wrong, lassie." Jeremy exaggerated his accent. "I saw how that rug reached up and attacked your shoe. Where I come from, rugs know how to behave when in the presence of a lady."

Kate laughed out loud. "Oh, so I am a lady now?" She put her finger on her lips and feigned deep thought. "Lady Katherine from the Shire of Slate. I like the sound of that."

Jeremy chuckled. "Shire? I thought this was West Virginia, not Middle Earth."

His joking tone eased her embarrassment, she smiled. "You came to West Virginia to wander, and you certainly got lost."

Suddenly, panic crossed his face. "Where are my pants?"

"Your pants?" The question took Kate off guard. "What pants?"

He looked desperately around the room. "The pants I was wearing when I came into camp. There's something very special in the pocket, a token my father gave me."

Kate remembered that his father had recently died, and she knew anything he'd given him would be of great emotional value. She tried to sound reassuring, "The men dressed you last night, but I don't know what they did with your muddy clothes. Would you want me to find one of them and ask?"

"No! Don't leave me!" he blurted.

Kate remembered Doc's warning about bringing pain and anxiety into the light. She made a dismissive hand gesture. "Leave and risk the wrath of Doc? Heck no, she gave explicit directions that I'm to stay with you until she returns, some silliness about you rolling off the bed and hurting your arm more." She shrugged. "Sounds overprotective to me, but she's the doctor."

Jeremy's body relaxed. "I don't mean to be such a dour crabbit. It's just a bit much, waking up in a strange place with your body all boggin' and broken."

"I can't imagine."

He looked around the room. "You said that this is some sort of holiday spot?"

"It's a wilderness resort that was supposed to open later this month." She paused, "That was until the flood hit. Not sure what will happen now."

"A new resort? This cabin looks really old."

"It is. Slate was a working lumber camp from the 1900s to the 1920s. Men would work eleven-hour days, six days a week cutting virgin timber and then send the logs down the mountain. Massive steam engines used to chug up and down the slopes hauling lumber to the pulp mill at the base. They harvested over a million-and-a-half foot of lumber each week." She took a quick look around the bedroom. "This cabin has undergone a full renovation to give it modern conveniences, but in the 1920s, it was where the workers would sleep. There would have been about fifteen to twenty men in this cabin."

Jeremy looked around the cabin, which was around five hundred square feet. "Fifteen to twenty men?"

"Workers' comfort wasn't a priority. Men were pieces of machinery: worked until they broke or wore out, then replaced."

"I wager some Scotsmen probably made up the group."

Kate nodded. "Many of the homesteaders who settled here were Germanic, but the area definitely has a strong Scotch-Irish heritage as well."

His eyes scanned the room again, this time more slowly as if trying to envision the history within its walls. "Perhaps a distant cousin slept in this same room."

"I wouldn't be surprised." Kate thought for a moment. "When renovations began, they found documents from when the camp was still running. Dalton Beamon is trying to get everything digitized. Perhaps he can help you with some genealogy research."

"I'd like that very much. I used to research historical stuff."

"Why did you stop?"

Jeremy scoffed. "No time, life heading off in a thousand different directions, always trying to catch up. I've had to give up lots of things I loved."

Kate looked at him inquisitively. She always thought celebrities had reached the penultimate of enjoyable lives; getting paid millions of dollars to do a job they loved, living their passions, and turning down any assignment they didn't feel like doing. Sure, getting your foot in the door was tough, especially the starving artist years. But once you had the clout and recognition of a celebrity like Jeremy Fulton, the world was yours to take.

Jeremy's voice pulled her from her thoughts. "Does anybody live here full time?"

She shook her head. "Not yet. Once the resort is finished, there'll be a full-time director who lives on site. For now, everyone in Slate is an evacuee from Riverside."

He nodded heavily. "Is Riverside flooded badly?"

Kate's shoulders slumped as if somebody had just placed one of the gigantic timbers upon them. "We don't really know what is happening in the valley, but we know it isn't good. The waters rose fast. We barely had time to gather food and irreplaceable items before it washed away the bridges. Nobody knows how long we may have to be here." She forced a smile. "We're lucky we have this place, though. We're safe and dry, that's what matters." It was the rehearsed response she'd given when trying to comfort scared, elderly residents.

"You really love Riverside, don't you?"

"Yeah, I do. It's my happy place." She cocked her head and smiled. "Actually, I grew up about an hour and a half away. My best friend, Penny, grew up in Riverside. We come back as often as we can to visit her grandmother, Nan."

"Where do you live now?"

"I live in Northern Virginia, about forty-five minutes outside of Washington DC. It's about as different as you can get. Life is so busy there, no peace and quiet. Whereas here, no traffic, no pollution, you can count the stars, everybody knows everybody's name and business." Kate rolled her eyes. "Of course, that isn't always a good thing."

"So, there are no secrets?"

"Well, when your great-grandmother went to school with your neighbor's great-grandfather, everybody knows each other's background, whether or not it's accurate." She grinned. "But we take care of each other. We're a family, we fight, we hold grudges, we can be petty and stubborn, but in the end, we love each other and protect each other."

"You talk about it with so much affection."

Kate smiled proudly. "Home doesn't always have to be where you live or where you grew up. I claim this town as my own, and the people here, they are my family."

Just as Jeremy began to reply, there was a knock on the door.

Kate stood. "Come in."

Doc carried a tray with applesauce, plastic ware, and a cup of water through the bedroom door. "So, what have you gotten yourself into since I last saw you?"

Jeremy flashed a million-dollar smile. "Kate and I were just blethering about."

Doc sat the tray on the nightstand. "How are you feeling now?"

He tried to raise himself to an upright position with his good arm but moaned and fell back onto the bed. "Aye, better until I tried to do that."

"You took a good spill, and you were dehydrated when you got to camp. So, you need to take it slow. Rest for most of today. I have to check on a few other residents, but I'll be back to see you this afternoon. Kate can stay with you until then." She looked at Kate. "Unless you have something else you need to do."

Kate frowned; Doc's words had jogged her memory. "Actually," she said hesitantly, "I told Sam I'd check on Lizzy after I got up."

Doc chewed her bottom lip. "Perhaps sending over a male would be a good idea. When the time comes for him to use the restroom, either he'll need help to get to and from, or he'll need to use a makeshift bedpan. Either way, I think a male would be better for the job. Let me see if Troy Whitacre is looking for a chance to get out. He could sit with the patient for a while."

Kate felt her heart rate quicken in irritation. Though she knew it was completely irrational, the insinuation that somebody existed who would be a better caretaker offended her. She started to protest, but Doc spoke first, "But I am glad you're here now. He needs to get something in his stomach before he takes any medicine, and he may need some help. I brought several bland foods. Before you feed him, elevate his head and shoulders, so he doesn't aspirate."

Kate looked at Jeremy. "Is that fine with you?"

He winked at her and gave a thumbs up.

Doc pointed to the tray beside the bed. "Drink all the water. You need to rehydrate. Then take the medicine. The red pill is Tylox, which is an opioid that will make you sleepy, and the blue one is an NSAID, along the lines of strong ibuprofen. With the extent of your injuries, I suggest the red pill, but I'll let you decide." She looked at Kate then back to Jeremy. "Can you think of anything else you need me for?"

Jeremy shrugged. "Not that I can think of."

"Well, if you do, I'll be around." Doc put her hands in her back pockets. "I'll leave you in Kate's competent hands. She's a great nurse."

## Chapter 12

THE SECOND KATE HEARD THE FRONT door click shut, her pulse quickened. Being the nurse sounded so easy when Doc was standing in the room beside her. Now that she was alone with a severely injured man, she didn't feel so sure of herself. She spun around and looked at Jeremy. "The Doctor lies," she blurted.

Jeremy cocked an eyebrow. "Excuse me?"

Kate sat in the folding chair. "She told you I was a good nurse; she lied. I couldn't even take care of a gerbil in my classroom when I was student teaching. Once I killed a cactus, do you know how hard it is to kill a cactus?"

"Well, that's reassuring."

She took a deep breath. "I figured I'd be honest with you. I have no idea what I'm doing. This is the first time I've taken care of somebody who is injured, much less in an old logging cabin in the middle of nowhere."

Jeremy gave a crooked smile. "Lucky for you, it's the first time I've been injured in an old logging cabin in the middle of nowhere."

Though the comment was made in jest, it made Kate more nervous. "Let's try to get some food in your stomach. That way if I injure you further, you can at least take meds." She untangled the I.V. tubing from the bedding and gathered several pillows. "Doc said we need to elevate your head, so you don't choke. Let's get these under your shoulders."

Jeremy tried to push himself into a seated position but immediately fell back to the bed. He held his bruised ribs. "Bloody hell. Can't even sit up by myself."

"I have an idea!" Kate sat on the edge of the bed and adjusted her body so that she was hovering inches above him. "Put your good arm around my neck."

Jeremy obeyed. When his arm was firmly secure around Kate's neck, she sat up slowly, pulling him with her. When his body was inches above the bed, she slid the pillows under his shoulders, and gently lowered him onto them.

When Kate pulled away, his brow was covered with sweat. "I'm sorry, I tried to be gentle," she said.

He gritted his teeth. "I'm okay. Really, I am."

She wiped the perspiration from his forehead. "Let's get food in your stomach so you can take the pain medicine. I say start with the applesauce." She reached for the tray. "How should we do this?"

"I'm right-handed, but I think I can manage with my left. Can you peel the foil off the top?"

Kate nodded and peeled the metal covering off the serving cup. She handed him a spoon and held the plastic cup while he clumsily scooped a spoonful of yellow goo. On his first attempt, his shaking hand was barely an inch away from the cup before it tilted and dumped applesauce over his chest. On the second attempt, he got the spoon to approximately his neck before dumping the contents on himself. Spoonful three almost made it to his lips but ended up dribbling down his chin and onto the pillow. Jeremy growled in frustration and threw his hand, which still held a spoon half full of applesauce, into the air. Yellow globs fell all around him, one landing, splat, on the tip of his nose.

Kate couldn't stifle her laughter.

He stuck out his bottom lip. "It's not funny."

"I'm sorry, you're right." Kate cleared her throat and tried to be serious, but the effort of holding in the giggles made her shoulders shake.

The corners of his mouth turned up. "Okay, it was a little funny."

She raised her eyes to meet his and instantly began to laugh. She laughed so hard that tears came to her eyes, and she snorted. When

Kate snorted, Jeremy burst out in hearty laughter. Immediately, he grabbed his ribs, and a look of anguish covered his face.

Kate gasped. "Oh no!"

"My ribs." He rubbed his side. "They say laughter's good medicine. I have to disagree."

Kate wiped at her eyes. "Perhaps I should feed you. Would that be okay?"

He gave her a small nod, and she rearranged the pillows. Then she carefully lifted a spoonful of applesauce to his lips.

He swallowed the yellow goo. "I cannot believe I have to be fed like a wee child."

"Oh, stop feeling sorry for yourself. You're a man with a broken arm and badly bruised body lying in a logging camp with an underskilled nurse. What do you have to be glum about?"

"I guess I'm being a bit of a baby," he said as he took a bite.

"Nah, you're not being a baby. Maybe a bratty teenager, but not a baby." Kate winked.

"To be fair, it erases any bravado, needing to be spoon-fed."

"This is temporary, though. Your body has been through quite a bit. Once you're healthy, you can do it all by yourself. There won't be a need for me to help you."

Jeremy swallowed another spoonful of applesauce. "You know, I did this for my dad when he was dying."

Kate remembered when his father had lost his battle with cancer. In fact, she had sent a letter of condolence through his fan site, a fact she kept to herself because many of her friends would balk at a thirty-seven-year-old woman religiously following a fan site.

"I'm sorry for your loss." The words sounded so generic and hollow, she wished she could find something more profound.

Jeremy didn't seem to mind her lack of eloquence, though. He nodded in appreciation. "Cancer took him a few months ago. He was a strong man, huge, powerful, with a monumental voice. In the end, he weighed less than sixty kilograms, and he could barely whisper."

He sounded like a brokenhearted child. "I miss him. He was a good man, a great man, my best friend. I hope that one day I can be half the man he was."

Kate looked into his eyes, the same eyes that she had looked into thousands of times. The eyes that made her stomach drop now made her heart ache. She caught herself before she reminded him that he was a very good man. It was a well-known fact that Jeremy was the first to offer his presence to raise funds for a worthy cause. He'd started an after-school program in destitute parts of Glasgow where students could study the arts and gain self-confidence. The Gates Foundation had named him one of the most philanthropic celebrities in the world. But that wasn't all. He had a reputation for being generally kind to everybody on set, from the coffee boy to his co-stars. He was generous to his fans. In his interviews, he was humble and socially conscious. By all accounts, he seemed like a truly good human being.

She knew she could never say these things. So, she reached with her right hand and placed her palm on his shoulder. He placed his hand over hers. "You need some rest," she said tenderly.

Jeremy nodded.

"The red pill or the blue pill?"

"What's the difference again?"

"The red pill is a narcotic; the blue is strong ibuprofen."

"I think I need the red."

"That's probably wise, it'll make you tired, which is good because you need your sleep." She handed him the small red pill then the glass of water. "Doc says you need to stay hydrated."

He swallowed the pill then placed his head back on the pillows. Then he grabbed Kate's hand. "Thank you, for everything. I feel bad asking for anything else."

"What is it?"

"Can you sit with me until I fall asleep?"

Kate whispered, "Of course."

"And you'll be back?"

"As soon as I can."

Jeremy lay back on the pillows, and Kate held his hand until his breathing slowed. Once she was sure he was lost in deep sleep, she pulled the covers to his chin and kissed him gently on the forehead.

She thought back to when she had become such a huge fan of Jeremy Fulton. They had both been in their late teens. She had loved his portrayal of a smart ass, 1900s deputy in *Wooden Dove*. When she was in college, she scored tickets to see him in *Hamlet* at the Kennedy Center. During that performance, she realized that he wasn't just some pretty-faced, comedic personality. He was a talented actor with an amazing gift that made her feel things that no performer had ever evoked.

She recalled the fresh and flawless face that she had seen on stage in DC that night, then looked at the man lying in her bed. His face had aged, but it was no less beautiful. The spattering of gray in his beard and fine wrinkles around his eyes made him look dignified, even more handsome.

As she walked into the living room she muttered, "Well isn't that just great. He ages like fine wine, and I age like cheap vodka."

## Chapter 13

A WHITE-HAIRED MAN IN A POLO SHIRT and creased blue jeans cracked open the front door. "Kate?" he whispered.

Kate walked to the door and opened it wide. "Hi Troy."

The hardwood floors creaked under Troy's penny loafers as he walked into the small living room. "How's he doing?"

"Doc said with rest and time, he should be fine." She glanced toward the bedroom. "He just fell asleep."

"I'm sure he needs rest. Did Doc leave any instructions for me?"

"If he wakes up, and he's in pain, give him another red pill."

Troy's kind, hazel eyes were reassuring. "I think I can handle that."

"I'm sure you can. How is Lizzy doing? It's a lot for you and Kathleen to handle." Lizzy, one of Riverside's most vibrant residents, was in the early stages of Alzheimer's Disease. Troy and his wife, Kathleen, had taken on the responsibility of being Lizzy's caretakers while in Slate.

Troy took a seat in one of the uncomfortable looking, antique chairs. "She has been pretty lucid and hasn't had one of her spells. That's a blessing."

"Hopefully, we can make it off the mountain without any episodes. Is she in your cabin?"

"She was asleep when I left."

Kate almost giggled like a schoolgirl. If Lizzy was sleeping, then Kathleen didn't need her, and she could remain at Jeremy's side. She tried to sound casual, "Well, if Lizzy doesn't need me, I can stay here. You can go back to your cabin if you'd like."

Troy waved his hand dismissively. "Nah, I'm good. You look like you're the one who needs a break, anyway. Why don't you take a nice walk or something?"

Kate laughed. "Last time I took a walk, I found a half-dead man on the edge of the camp."

"Good point. No more walks for you." Troy chuckled. "Kathleen said you had to sleep on the floor last night. Why don't you head to Nan's and take a nap?" He became somber. "I have a feeling the next few days won't be easy. We need to rest up while we can."

KATE CLIMBED THE WATERLOGGED WOODEN stairs of Nan's cabin and rapped on the door. Before the second knock, Penny's voice barked, "Come in."

Kate pushed open the cabin door and saw the two women were in the bedroom. She crept through the main room and stood in the doorway. Penny sat on the unmade king-size bed. Her hands were on her hips like a defiant teenager. "There's no need to sugarcoat things," she said through clenched teeth, "when we get off this mountain, don't you think they'll notice over half the town has been under water?"

Nan was leaning against the door that led to the bathroom. She was still wearing the brown leggings and white t-shirt she'd worn the night before. There was a cool edge to her voice. "We don't know how bad things are yet. Chris has heard bits and pieces on the radio, but right now it's mostly conjecture."

Penny threw her hands up in frustration. "How can you call it conjecture? Chris has been talking with the state police. I assume they know the facts."

Nan took a deep breath. "All we know is that the Greenbrier River is currently twelve feet above flood level and that streets are flooded. Those aren't enough details to share. It'll start mass hysteria."

Penny jammed her finger toward the door. "Don't they deserve to know what we know?"

"This is delicate, Pen, and I admit that I don't have the answers. I just know we're in a strange environment and tensions are high. People are barely hanging on, and mob hysteria isn't what we need. Once we have facts and details, we'll break the news to everyone, gently."

Penny buried her face in her hands. "I hope you're right."

Finally, Nan turned and acknowledged Kate. "Hello, sweetie. I'm sorry, we were just—"

Kate cut her off. "Really, it's fine. Everybody is at their wit's end." She crossed to the bed and pulled off her soggy shoes.

"I think you're right. We've all reached our breaking point." Nan walked to the bed and sat between the girls. "How's the patient?"

"Doc says he is making wonderful improvements, which is promising. This morning he was talking and cognizant."

Penny grumbled, "He's lucky he's even alive. Did he tell you why he was hiking in the middle of a flood?"

Penny's irritation took Kate off guard. "No... he didn't... I mean... I didn't ask."

A knock at the door ended her rambling. Sam pushed open the door and made his way to the bedroom. He cleared his throat then awkwardly nodded. "Penny, Kate, Faye," he acknowledged each woman.

Penny shot to her feet, her posture tense and voice pleading. "Has Chris heard from the state police? Have they talked to Tammie or my kids?"

Sam smiled warmly. "That's part of the reason I came. State Trooper Guthrie got a hold of your mother-in-law. They were worried, but now that they know you and Faye are okay, they're better. Homeland Security tracked down Lenard. He said he'll shorten his trip and be home tomorrow at the latest."

Penny's posture softened, and the hard lines around her mouth dissolved. "Thanks, Sam."

"It's no problem, Penny. If you have any other messages, I'll see what I can do." He turned his attention back to Nan. "Speaking of relaying messages, Chris also has found out more information about the valley. He wants to share it with us."

"Why can't he share with all of us?" Penny demanded.

Nan patted her shoulder. "It makes it easier to converse when we're in small groups. I promise I'll tell you everything when I get back, but now, you need to check on Milly. When we find anything definite, you'll be the first to know."

Penny's head bowed in defeat. "Okay, but as soon as you get back."

Nan nodded then gave Kate a tired smile. "Kat bird, I promise I'll find you this afternoon, and we can talk about everything."

Kate nodded. "Go. I'll be fine."

Nan looked at Sam. "Let's go find Chris." In a flash, the two were out the door.

Kate put her hand on Penny's knee. "How are you holding up?"

She fought to keep her voice level. "I want to talk to my kids. I worry. I never stop worrying."

"They're in good hands."

"I know they are. I just don't want them to be scared." Kate could hear the helplessness in her voice. "I feel bad that I snapped at Nan." Penny brushed her red ringlets behind her ear. "We got into an argument when I told her I didn't like the way she and Sam were keeping information from the rest of us. They snuck off to meet with Chris earlier this morning, too."

"That is peculiar." Kate looked toward the door. "And speaking of bizarre, why does Sam call her Faye? I've never heard anybody call her Faye. Even Oscar calls her Nan, and he's ninety-five."

Penny waved dismissively. "Everybody is acting strangely."

"Well, the circumstances are pretty strange."

"Yeah, but it's something more." Her voice was brimming with suspicion. "Last night, she didn't come back to the cabin until after midnight. When I asked her where she had been, she just said that she was meeting with other residents." Penny wagged her finger at the door. "Something's going on, and she's doing everything she can to hide it."

Kate positioned herself so she could lean against the wall. "I know she was sitting with Tim when I got back to the cabin."

Penny narrowed her eyes. "Tim?"

Kate's palms began to sweat. "Tim, the guy who came crashing down the mountain."

"Oh," Penny seemed suddenly irritated. "That's his name. Well, I know she was sitting with Tim for a while, but you relieved her around ten. What about the next two hours?"

Kate shrugged. "Maybe she was checking on some older residents, like your great Aunt Milly?"

Penny looked at her watch and swore. "Aunt Milly! I have to check on her every four hours and make sure she takes the medicine that keeps her from keeling over." She turned to Kate. "Will you be here when I get back?"

Kate sighed melodramatically. "Well, I was going to tear up the town, shoot out a few lights, but I guess that can wait."

"Save a place at the bar for me." Penny called as she walked out the front door.

## Chapter 14

KATE SCOOTED AGAINST THE WALL and closed her eyes. By the time she opened them, Penny had returned and was sitting beside her reading a book. "Welcome back to the present, Mrs. Van Winkle," she smirked.

Kate rubbed her eyes. "When did you get back?"

Penny looked at her watch. "About two hours ago. I brought back some fried chicken from Kathleen Whitacre. It's on the kitchen table."

Kate jumped out of bed. "Why did you let me sleep so long?"

Penny's mouth fell open in confusion. "Because you obviously needed it. You look like you didn't get a bit of sleep last night."

Kate slipped on her shoes. "I've got to go!"

Penny called after her. "At least take your fried chicken."

KATE LOOKED AT HER WATCH. It was almost three o'clock. *You are the worst nurse ever!* She berated herself. *What if Troy had to leave? What if Jeremy is sitting in bed, alone, in pain, scared?* She took the cabin stairs two at a time, anxious about what she would find inside. However, when she reached for the doorknob, she heard two male voices laughing.

She knocked on the front door and heard Troy's booming reply, "Come in."

By the time she was to the bedroom door, Troy was back to his story. "And we never got the hay made in that field all summer." He roared with laughter.

Kate looked around the room. Troy was sitting comfortably in the folding chair, his long legs sticking out in front of him. Jeremy laid flat on his back holding his ribs and smiling.

She cleared her throat. "Am I interrupting?"

Troy gave a toothy smile. "Kate, come on in. We were just shooting the bull."

"I hate to interrupt male bonding. I can come back later if you like."

Troy stood slowly. "Nah, I've got to get back to Kathleen." He turned his attention to Jeremy. "That's my wife. She's been baking all morning, casseroles and pies galore. She does that when she's stressed."

Jeremy said, "Well, I'm glad I got to chat you up. I thoroughly enjoyed it."

Troy gave a booming laugh. "I enjoyed chatting you up as well, son. I hope we get to do it again." He turned his attention to Kate. "I was wondering if I could have a word with you in private. I have a few things I need to run by you." He turned to Jeremy. "You don't mind if I borrow your nurse for a minute. Official camp business."

Jeremy gave a thumbs up with his unencumbered hand. "Camp business comes before nursing duties."

Kate scratched her head and followed Troy onto the covered porch. Five minutes later she returned.

"What was that about?" Jeremy asked.

Kate waved her hand dismissively. "Oh, nothing." She crossed the room and sat in the folding chair beside the bed. "You get any sleep?"

"A wee bit. When I woke up and saw a strange gray-haired man sitting beside me, it kind of shocked me into being wide awake."

"It looked like you and Troy got along pretty well, though."

"He's a fun bloke. I didn't understand what he was talking about half the time—picking rocks, spreading manure, and brush hogging, but he said it with such gusto. I couldn't help but pay attention. By the way, what does it mean to band a calf?"

Kate scrunched up her face. "Um... ah... yeah. Can you just take my word that you don't want to know the answer to that?"

"Well, now you really have me curious."

Kate got a puckish smile. "It's a way to castrate young male animals."

A look of horror crossed Jeremy's face. "You're right, I didn't need to know that."

Kate quickly changed the subject. "How's the arm? Do you need anything?"

"The meds are wearing off, and the pain is getting to be a bit much. I took one of the blue pills, but it didn't help. I think I need a red pill."

"It has only been a day since you fell, I'd be more surprised if you didn't. Doc said you should stay ahead of the pain."

"I know I need to eat something first." He looked at the tray beside the bed. "I could try toast this time."

"About that, I was talking to Troy. Today will be your last day of applesauce and toast." Kate stumbled over her words as she handed Jeremy a stale piece of bread.

"Why?" He asked nervously.

"Well, when you were resting, a few of the women from the camp came by to check on you."

"Whoa, wait... people came by and looked at me as I slept?"

"You make it sound so creepy. People came by to check on you, and since you were asleep, they chatted with Troy."

Jeremy furrowed his brow. "Still seems dodgy to me."

"I need you to remember you are in a small, tight-knit community. There is a level of comfort exercised with one another. I'm sorry if it seemed intrusive, but I promise you, the motives were pure."

Jeremy eyed her suspiciously. "Well, what did Troy and these visitors discuss?"

Kate took a deep breath. "You're in a village with farmers and their wives, old-time farmers, and their wives. They cannot allow you to just eat applesauce and toast. I need to know if you have any food allergies or if you're Jewish?"

"Why do they want to know my religion?"

"Because they're putting sausage in the casserole."

"Casserole?"

Kate had to suppress a giggle at the way the word sounded with his Scottish accent: 'case-a-roll'. She cleared her throat. "Yeah, casserole. In this one, you put eggs, sausage, cheese, and stale bread into a pan and bake until golden brown. Are you allergic to any of the ingredients that I just listed?"

"Not allergic to any of that, but I'm not sure it's something I'd like."

"You're not vegan, are you? That can be a sacrilege among a camp full of cattle farmers."

"Psh, no, I grew up on haggis and blood pudding."

Kate wrinkled her nose. "This will definitely be an upgrade. And you need to know, these ladies are making a total fuss over you. One of the ladies, or heck all of them, will be bringing food tomorrow."

Jeremy put his good hand on his stomach. "I don't know if Doc told you, but part of the reason I was in such bad shape is that I had food poisoning and spent most of the day before I got here, well... My stomach is still a little timid."

Kate nodded in understanding. "If it helps, this is one of the things Nan would make for us in the morning after Penny and I would have too much wine. It worked great for hangovers, maybe for post-food poisoning, too." She moved to the foot of the bed so it was easier for them to be eye to eye. "Listen, these are southern ladies, most of them mothers and grandmothers who no longer have anybody to nurture. You are patient zero and need to be nursed back to health with good food and lots of mothering. If you don't think you could handle the breakfast casserole, I'm sure they will think up something that would be easier on your stomach."

Jeremy gave a sly grin. "If I don't try it, will you put me back on the side of the mountain?"

Kate made her voice innocent and sweet. "No, you will have just broken the hearts of the mothers and grandmothers who are using their own limited rations to help you heal."

"Wow, absolutely astounding. That is probably the best guilt trip ever."

She shrugged playfully. "It's a gift."

Jeremy smiled and used his thickest Scottish accent, "Well, Mistress Katherine, you provide a compelling argument, so I must agree with your proposal."

Kate laughed. "Thank you. Like I said, these women need somebody to mother. This will mean a lot to them, and to me."

He choked down a bite of toast and took a drink of water. "Older women needing someone to mother. It seems some things don't change from culture to culture."

Kate fidgeted with the chain around her neck. "Speaking of culture, are you familiar with the phrase 'bible belt?'"

"I've heard it, but I don't know what it means."

She chose her words carefully. "Well, in the American south, especially among the older generation, religion is important, extremely important. They read their Bibles daily, go to church at least three times a week, not including board meetings, bible studies, and church socials. And they have a deep faith in prayer." She tried her best to explain the American colloquialism.

"I see."

"Are you religious at all?"

Jeremy was silent for several seconds. When he spoke again, his voice was almost robotic. "My father was a minister, and I was raised in the church, but I don't know what I believe now. I watched my father, a man who was so devoted to God, die a painful death. I don't know if I lost my faith or my faith lost me." He looked intently at Kate. "What do you believe?"

Kate hadn't expected the question to be turned back on her, and it took a moment for her to answer. "I call myself an X-Files Christian. I want to believe, but belief doesn't come easy. I have a degree in mathematics. I'm analytical, I want proof, the very opposite of faith. I spent years proving theorems. In math, one counterexample negates the entire theorem, and some people believe that if you disagree with any one part of the bible, you aren't a true believer." She took a deep breath. "Plus, religion has become such a caustic and dividing thing in America. The bible is used as a weapon to wound and justify self-righteousness. It makes me angry, and it makes me sad."

He looked at her sincerely. "But that doesn't tell me what you believe."

She brought her knees to her chest and wrapped her arms around her shins. "Well, I guess, with all the negativity, the lack of proof for my mathematical mind, it should be cut and dry. However, there is still something inside of me that believes in a loving God, the maker of the heavens, the architect of biology. I don't know if you call that faith, spirituality, religion, or if it even has a name, but that's me." She took a deep breath. "But this isn't about me, I have to ask you a question, and I hope it doesn't offend you."

"What is it?" Jeremy asked cautiously.

"There are members of the village that want to pray over you. If it makes you uncomfortable, I'll tell them no, but it means a lot to them."

He lowered his eyes. "I don't know."

"I understand. It's a very intimate thing. You hardly know us." She could see waves of different emotions wash over his face, sadness, irritation, uncertainty. She said cautiously, "I don't want you to do anything that would make you uncomfortable, but many evacuees are older. They feel like they cannot contribute to helping the community, this would make them feel useful."

Jeremy chewed his bottom lip. "It would give them a purpose?"

"It would."

He swallowed hard, then nodded. "You've all done so much for me. If this makes people feel like they are contributing, then yes."

"Thank you." Kate smiled. "Oh, and one of the ladies also wants to make you an apple pie. Do you like apple pie?"

He licked his lips. "Apple pie is my favorite. Could you find some vanilla ice cream and a nice glass of cold milk?"

"I'm not sure, but I can see."

He grinned mischievously. "I don't wager you could find some Aberlour A'bunadh. I could use a drink with that apple pie."

"I'm going to have to say no, especially since I have no idea what that is."

"It's a superb scotch whiskey."

"Ah, a Scot drinking scotch. How appropriate," she laughed. "I'm not sure about whiskey, but Mr. Coots brought some peach moonshine."

"A West Virginian drinking moonshine, how appropriate," Jeremy teased.

"Okay, now you are pushing it, kilt boy," She teased back. "You don't want to tangle with..." A knock at the door interrupted her comeback. She gave Jeremy a playfully stern look. "We'll finish this later," she quipped, then headed to open the front door.

## Chapter 15

KATE OPENED THE DOOR AND found a stocky man with red cheeks and kind blue eyes standing on the porch.

"CJ," Kate gasped. "Is everything okay?"

He made a dismissive gesture. "Yeah, everything's fine. I just hadn't had a chance to say hello to our guest." He lowered his voice to a whisper, "How's he doing?"

Kate said loudly enough for Jeremy to hear, "A lot better than he was yesterday. Would you like to come in and introduce yourself?"

"If you think he's up to it." CJ didn't wait for a reply, just clomped through the doorway, removed his mud-covered work boots, and continued into the bedroom. He smiled at Jeremy and stuck out his muscled hand. "Hello. I wanted to swing by and introduce myself. I'm CJ McDonald. I was one of the men who gave you a lift yesterday."

Jeremy shook the man's calloused hand. "Nice to meet you, Mr. McDonald. I'm Tim. I owe you my thanks and my life."

"All in a day's work and call me CJ. I stopped by to see how you are healing."

"I'm definitely not back to one hundred percent, but I am feeling stronger by the hour." He turned his face to Kate. "I forgot to tell you; Doc visited while you were out. She said I was no longer dehydrated and took out the I.V. See?" He lifted his arm to show her.

CJ nodded. "Doc's an amazing woman. Not only did she move to the sticks to help a town of stubborn old farmers, she's pretty good at triage, too." He put his hand in his pockets, and his face showed an expression of remembrance. "Almost forgot about this." When he pulled his hand from his pocket, an oval piece of brass sat in his palm. "When my wife, Connie, was trying to wash out your shorts, she found this. Thought I'd bring it to you."

Tears sprang to Jeremy's eyes. He held out his good hand and CJ placed the pendant in his palm. "Thank... thank you," he stuttered, "it's special."

CJ waved off the gratitude. "It's not a problem. I'm glad she found it. For some reason, I had a feeling it was important." He turned away to give Jeremy a moment. "Kate, there are a few residents who have been asking if you'd be making your rounds today. I told them I'd check."

Kate swore silently, she had just gotten back and didn't want to visit elderly residents. She wanted to stay by Jeremy's side, but she couldn't say that. "I hadn't planned on it, but if they need me, I'll go."

CJ lowered his eyes. "They need you."

His solemn tone made Kate feel guilty for wanting to stay in her cabin.

CJ added. "I can stay with the patient." He whispered to Kate as if he were sharing a secret. "To be honest, I could use a bit of time to hide out."

Kate looked back to Jeremy. "You good with that?"

"Yes, the medicine is kicking in already. I feel a bit knackered."

Kate tried to hide her disappointment. Though irrational, she wanted him to declare, *No, Kate don't leave me! I need you, just you.* She pushed her childish notions to the back of her head and asked, "Is there anything I can get for you while I'm out?"

"You know, I'd love something to read. Did anybody bring books or magazines with them?"

"I can check around for you," Kate said. "If I find any, I'll bring them back as soon as I can."

CJ interrupted, "I brought a few magazines. Not sure it's anything that will be interesting, but I can run back to my cabin and grab a few."

Without a word, he turned and walked into the main room, slipped on his boots, and was out the door.

"Looks like you get to spend some time with another of Riverside's finest." Though Kate didn't mean it to, the comment sounded sarcastic.

Jeremy frowned. "He seemed like a decent bloke to me."

Kate's shoulder's slumped. "He is, actually he's better than decent. CJ is one of the most generous men I know. I'm just tired and don't really feel like making my rounds." She wrinkled her nose. "That's selfish, isn't it?"

"Nah, just human, it's hard to be 'on' all the time. Hopefully, you can get some better sleep tonight." Pink crept into his cheeks. "Speaking of tonight, will you be back? Will you stay with me?"

Kate's heartbeat quickened. She cleared her throat and tried to sound nonchalant. "Yeah. That is, if you want me to."

"I do."

She fought the urge to squeal. When she felt she was finally in control of her voice she said. "I'll be right beside you on the floor."

He stammered, "You... ah... you can sleep... here... in the bed... if you like."

"Yes!" she blurted, her face turning fuchsia. "I mean, yeah, that floor is uncomfortable."

Thankfully, before she could say anything more embarrassing, she heard CJ's heavy work boots on the cabin stairs. "I found some magazines." He called from the living room, "But I'm not sure they are anything that would interest you." He walked through the bedroom door and laid copies of *Wild and Wonderful West Virginia* and *The Progressive Farmer* on the nightstand.

"I'm sure those are wonderful," Jeremy yawned, "but I'm suddenly quite exhausted. I think I may drift off soon." His eyes were already closed.

THOUGH JEREMY'S REQUEST FOR HER to return that night sent Kate over the moon, visiting the residents quickly brought her back to

Earth. Everybody had questions, and she felt useless when she couldn't give answers. So, she mostly listened. It seemed many just needed to feel heard, and that was one of the few needs she could fulfill.

By the time Kate finished visiting the last elderly resident, she felt broken and inadequate. She tried to find any shred of light to hang onto, then a thought struck her. Maybe if she could find books for Jeremy, she'd have accomplished something. She headed to Troy Whitacre's cabin to see if he had any reading materials.

She knocked on the door, and a perfectly made-up woman in her early sixties opened it. Kate suppressed a groan because Kathleen Whitacre was the last person Kate wanted to see. The manicured busy body was a countrified version of a Stepford wife. Everything she did had to be perfect or presented as perfect. Not a thing was out of place in her home, or in their barn. Her pies and cakes were made from scratch, and she made sure everybody knew it.

"Kathleen," Kate said with a forced smile, "it's nice to see you. Is Troy at home?"

"Why, hello Kate," Kathleen gushed. "What a pleasant surprise! How's that Scottish fellow doing?"

Kate continued in a business-like tone, "He's doing better and was wondering if anybody had brought reading material. Perhaps Troy would have something that would interest him."

"Troy took Lizzy to the Foreman's cabin." Kathleen's painted lips smiled a little too brightly. "I don't have any reading materials, but I'm making an apple pie if you'd like to stick around and help."

Kate had known Kathleen long enough to realize this wasn't just a request for help baking. "I'd love to, and any other time I would, but I have to visit other residents."

"I've seen you out tramping through the mud, it looked like you have visited all the other cabins already. I think it's time to give yourself a break and get some first-class cooking lessons," Kathleen insisted.

"I really think... I need to find Nan and see if there's—"

"Nan has asked too much of you already, you deserve some time to enjoy yourself." Kathleen put her hand on Kate's elbow and directed her toward the kitchen. "I bet you could use some girl time. It'll be fun."

The tone in Kathleen's voice made Kate's skin crawl. If circumstances were the slightest bit different, she'd have found a way out, or have been brutally honest about her lack of desire for cooking lessons. But the circumstances weren't normal. If she declined, Kathleen would carry a grudge, and the last thing she wanted to do was create friction in Slate.

Kate had no choice but to try to make the best of it. She clenched her teeth. "Sure, I have a few minutes."

After two hours of Stepford appropriate instructions on pie making, Kate had been pushed to the edge of her limits. As she was wiping off the counters, Kathleen said brightly, "You know Kate, it's a shame your mom didn't take the time to teach you how to cook. If she had, you may have a husband by now. Maybe if you can impress that skinny guy you found in the woods, things could work out."

Kate didn't take the bait. She looked at her watch and said, "Oh my, look at the hour."

Kathleen giggled. "Time has flown, hasn't it?"

Kate grabbed her windbreaker from the chair and mumbled something resembling, "Yeah, time flew."

She'd almost made it to the front door when Kathleen called, "Kate, I know you have a plateful. Tomorrow morning, I'll take that young man breakfast and then sit with him. I'm sure you're needed elsewhere."

Kate narrowed her eyes. "Troy said that some women in camp were bringing him breakfast."

Kathleen batted her lashes. "Well, yes. I am a woman, and I'm in the camp."

Kate clenched her jaw, of course Kathleen was behind all this. "Was the prayer vigil your idea too?" She couldn't believe she had made Jeremy feel uncomfortable just to fluff this busy body's ego.

"No, that was Sam and Dalton's idea, but the home cooked meals, that was all me."

Kate crossed her arms over her chest. "He's not up for visitors just yet."

"I think it's fine. Troy said that he and Tim had a long conversation this afternoon."

"But I think—"

"Kate, I have three sons and a husband. I've taken care of many men in my lifetime. You take care of what you need to take care of, and I'll tend to the young gentleman." The sugary smile never left Kathleen's face.

Kate couldn't fake it anymore. She used the voice she reserved for the most stubborn and insulant teenagers, "Do not stop by!" She stormed out the door and slammed it behind her.

She was still steaming when she threw open the front door of her cabin and found a man reading a book at her dining room table. "Mr. Coots, why are you here?"

A smile spread across his face. "CJ left about half an hour ago. When I heard you were spending time with Kathleen, I thought you would need some of this." He lifted a mason jar filled with clear liquid.

Kate reached for the jar and took a swig.

After a few more swallows and some colorful conversation, Kate was laughing when she walked Mr. Coots to the door. She bid the old man a giggly goodbye and tiptoed into the bedroom where Jeremy was curled up under the covers. Once again, she remembered that the dreaming man in her bed was the man about whom she had dreamt many a night.

She climbed into bed beside him, on top of the covers.

## Chapter 16

KATE'S EYES FLEW OPEN. She didn't know what had awoken her. It wasn't a loud sound or a dream. She didn't smell smoke, and nothing had touched her. Yet something had yanked her from a deep sleep. She frantically scanned the room. Nothing seemed out of place. She lay still as a statue, listening for any clue. Then she heard it: short gasping breaths. She looked to her right, and her stomach tightened. Jeremy lay beside her staring blankly at the ceiling. His body was rigid as a steel beam, and his jagged breaths shook the entire bed.

Remembering the training she'd received on tending to one having a seizure, she shifted so that she was poised above the gasping man and made sure his head was protected. To her surprise, there wasn't a vacant look in his eyes. Instead, they focused upon her.

Kate put her palm on his cheek. "Tim," she whispered. "It's all right, I'm right here".

He stuttered. "I... didn't mean to scare you... I dreamed... the water... I couldn't save him..." He sounded like a frightened child.

Without thinking, Kate lay beside him and wrapped him in her arms. She kissed his temple and whispered, "It's all right, I'm right here."

They lay in silence for several minutes, then Jeremy said, "Those are the first words you said when you found me."

"What words?"

"It's all right, I'm right here." His voice was weak and far away.

"I can't believe you could hear me, much less remember my words." In fact, she didn't remember any of the words she'd spoken when she found his broken body on the mountainside.

"I thought I'd died, and you were an angel," he paused. "Actually, the first words I heard you say were 'Holy Shit.'" He laughed then grabbed his ribs.

"Holy Shit?"

"I remember thinking it was strange that an angel would cuss, but I thought, I'd just go with it." His voice dropped. "I'm sorry if I scared you."

"You didn't scare me," she lied.

His entire body shuddered. "The dream seemed so real, my dad was stranded in a tree, and the water just kept coming. I couldn't get to him."

"It was just a dream." She pulled him tighter. "You're safe now."

"Thank you." He turned his head so he could look Kate in the eye.

Her stomach flip-flopped. She looked away before she did something inappropriate or stupid. "It was no problem," she stammered. "Try to get back to sleep."

He nodded and closed his eyes. After several minutes, Kate felt his body relax and heard the soft snoring sounds of peaceful sleep.

THE SUN HAD BARELY RISEN WHEN a harsh banging erupted from the cabin door. Kate opened her eyes and studied the man asleep in her arms.

He looked so peaceful and calm, nothing like he looked last night. Last night, the scene played like a looped video in her mind. She could still hear his ragged breath and feel the sweat on his forehead as it rested against her cheek. She wondered if he'd have any memory of the panic attack, and if he did remember, she wondered if he would want to talk about it. Should she broach the subject, or just let it be?

She gingerly pulled her arm from under his neck and immediately bit her lip. Pins and needles pricked from her fingers to her shoulder as blood flow returned to her sleeping limb. She was shaking her arm to restore circulation when the knock sounded again, this time, faster, louder, and more irritating.

Kate slipped on her rubber-soled slippers, crossed the main room in three long strides, and pulled open the front door. In the threshold stood a perfectly coiffed Kathleen Whitacre with picnic basket in hand. Her bright red cardigan matched her perfectly applied lipstick and her white capris were starched and creased.

"Good morning," Kathleen gushed. "I didn't wake you, did I? Troy and I are early risers. You know what they say: early to bed, early to rise, makes a woman, healthy, wealthy and wise." The older woman gave a smile so sugary-sweet; it could cause cavities.

At the present moment, Kate would have preferred cavities. She balled her fists and refrained from replying with a cute saying of her own; it rhymed with 'stow-away-you-rosy-witch'. Instead, she stood defiantly in the doorway with her arms crossed. "What are you doing here?"

Kathleen craned her neck to see into the bedroom. "I'm relieving you from your duties. You must be exhausted after sleeping on the floor these past two nights."

"Yes, I am tired and not in the mood for visitors."

"Of course, you're tired. Why don't you go to my cabin and lie down while I keep this fellow company? I bet you could use a nice sleep in an actual bed. Is he still asleep?"

Kate rubbed her temples, and Kathleen took advantage of the movement. She slipped through the cabin door, and in the blink of an eye, she was in the bedroom. By the time Kate could react, the busybody was sitting in the folding chair staring at Jeremy like he was a cut of meat she was considering purchasing. "I'll just sit here until he wakes up."

"I think waking up with a strange, elderly woman sitting in a chair staring at him may be a bit jarring." Kate gave a puckish smile.

Kathleen whipped her head around and glared at Kate through narrowed eyes. She stood and strutted into the kitchen. "I'll put the casserole and pie in the oven to keep warm, then I'll sweep up all the dirt and dried mud that's been tracked in." She gave a patronizing smile. "This is technically a sick ward. It needs to be kept clean, preferably by somebody who knows how to keep a home."

Kate was finished playing this game. "I'm not leaving. Plus, we agreed last night that stopping by wasn't a good idea."

"No sweetheart, you decided it wasn't a good idea." Kathleen's voice dripped with condescension. "You may be the one who found him, but you're a single woman with very little experience at taking care of men. I'm a mom and a wife. Let a woman who knows what she's doing have a chance."

Kate refused to give Kathleen the satisfaction of showing how much the comment stung. However, she knew if she stayed, the argument would escalate, and nothing good would come from that. She mimicked the older woman's fake smile. "You're right Kathleen, I do need a bit of air. He's been asking me about the history of Slate and the people who are staying here. I think you'll be perfect since you have your overly powdered nose firmly planted in the middle of everybody's business." With the last insult, Kate whirled and marched out of the bedroom. She grabbed her coat off the hook and slammed the cabin door behind her.

Holding her tongue was not one of Kate's strengths, and it took considerable effort to not storm back into her cabin and give Kathleen a piece of her mind. She took a deep breath and reminded herself that this was not a normal situation, and her normal behavior would accomplish nothing.

So instead of standing her ground, she stood outside her cabin wearing pajamas, bedroom slippers, and no bra. She looked down at herself and sighed. The pajamas wouldn't be a big deal. Her slippers had rubber soles, so that wasn't an issue. However, going braless on a chilly morning wasn't ideal. The residents would see enough destruction and sorrow soon, there was no need to inflict upon them the cruel effects of gravity on a thirty-seven-year-old set of double-Ds.

She zipped her fleece jacket up to her chin and stormed off in the direction of Nan's cabin.

Kate barreled through Nan's cabin door but stopped short when she saw the kitchen was full of people.

"Kate," Chris stood. "Have a seat."

"I need to stand," she snapped. Nothing was going right this morning; first the infuriating interaction with Kathleen, now she wouldn't even have Nan and Penny to vent to. "What's everybody doing here?" Her voice was abrasive and accusatory.

She looked at the room's occupants. CJ, Chris, Sam, Doc, Penny, and Nan all sat around the dining room table. Most were still in whatever they had worn to bed. Every set of shoulders was sagging, and every face looked exhausted. In an instant, Kate's sound and fury was stripped away. She made an extra effort to not sound bitchy. "I mean, why are we gathered in Nan's cabin?"

Nan stood and gave her a quick hug. "We're glad you are here, Kate. How's the patient?"

"He seems to be healing fast. Kathleen Whitacre brought him breakfast bright and early this morning. She insisted on sitting with him." Just saying the words irritated her.

Nan rolled her eyes. "Lawd, hasn't the poor boy suffered enough?"

Sam chuckled. "He fell down the side of a mountain, I think he can handle an hour or so with Kathleen."

Nan shook her head. "If you had to choose between tumbling down the side of a mountain and being held captive by Kathleen Whitacre, which would you choose?"

Sam shrugged. "Fair point."

Doc cleared her throat. "We met so Chris could share what he has found out about Riverside, not so we could gossip."

"We have news?" Kate asked anxiously.

Chris, who had been communicating with the outside world on his CB radio, pulled a crumpled piece of yellow paper from his pocket. "I don't know a lot, but here is what I've been told by the State Police."

He paused. "Ten inches of rain fell in thirty hours. The Greenbrier crested at fifteen feet above flood stage; all its tributaries are also out of their banks. Over half of Riverside is flooded. The post office, fire hall, and many homes had at least six feet of water, some are gone. Across the county, asphalt has been upended, and bridges have been washed away, the one at the bottom of the mountain included."

The room was enveloped in a deafening silence, as everybody tried to comprehend what fifteen feet above flood level looked like. Finally, CJ spoke. "So, nobody can return to their homes now, and some homes are completely gone?"

Kate exhaled in disbelief. "I guess we're lucky we got here when we did."

Chris leaned his elbows on the table. "Not all towns were as lucky as Riverside. Not everybody got out. Right now, the death toll is fourteen with at least twelve still missing."

A communal gasp rose from the group.

Chris continued, "The General Store is completely gone, and Kenny is missing." His voice broke on the last word.

Chris took a handkerchief from his pocket and wiped his eyes. Nan sat at the head of the table, tears streamed down her face, like a statue of a weeping angel.

Finally, Doc asked, "Other than Kenny, are any of the people who are dead or missing, relatives to anybody here?"

Chris shook his head. "They haven't released any names yet, so we don't know."

"Then, how do you know about Kenny?" Penny's voice sounded accusatory.

Chris didn't look up from the table. "Dan James is the one I spoke to. He wasn't supposed to give any details, but he knows that Kenny is one of us. Kenny has no next of kin to notify, so he told me."

Nan wiped a tear from her chin. "When will we know the other names?"

Chris composed himself. "They have to notify next of kin before they release any names. That's all I know. The conversations with the police have been short and sporadic. Communication with us is low on their priority list."

Penny shot from her seat. "We don't know when we can go home?"

Chris shook his head. "That's not what I said. If everything goes as planned, the National Guard should begin evacuations before the end of the week."

Tears spilled from Penny's eyes. "The end of the week?" she sobbed. Being away from her kids was taking and obvious toll.

Chris nodded sympathetically. "We are safe and dry, so evacuating us is low on the priority list. Some people are still stuck in their attics without food or water."

Penny slumped into her seat and put her head in her hands.

CJ motioned toward the door. "What are we going to tell them?"

Kate asked numbly, "Do we tell them anything? Maybe we should keep it to ourselves."

Sam said, "I thought about that, but they deserve to know. If not the whole story, at least something, anxiety and worry are eating people alive."

Nan looked at Sam then back to the tabletop. "I agree. Rumors and anxiety can be worse than truth, no matter how awful." She took a ragged breath. "However, we all know that there are members of our community who cannot handle so much stress. We need to be delicate when we let them know what's happening. We won't lie, but we need to be gentle."

Doc nodded. "Nan's right." Her eyes skirted the table, making brief eye contact with each person. "I know this is horrible, but we have to be strong. It may be asking too much to appear happy, but we must keep our anger and tears hidden when the others are around. They need to believe somebody will take care of them."

Chris asked, "So what now?"

## Chapter 17

NAN WHISPERED TO DOC, "Should we still do it?"

Doc looked around the room. "I think everybody needs it, but you have to be the one to tell her."

Kate felt like a child being left out of an adult conversation. Irritation laced her voice. "What are we telling and to whom?"

Doc looked from Kate to Nan and back to Kate. "Actually, we decided to meet even before we knew Chris had information. People need something to do, a distraction from fear and despair."

Chris furrowed his brow. "Like what?" It looked like he'd been left out of the loop, too.

Nan cleared her throat. "The foreman's cottage is almost finished. It doesn't have a kitchen yet, but the conference room and bathrooms are finished. We thought we'd have a meal, throw together a few casseroles, a few desserts and just come together. Some people have been trapped in their cabins since the moment we got here. They need to get out."

Penny sounded defeated. "Yeah, but that was before we knew all of this. I don't know if it's such a good idea."

Nan gently squeezed her hand. "I think we need it now more than ever. Besides, there should be some joy in their lives, because once they find out…" her voice trailed off.

Chris asked, "What about the short notice? What about food?"

Nan reassured, "Most of the food that was brought is canned food from people's gardens. We can warm it on the stove, and I'm sure Kathleen has baked enough for a small army."

Doc interjected, "Then we can have an impromptu camp meeting—"

Chris interrupted, "Won't people want to hear the information as soon as they get there? Everybody is on pins and needles. Making them wait is cruel."

Nan nodded. "We can initially say we don't know anything, and then you can get a message. We can go straight to the business meeting while we're all in one place."

Penny asked, "Don't you think that once everybody is together, all they are going to want to talk about is the flood?"

Doc said sheepishly, "We were thinking the residents could definitely use a distraction."

Kate felt unexplainably apprehensive. "Such as?"

Nan cleared her throat. "Such as a mysterious stranger."

Sam chimed in, "We were thinking it might be nice if—"

Kate cut him off. "Excuse me?" She shot to her feet. "Are you talking about the man in my cabin, Tim? The Tim that slid into camp the day before yesterday? *That* Tim? Because *that* Tim is still very sick. *That* Tim is still not walking without the support of two men." Words shot from her mouth like flames.

Nan stood and put her hand on Kate's shoulder. "Sweetheart, we know he's still ill, we were just thinking—"

Kate shrugged off the kind gesture. "Thinking what, exactly? That Tim is some zoo animal to be put on display so that residents can forget their lives are falling apart!"

"That's not what we're suggesting," Nan said patiently.

Doc's voice wasn't as sympathetic. "Besides, he has already said he's looking forward to it."

Kate crossed her arms over her chest. "When did you have time to ask him?"

Doc replied coldly, "When I checked in on him last evening. He and I talked about it at length. He said he'd like to get out a bit. I mentioned the gathering, and he was very excited."

Kate demanded, "Did you tell him that everyone in the whole camp will be tripping over themselves to get to him? Did you tell him he'd be put on display, like a specimen to be poked and interrogated? Do you realize how sick he still is? This is too much for him!" She wasn't sure why this bothered her so much. Jeremy wasn't hers to dictate what could happen to him. He didn't need her permission to go, and the townspeople didn't need her permission to ask him. She wasn't his nurse, she wasn't his... she wasn't *his* anything. With the wind stripped from her sails, she collapsed in her chair and covered her face with her hands.

With the confrontation over, Doc returned to her sympathetic tone. "I was honest with him. I told him the residents all wanted to meet him and that he'd be the center of attention. He knows what he's getting himself into. He said if he felt healthy enough, he'd like to attend." She took a deep breath. "I know you only want what's best for him. I hope you know we all feel the same."

Kate looked at Penny. "Did you know anything about this?"

Penny shook her head. "No, but Kate, I think it's a good idea. People need this more than you realize."

When Kate looked at Chris and saw his red-rimmed eyes, she felt ashamed of her adolescent outburst. She forced a smile. "Okay."

"So, the Foreman's cabin around five?" Doc asked.

"Sounds good." Penny put her hands on her knees and stood.

Chris asked, "How are we going to get everybody to the Foreman's cabin? It's slick out there."

Sam pondered the question for a moment. "I figure some of the younger men could help the elderly members."

"Yeah, but most of the 'younger men' are still over fifty," Penny added.

"Watch it there!" CJ protested, "Fifty is still young!"

Doc redirected the conversation. "After the meal, Chris can announce that he has gotten word from the State Police. We'll call an impromptu meeting."

Chris asked, "How are we going to let people know about the meal?"

Nan said, "I was thinking we could each visit two or three cabins and spread the word."

Kate pounded her palm on the table. "I am NOT visiting Kathleen Whitacre!"

"Fair enough," Nan smiled. "Do you think you could handle Hazel and Sally?"

"As long as it isn't Kathleen."

Nan patted Kate's back. "Don't worry, I'll take care of Kathleen." There was more than just a hint of mischief in her voice.

KATE TOOK AN EXTRA-LONG TIME WALKING to cabin number thirteen, which was shared by the widows Hazel Phelps and Sally Sparrow. The two were thick as thieves but fought like an old married couple. A visit with these two could either be a quick laugh or a tedious mediation.

Kate knocked on the cabin door. "Come on in," Hazel called.

Kate took a deep breath and stepped into the main room. The two women were sitting in burgundy armchairs, joking with one another. Thankfully, it didn't seem like this would be a mediation day. She joined their small talk and relayed the message about the gathering. Just when Kate thought the interaction had been unremarkable, she saw Hazel and Sally exchange puckish looks and knew she had overestimated the ease of the transaction.

"I haven't seen much of you, Kate, since that strange man rolled into camp. You must be doing a good job nursing him back to health." Hazel tapped her bubblegum pink nails on the end table. "How is he coming along?"

Kate recited the speech she had given the other residents. "He's doing well. He broke his right arm when he fell. He needed stitches. Other than that, plus a few bumps and bruises, he'll be okay."

Sally spoke up, "Will this mystery man be at supper?"

Kate replied, "Hopefully he can make it for a little bit; he still gets tired easily."

Sally turned to Hazel and said, "I heard that Phil Whitacre sat with him yesterday and that they had a good talk."

Hazel giggled. "Oh, good. I've been wanting to speak to this young man."

Kate was exhausted, and her patience was hanging on by a very thin thread. "He's still very weak, so we are asking the residents to not bombard him."

"Of course." Sally nodded.

Hazel had a Cheshire Cat grin on her face. "Okay, Katherine, we'll be there."

Sally giggled. "You tell Nan we can't wait."

Kate knew they were cooking up something nefarious, but she didn't have the energy to ponder their devious plan. She clenched her jaw and said, "I certainly will." Then she turned on her heel and walked out of the cabin.

In her mid-twenties, Kate had learned the hard way that her body could not handle drinking alcohol halfway through the day. However, today, she was tempted to visit Mr. Coots and retest the theory.

## Chapter 18

WHEN NAN WALKED INTO THE BEDROOM, Kathleen was sitting beside Jeremy's bed, rattling on like a toddler after an espresso. "All of Tommy's teachers told me he was the smartest in the class. He graduated valedictorian, perfect 4.0," Kathleen boasted.

Nan cleared her throat and interrupted the bragging. Kathleen spun around in her chair and glared. "Why Nan, what brings you here?" Her lips stretched in a fake smile.

Nan suppressed a giggle. "Looks like you two are having a grand 'ol time, but Doc has issued orders that the patient rest."

Kathleen narrowed her eyes in suspicion. "Where's Kate?"

"She's telling Hazel and Sally about the covered dish dinner we're having at the Foreman's Cabin."

"A covered dish dinner?" Kathleen exclaimed.

Nan smiled smugly. "Yes, we're throwing together a small fellowship meal. Everyone is bringing a dish. People are catching cabin fever, and this is a great way to get them out and about."

"People are making dishes to bring?" Kathleen sounded incredulous, like Nan had been keeping this a secret from her. She shot to her feet. "I need to get back to my cabin and start cooking." She muttered as she marched out the door.

Nan walked into the bedroom and sat in the chair beside Jeremy, who looked a little befuddled. He furrowed his brow. "Well, that was quite an exit."

Nan rolled her eyes. "Sorry about that. She can be melodramatic."

"Now I know why Troy talks so much. I bet he can hardly get a word in edge-wise at home." He licked his lips. "But man, the food was awesome. The casserole reminded me of something my mum used to make on Saturday mornings, and that apple pie, wow! I could survive for weeks on just those two dishes."

"Your stomach handled it okay?"

"Surprisingly, it did."

"Good, glad you are feeling better." Her kind eyes and warm smile put him at ease. "By the way, I'm Faye Kesner, but most people know me as Nan."

He nodded politely. "Pleased to make your acquaintance."

"It's nice to meet you, too. I'm so glad we can finally talk."

"Kate speaks very highly of you."

Nan put her hands over her heart. "I love Kate as if she were my very own. She and my Penny are as close as sisters."

"Penny is your granddaughter?" Jeremy asked.

"Yes. My husband, Arlin, and I helped raise her. She is the only child of my oldest, Joey."

"Oh?"

Nan nodded. "Joey is a brilliant man, but he didn't always think things through when he was younger. When he graduated from high school, he earned a full scholarship to Columbia University in New York City. We were nervous about our boy going straight from tiny little Riverside to the big city, but his future was so bright."

"How is that not thinking things through? Columbia is quite prestigious."

"It is prestigious, and he was doing very well. That is, until he came home for Christmas break with his pregnant girlfriend."

"Pregnant girlfriend?" Jeremy leaned closer. "He didn't tell you beforehand?"

"Nope. I knew he was bringing home a girl, but we knew nothing about the pregnancy." Nan shook her head. "They stayed in Riverside until after she had the baby. Six weeks after Penny was born, she just left. We haven't heard from her in thirty-five years."

Jeremy's amusement turned to disgust. "She just walked away?" The idea made him sick to his stomach.

"Oh, I was angry. I even hated her. But in time, I've come to realize that I didn't know her, and I didn't know her story. Fear makes us all do stupid things. Whatever her reasons, Joey was left a single dad, and he loved his little girl as no father has ever loved before."

"So, he gave up his dreams for his daughter?" There was admiration in Jeremy's voice.

"Not entirely. When Penny turned five, we told him to go back to college, but he wouldn't go to New York. He went to West Virginia University and got an engineering degree. Penny stayed with us, and Joey came back every weekend. When he finished his master's degree, the university hired him as an adjunct professor and paid for him to get his doctorate. Dr. Joseph Kesner. In two generations we went from dirt poor immigrants working in the coal mine to earning a Ph.D."

"You must be extremely proud."

"Prouder than you will ever know. When Penny was old enough, she went to the university for her accounting degree. They're still as close as a father and daughter can be. I have eight grandchildren. I love every one of them with all of my being, but if I'm honest, Penny and I share a special bond."

"It sounds like your bond is stronger than steel."

"It is. And when I met Kat bird for the first time, I felt my heart double in size. Do you understand?"

"Yes, ma'am, I do."

"Troy tells me that you're Scottish. Scottish mothers and grandmothers are very protective of their children aren't they, fiercely protective? They'd bring a grizzly bear to its knees if she thought it would hurt one of her babies. Isn't that right?"

He was slightly confused. "Yes, Ma'am."

Nan's soft smile was suddenly gone. She paralyzed Jeremy with a hard-as-steel gaze. "Well, there are two things I should tell you." She continued in a heavy Scottish accent: "The first is that I love Kate as if she were my very own. Second, my mum and dad hail from Bonnyrigg."

She lay her hand lightly upon his knee and said, "Remember that, Jeremy." Then without another word, she slipped from the bedroom and out the cabin door.

Jeremy chuckled. It was easy to see why Kate thought so highly of the spunky woman. He lay back on his pillows and stared at the knotty pine ceiling, the most entertaining parts of the conversation playing back in his mind.

Suddenly, the smile was wiped from his face as he realized the implications of Nan's last word.

## Chapter 19

KATE WAS GLAD SHE HAD MADE HAZEL and Sally her last stop. Her interaction with the two conniving old women left her tired, irritated, and ready for a nap. *Nan owes me for taking on those two. I'm talking homemade red velvet cake owes me!* She was so busy planning the guilt trip that she almost ran smack into Chris.

Though he stared intently at the ground, she could see that his eyes were swollen and rimmed in red. "Sorry, Kate," he mumbled.

"It's fine." She started to reach out to hug him, then remembered Doc's words from before. "I was just heading back to my cabin," she said in a casual tone.

"Yeah, heading back to mine, too." He kept his head down as he sidestepped her and continued in the other direction.

Kate stood rooted in her spot. Though, she prided herself on not buying into traditional gender stereotypes, seeing these usually stoic men reduced to tears set her world off-kilter. It made her feel like she was twenty-two again, standing at the head of her dad's casket and gazing at the line of well-wishers snaking out the door of the funeral home. Over five hundred people came to offer their condolences. Many times, she, her brother, or her mom ended up being the ones providing comfort. Grizzled old men whom Kate had seen stitch their own wounds without flinching, wept in grief. The memory still haunted her.

She trudged up the cabin stairs, each step taking more effort than the last. When she finally walked through the door, she felt like she was ready to fall to pieces. Not even the beautiful blue eyes and enchanting smile of the sexy Scotsman in her bed was enough to distract her.

As she walked into the bedroom, she heard, "Hey stranger."

She tried to smile. "How's the patient?"

"Better. I met Nan. She rescued me from Kathleen."

She sat beside Jeremy and leaned against the headboard. "Nan is everybody's rescuer."

He took her hand. The soft pressure of his fingers intertwined with hers felt natural and reassuring. "Do you want to talk about it, or do you want to be alone?"

"What I want?" She tried to laugh. "What I want is for Chris to walk through that door and tell me he was wrong, that he got the wrong message, that Riverside is not under water and people aren't dead. What I want is to wake up from this nightmare and not have to face eighty-year-olds whose lives have been washed away." She wiped a stray tear from her cheek. "I don't think I'll get what I want this time, huh?"

"It's obvious how much the people of this community mean to you."

"It's not just them. Some of my greatest memories are in Nan's house. It was my home. Thanksgiving dinner, Christmas mornings, gone, swept away."

He squeezed her hand tighter. "Oh, Kate, I'm so very sorry. When did you find out?"

Kate blinked hard to prevent more tears from coming. "Nobody said anything about Nan's, which is almost worse. Chris told us of a few buildings that are ruined. Logistically, if they're gone, Nan's probably..." Her voice broke.

"Oh, Kate..."

She shook her head as if the motion could protect her from the heartbreaking thoughts. "I bet when you came to the woods, you never expected all this drama."

"I came into the woods because I wanted to find answers, center myself, become one with nature, insert whatever new age rubbish you choose. Basically, I wanted to go where nobody knew me."

*Where nobody knew me*, the words repeated in her head. Now, she understood why he'd said his name was Tim. He was a celebrity, there were very few places where nobody would know him. He'd used an alias because he didn't want to be recognized.

Jeremy continued, "I came here so I could lose myself. I damn near succeeded, permanently." He laughed. "The thought that you may leave this world makes you think about things you never considered."

"Like what?"

"Like the people in your life, who you let in, who you don't, and why. Forgiveness, forgiving yourself and others. I pondered what's truly important, versus where we spend our time." He gave a sly grin. "You know, all that transcendental shite."

Kate, happy for the distraction, asked, "What conclusion did you come to?"

"Haven't come to one yet. I know that whatever I was doing up until this point wasn't working." He became very serious. "Working myself almost to death, trying to win the approval of strangers more than appreciating the relationships which should be important. There's just a lot I want to change when I get home."

"What is it that you do in Scotland?" The question left Kate's mouth before she could stop it. She reprimanded herself. *When talking to a celebrity who is trying to hide their true identity, asking what they do for a living probably isn't the swiftest thing.* She quickly turned the attention back to herself. "I'm a math teacher," she blurted.

"A teacher? My mom was a teacher." He smiled sincerely. "I should have known you have a nurturing profession. Your students are lucky."

Kate gave a light laugh. "I teach math. Most of my students feel like algebra should be outlawed by the Geneva Convention, cruel and unusual punishment."

"I never hated maths, but I was definitely more of a fine arts guy."

She dropped his hand. "I've always wondered why British people say maths, with an s? Why would math be plural?"

"Why wouldn't it be? You have a degree in mathematics, why would you not teach maths?"

"Because it's a single subject."

"No, there's arithmetic, algebra, geometry, different maths."

"No, those are different parts of the same subject." Her tone was barbed. The lack of sleep and overabundance of stress was making her irritable.

He crossed his arms over his chest. "I disagree."

His snotty demeanor increased her irritation. "You can disagree, but which one of us has a degree in math?" Her voice was sharp as cut glass.

He pulled so far away from her that no part of him was touching her. "You have a degree in mathematics." His voice dripped with sarcasm. "I, however, hail from the land that created the English language, so I think I'm a bit of an authority!"

Kate blurted, "You're from Scotland!"

"Which is a part of Great Britain, which contains England, where English originated. This conversation is over. Or as you mathS teachers would say, QED." He put extra emphasis on the "S".

She rolled her eyes. "So, you are dropping the mic?"

"Dropping the what? Bloody hell, you Americans murder the English language." He leaned back against the pillows and closed his eyes.

## Chapter 20

JEREMY DIDN'T KNOW HOW THE CONVERSATION had taken such a dramatic turn. When Kate had walked through the door, she looked so broken and weak. All he'd wanted to do was protect her. Now she was angry at him for… he didn't know what for.

After a minute of absolute silence, he felt the bed shake. He looked to his left. Kate was sitting with her hands covering her face, and her shoulders were shaking. His heart sank. Her world was falling apart, and he was arguing with her like a damned barbarian. "I'm sorry. I didn't mean to be such an argumentative arse."

Kate removed her hands from her face and looked directly at him. Tears were streaming from her eyes, but she was laughing.

"What's so funny?" he asked in complete bewilderment.

"This!" She let out a whoop of laughter. "This is so stupid! Are we actually getting into an argument over the annunciation of a single syllable word?"

The corner of his mouth turned up. "I believe we are."

They looked at one another and broke into a round of giggles. Jeremy grabbed his ribs. "You have got to stop making me laugh."

Kate bit her bottom lip. "I'm sorry." She lay her head on the pillow beside his. "You say you're a fine arts guy?"

"Sounds a bit pretentious, doesn't it?"

"No, in fact, I have admiration for those who have the guts to take the road less traveled instead of the safe route. I don't have that courage."

"Courage and stupidity are often confused."

"So, are you brave or stupid?"

Jeremy thought for a moment. "Depends on who you ask, I guess." He shifted so he could look at her. "Tell me, what's your favorite form of the arts?"

"My first love is photography, but I have so little time for it. Besides, I didn't discover my passion until I was thirty years old, too late to change course."

"It's never too late to change course."

"It is when you have those who rely on you financially," she stated.

"You have children?"

"I don't have kids. I always thought I wanted to, but that's another sad story for another sad day. There are others who depend on me, though." She quickly changed her tone. "After my first love of photography, my passion is live theater, especially musicals."

Jeremy had to physically suppress his glee. "You like live theater!"

"You sound surprised."

The prospect of being able to have a casual conversation about the stage made him feel like a bird whose cage door had been left ajar. "Not surprised, just excited. I never get to discuss the theater. My career requires me to interact with several of the biggest theaters in the UK. I never get to have honest conversations like this. Too many times, my words have come back to haunt me."

"Sounds exhausting, constantly having to be vigilant of everything you say."

"It is." He didn't want to discuss his heavy commitments, though. He wanted to revel in this time of noncommittal, non-consequential banter. His voice became lighter. "What type of theater do you enjoy the most?"

"Musicals, I have no earthly talent in either acting or singing. Perhaps that's why I enjoy them so much, admiration for those who do what I cannot."

His eyes sparkled. "What's your favorite musical?"

Kate chewed her bottom lip. "To narrow it down to just one, I'm not sure I could. There are so many I love: *The Lion King, RENT, Wicked, Spamalot*." She paused, "If I had to choose, I suppose it'd be *Wicked*. I love the story, and the lyrics are so powerful."

Jeremy nodded. "I like musicals, but I'm more of a theatrical purist; Arthur Miller, August Wilson. Ultimately, I'm a lover of all things Shakespeare."

Kate used an aristocratic tone, "Ah, the Bard."

Jeremy smirked.

"Don't give me that surprised look, that a girl from the West Virginia sticks could be cultured."

He held up his hands defensively. "No, it's just that I rarely hear many Americans use that term."

"Let me turn the tables, what's your favorite Shakespeare piece?"

"That's not fair, it's like being asked to pick your favorite child. I can't choose."

"You must!" Her chocolate eyes sparkled as she teased.

"You'll argue until you get what you want, won't you?"

She gave an impish smile. "That's usually the way it works, and don't change the subject."

"Fine, if I HAD to choose, *Hamlet*. The story: betrayal, love, lust, hubris, vengeance. It's as poignant today as when it was written. How about you? What is your favorite Shakespeare piece?"

"*A Midsummer Night's Dream*, it doesn't have the heart-wrenching story of *Hamlet* or *Macbeth*, but it has its own charm. It's fun and transports you to another place, where you can forget the chaos happening in your own world and spend a few hours romping in the woods with Puck. I hated Shakespeare when I was first exposed to it. My twelfth-grade English teacher tortured us with *Macbeth* for three months. I resembled one of the wicked sisters before it was over."

"American English teachers, Shakespeare's greatest enemy," Jeremy mused. "I've heard that same story from many of my American friends.

Shakespeare is meant to be experienced, reveled in, performed, not read like a novel. When did you stop hating Will?"

"The Shenandoah Shakespeare Express, a traveling Shakespeare company, performed *The Tempest* for us in a school assembly. I realized that Shakespeare didn't have to suck. I was still too immature to appreciate it, but it was no longer torture. My big epiphany came when I saw *Hamlet* on stage when I was in college. I fell in love with the nuances of Shakespeare."

"Isn't *Romeo and Juliet* the first love of most Americans?"

Kate wrinkled her nose. "I despise *Romeo and Juliet!*"

Jeremy placed his hand on his chest and feigned distress. "I'm not sure I can even share a room with you, much less a bed."

"There's the door," Kate teased. "Shall I call upon the men of the camp to lift you off of the bed so you can limp back to the mudslide?"

"Touché, mistress Katherine, touché." He smiled playfully. "So please enlighten me, what is it you hate about this famous tragedy?"

"I cannot see celebrating a pair of horny teenagers, who think each other are hot then decide to commit suicide when they aren't allowed to see each other."

"It's not a celebration. It's a tragedy."

"It's a tragedy that's celebrated, how about that? How often do you hear a man who is charming referred to as a Romeo or a young couple freshly in love referred to as Romeo and Juliet? Their so-called true love has been glorified, when it's just a tale of overactive hormones and lack of maturity."

He threw his unencumbered hand in the air. "But the story is so much more than that. It's the beautiful use of blank verse and iambic pentameter. It's about warring kingdoms, silly feuds that cost lives, murder, greed, the unquenchable thirst for power. The story of the Montagues and Capulets is so classic and poignant."

"I agree, but why throw two hormonal, whiny teenagers into the mix? They're exalted and romanticized, seen as martyrs for love. Love at first sight and all of that BS."

"Whiny?"

"You must admit, Romeo is very whiny."

Jeremy couldn't help but smile. "Okay, you got me there, but I still love the play."

"You're allowed to be wrong." There was a playful hilt to her voice. "I haven't even told you the best part."

"Of *Romeo and Juliet*?"

"Of my relationship to The Bard. I'm named after the lead character in *Kiss Me Kate*, the modernized musical version of *Taming of the Shrew*."

Jeremy stuck out his tongue in distaste. "Not a fan of *Kiss Me Kate*."

"I'm not either, but my mom loved the show. She's the one who planted the love of musical theater in my heart." Kate's eyes were wistful. "Each year we'd take one trip to New York City and see as many shows as we could fit in a twenty-four-hour period. It was our only vacation. I never realized what she went without so that she could save the money for our annual trip."

"She sounds like a great woman."

Kate's face darkened. "She was. I mean, is."

Jeremy cocked his head to the side. "I don't understand."

"Mom's technically still here, but she's gone a lot of the time. Alzheimer's Disease has almost completely taken her. For the past four years when I visit, she seldom knows who I am. Sometimes she's just a shell."

Again, he felt an overwhelming desire to wrap her in his arms and comfort her. "I'm sorry."

"My mom's in her seventies, I had thirty-three wonderful years with one of the most amazing women in history. I feel lucky to have had that."

He could tell she was trying to sound brave. "Is she with you in Virginia?"

"I wish," Kate said. "The reason I teach in such a wealthy district is so I can afford to put my mom in a decent care facility. However, even with my Northern Virginia teacher salary, I cannot afford a care center in Northern Virginia. She's in a little nursing home close to where I grew up. They don't have specialized Alzheimer's programs, but they're good to her. I grew up with a lot of the nurses. They all love mom, and I know she's cared for. It just makes it hard to be so far away from her. I only get to see her once a month, sometimes less. It's a three-hour drive each way."

"How does your dad deal with it?"

Kate shrugged. "He left us about fifteen years ago."

Jeremy's stomach hardened. His voice was full of disgust. "I'll never understand how somebody can walk out on their spouse as if the vows they took mean nothing."

Kate gave a small laugh. "He didn't walk out on us, he passed away when I was twenty-two."

He smacked his palm on his forehead. "Oh God, now I feel like a world-class arse, again."

"It's okay. Time has a way of turning gaping wounds into less painful scars."

"What happened?" Jeremy asked, then abruptly added, "I'm sorry, you don't have to answer that."

"No, it's okay." She took in a deep breath and continued, "He had a stroke. I'd just graduated from college and was visiting home. He was moving hay bales and stopped to have lunch. While he was sitting in the shade enjoying a sandwich and lemonade, he just died. I went to find him for supper, and he was leaning against a tree. He looked so peaceful, like he had just fallen asleep."

"You found him? How awful."

"Better me than mom. It would have been too much for her. I've made my peace with it. Dad was seventy. He didn't suffer or end up being a prisoner in his own body. He wasn't hooked up to machines in some sterile facility. I find a lot of comfort in that. Besides, he died doing what he loved, working on the farm."

Though Jeremy didn't realize it, the corners of his mouth turned up in a grin.

Kate glared at him through narrowed eyes. "What's so funny?"

"I'm sorry. It's not funny, just something you said reminded me of my mum."

"Oh?"

"My mum died suddenly of a heart attack three years ago. She died doing what she loved too."

Kate raised an eyebrow.

"Shopping for shoes. Don't get me wrong, I love my mum, and I miss her dearly. However, if you knew her, you'd see the humor. When we were growing up, things were tight. She stretched every dime. However, when my dad's job started providing better opportunities, my mum discovered the joys of shopping. Buying shoes became her obsession. When we cleaned out her wardrobe, we found over three hundred pairs of shoes. Most had never been out of the box."

"Three hundred? I'd definitely call that an obsession." Kate gave a small laugh. "Dad's obsession was farm machinery, more expensive of an addiction, but at least he could use his as a tax write-off."

"I don't know what a tax write-off is, but I'm not sure about the expensive part. You never saw my mom's shoe collection."

Kate smiled. "For my mom, the addiction became vacationing after dad passed. She'd spend Christmas in the Caribbean, Thanksgiving in Alaska, and Easter in Vegas. She finally got to live the life she could never have as a farmer's wife. That's how I came to spend every holiday with Penny and Nan in Riverside." A shallow dimple appeared in her cheek as she smiled. "It's nice to talk like this. I made peace with dad's passing long ago, but there are few people whom I can talk to about it without getting that *Oh, you poor girl*, look."

Jeremy felt a fluttering in his chest that had nothing to do with lost memories or bruised ribs. He opened his mouth to speak, and then quickly closed it.

"What is it?" Kate asked.

"I never do this. I don't share secrets or talk about my past, especially with somebody I just met." He chuckled. "Honestly, I've probably told you more in the last forty-eight hours than I've told most of my oldest mates."

Kate asked, "What makes me so special?"

"You don't seem like a stranger, there is something so familiar about you. Do you know what I mean?"

"Yeah, I think I do."

Jeremy wondered if there was more behind Kate's words because she quickly changed the subject.

"So, Doc told me you'll be the guest-of-honor at today's dinner," she said.

"She didn't tell me that."

"She didn't tell you about the meal?" Kate growled. "She swore that you'd discussed it, and that you were fine with it."

"No, she told me about dinner, but she left out the guest-of-honor part."

Kate clenched her jaw. "She didn't tell you that you'd be the center of attention, and that people would clamor to talk to you?"

"Oh, that's what you mean?" He breathed a sigh of relief. "She told me that. Being a guest-of-honor means something a wee bit different in my world."

Kate looked at her watch. "Ugh, I have to leave soon. I told Doc I'd help set up the tables for dinner. Troy and Sam will help you get dressed. Is that okay?"

"Perfect! I wonder if they could move a chair into the shower so I could wash."

Kate crinkled her nose. "I have a bit of bad news."

"What?" he asked, suspiciously.

"The showers don't work. Well, the showers work, but the hot water heaters don't. The water of Slate is fed by a freshwater stream, so it'd be a freezing shower. Most of us have been warming water on the stove and then taking a sponge bath."

Jeremy laughed. "If that's the worst news you have for me today, then it's a bonny day."

Her eyes clouded over. "I need to tell you something else."

"What is it?"

"Things below, in Riverside, are bad really, really bad. Homes are gone, people are missing or confirmed dead. The residents don't know yet, but after the luncheon, we're going to have a community meeting where we'll tell everyone what we know." Her brown eyes pleaded, "Please be patient with the residents if they seem too intrusive. You can be evasive, but please be patient. Soon afterward their worlds will be torn apart."

He put his palm on her cheek. "I can definitely do that."

FIVE MINUTES AFTER KATE LEFT, the front door of the cabin squeaked open. Troy's booming voice called, "Ya decent?"

Jeremy answered, "Sure, come on in."

Troy and a much shorter man walked into the bedroom. While Troy looked like he was preparing for a golf outing, wearing perfectly creased khaki pants and a designer polo shirt, the other man was dressed more appropriately for a flood evacuee, with dirty jeans, a faded NASCAR t-shirt, and a sweat-stained baseball cap.

Troy crossed the room in two long strides. "How are we doing today?"

"A bit lurgy, but on the mend." Jeremy grinned.

The shorter man held out his hand. "I don't think we've been formally introduced. I'm Sam Carr, I helped give you a lift to camp."

Jeremy took his hand. "Ah, you're one of my saviors."

"Nah, I just helped carry the backboard." He patted Jeremy on his good shoulder. "You certainly look much better now than you did then."

Jeremy didn't know why, but he felt an instant bond with the older man. "Nonetheless, I owe you my gratitude."

Troy plopped down in the folding chair. "Sure you're ready to meet the characters of Riverside?"

"I am. Kate's been giving me everybody's backstory, and it'll be nice to match the stories to the faces."

Troy chuckled. "Well, just don't believe anything Kate says about me. She may only be Nan's adopted granddaughter, but she has got Nan's spunk, feisty as a red-headed hen."

Sam, who seemed uncomfortable with Troy's assessment, cleared his throat. "We should get you dressed. I stopped by Jim's and brought you a pair of sweatpants and a button-down shirt. He's slightly bigger than you, but they worked last time, so I think it will again."

Jeremy's eyebrows squished together. "Last time?"

Sam explained, "When we carried you into camp, your clothes were not salvageable. Jim lent you pants and a shirt."

Jeremy remembered the faded cargo shorts he'd worn the day of the accident and how grateful he was when CJ brought him the pendant from the pocket.

He must have looked emotional because Troy touched a gentle hand on his back. "You okay? If you aren't feeling up to this, I can send Kathleen over with some food."

"NO!" Jeremy blurted a little too forcefully. He calmed his voice. "I mean, I need fresh air."

Sam said, "Let's get you washed up then into clean clothes. How's that sound?"

Jeremy nodded. "Sounds like a bonny plan."

It took the full support of both men to get Jeremy from the bed to the bathroom. Though the helplessness of needing to have two men help him with the basics of hygiene delivered a blow to his self-esteem, Sam and Troy did their best to keep him laughing and spare his dignity. When it was all said and done, he felt clean, refreshed, and even more indebted to the caring gentleness of the men.

After they got him in clean clothes, Troy asked, "Still sure you're up for this? It may get crazy in there."

"It's not what may happen in there that concerns me, it's the walk to and from." He tried to sound brave. "But I feel up for the challenge."

They helped him to his feet. "Take it easy, son," Sam said in a fatherly fashion. "Just tell us if you need to take a break."

Jeremy felt a warmness in his heart when he looked at Sam. The kindness in the older man's eyes touched his soul in a place he didn't realize he desperately craved being touched, the place reserved for a father's love.

He nodded. "Thanks, Sam. I will."

# Chapter 21

WHEN KATE WALKED INTO THE MAIN room of the Foreman's cabin, she saw that everything was ready to go. Though, the setup looked no different from any other community dinner in Riverside, this would be like no dinner the residents had ever attended.

Doc's voice interrupted her thoughts. "How's the patient?"

Kate turned to see Doc sitting in a metal folding chair in the far corner, her head leaning against the wall behind her.

"Even better than this morning." Kate tried to sound cheery. "I think he's looking forward to getting out of the cabin for a bit."

"Is he prepared to be the center of attention?"

"I think so." Kate crossed the room and sat in a chair beside Doc. "How are you, Iris? You look exhausted."

Doc exhaled. "As good as anybody else, I guess." She continued in an emotionless tone, "Chris got more information from the State Police. We know a little more about what buildings were affected and how bad." Her voice faltered. "The clinic took on over eight feet of water. It'll have to be completely gutted."

Kate wanted to say something comforting, but the words that sprung from her mouth were, "The clinic is in your house!"

Doc gave a sarcastic laugh. "It was."

"I don't know what to say."

"Not much you can say," Doc said numbly. "Wouldn't change things, anyway."

Kate didn't want to be insensitive, but she had to ask, "Any word on Nan's home?"

"Nan lives a few miles out. Chris didn't get information about anything outside of town."

"Oh," Kate sighed softly. She wanted to press for more information, but she knew Doc wouldn't keep anything from her. Continuing to ask questions would be rude. She tried to think of something comforting to say. "I know after Hurricane Katrina, FEMA helped set up temporary clinics."

Doc replied with a mirthless laugh. "I hope they can find a doctor to man it."

Kate's jaw fell open. "Where will you be?"

"Best-case scenario, Arizona, trying to find a new career. Worst-case scenario, prison." Finally, Doc looked at her. "It didn't strike you as strange a general practitioner would have vials of morphine and fentanyl on hand?"

"I... guess..."

"Remember Matthew Davis, Mike's uncle?"

Kate remembered Matthew very well. He was one of the most stubborn men she'd ever met. When she and Mike had been dating, Matthew was the one who had advised Mike to end things with her. He had counseled: "She may come from the country, but she has city girl longings. She'll never be satisfied as a farmer's wife." For years Kate resented him for his cruel accuracy.

Kate shook the memory out of her head. "Yeah, I remember him."

"When he was at the end, the old buzzard refused to go to the hospital or allow hospice nurses to come to the home. Two nights before he passed, Marilla called me, sobbing. By the time I made it to their house, he was in so much pain he'd lost control of his bladder and bowels." Doc shuddered at the memory. "I did what I could that night. Early the next morning, I visited a friend in Pittsburgh and got what I needed to make him comfortable. I promised my friend that if it ever came down to it, I'd lie and say I'd stolen it from his stock. I had seven vials left over from Matthew. I brought three and left four at the office. If the cleanup crew finds them and knows what they are... With the heroin epidemic, they're cracking down on doctors who have unexplainable opioids on hand."

"Can't you just explain? I'm sure they will understand."

"If I tell the truth, it could incriminate my friend. I refuse to do that. I'll take the blame." Doc growled angrily. "I should have crushed those vials after I pronounced Matthew. I kept them on hand, telling myself I'd never watch another friend suffer like that."

"But if you hadn't had the medicine, Tim... you would have had to set his bones without... he'd have gone into shock."

"If I had, if I hadn't, there is no reason looking back."

Kate could tell from Doc's tone that she didn't want to hear any more 'but what about' or 'it will be okay's'. So, she said nothing.

They sat in silence until people started to trickle into the meeting room. Kate excused herself, walked outside, and plopped herself on the wooden stairs. When she looked up, she saw a three-headed blob schlepping toward her. She squinted to make out the shape and laughed when she realized the creature was Troy, Sam, and Jeremy limping toward her.

She met them at the bottom stair and gave Jeremy an appraising once over. "You clean up pretty nice."

He gave a crooked half-smile. "Considering how I came to camp, I set the bar bloody low."

Kate looked more closely at his face. His brow glistened with sweat, and his eyes still looked exhausted. "Sure you're up for this? You don't look too well."

Jeremy set his jaw in determination. "It's the longest I've walked since the accident. I'm a wee bit winded, that's all."

"You'll be the center of attention in there. I can't protect you." She was only half-joking.

He smiled impishly. "I think I can handle it."

Troy interrupted, "Let's get you settled. I promised Kathleen I'd be back in time to help her carry dishes."

The moment they entered the room, all conversations came to an abrupt halt. Every eye was on the mysterious man. Kate worried that every head in the room turning to stare at Jeremy would make him nervous, but he hardly seemed to notice. Then she remembered he was probably very used to the phenomena. More and more, she was forgetting he was a movie star.

Jeremy's time in the spotlight was short-lived. Soon everybody's eyes snapped to the entryway as Kathleen made a huge production of struggling through the double doors with three casseroles in her arms. Troy followed close behind, balancing two pies and a cake. She sat her dishes on the central table then said in a voice loud enough for everyone to hear, "The room looks nice, what an efficient idea, going with no decorations." As she took the lids off her Pyrex, she flashed an overly bright smile. "I'd have brought more, but you know, limited resources."

Kate's eyes rolled so far back in her head she was surprised she couldn't see her brain. Luckily, Nan took the reins. "I think that's everybody," she announced. "Let's get things rolling."

Sam walked to the center of the room. "I'd like to thank everybody for coming this afternoon."

Zach Ryan called out, "It was tough to decide between coming to a catered luncheon or staring at the ceiling for hours on end."

Several members of the group laughed.

Sam grinned. "I know that for some of you getting across the muddy camp wasn't easy, so I really appreciate you being here. A special thank you to the men that helped." He nodded to Chris and CJ. "I'd also like to thank everybody who helped prepare the feast behind me."

Kathleen scanned the room to see who was looking in her direction, nobody was.

Sam continued, "I'm sure everybody is ready to get to eating, so let's have a moment of thanks and get on with the food." He bowed his head, said a quick prayer, and ended with a quiet "amen."

Jeremy made a small wave to get Sam's attention. "Um, can I say a few words?"

Sam's eyebrows shot up. "Sure."

Jeremy cleared his throat, and the room became pin-drop quiet. "I know I haven't met many of you. I'm Tim, that crazy foreigner who slid into camp a few days ago." A soft rumble of laughter permeated the room. "I just wanted to say thank you. I owe you my life. I know I'm a stranger, but the way you took me in and have treated me like family warms my heart. The kindness, the love, the support you've..." His voice broke, and he took a moment to collect himself. "I wanted to say, thank you."

The expression of emotion was enough to send every mother and grandmother into a tizzy. Gray haired women from every corner tripped over themselves to out nurture the one before. Jeremy was the center of attention more now than he had ever been at Comic-Con.

IN THE BRIEF MOMENTS WHERE SOMEONE wasn't asking him a question about Scotland, why he was camping, or inquiring about Kate's nursing skills, Jeremy watched the residents interact. There was an authentic affection among all. They laughed, they joked, they hugged, they gossiped. They were a community; they were a family. This realization made him forlorn.

When things finally seemed to wind down, Sam sat beside him. "How ya feeling, young man?"

"Much better."

Sam beamed with pride. "Good people are good medicine."

Jeremy scanned the room. "Then I've gotten a healthy dose today."

Sam nodded. "Listen, son, we'll start the meeting soon. I didn't know if you wanted to stay or head back to the cabin to rest."

Jeremy remembered what Kate had said about the meeting following the meal and the sorrow it would bring. The last thing he wanted to do was intrude upon their grief. "I think going back to the cabin would be a good idea. I didn't realize how knackered I was until now. How should I say goodbye to everybody?"

Sam thought for a second. "To be honest, it'd probably be easiest if you just slipped out without people noticing. Everyone will want their chance to say goodbye, which will just delay the meeting."

Sam scanned the room and spotted CJ standing by the dessert table. He made a jerking motion with his head, the old man sign language for *come over here*.

CJ sauntered over. "What is it, boss?"

"Our patient is ready to head back."

CJ grinned. "You tired of us Riverside folk?"

Jeremy shook his head. "No, just tired."

Sam and CJ got him to his feet, and as discreetly as possible, snuck out the back door. Once they made the trek to cabin one, CJ excused himself while Sam stayed and helped Jeremy get settled.

"How ya feeling?" Sam asked.

"I'm good." Jeremy yawned. The outing had tired him more than he realized. "Please tell everybody how much I enjoyed lunch and how much I appreciate it all. I wish I could've talked to each person and said thank you."

"I'll relay your thanks, but I think if we're here more than just a few days, you'll have an opportunity to speak to every person in camp. Everybody wants to spend quality time with the mysterious stranger. Savor the rest while you can. Sure there isn't anything else I can get ya?"

"Actually, if you wouldn't mind, my arm is hurting. Could you give me one of the little red pills on the nightstand with the glass of water?"

"Sure thing!"


WHEN SAM RETURNED TO THE MEETING HALL, Nan walked to the center of the room and announced, "While we've been eating, Chris has gotten some information on the CB radio. Since we're all here, I'll let him have the floor."

Chris shuffled to the center of the room and cleared his throat. "I know everybody's nerves are on edge, and there are many rumors floating around. I want to make sure everybody gets accurate information."

"Then hurry up and give us the information," Sy yelled.

"I've been talking to the state police. This is what they told me." He pulled the same yellow paper from his pocket that he'd read from that morning. "Eleven inches of rain fell over the course of thirty hours. Almost all runs, creeks, and rivers overran their banks. The Greenbrier crested at fifteen feet above flood level. Almost every valley in the county is flooded. Most of Riverside is under water." He kept his voice informative and devoid of emotion. "The post office, gas station, Kenny's store, and fire department all took on a lot of water. They may have to replace the fire trucks and ambulances. This will hamper cleanup efforts."

"Just who told you that?" Kathleen insisted.

"All of my information comes directly from the state police," Chris replied patiently.

"What about other areas, like Kimberly or Carrollton?" Adam Miller asked.

"Kimberly is at a slightly higher elevation; things are better there. Carrollton and Ellenridge suffered worse. The southern side of the county got hit even harder than we did."

"How about farms?" Sy asked. "Livestock, hay fields? That's how we put food on our table."

"I don't have details, but I wager any farmland close to creeks or rivers is under water. A large number of cattle were found dead downriver. It's probably safe to say most of the hay and corn at those farms are probably ruined."

Connie McDonald said, "Sounds a lot like the eighty-five flood."

Ellen Streyley added, "Thankfully we didn't get hit as hard in eighty-five as places like Pendleton County."

Sy snorted. "What's Pendleton got to do with us?"

Chris took a ragged breath. "Because, this time, we are Pendleton."

Kate's stomach dropped. She grew up in Pendleton County, and though she was only eight, she remembered the flood in vivid detail. Homes weren't just flooded, they were leveled. Levees broke. Entire towns were decimated. Fields were turned into lakes. Farmers lost their livelihood. However, the thing that haunted Kate the most were the deaths. In West Virginia, forty-seven people lost their lives, over a third being in Pendleton County. Farmers who lived close to waterways dreaded investigating their fields, fearful of finding another dead body.

Kathleen stood and demanded. "Didn't people die in Pendleton in 1985? Are people dead in Pocahontas?"

Kathleen's outburst was the tipping point for hysteria. Residents started murmuring, shouting, and sobbing. Chris tried to speak, but he couldn't be heard over the crowd.

Finally, Doc marched to the center of the room and shouted, "Let Chris continue!"

Chris thrust his hand into his dirty jean pockets. "When I talked to the state police, there were no report of deaths or missing persons. I assume many people did just like us, found higher ground to wait out the storm." It was a bald-faced lie, but a necessary one.

Doc put a gentle hand on his shoulder. "Thanks, Chris. I know it isn't easy to deliver bad news."

Chris bowed his head and backed out of the spotlight. Doc addressed the room. "I know this is hard to hear. Let us not forget, we're all here, we're all alive. We are all safe. Homes can be rebuilt, hay and corn can be bought, cattle can be purchased." Her tone softened. "This is horrible, worse than horrible, but we are stronger than any flood. Look at the way we have taken care of each other over the past two days. Heck, we found a stranger close to death and nursed him back to health. Some of us lost places that held a lot of memories, but we can rebuild, we can make new memories."

CJ asked the pre-rehearsed question, "How long are we going to be here?"

Chris answered from the corner, "A few days. All the bridges leading to Slate were washed away. We're safe, have food, and are out of harm's way, so we aren't a priority. People are still stuck in their attics with no food or water."

"What do we do until then?" Sy asked.

Doc tried to sound strong and hopeful. "What we've been doing all along, taking care of each other, being the community that we all know Riverside to be."

Sam walked to the center of the room. He raised his chin and squared his shoulders. "These waters may have taken our homes and damaged our land, but a community is much, much more than farms and wooden structures." He sounded like a coach giving a rally speech. "A community is the people who help each other; who shoulder one another's burdens, who pray for one another and risk their lives to save one another." His voice built to a crescendo. "No flood can take that away. These are the things that will never wash away!"

Sam's speech was just what the scared and tired citizens needed. Questions still flew, and tears still fell. However, residents knew they were not alone, they had each other, and that gave them hope.

WHEN THE MEETING WAS OVER, some residents returned immediately to their cabins, while others stayed to visit and gossip. Kate answered question after question about the raggedy man in her cabin. Instead of being annoyed at the prying questions, she was happy these questions helped distract from their personal anxiety.

When she, Penny, Nan, and Mr. Coots were the only ones left, Mr. Coots piped up, "Y'all like peach, right?"

Kate and Penny grinned as Mr. Coots pulled a flask from his back pocket. "I didn't want to have to share with everyone, so I kept it hidden. Plus, Kathleen Whitacre would be as mad as a wet hen."

Nan laughed. "That'd almost be worth it."

Penny said, "Yeah, but poor Troy would get the brunt of it."

"Poor Troy," Mr. Coots sighed. "She makes a mean apple pie, but apple pie only lasts for so long."

Kate shot to her feet. "Damn it!"

Mr. Coots stopped grinning. "Didn't know you and Kathleen were close."

"We aren't," Kate said through her teeth. "Did anybody see Hazel or Sally after Tim went back to the cabin?"

## Chapter 22

AFTER SAM GAVE JEREMY HIS PAIN MEDICATION, he fell asleep and began to dream. The voice of an older woman with a thick southern accent floated in the air above him. "Oh my, Kathleen is right. He is handsome, on the skinny side, and needs a good shave, but still cute."

A second voice, deeper and gruff, like an out of tune trombone, spoke. "Send him home with me, I'll get him clean and fattened up."

The first voice said, "Hazel, that's no way for a woman of character to speak, especially at your age."

The second voice huffed, "Lighten up Sally, I've been a widow for over ten years now. I could definitely be one of those bobcats you hear about on those reality shows."

"Bobcat?"

"You know, women who date younger men. I wouldn't mind being his bobcat."

"You mean cougar?" Sally asked.

"Yeah, cougar; I could be a cougar. And don't give me that look. I was reading the other day that seventy is the new fifty."

"Well, if seventy is the new fifty, then the young man lying in this bed is about sixteen, which makes you not only inappropriate but also a felon."

Hazel responded with a teenage appropriate humph.

Sally continued, "I wonder if there's something going on between him and Kate. She needs a good man. It's not right for a woman her age to be alone."

Hazel's voice dripped with scandal. "I heard that she dated this fellow for around six years. Kept waiting on a ring. Finally, she found out he had a family all along. She'd been his mistress! She swore off men after that."

"You don't know that's true."

"I can't remember who I heard it from, but I know it was somebody reliable. Then I heard she had a girlfriend, they lived together in one of those condominiums in DC."

"Just how do you know she had a girlfriend?"

"She brought her to meet Nan. She told Nan that they were living together, and it was working out real good."

"How do you know she wasn't just a roommate?"

"I guess that could have been what it was, but you know, once kids leave and have a taste of city life, it changes them. They forget all the morals you taught them. Did you hear about Erin's grandson and that Brazilian girl?"

"No, I didn't, and you need to stop gossiping," Sally scolded.

"Fine!" Hazel's voice took on a pouting tone. "I agree, though, Kate needs to find a good man."

"I'm telling you, give this man an hour with a good barber, and he'd clean up nicely." Sally's voice was maternal.

"He still needs to put some meat on those bones. And what *is* going on between him and Kate? She hardly leaves his side. There's things that need done instead of hanging out with her new beau. Just plain selfish, if you ask me."

Sally gave a dry laugh. "Then, I guess we're lucky nobody asked you."

"Kathleen said that when she came here early this morning, Kate looked like she had just woken up, and there wasn't a pillow or any blankets on the floor. You know what that means?"

"No, I don't know what that means."

Hazel sounded as if she were explaining something to a small child, "It means they slept in the same bed, and I'm sure there wasn't a lot of sleeping going on."

Sally made a sound like the air being let out of a tire. "Pssh! Even if that is true, I don't understand why it's any of your concern."

"Well, it's just not right. What would her father say if he were still alive?"

"I think her father would say that it's none of your damn business, Hazel Phelps."

After Sally's comment, neither woman said another word. In fact, there were no other sounds until the front door opened and then slammed shut. Kate's angry whisper rang through the cabin. "What are you doing here?"

JEREMY RUBBED THE SLEEP FROM HIS EYES. Kate was standing in the doorway of the bedroom, her shoulders rising and falling in irritated huffs. "Kate?" he asked.

She spun around. "Sorry, did I wake you?"

He pinched the bridge of his nose. "No, I was just having the most bizarre dream."

"Did it involve a conversation between two gossiping old women?"

Jeremy looked bewildered. "How did you know?"

"It wasn't a dream. You were being serenaded by two of the busiest busybodies in Riverside."

He shrugged. "I thought it was the morphine."

"Nope," Kate walked to the window and opened the blinds. "It was two old biddies trying to play nurse."

"Well, don't worry, you're my nurse. Nobody could take your place." The words were out of his mouth before he knew how true they were. He looked at Kate to see how she responded to his admission, but she was still facing the window.

She cleared her throat. "How's the pain?"

He didn't push it. "Better, but not good."

Kate turned and sat on the bed beside him. Her posture was open and soft. He was glad his comment hadn't crossed any lines. "How long since the last pill?" she asked.

"Sam gave me one when he walked me home from the meeting. Then I fell asleep."

Kate looked at her watch. "You can have another one."

"I wanted to hold off until after the prayer meeting. I don't want to be high as a kite when people are praying over me."

Kate winked. "I'll tell them you're full of the spirit."

"I'll be acting like I am full of Mr. Coots' spirits."

Kate laughed. "Sure you want to be the center of attention again?"

He didn't have a chance to answer. There was a knock, and Nan poked her head in the cabin door. "Can we come in?"

Minutes later the bedroom was packed with people. Jeremy recognized most of the residents from the luncheon. Ellen, the short spunky woman who had gotten him three plates full of food led the way, then came Penny, Kathleen, Troy, Sam, and others whose names he couldn't recall. Nan waited for everybody to shuffle into the room, then closed the door behind them. She looked so tired and sad Jeremy almost forgot about the last word of their previous meeting... almost.

A sturdy woman with graying blonde hair and a *World's Greatest Nana* t-shirt squatted beside the bed. "We've got to get more decent food in you. I brought the rest of my potato casserole and chocolate cake. I'll leave them in the fridge."

Jeremy smiled. "Thank you, ma'am."

Not to be outdone, Kathleen called out, "I'll put my sliced ham in the refrigerator, too."

Nan looked at Kate and rolled her eyes. Sam frowned at Nan and cleared his throat. "Why don't we get started?" He looked to Jeremy. "Are you ready, son?"

Jeremy nodded. "Yes, sir."

Sam placed his left hand upon Jeremy's injured shoulder and grasped Kate's hand with his right. Kate took Penny's hand and Penny grabbed Nan's. From there they formed a chain. When Chris, the final link, placed his hand upon Jeremy's other shoulder, Jeremy felt a soft electricity run through his body, as if a circuit had been closed and the current could now flow smoothly.

Sam closed his eyes and began to pray. He thanked God for the community of Slate, the safety of those in the camp, and for the comfort of those who weren't as fortunate. Next, Kate prayed for healing of Jeremy's body, and Nan prayed for his spirit to be renewed. CJ prayed for the waters to subside. Doc prayed for strength and wisdom for the coming days. Each person in the room took the time to say a few words. As the prayers were being lifted, Jeremy felt the anxiety that had slowly been devouring him dissipate, the dull thudding in his right arm lessened, and a calm peacefulness flowed from his toes to his scalp.

After the prayer, those who didn't have time to chat with Jeremy during the luncheon bombarded him with questions. Some asked questions about Scotland. Jamie Martin asked his thoughts on the EU. Zach Ryan said his mom was a McConnell and asked if he was related to any McConnells around Glasgow. A woman with a Bronx accent made him snort when she asked if there really was nothing covering him 'down there' when he wore one of those plaid skirts.

After an hour, Doc announced, "I think the patient needs rest."

As the residents wound their way out of the cramped bedroom, Jeremy said, "Thank you" over and over. He desperately wished he could find more profound words to express his gratitude, but 'thank you' were the only two words that could come to his mind.

FINALLY, JEREMY AND KATE WERE THE only two left. She sat on the bed, so they were face to face. "You look as content as a cat in a windowsill."

"A what?"

"A cat in a windowsill," she explained. "I used to have this cat, Little Mister. I got him my first-year teaching, and he was my best buddy. Anyway, he used to love to lie at the bottom of the window and sun himself for hours, just enjoying being fat and lazy."

"Are you calling me fat and lazy?"

She laughed as she rummaged through her pockets to find a ponytail holder. "No, actually as soon as I made that comparison, I knew it wasn't the wisest use of words."

Jeremy scratched his chin. "So, you're a cat person?"

"Very much a cat person."

He gave her a sly glance out of the corner of his eye. "What do you think I am?"

She knew the answer to the question. In fact, she knew that he'd named his first dog Spot so he could quote Lady Macbeth any time the dog had to potty. She pretended to pick an answer out of the air. "I'll guess, dog person."

"How did you know?"

"You just seem like a dog person. You're loyal, kind, and you shed a lot."

"So, what else do you think you know about me?" Jeremy asked the unbeknownst loaded question.

Kate frantically tried to find an unobtrusive observation, then in a moment of inspiration, she turned the tables. "No, I think you need to take a guess about me or to ask me something about myself."

"So, this is a getting to know you game?" Jeremy smirked. "Okay, I'll go first... Favorite movie?"

Kate fought the urge to say, *anything you are in*, but said, "*Dead Poet's Society*."

Jeremy thought for a second. "They perform *A Midsummer Night's Dream* near the end of that movie, don't they?"

"They sure do. Now, what about you? What's your favorite movie?"

"I like *Iron Man*."

"Interesting, I expected something serious and Victorian from a self-proclaimed thespian."

Jeremy used an aristocratic voice, "Well, I guess you're wrong." He winked at her. "To be honest, I'm a huge comic book geek. And before you ask, Marvel over DC."

Kate nodded appreciatively. "My turn, favorite food?"

"Haggis."

"Ew! Gross!"

"Fine, what does your refined palate desire?"

"Lobster."

"Fair enough, your turn to ask."

"Favorite childhood memory?"

Jeremy chuckled. "One summer my family visited the cliffs at Dover, we were having a picnic when suddenly, a bird flies overhead and craps right on my sister's head."

"Your favorite memory is a bird pooping on your sister's head?"

"My sister was very prissy. She danced around like she was on fire. I honestly thought she'd dance herself right over the cliff."

Kate rolled her eyes.

"Fine," Jeremy pretended to be offended. "If my memory's not appropriate, then tell me your best childhood memory."

Kate smiled big. "My dad was a workaholic. Actually, most farmers are, you have to be. Well, one summer day, when there were tons of things that needed to be done on the farm, he dropped it all and took me fishing. It was just the two of us. He taught me how to put a minnow on a hook, how to cast a line. It was a wonderful day."

"Wow, that does make my memory sound very pish-posh, doesn't it?" They were quiet for a moment, then Jeremy asked, "What's your favorite place on earth?"

A pained expression clouded Kate's face. "Nan's house." Her voice was no louder than a whisper.

He put his hand on hers. "I'm sorry. I didn't mean to."

"It's okay." She brushed off the comfort. "What's your favorite place?"

"There's this little stream in the glen behind my home in Scotland. There are these tiny little fish and frogs. It has a small bridge; it's so peaceful."

"It sounds beautiful." She pushed a stray strand of hair behind her ear. "Your turn to ask."

Jeremy got a puckish look in his eyes. "Favorite actor or actress?"

Kate's breath caught in her throat. Usually, the question required no thought, however, the person whom she usually would name was using an alias and sitting three feet from her. She stammered and stumbled, then finally said, "Robin Williams."

"He was a gifted man." Jeremy cleared his throat. "I love Sean Connery. It's probably a Scotsman thing."

"I'm not so sure about that. I know plenty of American women who love him too! I think it's that sexy Scottish accent."

Jeremy raised his eyebrows and grinned.

Kate mentally chastised herself. *You just told him his accent is sexy.* Desperate to change the subject, she began to ramble, "Okay, next question. Biggest fear? I'll go first, snakes. I hate snakes! I'm not just talking about poisonous snakes; I hate them all. Black snakes, brown snakes, yellow snakes, sticks that look like snakes. I hate them equally." When she finally took a breath, she looked at Jeremy, who appeared quite entertained. "What?"

"You hate sticks?"

"Only the ones that disguise themselves as snakes." She laughed. "Okay Mr. Slide Down a Mountain. What's your biggest fear?"

The laughter left his eyes. "Being a disappointment to my father."

The look on his face broke Kate's heart. "You're not…"

He looked away. "When I was in the cave on the other side of the mountain, I thought about giving up. I was sick, wet, tired, and I considered just falling asleep on the floor of the cave and never waking up. Looking back now, I realize I was being an overdramatic arse, but I was ready to give up."

She took his hand in hers. "What changed your mind?"

"I heard dad's voice," Jeremy laughed. "He said, 'Get up, son.' Just those three words. No huge revelation, no sage advice, just get your sorry, self-pitying arse up."

"Short, sweet, and to the point."

"Dad didn't raise me to give up without a fight. He'd be so disappointed to see me die sitting in a cave wallowing in self-pity." He stroked his beard. "He also didn't raise me to be a workaholic and wear myself tissue-thin. That's not the man who he'd want me to be, either."

"What kind of man do you want to be?"

"I don't know, but I know who I don't want to be. That's something at least, isn't it? Knowing who you don't want to be?"

"It's definitely something," she whispered. "I think everybody has a moment in their life where they take a step back and evaluate where they are, where they want to be, what they are proud of, what they regret."

"Do you have regrets?"

Kate laughed. "I'll just say that I did a lot of stupid things when I was younger. There's a lot I wish I could wipe from my timeline."

WHEN KATE MENTIONED HER YOUNG foolishness, Jeremy became jealous. He'd entered acting school at seventeen and was performing in the public eye by nineteen. He never had the luxury of youthful indiscretions. When he made mistakes, a gaggle of pseudo-reporters made sure that his misbehavior would be documented forever. He had to be constantly vigilant about not just what he did, but how it could be perceived.

Kate touched him on the shoulder. "Hey, you still with me?"

He shook his head and forced a smile. "Yeah, I was just thinking about some things in my youth I'd change if I could." He leaned back against the headboard. "That's the sticky wicket, though isn't it? If I could hop in a magic box and travel through space and time, change things, who would I be now? Would I be better off, would I be worse? If I'd go back and change the things I regret, what would my life look like now?"

Kate sighed. "Maybe, but the things for which I'm ashamed are times when I was selfish, judgmental, insensitive, just plain bratty."

"I understand." He dropped his gaze. "When mum passed, things with my sister, Meredith, got ugly. We were both still reeling from the sudden loss. I don't know who fired first or how the war started, but it was gory with lots of casualties. When dad got sick, we were both too childish to make amends. We couldn't even be in the same room to say goodbye. I think that's why dad chose to pass when neither of us was there. He didn't want the last thing he heard in this world to be his children arguing."

Tears sprung to his eyes as he remembered the last time the three of them had been together. He and Meredith had fought over something so inconsequential; he couldn't even recall what it was. What he did remember was the pain on his dad's face as he begged, "You are all the family you have left. Promise me you won't turn on each other. Promise!"

They had shaken hands and promised, but the moment they left the hospital, mean and spiteful texts were exchanged until the wee hours of the night. Until they got the call at 4:35 am. He blinked back the tears. "I have a niece who I haven't seen since she was two, and one that I've never met. I might risk being a different person now if I could take the things I said back."

"You said you spent a lot of time thinking about forgiveness. Could you forgive your sister?"

"I want to say yes. I hope that I'm man enough to."

Kate squeezed his hand. "One thing I've learned is forgiveness isn't for the sake of the person you're forgiving, it's a gift you give yourself. Even if the person doesn't deserve or accept your forgiveness, when you let go of the grudge you are free."

"What if the person you have a hard time forgiving is yourself?"

Kate shrugged. "I'm still working on that one. For things I've said, and things unsaid."

"I guess there was a silver lining to cancer. I had time to tell dad those things I never got to tell mum. It was selfish. He suffered, but we had time to talk. I got to hear the last of his wisdom, and I got to tell him how much I loved him. I believe he stayed with us as long as he did because he knew I needed him. He suffered for me."

Kate changed her position so that they were side by side. She lay her head on his shoulder. "I don't know if it's selfish. I'm the same way with mom. She may not be in physical pain, but she suffers. There are those windows of lucidity when I have her back, and I desperately cling to those moments. I don't want to let her go back into her own world, even though I know it's more peaceful there." There was anguish in every syllable of her words.

He took her hand, but he wanted to do more. He wanted to wrap her in his arms and protect her, the way she had held and comforted him when he'd awoken from his nightmare. He searched desperately for any words to ease her pain, but all he could come up with was, "At least you didn't have to watch your dad go through that."

Kate shook her head. "I still have a mountain of regret though. I never told my dad 'Thank you.' He was an interesting man. He wasn't the hugging, 'I love you' kind of dad. He was a farmer, a working man, the provider for his family. I wasted a lot of time being resentful that he wasn't the father I thought I deserved. He wasn't the dad that took us on vacations or played games with us. Now I realize it was because he was probably tired from working so damn hard." She exhaled heavily. "We were never poor, we had food on the table, we had clothes on our backs, but I knew we had less than other families. Sometimes I was ashamed I didn't have what my friends had. Instead of brand name, pre-packaged food in my lunchbox, I had fresh peaches from our orchard or canned green beans from our garden. It wasn't until much later that I realized how hard dad and mom had to work to provide what they did, and how it must have made them feel for me to be so unappreciative of the best they could provide. They sent us to college, my brother and I getting our degrees was my dad's greatest accomplishment. I wish I could go back and show appreciation, say thank you, be more understanding. It's funny, in college I made a lot of decisions I'm too ashamed to admit, but those aren't my biggest regrets."

"Do you ever talk to your dad? I don't mean 'I see dead people' talk, I mean..."

Kate smiled. "I know what you mean. I talk to the stars and I believe they relay the message to him." She changed her tone. "I wish you could walk. The sky is beautiful tonight. I'd love for you to see the stars."

"I know it seems odd, but I am feeling much better. Not sure if it's mind over matter, but I think if you help me, I could walk." It was true. Since the people of Slate had prayed over him, there was an indescribable feeling, a mild vibration resonating through his body. It was at the same time invigorating and peaceful, like he could feel the cells repairing themselves. "Can we try?"

Kate bit her bottom lip. "Are you sure? I'm not as strong as Troy or Sam. If you fall, I can't catch you."

"I want to try." Jeremy asked, "Please?"

Kate smiled. "Let me take the chair out so you have a place to sit."

When she walked back through the bedroom door, Jeremy was anxiously sitting on the side of the bed. The prospect of stargazing motivated him to sit taller. He put his good arm around her shoulders, and though he had to lean heavily upon Kate, he was able to walk from the bedroom through the small living room. When he reached the doorway, he stopped abruptly.

"What's wrong? Do you need to lie down?"

"No," Jeremy whispered. "I've never seen so many stars. Even when I was camping by the river, there were clouds. I never knew there were so many stars in the sky." It was as if an artist had expertly poked holes in a piece of black silk, allowing for the most delicate and magical designs to show through.

Kate wrapped her arm around his waist. "Worth the walk?"

The lump in his throat made it difficult to speak. "Definitely," he whispered.

Kate motioned toward the folding chair, and he sat. When he was finally situated, he tore his eyes from the velvet sky and looked at her face. It was enchanting. Though she looked nothing like the actresses or models with whom he usually gallivanted, her chocolate eyes, high cheekbones, and full lips were beautiful in an organic and unpretentious way. "Thank you," he whispered.

"For what?"

"For this." He motioned toward the stars. "For all of this."

"I can take credit for a lot of things, but this isn't my handiwork."

"Yeah, but I wouldn't be here to see it had you not rescued me."

Kate didn't respond. She sat beside his chair and leaned her head against his thigh. He ran his fingers through her brown tangled hair.

Finally, she looked up at him. "You look tired. Maybe it's time to go back in and get you to bed."

"You'll stay with me?"

"Of course, I will."

As she situated the pillows under his body, he gently slid his knuckles down her cheek. "You look like you need rest, too."

Without a word, she nodded and lay her head on the pillow beside him.

## Chapter 23

KATE FELT LIKE SHE HAD ONLY BEEN asleep a few minutes when she was awakened by a deafening banging on the door. She peeled herself out of bed. "I swear, Kathleen," she grumbled. "I'm done being nice!" She marched to the threshold and prepared to rain down a tsunami strength tirade upon the busy body.

However, before she could utter her first reprimand, something orange streaked past her and plopped onto the antique chair. "You know how Nan's been acting weird?" Penny bounced. "I figured out why!"

Kate yawned. "Morning to you too, sunshine."

Penny was back on her feet. "I don't have time for greetings, I've got BIG news!"

Kate looked out the open door at the fully risen sun. "What time is it?"

"It's after nine."

"Nine? We slept that long?"

"Yes, it's past nine, but I've got bigger news." She grabbed Kate's hand and drug her into the kitchen. "You know how Nan has been acting weird? I figured out why!"

Kate's mind was too foggy to gossip. "What?"

Penny looked left and right conspiratorially. "There's something going on between her and Sam Carr!"

"Whoa... what... Nan and Sam?"

"Yes, Nan and Sam," Penny spoke slowly as if she were talking to a small child. "She was peeved when I told her we'd be sharing a bed, getting back to our cabin after midnight, all the secret meetings." She counted off the items on her fingers. "It all adds up!"

"Are you sure? It could be a coincidence."

Pen crossed her arms like a sassy teenager. "I found them kissing."

"Wait! What? When?"

"About five minutes ago, I walked to the Foreman's cabin to see if Chris had heard anything new. When I came back, they were standing in our kitchen K-I-S-S-I-N-G," she sang the playground rhyme.

Kate smirked. "Well, that takes care of the coincidence argument." Then she asked tentatively, "How do you feel about it?"

"I'm not mad that they're dating. I'm not even pissed that she kept it from me. Everybody keeps secrets for their own reasons. I get that, but when I caught them kissing, you'd have thought I walked in on them hiding a body."

"Now, that's funny."

Penny frowned. "Nan shoved me out the door like I was a pushy vacuum salesman."

Kate could see Penny was trying to hide how badly Nan's reaction had hurt her. She put a hand on Penny's shoulder. "Everybody's been pushed past their breaking point. Nobody's acting like they usually would."

"I keep thinking she needs to be more understanding, that my hometown has been decimated, that my home may be washed away." Her voice broke. "Then I remember, her hometown has been decimated and that her home may be washed away. We're both worn threadbare and neither has the strength to be the bigger person."

Kate sat at the kitchen table and patted the seat beside her. Penny plopped down and covered her face with her hands. "I've got to get out of here, Kate, or I'll lose it! Between Kathleen telling me how to fix Spencer's 'little autism problem,' Aunt Milly refusing to take the medicine that literally keeps her alive, and Nan treating me like a misbehaving teenager, I'm going to have a nervous breakdown."

Guilt churned in Kate's stomach. She'd forgotten that her original reason for coming to Riverside was to be with Penny and Nan. With Nan spending so much time with Sam, and Kate spending all her time with Jeremy, Penny had been orphaned to deal with it all on her own.

"I'm sorry, Pen."

Penny waved off the apology. "I found Chris on the way here, though. The State Police say that the waters are finally starting to subside, but sixty percent of the roads in the county are destroyed. The water upended asphalt and took out all the bridges."

"You're kidding!" Kate felt her stomach harden. "Every bridge?"

"Any bridge less than twelve feet above the water was washed away or severely damaged."

Kate leaned back. "I keep thinking I'm going to stop being shocked when I hear things like that, but each time it floors me."

"There's some good news, though. We should be off the mountain by Saturday. The water is low enough for the National Guard to use rescue boats to evacuate the camp."

Kate thought she'd be happy about this news, but when Penny said the words, she felt her chest tighten. True, she craved civilization, the internet, a warm shower. However, she also realized that once they were off the mountain, she'd no longer be sheltered from the painful destruction in the valley.

Penny nodded toward the bedroom. "So, are you going to let him know?"

"Of course, I'll let him know about being rescued."

"That's definitely a good idea, however, I'm more interested in when you were going to let him know that you know who he really is?"

Kate's mouth became dry like the Sahara. "I don't know what you're talking about."

Penny leveled her gaze. "We've been best friends for decades. I can deal with the fact that you hid Jeremy's identity, but please don't lie."

Kate looked at her lap, after a long pause she mumbled, "I'm not."

Penny threw her hands in the air. "Yes, you are lying."

Kate shook her head. "I mean I'm not going to tell him—"

"What? The man you've dreamed about for two decades is asleep in your bed, and you won't confess your undying love?"

Kate squared her shoulders defiantly. "First, there's a huge difference between a celebrity infatuation and undying love." She glanced toward the bedroom and dropped the charade. "And he doesn't want to be recognized. From the very first, he's used a fake name, and he specifically told me he came into the woods to be where nobody knew him. I think he wants to be Tim, the ordinary guy."

Penny asked gently, "So what about Tim the ordinary guy?"

"He's anything but ordinary." Kate smiled as she remembered the intimate moments they'd spent together. "He's smart, funny, and kind. We've talked about so much, where we grew up, our families. We shared secrets, we joked, we..." She had no way to express what had transpired. They'd bonded? No, that made it sound like they'd stayed up all night on a college camping trip drinking beer. Gotten to know each other? Opened up to one another? None of these phrases came close to describing their time together. They had been vulnerable to each other, shared fears, discussed faith, talked about losing loved ones. Bonding, talking, sharing were all such inadequate words.

Kate shrugged. "I know that had he realized I know his true identity, he never would have shared so much with me." She paused. "It's more than that, though. Had I been allowed to be that fangirl, the 'Oh My God You Are So Awesome!' I'd have only seen him as Jeremy Fulton, celebrity crush. Instead, I got to know Tim, the really awesome guy."

Penny raised her eyebrows. "So, he is no longer Mr. Sexy?"

"I didn't say that." She shook her head and smiled. "I mean, look at him. When he looks at me with those blue eyes, I feel like I'm sixteen." She exhaled. "And he's brilliant. I could tell from his interviews he wasn't stupid, but I didn't realize he was flipping brilliant. Intelligence is so very sexy. Add all of that intelligence, coming from those beautiful lips, in that super sexy Scottish accent—"

"Lucky you!"

"Lucky me?" Kate laughed. "I have a super sexy, intelligent, Scottish man sleeping in my bed, sharing intimate secrets with me, and I'm supposed to exercise self-restraint? Not sure I'd call that lucky."

"But how are you going to tell him how you feel if you won't tell him you know he's really Jeremy Fulton?"

Kate shifted uncomfortably in her seat. "I have no idea what you're talking about."

Penny looked her directly in the eye. "Don't try that game with me. I've watched you watch Jeremy for years. I saw the way you looked at him on TV, on stage, at Comic-Con. I see the way you look at the guy laying in your bed." She pointed toward the bedroom door. "It's not even in the same ballpark. I recognize that look."

Kate started to give a defensive answer, but she knew Penny could see all the things she was desperately trying to hide. She lowered her eyes. "What do I say: Hi, I know you've been relentlessly trying to avoid being noticed, but from the moment you slid into camp I've known who you are. Oh, and I think I'm falling for your alter ego?"

"Maybe he'd find it endearing. Maybe he wants to find somebody who will let him be just Tim."

Kate scoffed. "Let's be honest, look at me. Girls like me never end up with guys like him, even as just Tim." She smiled sadly. "And we can't pretend he IS just Tim because he isn't. He's Jeremy Fulton, a super-star, a sex symbol. I've seen the girls on his arm, tall, size two, perfect body, flawless face, everything I'm not." She swallowed hard. "I'm a thirty-seven-year-old, size ten, math teacher with wrinkles, fat rolls, and sagging boobs. Even if we have an emotional connection in Slate, this isn't the real world. You'd never see a woman like me on the arm of *The Sexiest Man Alive*. Besides, if I had a choice between a one-night stand with Jeremy Fulton or the last few days with Tim, I'd choose Tim."

Saying the words out loud made her chest ache. She wrapped her arms around her stomach. "He came here seeking anonymity, and I will respect that. I cannot imagine what it's like to have millions of people thinking they have a right to know every detail of your life. I don't want him to worry I'd share his secrets. He came here as Tim; he'll leave as Tim." After a long pause, she met Penny's eyes. "And I'll really miss Tim."

Penny reached for her hand. "I love you to death, sweetie, and I respect your decision. But I think you're dead wrong."

"I can't think of any other way to handle it."

Penny exhaled heavily. "So, what now?"

"When he wakes up, I'll tell him we'll be rescued soon."

"What do you need from me?"

Kate's shoulders sagged. "Honestly, I just want some time alone."

Penny squeezed her hand. "Well, then I'll take your advice, find Nan and then take a nap. Speaking of which, you look exhausted."

"Yeah, I've gotten little sleep the last three nights."

Penny raised her eyebrows. "Not getting much sleep, eh? Sure there isn't something you are leaving out?"

Kate rolled her eyes. "You're ridiculous."

Penny made an exaggerated gesture of pushing herself to a standing position. "If I'm so ridiculous, I'll just leave."

Kate forced a smile. "Don't let the door hit you on the way out."

Penny strutted to the door, then turned to stick out her tongue. Though her mannerisms were sassy, her voice was gentle as she said, "Find me when you need me."

## Chapter 24

KATE RESTED HER ELBOWS ON HER KNEES. *So, Penny knows that Tim is really Jeremy,* she mused. *How could I think she wouldn't? I've forced the poor thing to watch every movie, TV show, and commercial he's ever been in. I've subjected her to countless ramblings about how Jeremy was the most talented, handsome, kindest, and sexiest actor in the universe. Of course, she would recognize him.*

Penny also knew how she felt about him. The words rang back to her. *The way you look at the guy laying in your bed. I recognize that look.* Her stomach tightened. Who else knew? Nan? Had Kathleen figured it out? Did Jeremy know?

He'd come to the wilderness of West Virginia to escape the trappings of stardom. If he found out she knew his true identity, would he think it had all been a fangirl's fantasy? Had she said anything that betrayed her feelings? She had held his hand, kissed his forehead, held him in her arms. Could he have interpreted those as nurse-like compassion?

The walls of the cabin closed in around her. She had to escape! She slipped on her boots, ran out the cabin door, and trudged through damp leaves until she found herself in the woods. Looking around she realized she was in the exact same spot where she stood four days ago and watched a stranger tumble down the side of the mountain. Her pulse raced as the memory of his broken body flashed through her mind. She sat on a fallen log and buried her head in her hands. The moisture from the wood seeped through her thin pajama pants, but she didn't mind because there were too many other issues battling for her attention.

For the first time in months, The Voice that she fought so hard to keep at bay reared its ugly head. Like a devil on her shoulder, it whispered in her ear, "What happens if he realizes that you knew all along?"

She balled her hands into fists, *I won't let that happen. He'll never know that I know.*

The Voice retorted, "What happens if he figures out how you feel about Tim?"

"I'll hide that too!" She said the words out loud. They'd be off the mountain in forty-eight hours. She would carry on with the charade. Jeremy Fulton wasn't the only person in cabin one who could act. If she had to play the role of a woman with no romantic feelings, she'd do just that.

KATE STOOD ON THE FRONT PORCH OF CABIN one and readied herself for the performance of her life. She would hide that she knew his identity, and she would hide her feelings for him. She slipped inside the door, and as she was removing her muddy boots, her stomach let out a monstrous growl.

She looked at her watch. It was after one o'clock, and she hadn't eaten anything all day. Luckily, some women from the prayer meeting left food in the refrigerator for the poor injured Scotsman. She piled a plate high with ham, mashed potatoes, and chocolate cake. Just as she was sitting at the table, there was a light knock at the door.

"Great!" she grumbled under her breath.

A sleepy voice came from the bedroom. "Kate, is that you?"

She ignored the knocking at the front door and walked to the bedroom. Jeremy rubbed the sleep from his eyes. "Hey stranger," he said.

Kate stared at the floor, not trusting herself to resist his magnetic cornflower blue eyes. "Somebody's at the door, you up for company?"

"Sure, unless it's Kathleen."

Kate laughed and walked to the threshold. Mike and Elle Davis were standing on the covered porch. Elle held a round Tupperware container. "Afternoon Kate, I got a pie-making lesson from Kathleen," she beamed. "The Scottish guy really liked the apple pie at the dinner, so I thought I'd bring him some."

Though Kate was amused by Elle's excitement, the expression on Mike's face held her attention. He looked at his wife with such affection, captivation, and pride, all the things she wanted a man to feel when he looked at her. She ignored the jagged pain piercing her chest. "Let me see if he's awake."

Jeremy was sitting up in bed smiling his cute sleepy smile. She spoke softly, "It's Elle and Mike. Elle made an apple pie and wants to know if you'd like to try."

He licked his lips. "Apple pie? Sure!"

Upon hearing Jeremy's reply, the couple walked into the bedroom. "How you feel today?" Mike asked.

"Better every day."

Elle proudly held out the pie. "I got lessons from Kathleen. Would you like to try?"

Jeremy smiled brightly. "I'd be honored. Mike, could you help me to the dining room table?"

Mike looked a bit worried. "Are you sure about that? We could bring some plates in here."

"Funny thing, yesterday I needed the help of two men to walk to the loo. Last night, I was able to walk to the front porch, just leaning on my nurse." He smiled affectionately at Kate. The way his robin-egg-blue eyes sparkled made her both want to run for the hills and run into his embrace.

Mike nodded. "Sure thing." He put his arm around Jeremy, and with very little effort, they made their way from the bed to the dining room.

Elle cut Jeremy a generous piece of pie. "You sure have made progress."

"I've received excellent care." He looked at Kate, but she was staring intently at the floorboards. He cleared his throat. "Sam said yesterday that good people are good medicine. I've received quite a healthy dose while in Slate. And the excellent food has helped." He took a huge bite of apple pie, and a look of sheer bliss covered his face. "Elle, this is amazing!"

It was hard to say who looked prouder, Elle or Mike. That same stabbing pain shot through Kate's chest. Would a man ever look at her with such pride and affection?ABrir Tears pricked her eyes, and she excused herself while she still had some semblance of self-control.

She walked to Penny and Nan's cabin, but nobody was home. "What to do, what to do?" she muttered to herself. She knew if she went to the Foreman's cabin, she'd be bombarded with questions about Jeremy, the very person she was trying to avoid thinking about. She could always go back to her cabin. When she had been putting on her shoes, Mike had asked Jeremy about the EU. Though Kate had little interest in foreign policy, eventually the conversation would morph into something more interesting, wouldn't it?

She sighed. Even if the conversation stayed on topics she found painfully boring, it would be captivating because it would be with Jeremy.

No, Jeremy was the reason to NOT return to the cabin. The more she was with him, the more she wanted to be with him, and the more likely he was to figure out how badly she wanted to be with him.

Then, a voice from the porch of cabin five called. Mr. Coots and Sy Rigglemen were sitting in lawn chairs. "Hey, Kate," Sy called. "CJ will be back in a minute, and we need a fourth for spades. You doing anything?"

"Just working up the energy to beat two old buzzards in cards." She grinned as she walked toward what would become a cutthroat series of card games.

## Chapter 25

THE FOURSOME WAS ON THEIR UMPTEENTH game when Nan sidled onto the porch. "Who's winning?"

Sy snarled at Kate and C.J. "Coots and I were ahead, then these two started cheating."

Kate crossed her arms over her chest. "We did not."

"Don't get your mule out of line," Sy guffawed. "I was just pulling your leg."

Kate looked to Nan. "What have you been up to?"

Nan winked. "Just spent a few hours staring at the walls."

Kate understood the code. Chris had gotten no new information. She shuffled the deck. "You gentlemen ready to get your tails beaten again?"

Nan interrupted, "Actually, Kate, I think the patient is missing his sentry."

Kate furrowed her brow. "Sentry?"

"Without you there to be the gatekeeper, there's been a steady stream of people through your cabin. When I left half an hour ago, he looked tired. Probably a good idea to check on him."

"Sure," Sy hooted. "Leave when you're winning. Don't give me a chance to redeem myself."

Kate handed her cards to Nan. "I promise a rematch," she called over her shoulder.

When she opened the front door of her cabin, nobody was loitering in the front room. She tiptoed to the bedroom door and peeked inside. Thankfully, no visitors awaited there either.

"Hey stranger," Jeremy smiled.

She met Jeremy's startling blue eyes, and the wind left her lungs. "Hey there yourself," she managed to say. "Heard you had a busy afternoon."

"Doc came by about ten minutes ago and shooed everybody away. Glad you're back, though. How is everyone?"

Kate walked to the bed and sat beside him. "As good as you can expect."

"Sam told me we'll be evacuated tomorrow or the next day."

"That's the rumor right now."

"I wouldn't mind staying here," he said sadly. "I could put off getting back to the real world for a little while longer."

Kate studied his face. There was a wistfulness in his eyes when he mentioned staying in Slate. For a moment, Kate imagined what his real world must be like. If the U.K. was anything like the U.S., people considered celebrities their personal property. A quiet evening out with friends was close to impossible. A trip to the store could become a photoshoot; an innocent, offhand comment could be used out of context to vilify. In all her daydreaming about what it would be like to be with Jeremy, she never thought about how hard it would be to be Jeremy.

She swept her eyes over his still-healing body. Suddenly, she felt very protective. She wanted to shield him from the paparazzi, from the chaos, from anything that could ever hurt him.

He took her hand. "You look troubled."

"I'm fine. I've been trapped inside my head all day."

He smiled playfully. "I'll tell you mine if you tell me yours."

Kate blushed, there was no way she could tell him the thoughts bouncing around in her head. "Why don't you go first?"

He shifted uncomfortably. "Do you remember me saying that when I was in the woods I did a lot of thinking about things said and left unsaid?"

She nodded.

His eyes became heartbreakingly sincere. "If we get off this mountain tomorrow, I don't want to have missed my chance to say thank you."

"For what?"

"For saving me, I mean, you literally saved my life. You nursed me back to health."

"It hasn't been just me; it was a team effort."

"True, everyone has been wonderful, but you... you've been..." His eyes were so intense, they pulled her in like a tractor beam. "You didn't have to stay by my side. You didn't have to hold me and comfort me after my nightmares. You didn't have to do any of that. Why did you?"

"I don't know. It just seemed like that's something I should do. It's what anybody would've done."

"I don't think so. When I think about everything you've done, the compassion, tenderness, and care that you showed me, it's not ordinary." His Adams apple bobbed up and down as he swallowed hard. "I've never asked, is there some lucky bloke in Virginia waiting for you?"

Kate laughed bitterly. "Nobody is waiting for me."

"Have you ever been married?"

She looked at her hands, which were now balled into nervous fists. "I got close once. I imagined the white picket fence, kids, happily ever after, and all of that shit." She scoffed. "Fairy tales don't come true, though, do they?"

"No, they don't." His words carried a heavy sadness. "I was married. I guess, technically, I still am. She left. According to her, I'm the most repulsive human being alive. Things got ugly, extremely ugly. I haven't spoken to her since the night she left."

Kate could hear the pain in his voice. She wanted to reach out to him, to comfort him, but she knew that each time she looked into his eyes, each time she touched him, it would be harder to hide how she felt. Even sitting beside him, feeling the warmth of his body, was making her heart thud uncontrollably.

He cleared his throat. "The leaving was bad enough, but then somehow the press got wind of it. We were both all over the tabloids, ugly secrets being aired for all the U.K. to see. I know some of the seediest stories made it to the U.S. papers too." He reached out, cupped Kate's chin in his hand, and tilted her head so they were eye to eye. "I hope you didn't believe any of the horrible things those tawdry rags said."

The walls of the room rushed in and the air became thick as mud. He knew! He knew that she knew! "What, I... you... what are you talking about, why would I know...?"

He gently ran his thumb over her cheekbone. "Kate, we've shared so much. Why keep up the facade? You know I'm not Tim Jones. You know who I really am."

"When, I mean, how?"

"I've suspected for a while you knew I'd lied about my name. It wasn't until I overheard you this morning that I realized you knew everything."

Shock and embarrassment crushed over her like a wave. "You listened in on mine and Penny's conversation?"

He pushed a strand of hair behind her ear. "It wasn't intentional. I was in that half-awake-half-asleep stage. I heard talking and thought it was part of a dream, like when those two crazy old bats came in after lunch yesterday. By the time I was fully awake, you were talking about me. I didn't know how to let you know I was awake without looking like some creep listening in on your conversation."

Tears pricked her eyes as she remembered all the things she had admitted to Penny that morning. He hadn't just heard that she knew his identity, he'd also heard how she felt about him. She shot to her feet. "I've got to get out of here."

He grabbed her hand. "Please, don't go!"

Though his pleading pulled at her heart, Kate knew that she was only seconds away from breaking down. She couldn't let him see that. She pulled from his grip and raced toward the door.

"Kate, please!" Jeremy pushed himself into a standing position.

The effort of trying to gain his balance so quickly was more than his body could handle. Kate turned just in time to see his knees buckle. She raced to catch him before he fell.

"Dumbass," she muttered as she lowered him onto the bed. "That's all I need, for you to fall, and hit your empty head on the ground."

With her arm still wrapped around his waist, she could see the deep purple bags under his eyes and feel his ragged breath. He was still not well. Her tone softened, "You've only had a few days of touchy medical help. You need to be careful." She sat down on the bed beside him. "Millions of fans' hearts would break if anything happened to the great Jeremy Fulton."

"Millions of fans." He covered his face with his hands. "Millions of adoring fans."

Kate was surprised at his sullen tone. "You're one of the most loved men in Great Britain, if not the world. People adore you."

He dropped his hands from his face. "Yeah, people adore me. They enjoy the roles I play, they like the pithy comments that I give in interviews. They even give me awards. They don't know me, they don't love..." He swallowed hard. "To be honest, other than my immediate family, I'm not sure anybody has ever known me enough to say they love me. And my only remaining family, my sister, bloody hates me."

He turned to look at Kate. "That's why I didn't let you know I was awake. I wanted to hear what you had to say. Everybody loves me when they want something from me, and everybody wants something all the time. I've never had the chance to find out what people think of me. I mean not Jeremy Fulton TV star, but just Jeremy."

She chewed her bottom lip. "I'm sorry. I shouldn't have kept it a secret that I recognized you."

"I'm glad you did. You pretended to not know who I am because you thought it would be best for me. I've never had anybody do that before."

She laughed. "To be fair, there probably aren't many people who have had the opportunity."

He looked into Kate's eyes. She looked back into those beautiful, stop-your-heart baby blues. The eyes that made her want to... her mind snapped back to reality. Blood rushed to her cheeks, and she covered her face with her hands. "You heard everything that I said to Penny and everything she said to me?"

"Yes, I heard everything." The humor left his voice, and he became very serious. "There was one part of the conversation I found disturbing. It made me angry and sad."

This pulled her out of her embarrassed stupor. "What did I say?"

"You read articles on the internet; you see pictures in tabloids..." His eyes bore into hers. "After all the conversations we had, after all the sharing, the connection, you took what you read from trashy gossip sites and believed that over the person that has shared so much of himself?"

"I don't understand."

"Do you really think I'm that shallow, that I only date starlets half my age, that bone thin models are my type, that I'm just another dick running around with no real standards or depth?"

She tried to look away, but Jeremy placed his hand softly upon her cheek. "Kate, I am a forty-two-year-old man. Did it ever occur to you that my type is a mature, thoughtful, intelligent, compassionate woman with beautiful eyes, sexy curves, and a smile that lights up a room?"

Before Kate could formulate a reply, Jeremy leaned in and softly kissed her lips. Pulling only a bit away, he pressed his forehead to hers. "Because that's the type of woman who I find extremely attractive."

## Chapter 26

KATE SAT PERFECTLY STILL. She didn't respond to his kiss. She didn't even blink.

"Kate are you—"

Then, she pulled back and smacked his good arm. "You're a real idiot, you know that?"

"Ouch!" Jeremy yelped. "Why did you smack me?"

"You just kissed me!"

Jeremy's face showed a hurt that had nothing to do with the slap. "I'm sorry. I shouldn't have. It's just... I heard you say to Penny... I thought you felt the same—"

Kate interrupted, "The past four nights, I've laid beside you, watching you dream, listening to you breathe." Giving a small laugh she continued, "Then YOU kiss me. All this time I've wanted so desperately to... exercising immense amounts of self-control. Do you realize there were times I literally had to leave the cabin because I couldn't trust myself?"

Her eyes were so bright, her smile so beautiful. Jeremy smiled back. "You're right... I kissed—" He didn't have a chance to finish the sentence. Kate urgently pressed her lips to his. He pulled her closer. This wasn't a soft and gentle kiss like he had given her. It was a kiss that communicated the tension and desires of the past four days.

When Kate finally pulled away, she was breathless. "That was worth waiting for."

"Hell, it was worth falling down the side of a mountain." He put his hand behind her head and pulled her closer, but before their lips met, there was a raucous banging on the cabin door.

"If we ignore them, will they go away?" she whispered.

As if directly answering her question the knocking returned, only louder and more desperate. She gave Jeremy a worried look and hopped out of bed. When she cracked the cabin door, Sam stood on the front porch looking scared as a lost child. "I'm sorry Kate, but we need you."

"What is it?" Her heart stopped beating. "Has something happened to Nan or Penny?"

"No. It's Lizzy, she's having one of her spells. We tried to calm her down, but everything we say just gets her more and more upset. She doesn't know where she is, she keeps screaming at Nan. I hoped that, you know, with your mom, you'd know how to handle her."

Kate breathed a sigh of relief then immediately felt guilty. She took Sam's hands in hers. "Is she somewhere safe? Are there any things she could hurt herself with, knives, guns, sharp objects?"

"We got all of that stuff out of her reach. We tried to calm her down, to help her remember." Sam rambled. "But she just—"

"Where's Doc?" Kate interrupted.

"She went for a walk. She said she needed a break."

Kate pinched the bridge of her nose. "Okay, take me to Lizzy," She slipped on her boots and looked back to the bedroom where Jeremy sat giving her a sympathetic smile. "Dementia has horrible timing," she uttered under her breath.

KATE COULD HEAR THE SHOUTING BEFORE she reached the cabin. She took the stairs two at a time. An agitated, white-haired woman plopped herself down at the head of the kitchen table. Kathleen kneeled in front of her, a bouquet of Queen Anne's Lace in her hands. "Look at the flowers, Lizzy. I picked them this afternoon. I know how you love flowers. Aren't they pretty?"

The old woman swatted at the bouquet. "I don't give a damn about some weeds. I want to see my Henry! Where's Henry? Josh was supposed to pick him up from the groomer. He hates that dog. Did he leave him there? I swear if he forgot Henry, I'll beat that little snot bag over the head with my cane."

Sam whispered to Kate, "We tried to remind her that her schnauzer died five years ago, and that Josh is now in the Marine Corps, but it only made her more agitated."

Kate squeezed Sam's hand then walked into the room. "Let me try. I have a bit of experience with this." She dropped to her knees so that she and Lizzy were eye to eye. "Mrs. Allen, who are you looking for?"

Lizzy's face was scarlet, and her fists were clenched so tight that her knuckles were white. "I want my Henry! Josh was supposed to take him to the groomer. I swear, that grandson of mine, so unreliable. If I could drive, I'd have taken him myself, but my arthritis has me all crippled up."

"That must be horrible." Kate nodded in sympathy. "I'm sorry you can't drive anymore. Arthritis is very painful." Then she asked, "Henry, he's a good dog?"

"The best dog in the world. My Alfred got him for me right before he passed. He had one of those aneurysms, the stupid asshole was dead before he hit the ground. Left me high and dry with a mortgage and not one penny in life insurance. We made due, me and Henry. Where's my Henry? Why am I in this strange room? Why are these people staring at me?"

"Well, Mrs. Allen, we're at the old lumber camp, Slate, you know the one on Mongold Mountain? They're turning the camp into a resort, to bring tourists to the area, to help the economy."

"That's just what we don't need, more outsiders traipsing around, bringing their drugs and dirty business. Before you know it, they'll build bars." She leaned closer to Kate. "That's when the whores come in, shaking their little behinds!"

Kate put her hand on Lizzy's. "Reverend Jim thought this would be a nice bonding weekend for the congregation. So, we're having a sleepover away from all the worldly influences. Josh is keeping Henry for the weekend. When you get home, he'll be so excited to see you."

"I don't remember planning a church revival. Are you lying to me, are you a friend of Josh's?"

"Reverend Jim wanted it to be a surprise. He said he wanted it to be just like when Jesus comes, like a thief in the night." Kate recalled the Reverend's brimstone filled sermons. "There will be a big lunch, Kathleen's been baking pies all day. She wanted me to ask what your favorite is."

Kate glanced at Kathleen, who was standing helplessly in the corner. Any irritation she'd felt for the uninvited visits or pie lessons evaporated.

Lizzy looked at Kathleen, her voice took a maternal tone, "Well thank the saints you're better at cooking than flower arranging. Bless your heart, those weeds look like you just found the first thing you could get your hands on. Why didn't you pick some of those lovely peonies from your backyard?"

Kathleen forced a smile. "When we get off the mountain, I'll bring you a beautiful bouquet of the magenta and white ones."

Lizzy whispered to Kate, "She has quite the green thumb. You should see her garden. She even has her own apple trees. Did you know she cans her own pie filling? Better than what that little hussy over there makes." She nodded in Nan's direction.

Kathleen stepped forward. "I'll have a fresh pie for you in the morning."

Kate nodded. "I think that's a great idea. Maybe she can even give me a baking lesson so I can catch me a man."

Lizzy put her hand on Kate's cheek. "What's a girl as pretty as you doing without a husband? What's your name again?"

"I'm Kate. I'm just visiting."

"Well, Kate if you get cooking lessons from Kathleen, you'll be married in no time. They say the best way to a man's heart is his stomach, at least that's the way it was in my day. Now with all the lustful and sinful things on TV, they'd have you believe that the way to a man's heart is through his pants." She scoffed. "No decency anymore. Shorts up to their butt crack, chest hanging out, they look like harlots running around half-naked." She glared at Nan. "I remember that one there. She used to wear tight slacks and use too much makeup. Looked like a Jezebel."

Nan looked befuddled, but Kate gave her a look that urged her to play along.

"Well, it's a good thing we're having this church retreat. Maybe some of the women can have a talk with her at the luncheon tomorrow, get her back on the straight and narrow."

"She definitely needs Jesus!" Lizzy used the judgmental voice reserved for older, southern women.

Kate tried to steer the conversation away from poor Nan. "Well, if we want Kathleen to make her famous apple pie, we should let her start cooking."

Lizzy crossed her arms over her chest. "It's still light outside, I'm not going to bed!"

Kate looked at Kathleen and then back to Lizzy. "Well, of course not. That'd be silly. I was just thinking there isn't much room for people to sit. If some of us go into the bedroom, there'd be more space."

Lizzy's face changed, and suddenly Kate was looking into the eyes of a wounded child. "I'm doing it again, aren't I?" Tears spilled onto her heavily lined cheeks.

Kate felt a vice close on her heart. She'd seen that same look of mortification and shame on her mom's face too many times. But seeing it on Lizzy wasn't any less painful.

Lizzy started to sob. "I'm making a spectacle of myself." She grabbed onto Kate's hand as if she were hanging on for dear life. "Kate, this isn't me. You know me, you weeded my flowerbeds last summer. You know who I am, this isn't me."

Kate put her arm around the wounded woman. "I know Lizzy. I know who you are, I love who you are."

"I hate this damn disease. I hate it!" Lizzy sobbed into her hands.

"Lizzy," Kate asked, "is there anything that would make you feel better?"

She sniffed. "Would you stay with me for a while?"

Kate exhaled, she really, really wanted to get back to Jeremy, but what kind of ass would leave a confused, hurting woman like Lizzy? She closed her eyes. "What would you like to do?"

Lizzy smiled. "I enjoy playing games. Kathleen brought a few, can we play a few games?"

They spent hours playing Chutes and Ladders, Farkle, and Checkers. Finally, Lizzy looked at Kathleen. "I'm tired. Can somebody help me to bed?"

Kate watched Sam and Kathleen lead Lizzy to the bedroom, then she walked onto the porch. The air was thick and muggy. The smell of rotting leaves made her nose itch. She heard the door open and close behind her and turned to see who had followed. "Kathleen?"

The usually perfectly put together woman was a mess. Mascara was running down her face and her skin was red and blotchy. She threw herself into Kate's arms. "Thank you so much. I didn't know what to do."

Kate hugged back. "I understand."

A sob escaped Kathleen's lips as she pulled away. "Her son and I have been talking about putting her in a facility, but I thought Troy and I could handle it. She's never had an episode like this."

Kate swallowed back the lump rising in her own throat. "It's a gut-wrenching decision, but eventually you have to admit you can't do it on your own anymore. Or else you'll wear yourself tissue thin. Trust me, I know."

"I'm sure you do." Kathleen smiled sympathetically. "How do you handle it with your mom?"

Kate shrugged. "Each episode is different. Sometimes, correcting her just makes her more agitated. If it isn't harmful, I just reassure her everything's okay, even if it means playing into the fantasy."

Kathleen wiped mascara from her cheeks. "I'm glad you got stuck up here with us."

Just as Kate was going to reply, Doc ran up the cabin steps. Kate fought the urge to scream, "Where the hell have you been?" but she knew that Doc deserved a few hours to herself. She was just as threadbare as the rest of them.

Doc whispered, "How's Lizzy?"

"Kate's a hero," Kathleen replied. "She knew exactly how to calm her down."

Doc put her hand on Kate's shoulder and squeezed gently. "Thank you. I can take it from here."

Kate nodded and walked toward cabin one. "Just one more hill and valley on this rollercoaster of a week." She mumbled as she climbed under the covers beside a beautiful, sleeping man.

## Chapter 27

KATE BURROWED FARTHER BENEATH the covers. The dream was so real that his smell even seemed to linger on the sheets. She forbade her eyes to open, but she could not prevent her ears from hearing the playful, "Good morning, beautiful."

She slowly pulled the covers from over her head, then sat bolt upright. "You're real."

"Excuse me?"

"You're real, this isn't a dream. I was sure when I opened my eyes, you'd be gone." She smiled sheepishly. "I mean, it wouldn't be the first time I dreamed about waking up next to you."

He chuckled and leaned his forehead against hers. "I'm not going to disappear. I swear this is all real."

Kate jerked away, her face a mix of horror and pain. She covered her heart with her hands. "It's all real. The flood, Riverside, the clinic... That's real too?"

Jeremy ran his knuckles along her cheek. "Yes."

She massaged her temples. "This is just so surreal. You, the flood, I just can't wrap my head around all of it, or hell any of it."

Jeremy lay back on the bed and gently pulled Kate down beside him. "How about this? We'll stay here, just the two of us, until at least one thing in your world makes sense."

She rested her head on his chest and ran her fingers up and down his sternum. "Can we stay here all day and pretend that the entire world consists of this little cabin?"

He kissed the top of her head. "Whatever you need."

They lay in each other's arms until reality, literally, came knocking on the cabin door. Kate squeezed her eyes shut. "Do I have to answer?"

"You don't have to, but you probably should."

Kate sighed and peeled herself out of bed. She stumbled to the front door and opened it just a crack. Nan and Sam were standing on the porch. "Hello sweetie, I hope you had a good night's sleep." Nan's words were crisp and fast.

Kate answered cautiously, "Yeah, I slept well."

Nan motioned toward the bedroom. "Is he awake?"

"No," Kate lied. There'd be fewer questions if everyone thought he was still sleeping.

"That's good. Chris just got off the radio with the National Guard. The rescuers will start evacuating tomorrow morning. We're having a meeting to devise a plan. Would you like to join us?"

Kate's pulse quickened. She'd never seen Nan this agitated. "Sure, yeah, I'll—"

Nan cut her off. "Get dressed, I'll wait right here for you."

WHEN KATE WALKED THROUGH THE double doors of the Foreman's cabin, she felt the weight of exhaustion bear down upon her. Chris, Doc, and CJ were sitting with their backs to the door, but she could tell from the way their shoulders slumped the ordeal was wearing on them.

Penny's voice interrupted her thoughts. "Good morning Briar Rose. You certainly slept late this morning."

Unsure of how to respond, Kate grunted, "Coffee," and walked toward the silver percolator. By the time she poured herself a cup of black coffee, the small council was seated around the table. She slipped into a folding chair and wondered how she became a member of this ragtag leadership team.

Though everybody looked tired, Nan and Penny looked the worst. Their eyes were rimmed in red and their bodies looked as if they carried an Atlas worthy load. Perhaps having the two women share a bed hadn't been such a great idea. She felt a twinge of guilt, not just because she had displaced Penny, but because she'd slept so wonderfully with Jeremy beside her.

Chris cleared his throat. "I'll start with the good news. The National Guard will be here tomorrow for evacuations."

Penny exhaled in relief.

Sam asked, "And the bad news?"

Chris set his jaw. "Things below are worse than we thought. In Pocahontas County alone, sixteen bodies have been recovered, and twenty people are missing."

Kate's jaw dropped. Thirty-six people dead or missing? She hugged her arms tightly around her stomach. "This can't be happening," she muttered.

Chris, who seemed to have switched his emotions to robot, replied, "It's happening, and we have to make some decisions."

Tears glistened in Sam's salt and pepper stubble as he nodded toward the double doors. "Do we tell them?"

Nan fiddled with the cross around her neck. "I think we keep the death toll to ourselves."

Penny sniffled. "Isn't that just prolonging the pain?"

Doc answered in a soft tone. "Yes, but we have to look at the big picture. If we tell them now, they aren't around family, unable to make phone calls, and away from their familiar surroundings."

Sam whispered, "But their familiar surroundings may no longer be standing?"

Doc exhaled. "That's a good point, Sam." She looked around the table at the tired faces. "That's why we need to come to a consensus about how to proceed. Personally, I think we should keep the deaths to ourselves. We aren't equipped to counsel and comfort forty elderly residents, some of whom have a loose grip on reality as it is."

Penny tugged at her red ringlets. "What do we say if they ask us? We can't lie."

Doc said patiently, "Yes we can, but whatever we say, we must all tell the same story. Inconsistency is how rumors get started, and we all know how rumors can balloon in this community." She looked around the table. "Are we in a consensus that we keep this to ourselves?"

Everybody nodded.

For the first time, CJ spoke, "What about the rescue team? What if they say something when they're in the middle of the river with someone like Sy?"

Chris answered, "I'll radio ahead and ask the guardsmen to not mention anything during the rescue."

Penny was becoming more frantic. "But what if they do?"

Nan put her hand on Penny's knee. "Then they do, and we deal with it then. We cannot prepare for every scenario."

Doc nodded. "Situations like this don't come with a manual. We're all unsure of how to proceed."

Sam's voice quaked. "Do we know if any of the dead or missing are family members of any evacuees?"

Chris answered, "Trooper Guthrie gave me a partial list. They still have to notify next of kin, which in some cases is proving to be quite difficult since some next of kin are trapped in their attics." His voice became as somber as a dirge. "Or have been evacuated to higher ground."

Kate watched as one by one people comprehended Chris' last statement. Higher ground, like in an abandoned lumber camp.

CJ sat open-mouthed, random words spilling forth. "Chris... What... Us?"

Chris held up his hand. "I was able to get Guthrie to open up just a bit. Nobody in this room will have an immediate meeting with the State Police when we get off the mountain, but others, won't be as lucky."

CJ cleared his throat. "Are there any names you can tell us?"

Chris nodded. "They'd only give me names if they'd reached next of kin." He pulled a worn piece of paper from his pocket. In a deep monotone voice, he began reading names. Each name read hit Kate in the chest like a sledgehammer. She knew these names; she knew the people who owned these names. In a small community like Riverside, there were no strangers.

When Chris finally stopped reading, he collapsed into a folding chair. "And they found..." his voice broke. "They found Kenny's body two miles from the store."

The room began to spin. Kate ran onto the porch, leaned over the railing, and vomited.

After the retching ended, she felt a calloused hand on her back. When she stood, Sam was standing beside her. "You okay, kiddo?" He asked, then corrected himself, "I guess that's a stupid question, huh?"

Kate collapsed into Sam's arms. When she finally lifted her head, a large spot on his shirt was soaking wet. She looked around, Penny and Nan had joined them on the porch.

Nan handed her a Styrofoam cup of water. "I'm going to visit folks and tell them about the Guard coming."

Kate took a long swallow of water. "Who do you want me to visit?"

Nan touched her cheek. "Why don't you go back and check on your patient?"

KATE TRUDGED THROUGH THE FRONT DOOR and into the bedroom where Jeremy sat beaming. With one look at her, the smile fell from his face. "Blimey! Kate, what's wrong?"

Her voice seemed detached from her body. "We just got a partial list of the dead and missing. I know them, not all of them well, but I know each person whose name was read." She seemed almost confused. "This doesn't make sense. It just doesn't..."

"Kate, I'm so sorry."

"I just can't wrap my head around this." The last word came out as a sob.

Jeremy pushed himself to his feet and limped to her. He pulled her close and kissed her forehead. "Tell me what I can do?"

Kate pulled back. A V-shaped line formed between her eyebrows as she looked him up and down. "What are you doing here?" she asked when their eyes finally met.

"I thought you wanted comforting."

"No, I mean, what are you doing standing here?" She pointed to the wooden floor. "You're in the middle of the room, away from the bed?"

Jeremy looked at Kate with wide, bewildered eyes. "I guess I am."

"You're standing, without help. How?"

"I don't know. I didn't think about it... You were standing there, looking so helpless. I wanted to comfort you."

"How do you feel?"

He smiled widely. "Lightheaded, but good."

Kate took his hand and led him back to the bed. He sat on the edge and rested his head in his hands. "I don't get it, Kate. You saw me yesterday, I needed two men to help me walk." He sat up straight. "Maybe it was the adrenaline. I wanted to get to you so badly that my body did something extraordinary?"

"Let's try it again." She stood and walked four paces from the bed and turned. "Walk to me."

Jeremy lifted his eyes and smirked. "Now, I feel like a toddler."

"Well, technically you are toddling," she teased. "But seriously, see if you can stand and walk to me."

Jeremy put his hand on the footboard and grunted as he slowly stood. He looked cautiously at Kate and took a shaky step forward, then another, and another. As he got closer, Kate took a step backward forcing Jeremy to walk farther. After a few unsure limps, he reached her. Kate wrapped her arms around his neck, and kissed him, hard.

He laughed. "Not sure I'm ready to be swept off of my feet right as I begin walking again."

Kate rolled her eyes. "That has to be one of the worst jokes I've heard, and I remember the writing for *Iron Ivy*."

"Ouch! You know, I worked on some of those scripts."

"Really?"

"No," Jeremy smirked. "I just wanted to see your reaction."

Kate gave an impish smile. "You just started walking again, I'd be more careful when addressing your nurse."

He pushed a strand of hair behind her ear. "I'll definitely keep that in mind. Now, Miss Nightingale, would you escort me back to our bed?"

Kate put her arm around his waist and slowly guided him to the bed. He propped himself against the headboard, and Kate took her place at his side. She put her head on his shoulder. "We'll be getting off of the mountain tomorrow," she said. "Luckily, the waters are tame enough to use the boats and we don't have to be airlifted."

"Darn, I was looking forward to a helicopter ride."

"Haven't you had enough adventure for the week?"

"What can I say, I enjoy taking risks."

Kate rolled her eyes. "Well, since you almost died last week, maybe you should spend a few days being tame."

Jeremy pretended to pout. "You always spoil my fun." Then he asked, "When does all the excitement begin?"

"Probably early in the morning. I think I'll pack all my things tonight. Do you need help packing?"

"Considering I was carried into camp with nothing except the clothes I was wearing, I'd say I'm pretty well packed."

Kate prepared to return the banter when Doc knocked on the cabin door. "Can I come in?"

"Come in," Jeremy replied as Kate moved to the folding chair.

Doc walked into the bedroom. "How's the patient?" she asked. Her eyes were red, and the cadence of her voice betrayed her exhaustion.

"Better, much better," he replied.

Doc looked at Kate and said, "I need to examine the patient, can you step onto the porch for a moment?"

As Kate sat on the stairs, waiting for Doc to finish her examination, she saw Troy and Sam approaching.

"Good afternoon, gentlemen," she said.

"Afternoon, Kate." They said in unison.

Troy asked, "Where's the tall and mysterious stranger?"

"In bed, with Doc." Kate slapped her hand over her mouth. "I mean he's in bed, and Doc is with him."

The men exploded with laughter.

Troy took out his handkerchief and wiped his eyes. "Imagine if you'd said that to Hazel."

THE THREE WERE STILL LAUGHING WHEN the cabin door creaked open. Doc and a slightly wobbly Jeremy walked through the door.

Troy's jaw dropped, and Sam uttered, "I don't believe it!"

Doc smiled at her patient. "I can hardly believe it myself, but I'm not questioning it. Not often I have a medical miracle standing beside me."

Sam beamed. "We were coming to visit a spell and keep you from being bored to tears, but I think that's a moot point now."

Troy added, "Now that you're walking, you could join us in the Foreman's Cabin if you like. I think some fresh surroundings would be great for you."

Jeremy looked at Kate and was torn. Even though she put on a tough face, he could see her brokenness under the veneer. He wanted to lie in bed with her head upon his chest and hold her until everything made sense. However, the cabin walls were closing in. Plus, the look on Sam's face was just as forlorn as Kate's. He had formed a great affection for the older man. Sam reminded him so much of his father that when he said, "It's still a bit slick out here." He could almost hear his father's Glasgow accent. He looked at Kate. "What do you think?"

Kate shrugged. "Do you want to get out for a while?"

"I do." He looked at Sam. "I'd appreciate that helping hand if you're offering it."

"Yes, sir, I am."

Jeremy took Sam's arm but found he really didn't need it. With each step, he felt steadier, so much that by the time he reached the Foreman's Cabin he wasn't leaning on Sam at all.

When they walked through the double doors of the meeting hall, every head turned, and all conversation stopped. He'd barely sat down when Jack Madison plopped himself in the chair across the table. "Looks like you are healing quite well."

Jeremy took a moment to catch his breath. "I am. Like I told Sam, good people are good medicine, and I'm getting a healthy dose in Slate."

"These here are good folks." Jack leaned closer. "I think having you here has helped. Gives everybody something to gossip about."

"Glad to help."

Jack leaned back and rubbed his bulbous belly. "So, how are you at poker?"

Jeremy shrugged. "Depends on the type I guess. What's the flavor: seven-card-stud, Texas hold'em, five-card draw, Omaha, thirty-two card draw, Americana?"

Jack slapped his knee. "Great Scott."

Jeremy winked. "I'm pretty average, but I thank ye for the compliment."

Jack's bellowing laughter echoed through the halls. When he could breathe again, he grabbed a deck of cards. "Let's start with Texas Hold 'em."


KATE STOOD IN THE DOORWAY POUTING. She didn't want to share Jeremy with anybody. She was so caught up in her self-pity, she didn't notice Penny walk up behind her. "Well, aren't we Miss Susie Sunshine?"

Kate stared resentfully at the table of poker players. "What do you want?" She wheeled to glare at Penny, but the moment she saw her friend's red-rimmed eyes and haggard expression, she felt guilty. "Sorry, I'm just…" she trailed off.

Penny waved off the apology.

"So how are things with Nan?" Kate asked.

"We talked, and things are fine." Penny nodded toward Jeremy. "So, did you tell him?"

"Tell him what?"

"Seriously? Have you already forgotten?"

"Oh, that!" Kate laughed. "No, I didn't have to. The little brat was listening to our conversation yesterday morning."

Penny raised her eyebrows. "And?"

Kate led Penny onto the porch, and gave a synopsis of the conversation, the shared feelings, and the kiss.

"I knew it!" Penny whooped. "I knew he felt the same way. I saw the way he looked at you. You were too blind or stubborn to see it, but we all saw it."

Kate took a step backward. "Who's we?"

"Anybody who saw the way you two looked at each other during the dinner."

Kate felt her stomach turn to ice. "So, everybody knows?"

"No, everybody's speculating and gossiping. My advice, don't let anybody know. If you do, there'll be a gigantic hubbub about the two of you sleeping in the same cabin."

Kate rolled her eyes. "Never thought about that."

"Trust me, some are already thinking about it. The River Song is being sung loud and clear."

Kate gritted her teeth. "You'd think they would have more important things to occupy their small little minds."

Penny stiffened. "They do realize there are more important things to occupy their small, little minds: sad, heartbreaking, terrifying things." She jabbed her finger toward the camp. "The scandalous behavior in cabin one is where they allow their small minds to wander to shelter them from the torment out here."

Kate's face flushed, and she hung her head. For the second time in a matter of minutes, she had been a self-centered ass. "You're right, I'm sorry." With her head still hung, she asked, "Any more word from Chris?"

Penny's voice was barely a whisper. "No."

Kate, embarrassed and ashamed, was eager to end the conversation. "I guess we should get back inside, huh? Don't want to start gossip about what we are doing out here." She tried to joke.

Penny wiped her hands on her jeans. "You go ahead. I'm in the middle of a good book. I want to get back to it."

Guilt pressed upon Kate's chest like a boulder as she watched her best friend stomp down the stairs. Though she desperately wanted to follow and make things right, she knew Penny needed time. She sulked for a while, then turned and walked back through the double doors.

A large group was gathered around the central table. Kate stood on her tippy toes and peered over the mass of gray and balding heads. In the middle of the crowd, Jeremy and Sy were sitting across from one another, engaged in an intense game of chess. Very few black pieces were still on the board.

She smiled. *How nice of Jeremy to let Sy win,* she thought. However, it quickly became obvious that there was no letting Sy win. The old curmudgeon was trumping Jeremy fair and square. The tension in the air grew increasingly thick, as over the next half hour, the two warred tit-for-tat. Finally, Jeremy sat back. "Check," he announced as he moved his queen into position.

Sy narrowed his eyes. "Don't get cocky, there, son." Then in a fluid motion, he used his knight to topple Jeremy's queen. Again, the two men were entrenched in an intense battle. Sy would check, Jeremy would escape. Jeremy would take a piece, Sy would reconfigure. The room was gripped in a tense silence when a raucous "Whew Wee, checkmate!" rang through the air.

Jeremy stared at the board in disbelief. But when he lifted his eyes and saw Kate standing behind the old man, he broke into a wide grin.

He looked back at Sy, stuck out his hand and said, "You're a worthy opponent, Sylvester. Where did you learn to play like that?"

Sy stared Jeremy in the eye. "Amache."

"Is that where you grew up?" Jeremy asked, and the room became deathly quiet.

Sy let out a humph of disgust. "It's an internment camp." His voice was rough as sandpaper. "Mom was half Japanese. That was enough. We were there from, '42 to '45. When we weren't doing our chores, we had nothing else to do. Didn't want to draw attention to ourselves, so my friend's dad taught us to play."

Nobody spoke or moved for what seemed like an eternity. Finally, Sy looked at Sam. "I need some fresh air. Help me to the porch."

"Sure thing, Sy." Sam put his arm around the older man and helped him to his feet.

Once they were out of earshot, Jeremy looked at Kate. "I'm sorry. I don't understand."

Dalton Beaman sat at the table. "It's okay, son. I'm not sure what you know about American history, but there are some dark spots we would all like to forget. Unfortunately, fear and ignorance can make people do bad things." He took a deep breath. "After the bombing at Pearl Harbor, there was widespread hysteria. Roosevelt thought it would be in the country's best interest to round up all the Japanese, even if they were U.S. citizens, and put them in internment camps. Sy and his family spent several years at the Granada Relocation Center in Colorado."

Kate mumbled, "I didn't know."

Jack said, "Not a lot of us did, until recently. In the past few years, Sy has opened up more about his time in Amache and even his tours in Vietnam."

Dalton added, "We'd started videotaping some of his talks. We did his, Nathan Clayton's, and Patrick Wilson's. We wanted to do a recorded history while they were still here to tell them." His face fell. "The tapes were in my basement. There's a good chance they're lost forever."

A heaviness fell over the room. Members looked from one to another, hoping somebody would end the awkward silence. Then, as if on cue, Kathleen paraded through the backdoor. "Have ya'll eaten yet? I've been baking all morning."

For once, Kate was happy to see the perfectly coiffed, nosy neighbor. With Kathleen's mention of food, others began offering his or her own side dish. Before you could say casserole, an impromptu potluck was organized.

Sam said the blessing and brought Jeremy a plate of food. "What ya' thinking about, son?"

Jeremy smiled. "I was remembering the sermon dad used to give about Jesus feeding the thousands with five loaves and two fish. I could write an equally compelling sermon about the casseroles and desserts of Slate."

"Son, I think there has been more than one miracle this week." Sam patted him on the shoulder. "I'm going to go check on Sy. I'll stop by the cabin later."

"Bye Sam," Jeremy called.

After he walked out the door, a loud tsk came from the next table. "Looky-there," Sally said. "Nan left five minutes ago, and now there goes Sam."

Hazel rolled her eyes. "Do they still think nobody knows what's going on?"

Doc added, "Even Lizzy has figured it out."

Elle smiled. "Ah, let them think it's still a secret. It's cute watching them try to hide it."

Sally added, "You can tell just from the way they look at each other that something's going on."

Kate and Jeremy locked eyes. If the women of Riverside were so adept to figuring out hidden romances, then they needed to be much more careful.

Jeremy cleared his throat. "Uh, Chris."

Chris walked to where he was sitting. "What can I do for you?"

"I'm feeling knackered. Could you help me back to the cabin? I can't help with the cleanup, and I'll just get in the way. No need for one more obstacle."

Though Kate wanted to be the one to take Jeremy back to the cabin, she knew he'd drawn attention to his exit for a reason. She dutifully stayed behind to sweep floors and wipe down tables, while Chris took the handsome Scottish stranger back to their cabin.

## Chapter 28

AFTER THE CLEANUP, KATE HEADED back to cabin one. As she opened the door, she heard a gravelly female voice coming from inside. She walked into the bedroom and saw Hazel standing beside the bed, looking as if she were about to pounce upon Jeremy. Kate crossed her arms over her chest. "Hazel, what are you doing in my bedroom?"

Hazel raised a drawn-in eyebrow. "Your bedroom? I thought you were sleeping on the floor?"

"I sleep on the floor of the bedroom, thus my bedroom. What are YOU doing in it?"

Hazel threw her shoulders back. "This young man was telling me about his homeland. I've always wanted to visit Scotland, ever since I saw that movie where Mel Gibson paints his face. I was just saying how much I'd LOVE to visit."

"Well," Jeremy said, "I'd love to have all my new Slate friends for a holiday. I'll talk to my travel agent friend about booking a group tour." He shifted his gaze to Kate. "Think Nan and Doc would like that?"

Kate stifled a laugh. "They'd be delighted."

Just as Hazel opened her mouth to argue, there was a knock on the door. Kate gritted her teeth and wondered who the next group of privacy invaders would be. She didn't have time to speculate before Nan, Sam, and Penny walked into the bedroom.

"Hello, sweetie," Nan said to Kate. "We thought we'd stop by for a visit."

Kate forced a smile. "Wonderful."

Hazel gave an exacerbated humph. "It's getting awful crowded in here."

"Yes, it is," Kate said through her teeth.

Hazel turned to Jeremy. "Hopefully, we'll be able to visit again soon," she said a bit too sweetly. Then she put her nose in the air and strutted out the door.

Nan winked at Jeremy. "Hazel has quite a thing for you."

Jeremy nodded. "Thank goodness Kate came along. It was getting uncomfortable."

He began to stand, but Nan motioned for him to sit. "Yes, yes, yes. We all know you can stand, no need to show off."

He smiled at Nan, then shifted his attention to Penny. "Nice to see you again."

"Well, I figured it was about time I get to know the man who stole my best friend." Penny laughed, but Kate could hear the resentment in her voice.

Sam spoke up, "Have you been getting bored?"

"Honestly, I haven't had time to get bored. You warned me that if we were in Slate for the whole day, I wouldn't have a free minute. You weren't wrong. My door's been opening and closing nonstop."

"Are you tired? Would you like some rest?" Kate asked excitedly.

"Nah, I'm fine. I'm enjoying meeting everybody and hearing their stories."

Sam sat at the foot of the bed. Nan, Penny, and Kate pulled in chairs from the kitchen, and for the next few hours, the stories and laughs came easily. However, as the rays of the evening sun slanted through the window, it became obvious Jeremy was wearing thin.

Sam looked at him. "Tired, son?"

"I'm a bit knackered."

Sam put a fatherly hand on his knee. "Maybe you should stop playing host for a few hours."

"I think that's a great idea," Kate said, praying the others would take the hint.

Nan stood from her chair. "Actually, now is a good time for us to head out." She turned to Kate. "Do you mind coming with me? We need to have a little talk."

Kate's stomach turned into cement. A 'little talk' was never good. She looked at Jeremy with terror in her eyes, then followed Nan and Penny onto the front porch.

"Let's take a walk," Nan said.

The trio set off into the woods. The smell of rotting leaves made Kate's nose itch, and the squishing sound of boots in the mud set her teeth on edge. But neither irritant upset her as keenly as the electricity bouncing back and forth between Penny and Nan.

Finally, they reached a small clearing. Penny mumbled, "I think this is as good a spot as any."

Kate tried to not sound accusatory, but her anxiety was mounting. "What's going on?"

Nan turned to look at her. "We talked to Chris. He got word about the house." Her voice broke, and Kate's stomach hit the ground.

Kate wanted to say something comforting, but all she could utter was an accusatory, "What?" She turned to Penny. "Tell me what's happening!"

Penny's red-rimmed eyes filled with tears. "The Calic Run was out of its banks. It made it across the driveway, and into the house."

"But we knew that could happen," Kate bargained.

Nan exhaled. "We knew there was a possibility that the Calic Run would overflow, what we didn't count on was the Greenbrier being at fifteen feet above flood level. The river pushed water back up the valley."

"But the house is still there, right? It's still standing?" Kate pleaded.

Nan put a hand on Kate's shoulder. "Part of it washed away, what's left will be declared a total loss and torn down."

If somebody had hit Kate in the chest with a sword, it would have been less painful. She looked back and forth between Penny and Nan and saw they were both holding on by a very thin thread. She realized how short she'd been with the two hurting women who stood beside her; the two women who'd always stood beside her. Grief and guilt crashed upon her like a tsunami. "Your home's gone?"

Penny gave a weak smile. "It's your home too."

With the strength and comfort that only a mother could provide, Nan wrapped Kate and Penny in a hug. They cried together in the dank woods. When the shock and tears finally lessened, Kate pulled away and asked, "How long have you known?"

"Chris told us last night," Penny said.

"Why did you wait so long to tell me?" Kate asked, there was no accusation in her voice.

Nan wiped a tear from Kate's cheek. "We figured after you dealt with Lizzy last night that you'd had enough drama."

"But... I could've helped," Kate uttered.

"Help what? Help us cry?" Nan gave a soft laugh. "We did just fine on our own."

"I could've cried with you."

Nan pointed back toward the camp. "Last night your gifts were better used elsewhere."

Kate thought back to the morning meeting, Nan's haggard expressions and Penny's red-rimmed eyes. How could she not have figured it out? She wrapped the two women in a hug and whispered, "I love you," the only words she could think to say.

The trio walked hand in hand back toward the camp. As they approached the Foreman's cabin, Penny broke the silence. "I'm going to take a walk. I need to clear my head."

"It's getting dark," Nan protested.

"I'll be fine. It's a clear night. With the moon and stars, I can traverse the woods," she called over her shoulder.

Kate looked helplessly at Nan. "I'm going to follow her."

"Give her time. She's clinging to the idea that everybody thinks she's fine. If she realizes that we see through her bravado, it'll be worse. You know how stubborn she is."

"But I haven't spent any time with her. I abandoned her to deal with this on her own." Guilt twisted in her gut like a sharp blade. "I've got to try."

By the time Kate had caught up with her, Penny was leaning against a tree trunk looking at the stars. "It's like they are mocking us." Penny spat the words, "Like look at us twinkle, and shine, while 'screw you, you minuscule peons.' No matter what happens here, who lives, who dies, who loses, who wins, the stars just sit there and sparkle. Nothing we do matters to them. Nothing we can ever do will affect them. They're in their own little existence, immune to the pain all around."

Kate chafed at this last comment. She knew the stars weren't the only ones who seemed in their own little existence. "Penny, I'm sorry. I've been spending so much time with Jeremy, I forgot why I came to Riverside."

"You had more important things to do. It's not every day you find an injured Scottish dreamboat who needs to be nursed back to health." Though Penny tried to joke, the resentment in her voice was undeniable. "Listen, I know what you're trying to do. I appreciate it, but I need time by myself."

"Pen, I'm so sorry."

"I want to be alone." The comment wasn't mean, but it was dismissive.

Kate hung her head and walked away. She trudged up the stairs of cabin one and threw open the door. Sam was leaning on the kitchen counter, and Jeremy was sitting at the table.

Sam put his hand on her shoulder. "You okay, kiddo?"

"Yeah, I was talking to Nan and Penny. I'm just," she paused, "really tired, that's all."

Sam nodded knowingly. "Where are they now?"

"Penny went for a walk, alone." Kate exhaled. "I don't know where Nan went."

"Well, I'll try to find her." He nodded at Jeremy. "See you in the morning."

"Sure thing, Sam," Jeremy replied.

Kate stumbled to the bed where she sat with her hands covering her face.

Jeremy limped toward her. "Do you want to talk?" he asked timidly. When she didn't reply, he sat beside her and rubbed her back.

"The flood swept away some of the house, and what's still standing will have to be torn down. Penny isn't handling it well. I can't blame her. I've deserted her to handle it all on her own." She wiped a tear from her cheek. "I tried to talk to her, but she's angry with me. I deserve it. I'm a shitty friend."

He kissed the top of her head. "You're not a shitty friend, you're a nurse to a narcissistic pansy who demanded your time." He put his hand on her cheek and directed her head so they were eye to eye. "She's upset, she's exhausted, let her sleep on it." Jeremy lay down and patted the spot beside him. "We all need the rest."

She placed her head on his chest. Once the numbness wore off, she began talking, recalling memories of Nan's home. When she told him about the rest of the destruction, she cried. When she told him about Kenny, he cried, too.

Finally, their tongues were too tired to talk, and they fell asleep in one another's arms.

## Chapter 29

A BRONX ACCENT YELLING, "YOU GUYS AWAKE?" yanked Kate from her sleep.

Kate willed it to go away, but the voice called out again, louder and more urgent. "Kate, wake up. Nan sent me."

Kate pulled the quilt from over her head. The obnoxious sunlight blinded her as she oriented herself. However, once her eyes fell upon the beautiful man at her side, it was all the orienting she needed. She tiptoed to the threshold and opened the door. "What is it?" she yawned.

Elle craned her neck to see around Kate then muttered under her breath. "I knew it!"

Kate rubbed the sleep from her eyes. "Knew what?"

Elle shrank back. "Look at me, I'm as bad as Hazel."

The memory of Hazel leering at Jeremy made Kate's skin crawl. She crossed her arms over her chest. "Exactly what did you know?"

Elle's cheeks turned red. "Kathleen said you were supposed to be sleeping on the floor, but that you'd been sleeping in the same bed. And well, you just woke up, and there isn't any bedding on the floor."

"And your point?"

"At the dinner and yesterday, I saw how you were looking at each other, and I just knew that there was something going on." Elle shrugged. "Pretty much everybody could see there was something between you two."

Kate couldn't help but smile. "You had it figured out at the dinner, huh?"

"I mean, who didn't? It's not like you tried to hide it."

Kate let out a deep laugh.

Elle bristled. "What's so funny?"

"Nothing." Kate smiled. "I guess everybody realized it except us."

Elle nudged Kate with her elbow. "So, what exactly is going on?"

"I'll let you know when we figure it out." Though Kate knew the people of Riverside needed a distraction, and that rumors would fly with or without her permission, she didn't feel quite like discussing her and Jeremy's newest developments. She steered the conversation in a different direction. "You said Nan sent you?"

"I'm here to tell you the National Guard will begin shuttling people across the river in about an hour. Sam will be up in a few minutes to help Tim get dressed. Nan wants you two to come to the Foreman's cabin as soon as you can."

"Thanks, Elle, we'll be down as soon as we get clothes on." Kate slapped her hand over her mouth. "I mean, we'll be down as soon as we get changed out of our pajamas and into regular clothes."

"I'll just tell her you'll be down soon." Elle winked.

When Kate walked back into the bedroom she heard, "Hey stranger."

"Hey, sexy stranger." She slid into bed beside Jeremy and lay her head on his chest. "It appears the time for evacuation has come. You ready for this?"

"If I'm being honest, I don't want to go. I want to stay right here with you, in this bed. I don't want to deal with the rubbish of the real world. I like Slate."

Kate ran her fingers through his chest hair. "I don't think we have a choice. We have to face reality."

"Before we do that, I have one thing." In a single fluid motion, he put his hand behind her head, pulled her close, and kissed her. It was a kiss of hunger, desire, and passion. Kate reciprocated, allowing her body to respond to the fire igniting inside her. When Jeremy finally pulled away, both were out of breath and looking at one another with a new appreciation.

Jeremy touched his fingertips to Kate's lips. "You have no idea how much self-control it took to not do that yesterday."

Kate nipped at his finger. "Why didn't you?"

"Each time we were alone, you'd just received devastating news. I didn't want to take advantage of your emotional state."

Kate watched him try to explain himself, but his sleepy smile and hypnotic blue eyes were more than she could resist. She pounced on him and initiated a passionate kiss of her own. When she pulled away, they were both breathing hard. "Feel free to take advantage of my emotional state at any time," she purred.

Jeremy wrapped his fingers around her frizzy curls and pulled her closer, but before their lips met, a knocking rang from the front door.

Kate bunched up her face. "I bet that's Sam."

"Hey, I like Sam."

"I like Sam too, but not at moments like this." She untangled herself from his arms and dragged herself to the front door.

Standing on the front porch was a freshly shaven man wearing clean blue jeans, faded t-shirt, and a too-bright smile. "How's everybody this morning?"

Before Kate could answer, Sam was already to the bedroom. He peeked inside and smiled at Jeremy. "Hello, son, brought some new clothes. I figured you'd like to clean up a bit."

Kate left the men to their business and scurried to the bathroom. As she closed the door, she resisted the urge to giggle like one of her fourteen-year-old students. She looked in the mirror and said to her reflection, "You just made out with Jeremy Fulton!" Then a thought even more exciting, and terrifying struck her, *you just kissed a man who could easily steal your heart.*


WHEN THE TRIO WALKED THROUGH the double doors of the meeting hall, Nan crossed the room to meet them. "How's the patient?"

Jeremy replied, "Much better, thanks."

Kate grabbed Nan's hand. "How's Penny?"

"She came back to the cabin about an hour after our talk and seemed much more at peace. We also got word last night that Lenard made it home, so that helped a lot."

Kate's eyes darted around the room. "I need to find her. I need to talk to her."

Nan smoothed the collar of Kate's shirt. "There'll be plenty of time to talk when we are off the mountain. For now, evacuation is the priority." She turned her attention to Jeremy. "You'll go in the first round. Sam and Chris will be here soon to help you get to the boat. I know you've been walking around a bit, but the ground is uneven in places. I think you should let the men help you."

Kate asked, "And me?"

Nan replied, "You'll go last, that way you can stay here and keep the natives from going loco."

Jeremy looked anxiously at Kate then back to Nan. "I'd like to wait and go with my nurse."

"You sure about that? We could get you to an ER with an x-ray machine faster if we took you in the first round."

He shook his head. "Doc said that I can wait until tomorrow to get the x-rays. I want to stay with Kate."

Kate interjected, "Nan, if he goes down without me, he'll get pounced on like a steak in a lion's cage. We can't do that to him."

Nan thought for a moment. "You're right. I don't want to leave him at the mercy of Hazel. I'll take Lizzy Allen with me in the first boat. Chris has been communicating with her son, and he's very eager to get her off the mountain." She glanced at her watch. "Just don't forget there will be a meeting at the fire hall in Kimberly around five." She began to walk away, then turned on her heel and faced Jeremy. "Oh, and just in case you were wondering, this 'I want to stay with my nurse' isn't fooling anyone. I had it figured out before you two did."

Kate looked at Jeremy. "From what I hear, everybody did." She gave Nan a sly glance. "It's extremely difficult to keep a romance under the radar in a situation like this."

Nan's back straightened. "Yes, well, I'm going to help Troy get Lizzy loaded."

Minutes later, Nan followed Troy, Kathleen, and a puzzled-looking Lizzy onto the porch. Sam opened the rear door of his truck, and Lizzy climbed into the back seat. Nan helped her with the seatbelt then turned her attention back to Jeremy. "See ya' at the bottom. Take care of Kat bird, Jeremy."

Kate's throat constricted. "I swear I didn't tell her, I haven't told anybody. I promised you I'd keep your secrets, and I did."

Jeremy smiled. "She's known for a while."

Kate gaped at Nan. "Since when?"

"Since the moment I saw him." Nan smiled at Kate. "You've spent countless nights in my home and most of those nights you were watching this man in some TV show. Did you honestly think I wouldn't know who he was?"

Kate felt crimson creep up her neck.

Nan turned to Jeremy. "You know, you're not a bad actor."

Jeremy laughed uncomfortably. "Thank you?"

"I really liked the comedy set in the 1800s, where you were a sheriff. What was the name of that town?"

"*Wooden Dove*?"

"Yeah, that one I really liked, but then after that, there was a show where you played an astronaut that traveled through time." Nan tapped her index finger to her chin. "What was that one?"

"*12 o'clock Moon*?"

"Yes, Gawd! I hated that show!"

Jeremy broke out into loud laughter. He wrapped Nan in a strong, one-armed hug. "Nan, meeting you has been one of the most unforgettable and enjoyable experiences in quite some time!"

Nan hugged back. "It's been a pleasure on my end as well." She pulled back and put her hand on his uninjured shoulder. "And you're not done with this old grizzly bear yet."

## Chapter 30

WHEN THEY ARRIVED AT THE BASE of the mountain, Kate couldn't believe her eyes. The small stream that used to meander between boulders, was now a tan, churning cauldron of debris. Once towering pines lay uprooted and limbs littered the creek-sides. All that remained of the single lane cement bridge was two, ugly lumps of gray on either side of the creek.

Before the tears could spring to her eyes, an African American woman with mud splattered on her boots greeted them. "I'm Private First-Class Marissa Lee, and I'll be helping you back to civilization today?" Though the woman tried to sound positive, Kate could hear the weariness in her voice.

Jeremy's arm tightened around Kate's shoulders. "I cannot express how thankful we are for your aid."

Marissa nodded in acknowledgement. "Right this way, please," she motioned toward the evacuation raft. Kate gaped at the red rescue boat. "I think we are going to need a bigger boat." The red raft looked like a child's bathroom toy bobbing in the current. "The water's moving really fast."

"Trust me, ma'am." Marissa smiled. "We've been shuttling people across all day, you'll be fine."

Once they were safely docked on the other side, they bid their farewells to Marissa and made their way toward the silver pickup truck waiting on the rutted dirt road. A round man with thinning hair climbed out of the driver's side. "I'm Dan Thacker." He extended his hand. "I'll be your chauffeur today."

Kate took his hand. "Thank you. I'm not sure we need chauffeur service, but we'd be mighty thankful for the ride."

Dan shook Jeremy's hand. "Well, a chauffeur is definitely fitting for a celebrity like you."

Kate's stomach dropped. "Celebrity? How did you find out?"

Dan laughed. "The survivors of Slate and the Scottish guy you nursed back to health are the talk of the town. Don't be surprised if gaggles of people gather to hear your stories."

Kate's pulse returned to normal. "Oh, yeah. I bet we are the talk of the town." She glanced at Jeremy. "I'm not sure how interesting we are though. We're just ordinary people."

Dan said, "Well, let's get you ordinary people on the road and back to civilization."

Kate climbed into the back seat while Dan helped Jeremy into the passenger side. Once everybody was situated, Dan turned the ignition, and the mighty diesel engine roared to life. As the truck tires climbed over rocks and debris, Jeremy asked, "Have you done a lot of driving today?"

"You're my third and last trip," Dan replied. "I took Lizzy to meet her son earlier this morning. Don't know if I've ever seen a son so relieved."

The statement was like a blade in Kate's heart. She changed the subject before the full weight of it could take hold. "We're extremely thankful for the ride. Everyone has been so helpful."

Dan smiled proudly. "That's the way we do things in West Virginia."

"I've heard that quite a few times," Jeremy said with a smile. "If I had to get stranded anywhere, I'm glad it was in West Virginia."

Dan nodded. "A wise man once said, *'The sun may not always shine in West Virginia, but the people always do.'*"

"Is that a Sam quote?" Jeremy asked.

Dan's booming laughter reverberated in the truck cabin. Jeremy raised his eyebrows and turned to look at Kate.

"It was President John F. Kennedy," she explained.

Dan wiped tears from the corner of his eyes. "Wait until I tell Sam you think he sounds like a Democrat!"

Kate tensed. West Virginia had recently swung from being a deep blue to a staunchly red state, and the last thing she wanted today was any mention of politics. She breathed a sigh of relief when Dan changed the subject. "I've got a cooler in the back. It's full of waters and snacks. You guys want anything?"

"Thanks," Kate said as she fished a bottle of water from the cooler and handed one to Jeremy. "Now if you only had a hot shower in there."

"A hot shower," Jeremy lamented. "I think I want one even worse than you do! Remember, I came to camp via mudslide."

Dan interjected, "You know, my house is on the way to the shelter. You have time before the meeting in Kimberley. My wife's home, you could use our shower. I bet you need some clean clothes, too." He looked at Kate in the rearview mirror. "You seem a little smaller than my daughter, we have some of her clothes for when she comes home from college. Might be big for you, but you're welcome to them." He looked at Jeremy. "My stuff will be baggy on you, but I have a few of my dad's old things. You'll need a button-down shirt with that arm."

"That would be wonderful! Thank you so much!" Kate gushed.

"Don't mention it. It's the Christian thing to do," Dan said, then launched into a twenty-minute narrative about when he had broken his arm while making fence and how difficult it was to get things done around the house. Just as he was finishing the tale, the truck pulled up to a cute, gray colonial with beautiful peony blooming in the flowerbed.

A petite woman with blonde hair and warm green eyes met them in the driveway. She gave Kate and Jeremy warm but gentle hugs. "I'm so happy y'all are safe!" She said as she led them into the kitchen. "I'm Paige.

You make yourselves at home. Coffee is on the counter, help yourself to anything in the fridge." Before they could even say thank you, Paige disappeared up the stairs. She returned minutes later. "I put clothes in the two bedrooms. There's a Jack and Jill bathroom between them. I laid out towels and washcloths. If you need anything else, just holler."

Jeremy looked at Kate. "Ladies first."

"Don't have to tell me twice," Kate called over her shoulder as she took the stairs two at a time.

She quickly undressed and stepped into the white tile shower. Water weaved its way through her tangled locks and caressed her skin. The cadence of water against tile had a hypnotic effect as the dirt of the past days spiraled down the drain. After rinsing the conditioner from her hair, she stepped out of the shower, wrapped a towel around her, and scurried into the bedroom.

On the bed was a perfectly folded pair of black yoga pants and a Virginia Tech t-shirt. Kate grimaced at the maroon and orange shirt. It was fitting that in the bizarro-world of flooding and evacuations, the clothing offered to her would be from one of her alma mater's most hated rivals. "Well, at least it's clean," she murmured as she hung the towel on the metal footboard.

In the corner of her eye, she saw a slight movement. Kate dropped the t-shirt and spun around. To her horror, she found herself staring at a full-length mirror. She studied her naked reflection, and she wanted to cry. Her hips were wide, definitely no thigh gap. There were rolls on her stomach, and her breasts no longer defied gravity. There were bags under her eyes, and the skin on her jawline had lost the elasticity of youth.

She remembered watching countless award shows where Jeremy had beautiful, un-aged, thin women on his arm. They were actresses, models, women who looked nothing like her. The Voice hissed in her ear, "How could Jeremy Fulton ever be attracted to a saggy, middle-aged woman with curves that are no longer in the right places?"

"I don't have time for you right now," she answered out loud then forced herself to turn away from the mirror and pulled on her clothes.

She put a palmful of leave-in conditioner in her hair then made her way downstairs to where Jeremy waited. "Thanks for letting me go first. I left some hot water for you."

He rubbed the back of his neck. "I, uh, need your help."

Kate blushed. No matter how much she wanted, there was no way she could shower with him in a house full of Baptists!

Jeremy motioned to the soft cast on his arm. "I need help getting my shirt off so I can take a shower. Can you help me?"

Kate felt her cheeks turn scarlet. Of course, that's what he meant. She was his 'nurse' after all. "No problem." She looked cautiously toward Paige, who didn't seem to pay any attention to them, then followed Jeremy upstairs.

The moment Kate closed the bedroom door, Jeremy grabbed her arm. He spun her around, pushed her against the wall and kissed her. It was a hard kiss, a kiss with passion, with desire. It was a kiss that made every molecule of her body come alive. She kissed him back, her body melting against his. His bandaged arm was the only thing between them.

Suddenly, Kate felt the muscles in his body tense, and he pulled away. Her heart sank. What had she done wrong?

His brow was furrowed in pain, and he was holding his right arm. "For a wee bit, I forgot about this." He grinned. "That kiss made me forget a lot of things."

Kate knew she was probably giving the widest, cheesiest grin, but she didn't care. The kiss had made her forget a lot of things too.

Jeremy tugged at his shirttail. "I need your help getting this off, so I can shower."

"Is a shower a good idea? Doc said to not get your bandages wet." Kate thought for a moment. "What about a bath? You could hold your arm over the side."

"A long soak would feel amazing. You're so smart."

"I know," Kate teased as she stepped closer to him. "Here, let me help you with your shirt."

As she began pushing buttons through the slits, a dry electricity filled the air. For some reason, the act of unbuttoning his shirt felt so intimate. It was something a lover would do. She looked up, and Jeremy was staring at her. With his good hand, he tilted her face and kissed her gently. "I don't know what I'd have done without you." His eyes were so sincere and vulnerable, that Kate was speechless.

She removed his shirt and, though she tried not to stare at his half-naked body, she couldn't help herself. His torso was lean and flawless. His shoulders were wide, his waist was small. She dropped her eyes to the shag carpet. "I should go," she mumbled and quickly backed out of the room before she lost total control.

AS JEREMY SAT IN THE TUB, he thought about the last eight days. He thought about his brush with death, but his thoughts didn't linger there. He thought of the compassion of the doctor and the men who carried him to safety. His mind replayed the moments spent laughing with the members of Slate, the first time he had authentically laughed since he'd lost his father. He remembered the calming energy that coursed through his body when people prayed over him. And he thought about Kate. Kate, who had saved his life. Kate, who'd stayed beside him. Kate, who'd hidden the fact that she knew his true identity because she thought it was what he needed. Kate, who'd shown him more tenderness and kindness than he'd experienced for a long time. Kate, a woman who two weeks ago he'd have walked by and not noticed, but now constantly occupied his thoughts. Her brown eyes with flecks of gold reflecting the afternoon sun, her high cheekbones, the luscious curves of her body. Now he couldn't remember ever seeing a woman so authentically beautiful. Everything about her turned him on.

Though remembering the stolen kiss in the bedroom made his heart race, it paled to the undeniable electricity he felt when she was unbuttoning his shirt. The care that she took with each button, the closeness of her body, the smell of her freshly shampooed hair. It was more intimate than any kiss he had ever stolen.

## Chapter 31

PAIGE DROVE THE COUPLE TO THE Kimberly Fire Hall. After they said their goodbyes, Kate gestured toward the cinder block and stucco building. "You ready to be bombarded with questions?"

"Worse than Slate?"

"It'll be way worse than Slate."

He pointed to a white sign atop a metal pole. "What's this?"

"It's a historical marker." Kate motioned to the surrounding landscape. "See how we're on top of a hill and you can see the entire valley? This was once the site of Fort Kimberly, a strategic outpost during the French and Indian War."

Jeremy read the sign aloud, "Site of Fort Kimberly, one of the forts erected under Washington's Orders. In 1758, Indians captured and burned it. Captain James Conrad and twenty-one others were killed. No one escaped." He turned to look at Kate. "This was the site of a massacre? Is it morbid I find that fascinating?"

"Just a little bit."

"I love history, and this area seems to hold so many stories. I wish things were different. I'd love to have time to really explore."

Kate watched a haggard-looking woman with a baby on her hip walk toward the fire hall. "I have a feeling we aren't the only ones wishing things were different."

The moment they entered the fire hall, Jeremy resumed the role of the injured foreigner, and Kate resumed the role of the nurse and go-between. Soon, the heartache which permeated every inch of the building attached itself to her. It weighed her down like tar. After two hours, she was spent. She grabbed a granola bar and escaped out the back door.

Behind the fire hall sat the community cemetery. Kate weaved between gravestones until she arrived at the fence on the opposite side. She'd always found an eerie peacefulness in cemeteries. Everybody is equal in the grave. Race, orientation, social standing didn't matter.

However, today she found no peace. To her left, massive yellow machines sat ready to dig six-feet-deep holes; the final resting place of those who hadn't fared as well as the Slate evacuees. The valley below, which should be full of knee-high corn stalks and first cut hay, was littered with debris. Tree limbs and parts of houses lined the riverbanks. There was so much clean up to be done, it would be weeks before they could even begin thinking of rebuilding. At least she'd have the summer to help Nan before she returned to northern Virginia.

She was so lost in thought she didn't notice the figure shuffling its way across the cemetery. By the time she realized she had company, Jeremy was standing beside her. "Hey stranger," he whispered.

"What are you doing out here?"

"I borrowed Sam's phone to make a call, and it took me forever to find a cell signal." He lowered his eyes. "I got in touch with my agent, Phil. He wants me on the first flight tomorrow to Glasgow."

"You're leaving?" Kate felt the ground under her feet shift. She put her hand on a fencepost to keep her equilibrium.

The Voice hissed in her ear, "Of course, he's leaving, you idiot. He has a life in Scotland, he was bound to return to it."

She took a deep breath. "I'm sure you're ready to get back to your life."

He cupped her chin with his good hand. "Come with me."

Kate's mouth went dry. "Excuse me?"

"Come back to Scotland with me." His eyes looked so desperate it made her chest hurt. "When I went into the woods, I didn't bloody care if I ever walked out. Then you found me. You nursed me back to health. You made me laugh for the first time in years. I told you things I've never told anybody. Even when I was in immense pain, I was happy with you. You're the reason I'm standing here, you're the reason I'm glad I didn't stay in that cave. I'm selfish. I know people here need you, but Kate, I need you. When I get on that plane tomorrow, I need you beside me."

She tightened her grip on the fence post for support as she processed what he had said. If Kate hadn't thought about Jeremy returning to Scotland, she had certainly never considered being asked to come with him.

Everything in her wanted to grab Jeremy's hand and run to the closest airport, but when she raised her eyes, she saw Nan carrying boxes from the firehall to a white box truck. There was no way she could go. There was no way she could leave the woman who had brought her back from the brink too many times.

She squeezed her eyes shut. "I can't." A sob caught in her throat. "They need me."

"I need you!"

"No, you don't. You'll be just fine. I have mission trips to organize, clean-up crews to recruit, people to comfort."

"I need you to comfort me!"

Jeremy sounded like a hurt child, and it ripped Kate's heart in two. "You don't need me," she whispered. "You'll be fine without me. You'll go home to—"

"Home to what?" Jeremy interrupted. "Home to people who want me, but don't care about me. To people who feel the right to intrude in my life? To people who rely on me for a job, but would hop to another celebrity if given just a few euros more?"

"You'll be fine, you're a survivor."

"What if survival is insufficient? What if fine isn't enough? What if I want to be happy? What if I want somebody who can make me authentically laugh? What if I want somebody who makes me look forward to the night because I get to lie down beside them, somebody who makes me look forward to the morning because I get to wake up next to them? What about that?" He raised his hand to brush away the tear running down her cheek, but she moved out of his reach.

"You don't understand, I don't have a choice."

"Rubbish! You have a choice."

Kate turned to look at the desecrated valley. "I can't leave Nan." Her voice was non-accusatory. "I know it's hard to understand. There are things about me that you don't know. Nan and Penny stood beside me in the darkest times of my life. They were there when everybody else walked away." She sniffed. "Actually, it's more like I shoved people away. I wouldn't have blamed them if they had walked away too." She tried to sound brave. "They didn't walk out on me when I needed them the most, and I won't do it to them. Penny will return to work. I have the entire summer to help Nan rebuild her life. She's done that for me more times than I can count."

Jeremy asked softly, "Do you want to come with me?"

"That's not fair."

"Why? Why is asking what you want not allowed?"

"Because this isn't about me." She turned on her heel and ran toward the fire hall. She'd been strong, she'd made her stand. One more look into those blue eyes would be all it took to make her granite facade shatter.


AT 4:30, KATE FOLLOWED PENNY from the fire hall to an older model Ford F200 pickup. "Whose truck is this?" she asked.

"It's Sam's. He mostly uses it on the farm." Penny was practically giddy as she turned the ignition. "You know how I love driving BATs."

"BATs?"

"Yeah, Big Ass Trucks!" Penny chatted on and on about her love of pickups and then about how excited she was to return to Pittsburgh, but Kate didn't hear a word. Instead, she moped in the passenger seat like a brooding teenager in a vampire novel. Finally, Penny put her hand on her knee. "You didn't hear a word of that, did you?"

Kate stared out the window. "Sorry, I'm just sad about the house, about Kenny, about everything."

Penny nodded. "Those are all heartbreaking things, but there's more to this." She paused. "Is this about Jeremy?"

Kate let the tears fall. "He's leaving tomorrow. He'll get on a plane, and I'll never see him again." Her heart hurt just saying the words. She turned to look at Penny, anger colored her voice, "How could I have been so stupid? I mean, in all of this, somehow I forgot that he'd return to his own life, and I'd have to return to mine?" She wiped her nose on the tail of her shirt. Wiping her snot on something from Virginia Tech made her feel a little better.

Penny put her hand on Kate's arm. "Oh sweetie, I'm so sorry. I thought for sure he'd ask you to go with him."

"He did. I said no." Her voice was barely audible.

"Why?" Penny demanded. "Why on earth would you say no?"

"I can't."

"Why can't you?"

Kate's voice broke. "I don't want to talk about it. Can we just get to the church and get this over with?"

They rode in silence until they arrived at the Kimberly Church of the Brethren. Penny climbed from behind the wheel, but before she closed the door, she said gently, "I'll get us seats. You stay out here as long as you need to."


KATE WALLOWED IN SELF-PITY for a good ten minutes before she dried her eyes and followed Penny's path into the gray stone church. She slipped into the back pew just as the first politician, the local house delegate, began his gratuitous 'We'll get through this together!' speech. Other politicians followed with promises for funding, mournful laments, and thinly veiled jabs at the other party.

By the time the Governor took the pulpit, Kate had heard enough. She slipped from her pew and onto the church's crumbling stone steps. The clouds from earlier in the day were gone, and the sun's harsh rays beat down upon her. She searched for shade and spied a patch of woods bordering the church's graveyard. She walked toward the trees, then began jogging. Before she knew it, she was on a full-on sprint. The sprint didn't last long. Mud congealed around her shoes adding extra weight, and she was horribly out of shape.

She leaned against an aged oak to catch her breath and looked around the small patch of woods. The trees, bright green with spring foliage, cast cartoonish shadows on the surface of a small pond. Kate picked up a stone and threw it into the water. It barely made a splash. She picked up a bigger stone and threw it. She threw another rock, then another, then another. With each throw, her rage grew. Kate was so engrossed in her anger that she didn't hear Nan approach.

"Kat bird?" Nan asked gently, "Do you want to talk about it?"

Kate spun around. The floodgate of emotions she'd been holding back burst open. "After a hellish year of school, I come to the one place I can find peace. But instead of peace and quiet, there's a hundred-year flood. I lose the place I call home, for a second time. We could have died. People did die! Yet somehow, I'm supposed to keep my shit together because, for some reason, people think I have answers. And I don't have answers. I didn't have any answers in Slate, I didn't have them at the fire hall, and I sure as hell don't have any now!"

Nan's face was pure compassion. "I'm sorry, sweetheart. I shouldn't have asked so much of you."

Kate looked at the grossly bright sky and tried to sound stronger than she felt. "No, you're fine. You've done more than enough for me over the years, I'm glad I could help." She felt like an ass for making Nan feel like she was to blame for her temper tantrum. "I'm just tired and overly emotional."

Nan took her hand. "This is an emotionally charged situation, and I know you're tired." She looked Kate directly in the eyes. "But something else is bothering you, isn't it?"

Kate hung her head. "Yes."

"Penny told me that Jeremy asked you to come back to Scotland with him."

Kate's shoulders slumped. "This has all been so screwed up. What was supposed to be a relaxing family weekend turned into a mandatory evacuation that resulted in me finding a half-dead man at the bottom of a hiking trail." She gave an ironic laugh. "Of course, the story doesn't stop there, does it? Somehow this strange man ends up in my bed, and when he wakes up, he's funny, and kind, and sweet, and loyal. He's handsome as hell, intelligent, cultured, and pretty much perfect in every freaking way. Every night, I lay beside him and share these unbelievable conversations about God and love and family and belief. The amazing man should be a complete stranger, but every time I look into his eyes, it's as familiar as an old friend. Each time I see him smile, I feel like I have seen that same smile a thousand times. Because I *have* seen that same smile a thousand times, just not in person! Yet, I have to pretend that it's the first time because I cannot let him know that I know who he really is. When he tells me some aspect of his life, like his father was a minister or that he lost his mom three years ago, I have to pretend like I don't already know, because he's supposed to be a stranger. And he is, but he isn't. Then I lose sight of reality because I don't know where Tim ends and Jeremy begins." She wiped a tear from her chin. "Because who he really is, is the man I could easily fall in love with. Tomorrow I'm going to watch this wonderful, amazing man get on a plane and leave my life forever."

She had expelled her rage, and all that was left was her brokenness and shame. "Here I am, crying in the woods like a little baby, because I don't know what to do about a boy, and there are eighty-year-olds sitting in that church who have lost everything."

Nan squeezed Kate's hand. "You've been keeping all of that bottled up for a long time."

"I need to get it together. Look at me, I'm a complete mess. How could anybody think of looking to me for answers?"

"Sweetie, I don't know how I would have gotten through this without you." Nan wiped a tear from Kate's cheek. "Do you remember all those long talks we had on the front porch over the years?"

Kate smiled. "How could I forget? Some of the best lessons I learned were during those talks."

"We used to talk a lot about God, and His plans. Do you still believe in God?" There was no judgment in her voice.

"I honestly don't know what I believe anymore," Kate replied, though she wasn't sure who she was answering.

"I still believe God has a reason for everything that happens, even if those reasons are beyond our comprehension. God brought you here because He knew Riverside would need you. God put you on that path, so you could find Jeremy, so you could be the one to nurse him back to health. There's a reason God brought you into Jeremy's life and He brought Jeremy into yours."

Kate looked at Nan with shock. "Are you saying that God caused a flood that devastated an entire community, where people lost their homes and their lives so Jeremy and I could meet?"

"No sweetheart," Nan used the wise voice only older women possess. "I don't know why this valley flooded. I don't know why those who were lost were called home at this time. What I'm saying is that God can create beautiful miracles out of ugliness and destruction."

Kate sniffed. "What's the reason Jeremy came into my life?"

"I don't know why, Kat bird. I just know that he did. Why did you say no when he asked you to go with him?"

"How can I go when there's so much work to be done? It's going to take years to get everything back to any semblance of normal."

Nan looked at the sky. "You're right, it's going to take years."

Once again, tears were rolling down Kate's cheeks. "There's so much to do. I can't just up and leave the people here. I have a responsibility to them, to you."

"What about the responsibility you have to yourself?"

Kate was silent.

"Go with him, Kate."

"I can't."

Nan pulled her into a strong hug. "Yes, you can. Go back and tell him yes."

"What about the cleanup effort?"

"Someone else will take over." Nan released Kate from the hug but kept her hands on her shoulders. "I don't want to minimize what you've done for us. We're beyond thankful, but we're stronger than you give us credit for."

"That's not what I meant."

"I know what you mean, and we appreciate all that you've done, but sweetheart, we'll be okay without you."

Kate looked at the muddy ground. "You and Penny, you never turned your back on me, even when I didn't deserve you. You saw me through my bi-polar episodes, the mood swings, the mania, my ugliest and meanest phases. You were always there for me."

"And we always will be."

"How can I turn my back on you now?"

"Hush!" she put her finger under Kate's chin and gently lifted her face. "Following your heart is not turning your back on us! If you don't go, if I have one iota of blame for you not going, I'll never forgive myself." Her tone was still compassionate but held a hint of sternness. "Kate, go to Scotland."

## Chapter 32

KATE WALKED THROUGH THE FRONT door of the parsonage and found Jeremy sitting on an outdated velvet couch. "Hey stranger," her voice quaked.

He stared at his arm. "It hardly hurts anymore, unless I try to do this." He made a looping action with his forearm and grimaced.

"Well, then don't do that," she tried to joke.

He didn't look up. "Sam took me to a place called Buckeye to get X-rays."

"I thought they'd put you in a cast. It's still just wrapped in an ace bandage."

Jeremy continued as if she hadn't spoken. "The doctors couldn't believe the break was less than a week old. You saw how well I can walk. People are saying I'm a bloody miracle."

"I think they're right."

He scoffed. "Maybe I'm converting to your X-files Christianity."

Kate knew she had to say what she'd come to say soon, or else she'd lose her nerve. She took a deep breath. "Tim... I mean Jeremy..."

He raised his eyes to meet hers, and she wished he'd continued to stare at his hand. There was a coldness in his eyes she'd only seen on-screen.

"You still don't know who I am?" His tone was more frigid than his gaze.

She took a step backward. "When I found you five days ago, I knew you as Jeremy Fulton. During our time at Slate, I got to know you as Tim. Now you're Jeremy again. It's been a bit of a mind trip."

"Yeah, it's been extraordinary for me too." His posture stiffened. "Did you come to say goodbye?"

Kate felt like someone had slapped her in the face. "I came to—"

He cut her off. "I contacted Phil. He's having a car delivered. Sam said Pittsburgh is the closest international airport. In a few hours, I'll be out of your hair." His tone bordered on cruel.

"I didn't realize you're that eager to get back." She blinked back tears. How could things have changed so much and so fast? At the fire hall, he'd begged her to come with him, now he wouldn't even look at her. After everything that had happened, after everything they'd been through together, why was he treating her like this?

Kate's cheeks turned pink as her hurt turned to anger. She fought the urge to lash out at him, call him a world class jackass and every other name he deserved, but showing anger would show her weakness. He'd not have that power. She took several breaths then leveled her voice. "I don't deserve to be spoken to like this."

Jeremy's eyes flashed at her, then he bowed his head, and his shoulders slumped. "You're right."

"Then why are you doing it?"

He kept his eyes on the ground and shrugged. "Because I am an arse."

Kate felt the anger fade, she crossed to the couch and sat on the cushion farthest from him. "Why are you here, Jeremy?"

He frowned. "Because Nan said the church would be packed, and it'd be better if I stayed here."

Kate gave a small laugh. "No, I mean, why are you in Kimberley, right now?"

Jeremy tilted his head and looked at her like a confused collie. "This is where Paige dropped us off after we took showers at her house?"

"No, you moron!" Kate rolled her eyes. "Why were you in Slate? And don't say because I found you on the side of the mountain. I'm talking about more than that. Why did you choose Riverside?"

"I picked a random spot on the map."

Kate threw her hands in the air. "That's just it! Why is it that the randomly chosen spot was Riverside? Why did you pick Snowbird creek, right on the other side of Slate? Why were you hiking toward Slate at the exact time I was trying to escape? Why did it work out that this was the week your agent could clear your schedule? Hell, why is this the very week Penny and I decided to help Nan with the canning?"

"Blimey Kate, I don't know."

Kate's eyes locked with his. "If any of these tiny coincidences occurred differently, had you chosen a different week to travel, had you chosen a creek two miles away, had you fallen down the mountain an hour after you had, we wouldn't be sitting here, right now." She touched his cheek. "Why was I, the person who sees your face every night when she dreams, the one to find you?"

"What are you asking me?"

Kate was on her feet, pacing back and forth. "What if I'm wrong? I told you I'm a woman of reason, that faith's hard. So why am I having such a hard time seeing what's right in front of my face? What takes more faith, to see all these things lined up perfectly and think they're pointing to an answer or to just see them as random, unconnected events with no grand design?"

"I don't know what you want me to say."

Kate's eyes flashed fire. "I want you to ask me again."

"What?"

"Ask me again. Ask me to come with you."

Jeremy hesitated. "Come with me?"

She knelt in front of him. "YES!"

"YES?"

"Yes, I want to come with you. Yes, I will come with you!" She wrapped her arms around his neck and kissed his lips.

After a moment of shock wore off, he kissed her back, and she kissed him back until they were both brought out of the moment by an uncomfortable "Uh, hmm."

They turned to see a very embarrassed looking Sam standing in the doorway of the living room. "Ah Kate, Penny was looking for you."

Kate pushed herself onto her feet. "Thanks, I'll find her."

Sam mumbled a reply then shuffled out of the door.

Kate turned back to Jeremy. "I have bad news for you though."

"Nothing you could say would be bad."

"I can't go WITH you. You're flying out tonight. I can't leave now. I promised Nan and Penny we could spend time together before I left. This week was supposed to be our special time, and even though we've been together since Sunday, it wasn't exactly the girl time we'd planned."

Jeremy smiled playfully. "I heard you had to take care of some spoiled, TV diva. That must have sucked!"

Kate rolled her eyes. "You have no idea, by the end I felt like pushing him off the side of a mountain."

"Was he more or less whiny than Romeo?"

"This guy had more of a tortured Danish prince thing going on."

"So instead of being whiney, he was batshit-crazy and drove you to the point of suicide? I do have a lot to make up for." He pushed a strand of hair behind Kate's ear. "Seriously though, I'll rearrange my travel plans, we can leave first thing tomorrow."

"Actually, there are a few more things I need to get done. I need to swing by my apartment in Virginia to get some things, clothes and stuff."

"Can I share a secret?" He made a 'come here' gesture with his index finger, and she leaned in close. "There's something I should share with you, that I don't tell many people."

"What is it?"

He whispered in her ear, "I'm rich."

Kate let out a laugh.

"Seriously." He gave a crooked smile. "I have a job that pays really, really well. When we get to Scotland, I could afford to splurge on a shopping excursion for you."

She kissed him gently. "You don't have to do that."

"I know I don't have to, but I want to. You saved my life; a shopping spree is a minor repayment."

Kate batted her eyes. "What am I going to wear on the plane to Scotland?"

"Well." He pulled her in for a long, deep kiss.

Kate finally pulled herself away. "As tempting as that sounds," and she truly was tempted. "I'm thinking the TSA may have a problem with that."

"There wouldn't be any issue about metal detectors or pat downs." He kissed her neck.

Kate forced herself back into reality and away from his lips. "True, but I might get cold, and those airplane blankets are scratchy."

He pretended to pout. "You West Virginia girls are so high maintenance."

"Plus, where would I keep my ID and passport?"

"I guess you have a good point there. We'll stop by your apartment in Virginia then fly out of that little airport that I flew into."

"Jeremy," Kate was suddenly very serious. "I need to see my mom. I cannot leave without seeing her."

"Of course." His tone was full of compassion. "I'll have our driver meet us here and take us immediately to where your mom is. You take as long with her as you like. I'll be waiting for you in the car when you are done."

She looked at him through her lashes. "I'd like for her to meet you."

Jeremy put his hand across his heart. "I don't know what to say. I would feel honored." He ran his thumb over her cheekbone. "I was afraid that you were going to say that you couldn't come with me for a few weeks."

"I can't do that. If I have too long, I'll talk myself out of this." She looked him in the eye. "You don't understand. This is SO not me. I don't leap without a firm understanding of where I will land. With you, I don't know if I'll land on dry land, the ocean, quicksand. Coming with you is the greatest risk that I've ever taken."

He kissed her gently on the nose. "Well, this tortured prince is happy you think he's worth the risk."

---

THANKS TO HAZEL, THE SCANDAL of the unmarried Kate Thorn spending every night in Slate with the mysterious foreigner spread through the town like a stomach virus on a cruise ship. Rumors flew and grandmothers tsk-tsked. As a result, when it came time for Slate evacuees to be welcomed into different homes, careful consideration was put into each placement. Ultimately, it was concluded that while it was acceptable for Kate to spend the night with Jeremy when she was his nurse in camp, now that they had made it back to civilization, things were different. An unmarried woman and an unmarried man staying in the same home was just too scandalous.

Ten years ago, this type of intrusion would have irritated Kate to no end. However, tensions were at a fever pitch, and she obliged. So, Jeremy and Sam headed to Sam's home in Trig. Nan, Kate, and Penny headed to the home of Michelle and Matt Mullinax on the "outskirts" of town.

While Kate helped Michelle in the kitchen, Nan and Penny got their much-appreciated warm showers. After dinner, their hosts opened a bottle of red wine, and everyone sat around the fire pit in the backyard. Not long into the second bottle of Shiraz, Matt and Michelle excused themselves for the night, leaving the trio to talk and finish the bottle.

As soon as the hosts were out of earshot, Kate asked, "So Pen, are Lenard and the kids coming to pick you up tomorrow?"

"No, Sam will give me a lift to Elkins. My insurance will have a rental car waiting for me." She put her hand on Nan's. "And I'll be back next weekend to help sort through things."

Tears threatened to spill onto Nan's cheeks. "Don't you worry about me. Your family needs you more than I do."

Penny squeezed her hand. "You are my family!"

"You know what I mean, dear." Nan sniffed.

The guilt of leaving Nan gripped Kate's heart like an iron fist. "I can stay." She blurted. "I can tell Jeremy—"

"No," Nan said with authority. "You'll get on a plane tomorrow, that is what you'll do."

"But your house... where will you stay?"

Nan shifted uncomfortably in her seat. "I'll be staying with Sam for a while."

"With Sam?" Both girls exclaimed in unison.

Nan's voice was prim and proper. "Yes, with Sam."

Penny laughed. "What will the likes of Kathleen and Hazel have to say about that?"

Nan smiled slyly. "Any time it gets brought up I'll just change the subject to that girl who ran off with the Scottish movie star."

The three women fell into gales of laughter. When they were able to breathe again Penny asked Kate. "When are you two jetting across the pond?"

"Jeremy has a car coming for us around noon, then we are heading to visit mom. After a quick stop at my apartment to get my passport and a few necessities, we're off."

"Are you nervous?" Penny asked gently.

"How could I not be? You know me, Pen; this is SO not me. I don't take chances like this."

"I know you're scared." Nan put her hand on Kate's cheek. "That's why I'm so proud of you! Since Max, you haven't let anybody close to you."

"Well, when you find out the man you thought you would marry had a family all along, it gives you trust issues," Kate laughed. The third glass of wine was helping her relax.

"We all have asshole stories." Penny took a sip.

Kate placed her glass on the table a bit too hard. "Secret life! Married! With kids!"

"Okay, so you win with the most messed up story, but do you remember that loser I dated before Lenard? He may not have had a secret life but talk about mommy issues." Penny cupped her hand around her mouth like a megaphone: "Paging Dr. Freud." She belly laughed. "Do you remember when I broke up with him? He started showing up at my work, following me home. I ended up having to get a restraining order."

Kate rolled her eyes. "I remember him. I also remember the night you called me, crying hysterically. It took every ounce of effort I had to not drive to his mama's house, pull him out of his 'basement apartment' and smack the snot out of him."

"Instead, you showed up on my doorstep saying: get your toothbrush and a change of clothes, that's it. No explanation, no idea where you were taking me, nothing." Penny took a long sip. "We didn't stop until we were sitting in traffic in Manhattan. I thought for sure we'd end up at some overpriced Shakespeare production starring a certain Scottish actor."

Kate tipped her glass. "Not this time."

"I don't want to know what an outrageous amount of money you paid to get those tickets to *Wicked*." Penny sat back in her chair. "That was an unforgettable weekend, but Monday morning was rough. I could barely pull that stuff in my twenties. There's no way I could do that today."

Kate scoffed. "You had a rough Monday. You're a CPA, you work in an office. I had to deal with teenagers!"

Penny laughed. "Hello children, the word of the day is hangover."

The retelling of the night in Manhattan segued into another story and into another and another. Reminiscing continued until after midnight. Finally, Nan rose from the table. "I'm not as young as you two chickadees. I have to get some sleep; tomorrow is a big day. Goodnight, my loves." She kissed each girl affectionately on the forehead and walked toward the house.

"Goodnight, Nan," the girls said in unison.

As Kate watched Nan walk through the French doors, her eyes filled with tears. "What is it?" Penny asked.

"Nothing, everything; I'm excited and terrified. I feel like I need to stay and help, but I feel like I need to do this." Kate exhaled. "But mostly, it's that I'm going to miss you and Nan so much."

"Ah sweetie, you've had too much wine. I can tell, you get all emotional like this. I know you're scared. I know you'll miss us. This is a huge risk, but you'd never forgive yourself if you didn't see where this could go. Nan and I will always be here. Riverside will always be here." Penny raised her glass in a mock toast. "Go, proceed with reckless abandon, carpe diem and all that crap."

Kate clinked her cup to Penny's. "And I'm the one who gets emotional when I'm drinking?"

AS KATE CLIMBED INTO BED THAT NIGHT, she was surprised by how bizarre it felt to not have Jeremy beside her.

## Chapter 33

WHEN KATE ROLLED OVER THE NEXT MORNING, instead of seeing the face of a sexy Scotsman saying, "Good morning," she saw the face of an antique clock saying it was seven o'clock. The morning she left for Nan's, a seven a.m. wake up would have been annoyingly early for summer. Now, not only did she consider it sleeping in, she was irritated by the fact she'd slept so long. She took a quick shower, pulled on the clothes that had been graciously laundered by her hosts, and was on her way by seven-thirty.

As they walked toward the front screen door of the Kimberly Fire Hall, Kate peered through the window. Between the faded 1970s orange, paisley curtains, she saw the main room was being transformed from a temporary shelter back to a dining hall. Along the far wall, a guardsman in BDUs was stacking sleeping cots while two other guardsmen were setting up folding tables and metal chairs.

"How many people stayed here last night?" she wondered out loud.

"The National Guard brought twenty-five cots. Not sure if they were all full," Nan replied. "I'm sure somebody counted, and the number will be exaggerated by this afternoon to at least double."

The minute they walked through the front door, the smell of bacon and eggs teased her nose. Her stomach let loose a bear worthy growl.

Nan raised her eyebrows. "Hungry?"

"Matt offered to make us breakfast, why didn't you eat something?" Penny asked.

Nan smirked. "It's almost like you couldn't wait to get here."

Kate was ready to retort when a short woman with gray curly hair and hazel eyes bustled up to them. "Nan, thank the Good Lord you're here. We're very shorthanded."

Nan smiled. "Hello Macy. How can we help?"

Macy didn't bother with greetings. She glanced at the clipboard in her hands. "Penny, help unload donations. Nan, you go to the office. We have to log every single box and account for every single can. Kate, follow me. You'll help in the kitchen."

Kate had only met Macy a few times, but those few times had taught her that the older woman ran a tight ship and did not like to be questioned. If Macy had assigned her a duty, her chances of sneaking a few minutes for breakfast were slim. She hushed her growling stomach and traipsed through the main room.

In the back-left corner of the room, volunteers had set up tables where representatives could help flood victims make sense of their insurance policies. A woman with torn sweatpants sat with her head in her hands and her hair hiding her face. Her tears splashed onto the plastic tabletop, tears the woman was trying to hide from the curly haired little girl sitting on her lap clinging to a one-eared teddy bear.

Kate stopped dead in her tracks. Tears pricked her eyes, and her stomach hurt, but it was no longer from hunger.

Macy put a hand on her arm. "I know it's horrible, dear. Your tears won't help them, but your hands can." Kate sniffed and followed the gray-haired woman into the kitchen where she was immediately put to work. So many flood victims came in for a warm meal, that for the next few hours, Kate spent each second either filling plates or washing them. Before she knew it, it was past noon, which was when Hazel Phelps made her grand appearance.

The pastel-clad busy body pranced straight through the firehall and found Kate in the kitchen. "Well, Katherine. How did you sleep last night? Did you find out any interesting information?"

Kate shook out the dish towel she was using to dry a huge saucepan. "What on earth are you talking about?"

Hazel smacked her bubblegum-pink lips. "Oh nothing, dear lamb." There was a taunting in her tone. "I had a very educational evening, I thought you might have too." She turned on her gaudy gold heeled sandals and strutted out the kitchen.

Ellen, the woman in charge of frying bacon, gave Kate a confused look. "I think all of that cheap hair dye finally fried her brain."

Kate shrugged. "If it's something juicy, she won't be able to hold it in very long. I give it twenty minutes before she spills, and everybody knows."

Kate was wrong. It took less than ten. She was drying a cast-iron skillet when she heard the words: movie star, TV, celebrity, and finally the name Jeremy Fulton come from a circle of women. When all blue-haired heads turned to look at her, she knew what Hazel meant by educational evening.

Bony fingers wrapped around her wrist, and before Kate could comprehend what was happening, Macy pulled her down so that they were eye to eye. "Best get out of here before you get mobbed."

Kate couldn't tell if Macy had warned her out of compassion or because she didn't want chaos in her kitchen, and it didn't matter. She nodded appreciatively and slipped out the side door. She walked into the main room; it was deserted. "That's weird," Kate muttered to herself as she looked at the empty chairs and tables. She walked to the front of the fire hall and looked out the window. Through the dirty glass, she could see everybody was gathered in the front parking lot around a large black SUV.

She pushed open the screen door. A hand clamped around her upper arm and jerked her to the side. "Get over here," Penny hissed in her ear.

"What's all this about?" Kate asked.

Penny's voice was now tauntingly innocent. "Rumor has it a celebrity has stopped by."

The irritation Kate felt earlier burned bright white. "I'm going to kill Hazel."

Nan was now beside her. "It was bound to come out eventually."

"Does Jeremy know word has gotten out?"

Nan put her hand on Kate's elbow. "When I heard the gossip, I called Sam to give him a heads up."

Kate clenched her jaw. "I'm still going to hunt down Hazel and—"

Nan said in an irritatingly calm tone, "This gives him a chance to explain himself and make amends."

"Make amends?"

Penny explained, "When word got out that Tim Jones was a phony..."

Kate rubbed her temples. "I never thought about it. How are people from Slate reacting?"

"People are falling into one of three categories," Nan explained. "Group one, like Hazel are star-struck, even though they have no idea of who he is. Group two, like Troy and Chris, couldn't care less."

"And group three?" Kate asked anxiously.

"People like Sy, are angry and hurt."

Kate made a pfft sound. "That's just stupid."

"Maybe to you or me," Nan said wisely. "But to people who have a well-founded distrust of outsiders, or to those who are barely holding onto reality, finding out someone you trusted has lied to you... it's a bitter pill. No matter what the reason was for the lie."

Kate frowned. She hated it when Nan's sage logic one-upped her self-righteous indignation. "The fact that people are angry with him will really bother him."

Penny raised her eyebrows. "Perhaps he can find comfort in the arms of a sexy schoolmarm."

Kate shoved her playfully. "You're horrible!"

"Maybe," Penny said, "but it looks like our mystery celebrity is handling this in stride."

Kate watched Jeremy interact with the displaced. Each person he met, be it fan or not, got all his attention at that moment. He shook hands and posed for selfies. He dropped to his knees to mimic the voices of cartoon characters for every child he met. He hugged those who wanted to hug and autographed what people wanted autographed.

Finally, he made his way to Kate. He grabbed her hand, raised his eyebrows, and whispered, "I guess the feline's out of the sack."

Kate snickered. "You mean the cat's out of the bag?"

"Ah, that's the saying." His eyes twinkled with mischief. "I guess the cat's out of the bag. Are you packed and ready?"

Kate lowered her eyes. "Jeremy, I can't leave with you."

A look of agony crossed his face. "You changed your mind?"

"No." she whispered. "But we didn't think this through. I can't be seen getting into a car and leaving with you, not now that everyone knows who you are."

Penny and Nan had joined them, forming a tight circle that would make any teenage clique proud. "Kate's right," Penny agreed.

"Then what do we do?" Jeremy asked.

Penny chewed on her lip for a moment. "Jeremy, you leave now. Kate and I'll meet you at Sam's house."

Jeremy looked at Kate. "Are you fine with that?"

"I don't have a better idea."

Nan added, "And make a production of saying good-bye. Cry if you have to."

"She's right," Jeremy said. "We have to make it look like this is us parting ways."

Kate looked back to the crowd. She was white as a ghost and tears were in her eyes.

"Perfect!" Penny directed. "Go with that look, despair, and sadness."

"This is my so scared I might throw up look."

"Well, it works! Stick with it."

Nan looked at Jeremy. "You play it up, too. Be melodramatic and whiney like your last episode on that time travel show."

He crossed his arms over his chest and stuck out his bottom lip. "I played the scene the way the director told me to."

Nan made a dismissive motion with her hand. "That's not important, now. Get to saying goodbye and leaving."

Jeremy glanced over his shoulder to make sure everybody was watching, then he wrapped Kate in the warmest of embraces. The moment his arms were around her, she forgot about the crowd, and let herself melt into him. She lay her head against his chest, the steady rhythm of his heartbeat drowned out the anxiety echoing inside her head.

Before she was ready, he pulled away and kissed her gently on the forehead. "Goodbye, nurse Kate, and thank you." Melodramatic sadness glazed over each syllable.

She lowered her gaze. If she peered into those cornflower blue eyes, she wasn't sure she'd have the willpower to not follow him. "Goodbye," she whispered then turned and ran back into the firehall.

KATE WAS HIDING IN THE LAST STALL of the women's restroom when Macy found her. "You okay, sweetie?" she asked. This time, there was no question in Kate's mind about the older woman's intention. Macy's voice was so full of compassion, Kate felt bad for deceiving her.

She pushed open the stall door and walked out. "I will be," she answered.

Macy put her hand on Kate's shoulder. "You made the right choice, not going. It all looks so glamorous now, but you're better off. Eventually, he'd have forgotten about what you did, and a plain old West Virginia girl wouldn't be enough to keep him." Tears filled the older woman's eyes. "My first husband was from France, we were married less than a year before he was off and... European men roam, it's in their blood. You did the right thing, Kate. You'd regret it if you went."

Kate's throat constricted, her mouth opened and closed like a fish gasping for air.

Macy wrapped her in a warm hug. "I know watching him leave was hard, but in time, you'll see."

When Macy released her, Kate straightened her shirt and stammered. "I need to find Nan."

"I think I saw her in the main room."

"Thank you." Kate nodded and exited the bathroom. As she walked down the hallway, the words, *'a plain old West Virginia girl wouldn't be enough to keep him'* bounced around in her head. She was so lost in thought she didn't notice the sea green object coming toward her.

"Ouch!" the object said.

Kate looked up and saw a teenage girl with green hair and a nose ring glaring at her. "Sorry," she mumbled.

"It's you!" The girl's chocolate eyes got big. "You're the one who let that movie star just walk away." Kate kept her head down and tried to maneuver around the girl. The last thing she needed was the wisdom of a fourteen-year-old. But the girl stood blocking her way. "I think you're a total moron for not going with him! He's hot, he's famous, I'm sure he's loaded."

The teen pulled her phone from her back pocket and held it inches from Kate's face. "I mean, what kind of celebrity does this?"

Kate stared at the cracked iPhone screen as the girl pushed play. Jeremy was standing at the front of the black, shiny SUV. He raised his hands and yelled, "Can I have your attention?"

The parking lot went silent. Jeremy spread his arms wide, as if to embrace the entire crowd. "By now, many of you've heard about how I came to Slate, bloody, broken, and using a fake name."

Various reactions rose from the crowd: murmurs of agreement, grunts of aggravation, hisses of betrayal.

Jeremy continued. "If you haven't heard, I'm an actor in England. In my own land, I cannot walk down the street, visit a pub, or have a pint with my mates without being assaulted by cameramen. Fame is a fickle mistress. She lures you in with promises of adoration, then shackles you with an inability to live a life without constant scrutiny and scorn." He let the words sink in. "I came to West Virginia, so I could be where nobody knew me, so I could discover who *I* was again. What I found was some of the most amazing, caring, resilient, and wonderful people on Earth. You took me in and treated me as one of your own." His voice broke, and he dabbed at his eyes. "I can never thank you enough for saving my life, for showing me what life is about. You gave me so much. I feel guilty asking for anything more, but I guess I am." He paused for effect. "If I offended you, with my lies about my identity or in any other way, I beg you to forgive me."

The murmurs were kinder, perhaps even forgiving.

"I'll not be mentioning my stay in West Virginia to the media. It's not because I wish to hide what happened here. It's because what happened was so dear, I want to keep it for just me... just us. But there's a bigger reason. I care about you. If the paparazzi were to find out what happened in Slate, they'd swarm these mountains like greedy locusts. They'd invade your privacy, they'd intrude upon your grief, and they'd hamper the cleanup efforts."

The crowd grumbled.

"I can't tell you how to proceed with the information about my time here," Jeremy continued, "but I'll caution you, the people who would contact you do not have your interest at heart. These rubbish reporters want a story and a paycheck. They'll exploit you and your pain to get a headline."

The video ended.

Kate looked at the teen. "Is that it?"

"Ran out of memory." She shrugged. "He said a few thank yous, then just got in the car and left."

A tear trickled down Kate's cheek. The girl's demeanor softened as she raised a pierced eyebrow. "Maybe you were right. You don't look like the celebrity girlfriend type."

From years of teaching, Kate was used to the acidic tact of a teenager, but this comment cut deep. She was keenly aware she didn't look like the woman who would be on the arm of a celebrity. Kate was about to reply when she felt a hand on her shoulder. She spun around. "Nan, thank goodness."

"I've been looking for you." Nan smiled.

"I need to get out of here."

"Why don't Penny and I take you someplace where you can rest."

Macy, who was standing behind Nan, asked, "But you'll be back later?"

Guilt punched Kate in the stomach. "I wish I could. I volunteered to teach summer school. I have to be back in Leesburg tomorrow." Lying made the guilt triple.

Macy put on a brave smile. "I guess those kiddos need you as bad as we do."

Kate opened her mouth to reply, but no words came. Thankfully, Nan interjected, "Why don't we get you to Sam's?"

The fifteen-minute drive to Sam's was torture for Kate. The guilt of leaving so much undone crashed upon her like a tsunami. However, when they pulled into Sam's driveway, and she saw Jeremy leaning against the back bumper of the SUV, she knew she'd made the right decision. After a teary goodbye to Penny, Nan, and Sam, she was securely belted into the back seat of the black Lincoln. Jeremy slid in beside her. "You ready for this adventure?"

"I still can't believe I'm doing this," she said.

He kissed her gently. "You're doing it, love. No turning back."

Butterflies traveled from her lips to her stomach. "No turning back," she repeated.

Jeremy took her hand. "How long will it take to get to your mom's facility?"

"Around two hours."

He leaned back against the seat and put his arm around her. "Let's just sit back and enjoy the scenery."

JEREMY REMEMBERED THE QUIET VALLEYS and breathtaking views from his journey to Riverside. What he saw out the window now was startlingly different. Instead of a drive through lush green forests and quaint towns, this was a crawl through a labyrinth of destruction. Bridges had been swept away. In several places, flood waters crumbled the asphalt like crackers in the hands of an angry toddler. Debris, clothing, parts of homes, pieces of lives littered every inch of the landscape.

Kate stared out the window. She didn't say a word, but periodically a tear would fall from her chin. Though Jeremy wanted desperately to comfort her, once they started across the mountains, he began fighting a battle of his own. At every switchback, his stomach seemed to turn over. By the time they reached the base of Allegheny Mountain, he felt almost as bad as he had in the cave before his journey to Slate.

As they passed through the tiny village of Onego, Kate finally turned to look at him. Her eyes got big, and she put her hand on his cheek. "You okay? You don't look so good."

Jeremy swallowed back the vomit rising in his throat. "I've never ridden across mountains like that in the backseat of an SUV." He rubbed his temples. "Now I know why."

Kate leaned forward and tapped the driver on the shoulder. "At the stop sign, there's a little store on the right. Stop there."

The driver pulled into the parking lot of Yokum's general store. While Kate went inside to get ginger ale, Jeremy slid from the backseat and leaned against the SUV. He stared at his feet, taking in gulps of fresh air, until he was sure he wasn't going to lose his breakfast. When he finally raised his head, he gasped. Before him stood the most beautiful rock formation he had ever seen. A massive expanse of limestone rose from the mountainside, like a stone eagle rising from the earth.

Kate's voice came from behind him. "That's Seneca Rocks, it's the most photographed natural rock formation east of the Mississippi."

For a moment he forgot about his stomach. "I can see why. It's gorgeous."

"If you were feeling better, we could climb to the top. The view is breathtaking."

Jeremy patted his queasy stomach. "Perhaps another day. Besides, I know you want to get to your mom's."

At the mention of her mom, Kate's shoulders sagged. "You're right. Do you feel you can ride some more?"

Though the idea of getting back into the SUV was about as appealing as being waterboarded, Jeremy knew it there was no way to avoid the winding roads. He took a few sips of ginger ale then nodded.

Kate said, "Why don't you sit in the front, so you don't get sick?" Her eyes were sad, and the cadence of her voice betrayed an exhaustion that had nothing to do with sleep.

It melted his heart. He shook his head. "I want to be by your side."

Kate didn't argue. She held opened the door of the SUV, and Jeremy climbed in beside her. She touched the driver on the shoulder. "Make a left at the stop sign."

The driver tapped the car's GPS screen. "This says to make a right."

"If you make a right, we'll have to cross North Mountain. Unless you want to be cleaning vomit out of the upholstery, I suggest you make a left and go through Petersburg."

## Chapter 34

AS THE SUV SNAKED ALONG THE rural routes, Kate wanted to point out places which held precious memories. But Jeremy's complexion still had a green tinge to it. So, she sat in silence and allowed the flatlander to keep his eyes directly ahead. Finally, they passed a blue-painted sign with the words, "Welcome to Franklin, West Virginia."

Jeremy said. "Isn't Franklin where you grew up?"

Kate smiled. "No, I grew up in a little town called Upper Tract. We passed it about twelve miles ago."

Jeremy wrinkled his brow. "We didn't pass any towns twelve miles ago."

"Remember me pointing out that old elementary school and post office?"

"That's a town? You weren't kidding when you said you grew up in the country!"

Kate chuckled then touched the driver on the shoulder. "At the stoplight, take the left onto 33 East," she instructed.

The driver tapped the in-dash GPS. "I got it, ma'am. Still heading to the Pendleton Manor?"

Kate tensed at the name of the nursing home. "Yes," she exhaled as she slumped back in her seat. She was silent for the rest of the ride through town, all thirty-seconds of it.

The SUV parked in front of a white picket fence guarding geranium laden flowerbeds. Kate took Jeremy's hand. "How you feeling?"

"Much better. Thanks for taking the gentler route."

"No problem." Kate kissed him on the cheek, then opened her door. As she slid from the leather seat, heat from the June afternoon hit her in the face like a fist. She squinted at the sun reflecting off the asphalt. "This is the place," she exhaled.

Jeremy stood beside her. "I can't believe the difference in weather from Slate to here."

"We just crossed the eastern continental divide. The Allegheny front creates two different climates."

Jeremy smirked. "In Scotland, it just drizzles everywhere, all the time."

"Sounds cheery."

"It has its own charm. How are you holding up?"

Kate tried to sound brave. "Fine, I just need a moment to prepare myself. I never know who I'll meet when I walk through her door. Sometimes mom is catatonic, sometimes angry and cursing like a sailor, sometimes she sobs for reasons she doesn't understand. Every time, I think I'm prepared, but every time I walk into the room and see a stranger wearing her skin…"

He touched her cheek. "I cannot imagine."

"Once in a great while, I get to see a glimmer of the spunky woman who raised me." Her voice broke. She leaned against his shoulder. "Listen. I don't always know how I'll react to who she is." She bit her bottom lip until it hurt.

He pulled her closer. "However you are, I'll be right beside you."

Walking through the doorway of the nursing home always had a dizzying effect on Kate. The pungent odor of disinfectant stung her nose, and the high-pitched humming of fluorescent lights set her teeth on edge. She tightened her grip on Jeremy's hand and resisted the urge to turn and run out the door. Then, she heard a friendly voice say. "Kate, are you okay?"

Kate focused her eyes on the woman behind the desk. She was in her early forties, with corn silk blonde hair, and compassionate blue eyes. "Kate, do you need to sit?" she asked.

"Shelly," Kate exhaled. "I'm so glad you're here."

Shelly walked from behind the desk and wrapped Kate in a warm hug. "Bless your heart, you look like you haven't slept in a week."

Kate relaxed into the hug. Shelly was not only Kate's favorite nurse, she was a longtime friend. Kate didn't feel like she had to put on a brave face when she was discussing her mom's illness or the toll it took on her. Sometimes, being able to visit with Shelly was the only thing that made a visit with her mom bearable. "I'm fine. Coming here is always rough, and I've had a very trying couple of days."

Shelly released her from the hug. "The flood has been all over the news, and I heard about you getting stuck in that old logging camp. How awful!"

"We were lucky. The older residents knew what was coming. They had the good sense to talk everybody into evacuating. We even had enough time to gather supplies before the waters got too high. It's bad though. I haven't seen anything like it since 1985."

"That's horrible," Shelly shuddered. "I talked to my dear Aunt Sally this morning for a few minutes. She was up there with you."

"Sally Sparrow is your aunt? How did I not know that?"

"Yeah, she was daddy's sister. Please excuse her if she was a super busy body. She's like that with everybody." Shelly rolled her eyes. "Aunt Sally said Doc Kile got stranded with you. That was lucky, especially for the Scottish guy who almost died. He'd better be thanking his lucky stars." As she said the words, Shelly's eyes drifted to the man standing at Kate's side. "Oh, hello, sir."

Jeremy stuck out his hand. "Pleasure to meet you."

His thick Scottish accent echoed off the walls, and Shelly's eyes opened wide. She leaned closer to Kate and whispered, "Is this the guy?"

"Yes, he is," she chuckled. "Jeremy and I became friends when we were at Slate."

"But Aunt Sally said he left you crying in the Kimberly Firehall parking lot?"

Kate's eyes darted to Jeremy. Heat crept up her neck, staining her cheeks magenta. She cleared her throat. "We talked later and decided it would be best if I helped Jeremy get to the airport safely."

Shelly pursed her lips in disapproval. She knew about the long list of men who Kate had let take advantage of her trusting nature. She moved her hand to Kate's shoulder. "It's none of my business, whatever you decide."

Jeremy shifted uncomfortably. "Did the news mention anything about me?"

Shelly gave him a good once-over that said: What makes you think you are so special? "No, it didn't." Her words were crisp.

Kate felt Jeremy relax. She looked back to Shelly. "Could you do me a favor, and not mention to anybody that Jeremy is with me? We don't want to restart rumors."

Shelly eyed Jeremy suspiciously. "It's unprofessional for me to say anything to anybody about who visits my patients."

"Thank you." Kate glanced toward the left hallway. "So, how has mom been?"

Shelly's posture relaxed. "She's had some good days and some bad days. She slept most of the morning. Yesterday, she yelled at your dad most of the day. I guess he wrecked the car and she gave him one heck of a tongue lashing."

Kate asked apprehensively, "Did she ever realize that dad wasn't here?" Sometimes when her mother realized that her husband wasn't really there, that he had passed away fifteen years ago, she would sob for hours. With Alzheimer's forgetting is the blessing. It was remembering what you had forgotten that was hell.

Shelly shrugged. "No, she fell asleep murmuring about snorkeling off the coast of St. Martin with somebody named Javier."

Kate didn't know if she wanted to laugh or cry. "Has she recognized you this week?"

"Off and on. She's slept a lot the past few days."

"Thanks for taking such great care of her. I'm lucky to have you here with her."

"Faith is a great woman. I'm glad to do it." Shelly glanced toward the patient rooms. "Want me to check on her frame of mind before you go in?"

"No, but thank you." Kate took a deep breath, looked at Jeremy, then turned toward the hallway that led to the four-hundred wing where the memory patients lived. The fluorescent lights reflected off the freshly waxed floors, and her sneakers made an annoying squishy sound as she walked. Finally, she stopped in front of door 403. "Mom," she called as she pushed the door open.

A petite woman in a turquoise dressing gown sat in a hospital bed. Her gray hair was disheveled, and her eyes were fixed intently on something out the window.

"Mom, would you like company?" Kate tried to keep her voice steady.

The woman in the bed spun around, the lines around her gray eyes crinkled as she smiled. "Katherine Beverly, what a nice surprise!"

Kate's breath caught in something between a laugh and a sob. She couldn't recall the last time her mom had recognized her without being introduced. She slipped quietly into the room. "What are you doing, mom?"

"I was just enjoying watching the birds. I swear I thought I saw a cardinal a few minutes ago. At least I think I saw it, it may have been my mind playing tricks on me like it always does," Faith added, matter-of-factly.

Kate smiled so big her cheeks hurt. She sat at the foot of the bed. "Shelly said you have had a good couple of days."

"I have. I thought I saw your dad yesterday." Faith winked. "He was irritating as ever!"

"Shelly told me you were giving him hell for wrecking the car again." She'd heard the story hundreds of times about how her dad swerved to avoid hitting Mrs. Smith's chickens and ended up hitting a huge oak tree on the corner. It was the first new car they'd ever purchased, and the insurance company declared it a total loss. Mom hated Mrs. Smith and her chickens from that day forward.

Faith sighed. "Swerving to miss a five-dollar piece of poultry. Do you remember how crazy Mrs. Smith was over those stupid birds?

Was she worried about your father? No, she was just worried about that damn rooster." She rolled her eyes.

"She was an interesting lady, that's for sure." Kate's eyes sparkled with joy. These moments were more precious than gold.

Faith's face fell. "The hallucinations had been better until today."

Kate put her hand on Faith's knee. "Why, what happened today?"

Faith lowered her head. "When you came into the room, I saw a man following you. He was skinny and scruffy, and he hardly takes his eyes off you."

Kate laughed. "He isn't a hallucination. Mom, this is my friend, Jeremy. Jeremy, this is my mother, Faith."

"Nice to meet you Faith," Jeremy nodded his head in a greeting.

"So, he's real?"

Kate wrinkled her brow. "Have I been single so long that when a man accompanies me for a visit, the most logical assumption is a hallucination?"

Faith chuckled. "No, dear. I thought he was an illusion because he looks like that fellow you used to watch on TV all the time." She turned her attention to Jeremy. "You should have seen how crazy she was over that foreign actor. I've never seen a grown woman with such a crush." She lowered her voice to a whisper, "It was almost shameful."

"Mom!" Kate gasped.

Jeremy smirked. "She really liked that bloke, huh?"

"It was ridiculous. She tried to convince me she liked him so much because he was a good actor, but if you ask me, it was because he was a looker. She always liked them skinny." Faith wrinkled her nose. "Do you know what my Kat Bird did? That actor was in New York, doing some Shakespeare Play, and she paid over six-hundred dollars for a ticket! She spent an entire month's pay from her summer job at the farmer's market. Can you believe that? I was livid." Then Faith used the voice reserved for older women when passing judgment. "I don't know of any actor that is worth six-hundred dollars a ticket."

Jeremy laughed. "No ma'am. I agree."

"Well, Kate told me more than once how worth it he was, but if you ask me, he'd have to been sweating solid gold for that much."

A pink blush tinged her cheeks, but it wasn't from embarrassment. True, if anyone else had told that story, she would have dug a hole and crawled inside. But having her mom back for these fleeting moments... it was worth more than gold. These precious windows of time were definitely worth the embarrassing stories.

Faith leaned in closer to Kate. "I wonder if he ever gets told he looks like that celebrity."

Jeremy chuckled. "From time to time."

Faith nodded to Kate. "For a skinny guy, he's kinda cute." She turned her attention to Jeremy. "If I were younger, I just may give Kat Bird a run for her money."

Jeremy winked. "Well, Faith, Kate would have some competition."

Faith sat up straighter. "Kate hates it when I tell this story, but when she was in her mid-twenties, we vacationed in Grand Turk. This Egyptian fellow walks up to me on the beach and offered me ten thousand dollars to let him marry my daughter. He said he'd make it twenty if I'd come too!" Faith put her hands on her hips. "Well, I looked him straight in the eye and told him we were from America, and women couldn't be bought!" Faith continued, "Then Kate stares him down and says, 'And even if we were for sale, you couldn't afford women like us!'"

Jeremy shot an amused look at Kate. "So, you were feisty then too?"

Faith smiled. "That's why she made such a great traveling partner. We had some great adventures, didn't we Kate? Do you remember that one time when..."

That story led to another, which led to another and to another. Before anybody realized it, hours had passed. Through it all, Kate never stopped smiling. Her mom hadn't been this lucid in years. After Faith's story about Kate's photography project winning a blue ribbon in the state fair, Kate lay her head on her mom's bended knees. "I love you so much, mom."

"I love you too, Kate." Faith gently patted her head. "If my old woman intuition still rings true, from the way this gentleman looks at you, he holds quite a bit of affection for you, too." She turned to address Jeremy. "So, are you sleeping with my daughter?"

Kate sat upright. "Mom!" she gasped.

"Oh, don't be such a stick in the mud. What good is having dementia if you cannot use it as an excuse to say whatever you want?" She looked at Jeremy again. "You didn't answer."

Jeremy seemed unfazed. "No, ma'am, I'm not."

"Why the hell not? She is a beautiful woman."

He said looking at Kate. "Aye, she is."

Faith giggled. "Listen to that accent. It makes up for the lack of meat on his bones. You always liked exotic men. Do you remember when you lost your virginity to that foreign exchange student? You thought I didn't know." She tapped her fingertip on her temple. "But a mother always knows."

Kate felt a rock hit the bottom of her stomach. All the banter up to this point had been playful and in Faith's regular repertoire. This statement was outside the norm. She did her best to hide her shock. "Yes, I remember."

A look of horror covered Faith's face. "Oh, God I didn't mean to say that? I never know what's too much to say anymore."

"You said nothing you wouldn't have said five years ago," Kate tried to make her voice sound cheery. "Besides, Jeremy needed a good laugh. He has had a rough couple of days."

Faith's eyes filled with tears as she looked at Jeremy. "I used to be really smart. This stupid disease has made me an idiot." She looked at Kate. "I used to be a good mom, too."

Kate walked to the head of the bed. "You're still a good mom. You're the best mom in the world."

"I feel like a child." Faith looked at Jeremy. "Do you know I need to have somebody wipe my ass? Do you know how that makes me feel?" Tears streaked down her powdered cheeks.

Jeremy knelt beside the bed and took Faith's hand. "When my dad had cancer, he was so weak that I had to do that for him, too. You know what? I was proud to do it. It made me feel like I was being a good son, taking care of him. I was re-paying all the times he'd taken care of me. It's not a bad thing to allow others to take care of you."

Faith placed her palm on Jeremy's cheek. "You're a good man."

Kate's throat tightened as she watched the tender moment. "Mom," she squeaked.

"Yes, Kat Bird."

"I brought you some books. I brought the Bible, the Laura Ingalls Wilder series, and Harry Potter. Would you like me to read to you?"

Faith dried her tears. "I would actually like for this handsome fellow to read to me if that's okay with him. I think his accent is sexy."

"I would be honored to read to you, Faith," Jeremy replied. "How about *Harry Potter*?"

"Sounds lovely." Faith lay back on her pillows and closed her eyes.

Kate pulled the well-worn paperback from her bag and handed it to Jeremy. A single tear streaked down her cheek. He reached to wipe it away, but the moment his hand touched her face, Kate ran from the room. The tenderness in his touch had pushed her over the edge. She sunk to the floor outside her mom's room and allowed a flood of emotions to sweep over her. She began to sob, sobs that shook her entire body.

Between her sniffles, she heard a kind Scottish voice softly recite, "Chapter One, The Boy Who Lived."

JEREMY READ TO FAITH UNTIL SHE fell into a restful sleep. Once she had drifted off, he peeked his head out the door and saw Kate sitting in the hallway, hands on her knees, and tear stains on her face. She looked so helpless, so hurt, so fragile. The woman who had nursed him back from the brink of death needed him, and he didn't know how to comfort her. He sat beside her on the linoleum. "Hey stranger," he whispered.

She gave a sad smile and wiped a tear from her chin.

He put his arm around her shoulders and pulled her close. "Thank you for allowing me to come."

"It's the first time she has recognized me in over a year."

He kissed the top of her head. "I'm sorry."

"No, it's a good thing. These moments don't come often," Kate whispered "I miss her so much. I mean, she's here, but she... I miss her."

Jeremy didn't speak, just tightened his grip around her shoulders and lay his head against hers.

After a few minutes, Kate sighed. "I guess we should get going."

"We can stay as long as you like."

Kate lifted her head from his shoulder. "You know you are pretty amazing?"

Just as Jeremy was to reply Shelly walked out of room 404. "Oh, sorry!" she said. "I didn't mean to interrupt. I needed to change the dressings on Mr... on a patient."

"It's okay, Shelly." Kate pushed herself into a standing position.

"How was it today?" Shelly asked.

"Wonderful! She remembered me." Kate was almost in tears again. "We have to get going, though. We have a long trip ahead of us. Can you tell her that I had to leave when she wakes up?"

Shelly took Kate's hand. "Sure thing, sweetie."

Jeremy wondered how Faith would react when she woke up and Kate wasn't there. Would she even remember, would she be heartbroken they had left? He looked at Kate. What a burden, what a weight to carry upon one set of shoulders. He wished they were still back at Slate, laying in the king-size bed. He could wrap her in his arms, comfort her, let her cry.

When they climbed into the back of the SUV the driver asked for Kate's address.

"221B Baker Street, Leesburg, VA." She replied, "And take a right out of the parking lot."

The driver typed the address into the GPS. "That's not what this says."

"Do you remember what I said about switchbacks and vomit?"

Jeremy couldn't help but smile. After everything they had been through that day, Kate was still watching out for him. As they drove through luscious green farmland and through quaint small towns, Kate was unusually quiet. Jeremy understood. There had been too many silent drives from the hospital when his father was ill. He knew Kate needed to be with her thoughts. So, he held her hand and allowed her the time.

AFTER A QUICK STOP AT KATE'S APARTMENT, they drove to the private airstrip where Jeremy had arranged a plane to meet them. Kate gasped at the beautiful antebellum mansion. "Do you own this?" she asked.

"No, it belongs to a friend of a friend." He helped her from the backseat of the SUV. "Are you ready to depart?"

Kate nodded and walked across the small landing strip. She climbed the staircase to the jet and stopped in the cabin's doorway. "What in the..."

Jeremy bumped into her back, sending her stumbling forward. "You stopped short!"

Kate's mouth was agape. "It's so much bigger on the inside."

"It seems that way, doesn't it?"

Kate motioned to the interior of the jet. "I know that this may be an everyday occurrence for celebrities like you, but for me, this is definitely not normal."

"Actually, I seldom do this. Usually, I fly commercial. It would be excessive to rent a private jet every time I needed to get somewhere."

"Why did you choose it this time?"

"I wouldn't be surprised if the media has gotten wind of my disappearance. I don't want to get off the plane to a bunch of ravenous pseudo-reporters."

The butterflies in Kate's stomach went from fluttering to slam dancing. "Oh God, I never thought about the paparazzi." She began to hyperventilate. "I don't want them to see me. I don't want to be on the front of some trashy magazine. I don't want people going through my dirty laundry, trying to find trash on the fat girl dating Jeremy Fulton. I can't do this!" She turned and tried to leave the plane.

Jeremy put his hands on her shoulders. "Kate, wait!"

"I can't do this, I'm sorry, Jeremy. I just can't."

He gently moved his hands to her cheeks and directed her face, so they were eye to eye. "Kate, look at me. I won't let you be hounded by the press or followed by paparazzi. I'll protect you." He ran his thumb over her jawline. "The reason I chartered a private plane is so we can get a car at the airstrip and drive directly to my home. We won't even be seen by the media."

Kate took a deep breath. "Okay, I trust you."

Jeremy took her hand and led her into the cabin. He sat in one of the recliner style chairs and pulled Kate into the seat beside him. He kissed her lightly. "There is a small kitchenette in the back. I had it fully stocked with food and alcohol." He winked. "Sorry, I couldn't find any peach moonshine."

"Well, then it's not fully stocked, is it?" Kate teased.

Jeremy walked to the back of the cabin and rummaged through the fridge. "I think I'll stick to fizzy juice. Is there anything you would like?"

"I want something strong, preferably with tequila."

He rummaged through the liquor cabinet. "Are you nervous about flying?"

"No, I am nervous about flying to another continent with a man I have known for eight days and may bring about a hailstorm of ravenous paparazzi."

He poured Don Julio over ice and handed it to Kate. "Thank goodness, I was afraid you didn't like to fly."

## Chapter 35

AFTER NAVIGATING THE BUREAUCRATIC hoops of international travel, Kate and Jeremy arrived at his estate around three a.m. Too exhausted to change from their clothes, they collapsed into bed and fell right asleep.

Eight hours later, Jeremy reluctantly peeled himself from the bed. He kissed the still-sleeping Kate on the forehead and slipped into the kitchen.

He called Constance, a friend who was an orthopedic specialist. He explained that he had broken his arm on holiday and begged her to work him into her schedule. With a promise for front row seats to his next performance, she agreed to meet him at her office.

Half an hour later he was sitting in an eclectically decorated exam room talking to a woman with bright purple hair. "Those tickets must be front row center, Mister," she chided him as she gave him a hug.

"Of course." Jeremy tugged playfully at her violet braids. Constance wasn't just a chum, she had been like a sister when they were growing up. Her mom was the superintendent of his dad's first parish. Jeremy would chase her with pencils between his fingers pretending to be Wolverine. She would force him to play the victim of all sorts of false calamities, so she could wrap, bandage, and mend his broken bones.

"Touch my braids again, and I'll break your other arm." She ripped the manila folder from his hand. "Give me this."

She rifled through its contents until she found the x-rays, then clipped the films to the light box. "Where and when were these taken?" she asked.

"In the US and two days ago," Jeremy answered.

Constance glanced from the films to the notes and back to the films. Her lips tightened over her teeth. "That bloody American doctor screwed up your chart." She threw Doc's notes on the exam table. "These say you broke your arm ten days ago. Any idiot could look at this film and see the injury is at least six weeks old. Look at this." She pointed to a thin line on the x-ray. "A first-year medical student could see this wound shows advanced stages of healing. This may seem like a small detail here, but medical errors like this can be devastating in other situations."

"Constance," he said smoothly, "Doctor Kile didn't make a mistake. I broke my arm ten days ago when I fell during a mudslide."

She lifted a pierced eyebrow. "In a mudslide?"

"I was camping in the U.S. where that flood devastated all those small towns. You may have seen it on the news; it was just last week."

"I think I saw a blurb about it on STV."

"I was camping when the flood hit. I got lost in the forest. When I finally found a small camp, I was so excited to get to civilization, I didn't watch my step and caused a huge landslide. I broke my arm while getting tossed down the mountainside."

Constance looked at him empathetically. "Jeremy, you don't have to do this. I know you must be very careful about what gets to the media, but I'm a professional. More importantly, I'm your friend. Anything you say in this room is between us."

"I swear, it was only ten days ago."

She looked at her watch. "Jeremy, the truth, or I'm going to leave."

"When is the last time you talked to your brother, Nate?"

"Last night, why?"

"Fourteen days ago, we met for a pint at Frankie's. My arm was fine then. Ask him."

Constance pinched the bridge of her nose. "Fine, then how is it possible for a wound this bad to show six weeks of healing in ten days? It would have to be a miracle."

"In the past two weeks, my attitude on miracles has greatly changed." Jeremy sat on the exam table and launched into a detailed narrative of his time in West Virginia. He told her about the flood, the landslide, the residents praying over him. And he talked a lot about Kate.

Jeremy put his hand on hers. "Do you remember chasing each other around the pews at dad's first parish? We used to have faith in things like miracles." He looked at the ceiling. "What happened? Why is it that when a miracle is staring us right in our face, we'd rather believe a friend is lying?"

"I don't know, Jeremy, I really don't know." She sounded sad. "I guess it's called faith of a child for a reason. When you see all the shit that is out there, believing in miracles becomes harder and harder." She looked him in the eye. "But if you tell me that this happened ten days ago, I believe you."

"I give you my word."

"Well, then." She pushed herself up from the table. "In my professional opinion, keep a brace on for another two weeks. I'll reevaluate the wound then. For now, I would say it is healing miraculously."

Since Constance had come in on her day off, there were no other patients to see. She and Jeremy visited until it was past noon.

As he hugged her goodbye, Constance said, "Let me know when I can meet your swearing angel, this mysterious Kate."


THE AFTERNOON SUN SHINED LIKE a halo around the blackout curtains. Kate pushed herself onto her elbows and blinked the sleep from her eyes. She glanced around the room. *Where am I?* She panicked. Then she remembered, Jeremy, the man she had saved from certain death. Jeremy, the person with whom she had shared countless late-night talks. Jeremy the international celebrity she'd known for nine days... and flew to another continent to be with...

Her chest tightened. She reached for him but found only empty sheets.

*Where is he?* She needed to see him, touch him, hear his voice. She needed him to reassure her the way he had on the flight over, but he was nowhere to be found.

She pushed her frizzy curls from her eyes, and a yellow post-it-note on the nightstand caught her attention. She plucked it from the marble top and read aloud, "Going to the doctor to see about my arm. Be home soon. Fridge and pantry completely stocked. Sorry, couldn't find moonshine."

Kate climbed from the massive four post bed. In the bathroom, she undressed and stepped into the slate tile shower that looked big enough to play a game of racquetball. The multi-head shower sent rivers of steaming water over her skin, melting away her anxiety. Once she felt centered, she dried off with an Egyptian cotton towel. She slipped on jeans and a t-shirt then went downstairs to explore.

Though Jeremy's home was spacious and impeccably decorated, it wasn't extravagant. In fact, it wasn't much bigger than the homes of the doctors and lawyers whose children she taught in Northern Virginia. She descended the staircase and searched until she found the kitchen.

She was standing in the luxury walk-in pantry looking for a coffee maker, when a voice behind her said, "Do you always rifle through other people's pantries when they have a doctor's appointment?"

Kate jumped. "You scared me," she admonished.

"Sorry about that." Jeremy gave a lopsided grin. "Have you been up long?"

"I just woke up."

He pushed a lock of hair behind her ear. "Aye, my sweet Briar Rose."

Kate laughed. "You mean your jet lagged, Briar Rose?" She turned back to the pantry and called over her shoulder. "Do you have coffee?"

He hooked his finger through one of her belt loops and gently tugged. "It's out here."

Kate followed him from the pantry and looked around the kitchen. The mahogany cabinets, marble countertops, and black steel appliances all but broadcast the decorator's possession of a Y-chromosome. She ran her fingers over the pewter backsplash. "I love the color scheme in here."

"Thanks, I had the whole house redecorated about six months ago." He quickly changed the subject. "You need coffee, eh?" He walked to the cabinet beside the gourmet stove, rifled through the contents, then pulled out a Mr. Coffee electric coffee pot that looked like the one she'd had in college seventeen years ago. "What's your pleasure? I have a dark Sumatra, a Costa Rican light roast, a middle of the road American."

Kate cocked her head and stared at the antique coffee maker.

"I see you are wondering about this." He nodded toward the outdated machine. "It belonged to my dad. I always told him to get a better one. I even bought him one of those that has the individual cups, but he said, 'You don't throw away something that works just because something prettier comes along.'" Jeremy smiled nostalgically. "He said a lot of things I didn't see the wisdom in until recently."

"I'm sure it will brew a lovely Sumatra." Kate smiled. She sat on a barstool at the island, as Jeremy brewed a pot of coffee. "I just noticed the wrap on your arm has been replaced by a brace. Does that mean your friend said you are healing well?"

"Constance said it looks great for a break six weeks old."

"Six weeks?"

He wriggled his fingers. "She said that it's in the advanced stages of repair, and it's healing miraculously."

"Miraculously," Kate repeated in a low tone.

"Her words, not mine." Jeremy took a sip of coffee. "How do you feel about a picnic?"

"A picnic?" Kate said, surprised by the change in subject. "Why a picnic?"

"Remember that glen I told you about when we were in Slate? I want you to see it."

Fifteen minutes later they were hiking across the vibrant Scottish countryside. When they crested a small knoll, Kate stopped in her tracks. At the bottom of the shallow hill, a narrow stream snaked through the emerald grass. A white-painted bridge connected the sides, like a Monet come to life. "This is the place." Jeremy smiled as he spread the blanket.

"I can see why it would be your favorite place." Kate inhaled, and the rich sent of hawthorn in bloom filled her nostrils. "I'd always believed no place could rival the beauty of West Virginia, but Scotland makes me second guess that."

They whiled away the morning laughing, talking, and acting as new lovers act. After a bit, Jeremy escaped into the woods, leaving Kate alone. She sat on the little wooden bridge and dipped her toes in the crisp water. It reminded her of the brook by Nan's house. Nan's house where she celebrated holidays, Nan's house where she had retreated when the world was too much, Nan's house where so many memories were forged, Nan's house, which had flooded, Nan's house which was gone.

Kate's mind replayed the events of the last week in vivid detail. When she was in the thick of the chaos, she was in survival mode. Getting from one moment to the next required all her attention and had kept her from truly comprehending the destruction. It had sheltered her from experiencing the pain. Now, there were no distractions, and the pain washed over her like the flood waters that had taken her second home.

Her home was gone. People she loved were hurting. People she had called friends were dead. People whom she considered family were desperately scrambling to regain any sense of normalcy. And she had deserted them. While they were picking up the scraps of their lives, she was having a picnic on a beautiful Scottish hillside with her new boyfriend. The pain, the frustration, the anger, and the guilt bubbled to the surface and hit her all at once. She buried her head in her hands and cried.

When Jeremy returned, he found Kate sitting on the bridge, tears streaming down her face. He didn't say a word, he didn't ask what was wrong, offer suggestions, or try to fix anything. He pulled her onto his lap and let her cry. He stroked her hair and held her to his chest as he whispered over and over again, "It's all right. I'm right here."

It wouldn't be the last time she cried and mourned for the town of Riverside, and Jeremy was true to his word. He was right there every time.

THAT EVENING BOTH KATE AND JEREMY were exhausted. They decided on watching a movie and ordering Chinese food.

As Kate stuffed an oversized piece of General Tso chicken in her mouth, Jeremy looked at her and said, "I want you to meet my friends."

Kate choked. "Excuse me?"

"Today when I was talking with Constance, I realized just how far I have grown from my friends. I want to see them; I want them to meet you. How do you feel about inviting a few people over one evening?"

Kate was not excited about the prospect. She didn't really want to be put on display for Britain's rich and famous. She was afraid she would be judged for her Appalachian accent or lack of proper upbringing. Mostly, she had no desire to spend an evening being the fattest and least attractive person in the room.

Jeremy took her hand. "You can say no if you like."

He looked so pathetic, like her six-year-old nephew when his birthday party at Chuck E. Cheese got snowed out. There was no way she could take this from him. She pushed her apprehension to the back of her mind. "I think that would be nice."

"Great!" He sprang to his feet. "I have got to make a list of guests, a list for the bartender, a list for the caterer."

"Why don't you start with a list of lists you need to make?" Kate said a bit too cheerily.

"Great idea!" Jeremy kissed the top of her head and bounced out of the room.

## Chapter 36

WEDNESDAY MORNING, THE BRIGHT sunlight streamed through the craftsman windows and pulled Kate from a peaceful sleep. She rolled over and reached for Jeremy's arm, but only found crumpled sheets. Jeremy's words from their argument in Kimberly played in her ears, *What if I want somebody who makes me look forward to the night because I get to lie down beside them, somebody who makes me look forward to the morning because I get to wake up next to them?* She sighed, if Jeremy continued to be such an early riser, she'd have to be content with just laying down beside him.

She tiptoed downstairs and found Jeremy sitting behind a gargantuan desk in a mahogany-paneled room. To her delight, he was wearing flannel pajama pants and nothing else. She slid into one of the leather chairs across from him and playfully propped her feet on the desktop.

He gave her a sexy half-smile, then sat bolt upright. "Sorry, can you repeat that?" he said into his phone. "No, I was listening, I just want to make sure I understood you fully." He flashed Kate a mischievous grin and shooed her out of the room.

She gave an exaggerated pout and tiptoed to the hallway. Suddenly the peaceful silence was shattered. Jeremy's angry voice echoed in the hall. "I never agreed to that!"

Kate peeked through the crack in the door. Jeremy was on his feet, his face in a fierce scowl. "I don't bloody care what you told the studio, I told you I won't do that anymore!"

Kate turned on her heel and scurried away. As she was making coffee, Jeremy stormed into the kitchen wearing jeans and a Beatles t-shirt. His mischievous smile was gone. "I have to talk to my director, Robert Forrest. That freaking eejit didn't listen when I told him I wasn't coming to the premier."

"Would it make you feel better if I told you I think Forrest is an idiot too?" Kate tried to lighten the mood.

"I don't want to meet with the bloody dobber." He stopped right in front of her, as if noticing her for the first time. His expression softened, and he kissed her lips. "And I definitely don't want to leave you."

She wrapped her arms around his neck and pulled him even closer. "I should tell you to not worry about it and go, but having you here in front of me makes me want to beg you to stay."

He kissed the ticklish spot above her collarbone. "It shouldn't be long. Less than three hours, I promise."

WHEN JEREMY ARRIVED HOME at eleven that night, Kate was asleep. As he slipped into bed, she rolled over to face him. "Is everything taken care of?"

"I'll never work with that wanker again." He lay his head on her chest. "Are you mad?"

Kate closed her eyes. "I'm not mad at you."

He lifted his head to look at her. "You're upset. I can tell from the way you cut your words short, and you have that v shape forming in your brow."

Kate touched the spot between her eyebrows, thinking the cursed v was probably causing wrinkles. "I get it, this is your life, and I'm just a guest in it, but when you're gone, I'm alone. I know you can't help it, but isolation's something I've never dealt with well."

Jeremy took Kate's hand and kissed the tip of each finger. "I'm sorry. I never considered that I'm the only person who you know here. I didn't think about how alone you'd be."

Kate shrugged. "It's inevitable. Every time I've chased a sexy Scottish man across the Atlantic, I always end up spending days alone."

"Exactly how many Scottish men have you chased across the Atlantic?"

"I can think of only one worth mentioning."

THURSDAY MORNING, KATE AWOKE to a heavenly mixture of aromas: fresh baked bread and Italian roast coffee. She opened her eyes to see Jeremy beside her, a breakfast tray balancing in his arms.

He handed her a cup of coffee. "I wanted to do something nice for you."

She took a long drink. The hot coffee mixed with the kind gesture melted any resentment left over from the day before. "Thank you," she said. "What are our plans for today?"

"I've put it off long enough. I must meet with Phil, my agent, and Jackson, my publicist. The entire voyage into the wilderness hasn't made it into the news. I'd like to keep it that way."

"Think they'll respect that?"

"I'll make them an offer they can't refuse," he said in a Marlon Brando voice. "Besides, there are many things I will say today that'll leave them unhappy. Keeping Slate out of the public is the least of their concerns. It'll be a long day; I probably won't be back until late this evening."

Kate narrowed her eyes. "What about 'I'm so sorry? I won't leave you alone all day again?'"

Jeremy kissed the top of her head. "I've taken care of that. My sister is coming to take you shopping and then to the spa to get pampered."

"Wait, wait, wait." Kate slammed the coffee cup down on the nightstand, splashing the dark roast onto the marble. "You set up a playdate with your sister?"

"It's not a playdate."

"Then what is it?"

"A wee shopping trip. When you were picking up a few things from your flat, you promised me when we got to Scotland you'd let me buy you a whole new wardrobe."

She crossed her arms over her chest. "No, I told you I could wait until we got to Scotland to pick up a few items."

"Same thing."

"No, it isn't." With each exchange, Kate was becoming more and more annoyed.

A frustrated growl escaped his throat. "Why won't you let me do something nice for you?"

Kate tried to keep the irritation from her voice. "I appreciate that you want to do something special for me, but I really don't want to spend the day with a complete stranger."

"She isn't a stranger, she's my sister."

"She's a stranger to me." Then Kate sat up straight and pointed at Jeremy. "Hold on, your sister, Meredith? You talked to her? She's coming to your home?"

Fine lines creased around his eyes as he smiled. "Yeah, I called her early this morning, and we had a long chat."

Kate leapt to her feet. "That's wonderful!"

Jeremy wrapped his arms around her waist. "There are a lot of things between Meredith and me that cannot be undone. We've hurt each other a lot over the years, but she's all the family I have left. There's no magic solution to fix what we did to one another, but we both want to try."

"What have you told her about me?"

He got a mischievous glint in his eye. "Only the things that are appropriate to tell your sister." He ran his knuckles along her cheekbone. "Meredith asked to do this. It means a lot to me that she wants to meet you."

Now Kate understood why this was so important to him. She felt ashamed for being such a brat about it earlier. She tried to lighten the mood. "Meredith wants to meet me as in, 'Hey this Kate chick sounds cool' or 'I need to make sure this wench is worthy of my baby brother?'"

"Maybe a little of both," Jeremy smiled. Meredith acting like a protective big sister obviously made him happy.

Kate chewed her lip. "Wait, doesn't Meredith live in London?"

"Luckily, she was in Glasgow for a conference." Jeremy looked at his watch. "She'll be here in about twenty minutes."

"Twenty minutes? Are you effing kidding me? I need a shower, I haven't brushed my teeth, I have to do my makeup." Kate muttered as she ran toward the bathroom. "You're such a guy."

EXACTLY TWENTY MINUTES LATER, the doorbell rang. "She certainly is punctual," Kate grumbled as she pulled her hair in a tight ponytail and slapped on a little makeup. After an overly critical look in the mirror, she made her way downstairs.

A thin woman in designer jeans, black t-shirt, and high-heeled boots was standing beside Jeremy. They had the same cornflower blue eyes, thin nose, and full lips.

When Kate reached the last step, she stuck out her hand. "You must be Meredith. Nice to meet you."

Meredith gave her hand a business-meeting-worthy shake. "And you must be Kate. I'm happy to finally meet the woman I've heard so much about."

Jeremy spoke up. "I told Kate that I'm going to talk to Jackson and Phil today about upcoming events, but I should be home for dinner. Why don't I bring something home from that little place on Highland Avenue?"

Meredith nodded. "Sounds great." She turned her attention to Kate. "Are you ready for this? I've procured the credit card of a millionaire, and the sky's the limit."

Kate swallowed hard, she kept forgetting Jeremy was an internationally known actor and millionaire. Being reminded of that, on top of meeting the family for the first time, made her stomach twitch. But, before she could even wrap her arms around her middle, Meredith grabbed her by the elbow. "Let's be off."

They stepped onto the front porch, and Kate froze in her tracks. A shiny, black stretch limousine was sitting in the driveway. Meredith's grip on her elbow tightened. "Our chariot awaits."

The women slid into the supple black leather seats, but when the car door slammed shut, the bright smile that had been plastered across Meredith's face was gone. When she spoke again, her voice was deep and full of emotion. "I need to say something." She fidgeted with the diamond pendant at the nape of her neck.

The sudden change in demeanor put Kate even more on edge. Meredith shifted uncomfortably. "I don't know what Jeremy told you about me." She lowered her eyes. "I want you to know, I acknowledge I've made mistakes, things I wish I could take back."

Kate made her voice as gentle as possible without sounding condescending. "He told me that there are regrets on both sides. He hopes you both can put the hurt behind you and have a relationship. He really missed you."

Tears clung to Meredith's perfectly mascaraed lashes. She reached across the aisle and squeezed Kate's hand "I can see why my brother is so taken with you." For the first time her voice was natural, neither forced nor weighed down. "Now for shopping, I thought we'd start at the Edinburgh. They have the most amazing shops there!"

Kate smiled a bit too brightly. "I'm the tourist, you're the expert."


THE LIMO DROPPED THE TWO WOMEN at the entrance of a gray stone building with faceless mannequins in the window, the name Jane Davidson was written on navy and white signs.

Kate followed Meredith into the store where perfectly made-up patrons browsed through racks of designer names she'd only heard on tv. She'd never felt more like a poor country mouse in her entire existence. She was more at home in stores like Old Navy, Target, and Marshalls, places a teacher could afford.

Before she could protest, Meredith shoved a navy and white striped sundress into Kate's hands. "This will look adorable on you!"

Kate looked at the price tag and suppressed a laugh. *Who'd pay that much for a simple cotton dress?* She looked at Meredith, who was staring at her expectantly, and realized that today she'd be spending that much for a simple cotton dress. Before she could protest, Meredith gently shoved her toward a dressing room. "Try it on," she urged.

Kate barely had time to strip off her Lee jeans and Walmart brand t-shirt before Meredith returned with jeans, sparkly shirts, even lacy underwear. "Jeremy said you only picked up a few things at your flat on the way here," Meredith called as she slid the garments under the door. "I hope you don't mind me picking out some things that look like they're your size."

"Thanks," Kate choked as she picked up the sundress. She slipped it over her head and slowly turned to look in the mirror. A huge smile covered her face. The way the cotton clung to her curves in the right places made her look, dare she say, pretty. With a new fervor for shopping, she whipped off the dress and slipped on blue jeans and a fitted t-shirt with a jeweled neckline. The jeans were too small and made her thighs look like sausages in denim casing, but the fitted t-shirt made her boobs look amazing. By the time Kate had removed the jeans and put them in the reject pile, Meredith had gathered a stack of new things to try on. There were jeans, socks, shirts, and even a bathing suit.

When the two were back in the limo, Kate said to Meredith "I just don't get Jeremy. He runs around in frayed jeans then sends me out to pay $750 for a purse."

"He used to do that with mum. He'd wear ten-year-old trainers, then buy mum $600 shoes that she'd only wear for Sunday morning. I stopped trying to make sense of it."

"I guess if you haven't figured him out in forty-two years, then I have no chance."

After a quick lunch, they were off to the spa where they got spoiled with manicures, pedicures, massages, facials, custom made makeup and decadent chocolates. By the time they were ready to head back to Jeremy's, Kate was beginning to enjoy being spoiled.

WHEN THE LIMO PULLED UP THE DRIVEWAY Jeremy was waiting on the front porch. As they walk toward the house, Kate could feel the anxiety on his face as his eyes darted from her to Meredith and back to her. "How was your day?" he asked.

Kate put her hand on his shoulder. "I had a wonderful time."

Meredith's posture softened at Kate's reply. "It was great, thanks, Jeremy."

"Excuse me." A strained voice came from behind them. Kate turned to see their driver struggling up the walk, his arms laden with bags. "Where would you like your things, Ms. Thorn?"

Jeremy rushed to the driver's aid. "Let me help you with that." Before the driver could object, Jeremy had taken half the bags from his arms. The two men carried the ridiculous number of packages into the foyer and sat them beside the stairs.

Kate looked at the pile, then hung her head. When they were in the boutiques, she'd gotten caught up in it all. Now that she saw the absurdly large pile, she felt selfish and ashamed.

Meredith piped up, "It was like pulling teeth to get her to buy anything. I practically had to bully her into purchasing what we did." She dug around in her purse then handed Jeremy back his credit card. "I hope you don't mind, I picked up something for Lillian and Alexandra."

Jeremy scoffed. "I'd be upset if you didn't. I can't wait to see them. I've missed my nieces so much."

A sad smile tugged at the corners of Meredith's mouth. "There's so much to catch up on, brother." Just then, her stomach let out a ferocious growl. "But can I catch you up over dinner? We haven't eaten in hours."

The conversation moved to the dining room. As Kate devoured her eggplant parmigiana, Jeremy and Meredith caught up on the missed years. Though Kate was seldom in the conversation, the smile on Jeremy's face made her heart happy.

## Chapter 37

FRIDAY MORNING, KATE AWOKE with a ball of dread in her stomach. The small get together Jeremy proposed had morphed into a full-scale party, and tonight was the night. She gave herself a stern pep talk. "You need to snap out of this self-pity. It's about Jeremy, his need to connect with his friends, his need to recreate the life that fame stole from him. Get your head in the right place, or you'll ruin it."

Kate put on her game face and made her way downstairs. The house was already in a frenzied state, with cleaners, caters and bartenders milling about. Jeremy conducted the chaos with a huge smile, and Kate knew that tonight would be good for his soul.

Her soul, however, was not as pleased. That evening, as she got out of the shower, she caught the reflection of her naked form in the mirror. It was a harsh reminder of just how different she was from the beautiful people who would soon begin arriving. She slipped on one of the bathing suits from her shopping expedition with Meredith, a black one piece with tummy control panels, then made her way downstairs.

She was finishing her second margarita when the doorbell rang for the first time. It didn't stop ringing for an hour. Jeremy, ever the gracious host, welcomed each guest and proudly introduced her as "The Kate." Even with his adoration, she felt like a velvet Elvis in a room of Van Gogh's. She excused herself to the pool where she sat with her toes in the water.

Though she was no longer bombarded with introductions, things were no less surreal. Beautiful people littered the backyard. Kate tried to not gape open-mouthed because these weren't just beautiful people, they were beautiful people whom she had watched for years. Standing by the diving board was Jeremy's love interest in the romantic comedy where he played a single dad. Sitting cross-legged on a beach blanket was the villainess who tried to assassinate him when he played a member of parliament.

Kate looked down at her body. It was easy to tell that she didn't have a personal trainer or dietician. A song from her childhood played in her head, *One of these things is not like the others, one of these things just isn't the same.* She pulled her legs from the pool and wrapped her towel around her waist.

Then she heard a familiar voice call, "You're Kate, aren't you?"

She spun around, and her breath caught in her throat. Standing three feet from her was William Remy, *The Magician*. He was one of the most recognizable faces in all of England, if not the world. He had been in American sitcoms, British sitcoms, blockbuster movies, Broadway. You name it, he'd mastered it.

He looked just as handsome as he did on TV, standing there wearing nothing but turquoise swim trunks. Kate said something she hoped sounded like "I'm Kate," but her mind was so discombobulated that she could have said, "I have a purple toupee," and not realized it.

He flashed a million-dollar smile and held out his hand. "I got here late, so I missed introductions. I'm Will."

"Yeah, I know!" Kate exclaimed before she could stop herself. At some point during the night, she'd stop being so star-struck. Obviously, this wasn't it.

Will took it all in stride. "I've heard so much about you, I wanted to introduce myself."

"I'm... I'm sorry." Kate stammered, "This entire thing is such a mind trip."

"I can imagine. Even though I'm a part of this whole universe, it's still a mind trip for me too."

Will's presence was so genuine, that Kate felt more comfortable than she had with any of the other guests. She took a sip of her third margarita. "It's definitely strange."

"When I got into this crazy circus, I was only twenty. Jeremy took me under his wing and showed me the ins and outs of the business. He's one of the most humble and grounded people I know, much less in this crazy rat race."

Kate exhaled. "He's special. I've never met anybody like him."

"He says the same about you. He told me everything about the flood and the time the two of you spent together. He told me you saved his life and his sanity."

"I'm not sure I did all that. He'd have been fine with anybody."

"That's not what he thinks, and it's not what I think either. He said you are one of the most authentically beautiful and compassionate people he's ever met."

Kate looked around at all the perfect bodies. "Beautiful?" she scoffed.

He gave Kate a sincere smile. "He's one of my closest friends, and I can tell he really cares about you. I haven't seen him this happy in a very long time. Probably since..."

"Meghan," Kate looked Will in the eye. In all their talks, Jeremy had hardly mentioned his ex-wife, but Kate remembered the stories from the tabloids.

Will slapped his hand over his mouth. "Damn it, too much wine!"

"It's okay." She pulled back her shoulders in faux confidence. "He hasn't really talked a lot about Meghan, but I know she hurt him badly." She put her hand on his elbow. "I don't know where this is heading, but I promise you, I do care about him deeply."

"I believe you."

Suddenly somebody from the patio yelled. "Hey Will, we need your bar tending skills."

Will rolled his eyes playfully. "I should go. It was nice to finally meet the woman that Jeremy constantly talks about."

"It was great meeting you too." Kate watched him walk away then tightened her towel around her waist and snuck upstairs.

That night as they lay in bed, Jeremy asked, "Did you have fun this evening? I saw you talk to Will, and then you were gone. Was everything okay?"

Kate exhaled heavily. "I had a great time, I really did, but I felt a bit out of place. All the beautiful people, stars with so much in common. I was the only plain, ordinary person there. It was weird."

Jeremy put his finger under her chin and lifted her head, so she was looking at him. "First, you're anything but plain and ordinary. Second, I'm sorry. I got so excited to see everybody and to introduce them to you, I completely forgot how it would make you feel. I keep forgetting what different worlds we come from."

"Don't be sorry, this IS your life. If I'm going to be in your life, I'll have to find a way to be a part of all of this."

She instantly regretted her words. Of all the things they had talked about, the future is the one thing they never discussed. Both had silently decided to live in the moment and not worry about what tomorrow brings. By insinuating she may become a part of his world, she'd crossed a line.

Either Jeremy didn't hear Kate's words, or he ignored them. He kissed the top of her head. "Goodnight, my dear," he said then rolled over and turned off the lamp.

## Chapter 38

SATURDAY MORNING, KATE STOOD on the front porch. She took a sip of her coffee and watched the morning fog lift from the wet grass. "I have never seen greens so vibrant."

Jeremy wrapped his arm around her waist. "Mornings are my favorite times. Perhaps one day you can get out of bed early enough to watch the sunrise with me."

Kate lay her head on his shoulder. "If only mornings weren't so early."

Jeremy chuckled. "Speaking of mornings, there's something I want to talk to you about. I want to do something I haven't done in a very long time." He exhaled. "I want to go to church, my dad's church, not the big church with a thousand people. I want to go to the little chapel where he preached when I was a child, where my sister and I were baptized." His eyes became moist. "I know nobody there would probably remember dad, but I'll remember him there."

Kate put her arms around his neck. "I think that would be nice. When would you like to go?"

"Tomorrow." He pulled her closer. "And I want you there with me."

Tears pricked her eyes. She felt honored he'd ask her to be part of such an intimate thing. She kissed him lightly on the mouth. "I'd love to go with you."

SUNDAY MORNING, THEY STOOD on the steps of a beautiful, gothic brownstone church with spires that seemed to touch the sky. Again, Kate was reminded of the different worlds from which they came. Jeremy told her they would be attending a small church. This beautiful, historic cathedral was five times the size of the little white wooden church she'd attended as a child. She turned to tell him so and saw him nervously fidgeting with his bowtie.

She winked at him to lighten the mood. "I can't believe you went with the bowtie."

"Bowties are cool."

"On you they are."

He chewed his bottom lip. "Thank you for coming with me."

There was a steely vulnerability to his voice that made her heart both swell and break. She wanted so badly to hold his hand or comfort him, but they had discussed on the drive over the possibility of being seen or photographed showing physical affection. The days of cell phone cameras and social media made anonymity almost impossible. Again, she was struck with the immense pressure Jeremy had to face to do ordinary things.

As they walked into the sanctuary, Jeremy inhaled deeply. Kate could see his whole body tense with the ache of grief when he looked at the pulpit where his father used to stand. Once they were both seated, she discreetly squeezed his hand.

Everything was beautiful, until the closing hymn. The moment Kate heard the opening notes, her heart hammered against her ribs. From the change in Jeremy's body language, he recognized the tune too. As the congregation began to sing:

*Faith of Our Fathers, living still*
*In spite of dungeon, fire, and sword;*
*Oh, how our hearts beat high with joy*
*Whene'er we hear that glorious word.*
*Faith of our fathers*
*Living faith; We will be true to thee til death.*

Kate reached for Jeremy's hand but grasped only air. She turned in time to see the heavy wooden doors of the sanctuary swing shut. She looked at the sky, and anger coursed through her veins. "Jeremy's first time returning to his dad's church, and *Faith of Our Fathers* was the closing hymn?" She raged at God, "How could you be so cruel?"

She raced down the church stairs and got to the corner just in time to glimpse Jeremy walking toward the church cemetery. She followed, keeping a respectable distance, but never losing sight of him. Finally, he stopped in front of a massive granite stone. He sat on the ground, wrapped his arms around his knees, and began to sob.

Kate knelt in front of him and placed her hand on his shoulder. Before she could ask if he wanted her there, he reached for her like a drowning man reaching for a life preserver. In one swoop he pulled her onto his lap and held on to her as he cried. She wasn't sure how long they were sitting at the base of the statue, but when Jeremy released her, the fabric where he had buried his face was soaked.

He brushed a tear from her cheek. "Why are you crying?"

Kate touched her cheek and realized it was wet. She ran her fingers over his freshly shaved scalp. "Because you are."

Jeremy pulled her closer. Over his shoulder, Kate noticed a couple in their late sixties staring at them. White-hot anger flooded her veins. She glared daggers at the asinine voyeurs. Fans wanting to see their favorite star was one thing, but this was ridiculous. Celebrities deserve to mourn without being made into a spectacle. To her horror, the couple began walking toward them. She leaped to her feet, her hands balled in fists of rage.

Just as she was prepared to unleash the wrath of a hurricane upon the insensitive jerks, Jeremy looked up to see the couple approaching.

The woman bent down so she and Jeremy were eye to eye. She put her hand to his cheek. "You look so much like your father. He was so proud of you."

And with just those words, the nice couple walked away.

## Chapter 39

THEY ATE A LIGHT LUNCH ON THE PATIO. As gray rain clouds encroached upon the sky, Jeremy reached across the table and took Kate's hand. "I have to talk to you about something."

Dread infiltrated her happy mood. She fought to keep her face stoic. "What is it?"

"I have to work for the next few days. It should be a simple eight-hour day."

She let out a sigh of relief. "That's it? The way you said it made me think it was something catastrophic."

He crossed his arms over his chest. "You were cheesed off when I had to work the other day."

"I wasn't upset you had to work. I was upset you promised me it would be a four-hour meeting, and you were away for twelve hours."

Jeremy reached across the table and ran the bud of his thumb over her soft cheek. "When I asked you to come with me, I never thought about how hard it'd be on you when I went back to work. I'm the only person you know in this entire country."

"Please don't set up another playdate for me! I enjoyed my time with Meredith, but…"

He chuckled. "No playdates. However, I have something for you. Hopefully, it'll stave off the boredom." He reached behind his chair and pulled out a white box with a bright red bow. He slid it across the table. "Open it."

Kate slowly lifted the lid and gasped. The box contained a Canon EOS-1D X Body Digital SLR Camera with three professional-grade lenses. "Jeremy!" she choked. "You didn't have to…"

"I remember you telling me when we were in Slate photography was your first love. You may not be able to quit your day job, but maybe you can have some fun during your downtime."

She leaned across the table and kissed him. "I love it… thank you!"

He smiled proudly. "I have a friend who is a photographer, it's what she uses."

Kate reached into the box and lifted the camera. "This is too much! I know how much this thing costs!" She'd coveted this model for years, but the camera plus all the lenses would be more than an entire month of her take-home pay as a teacher.

Jeremy waved off her objection. "My friend recommended this model. She also said she uses Adobe for her editing, so I got you a laptop and loaded the entire suite."

"You bought me a laptop with Adobe Photoshop? That program alone costs—"

"None of that," He pressed his fingers gently to Kate's lips.

Kate kissed his fingertips, then turned her attention to the white box on the tabletop. She reached inside and lifted the camera body. She cradled it next to her chest, as gently as she had her niece when she held her for the first time. Somewhere to her left, she heard Jeremy say, "I'm glad you like it."

Kate gently placed the camera back in the box. "You really know how to spoil a girl." She walked around to his side of the table and wrapped her arms around his neck. In a single motion, he pulled her onto his lap, but she didn't melt into him like she normally did. He followed her gaze, which was lustily fixed upon a white box on the tabletop. He chuckled. "You want to try out your new toy?"

Kate bit her lip. "No, I mean, cuddling like this is nice."

Jeremy playfully pushed her off his lap. "Go, take pictures."

Kate beamed. "I've waited my entire life to hear a man say those three words!"

MONDAY MORNING WHEN JEREMY rolled over, Kate was not there. He found her in the kitchen making coffee.

"Well, good morning sunshine." He said as he kissed the ticklish spot behind her ear. "Is your inner clock finally adapting to the time change?"

"No," she bubbled. "I set the alarm on my phone so I'd be up before dawn. I wanted to take pictures of the sunrise. Thank you so much for the camera. I love it!" She wrapped her arms around his neck and kissed him, appreciatively.

Jeremy pulled away from the kiss before it led to a place that would make him late for work. "Are you going to go out shooting today?"

"Yep, this thing is amazing, look at what I took this morning!" She held out the camera so he could see the view screen.

"As much as I'd love to see them, I have a meeting at eight o'clock, and I can't miss it." He wrapped his arms around her waist and pulled her tight. "I can't wait to see what you have to show me tonight, though," The double entendre was clear.

KATE SPENT THE ENTIRE MORNING and afternoon taking photographs. Around two, she realized that she hadn't eaten. She made herself a sandwich and began editing her photos on her new laptop. When she finally looked at the clock, it was after five.

Butterflies began to flutter in her stomach. Jeremy would be home soon, but she wanted to finish a few more photos before he arrived. She was proud of her work and couldn't wait to show off what she had accomplished. When Kate looked at the clock again, it was almost eight.

At eight-thirty, Jeremy walked through the door, and he was in a foul mood. He stormed to the wine rack and opened a bottle of red.

"Those effing eejits want me to 'share my story' of survival on some bloody talk show. They said it would endear me to viewers. I don't want to go on a talk show and answer questions about boking on the side of a mountain. I couldn't care less about what this does for my next film!" He took a gulp of wine. "And now, I have to make more bloody phone calls to ensure that those two jackasses don't mention this to anybody else."

Finally, he looked at Kate as if he'd just realized somebody was in the room with him. "I'm sorry, I'm just blethering about. How was your day?"

Kate put a dutiful smile on her face. "It was good. I love your gift. I got some great shots."

He gave her a quick kiss on the lips. "I want to see them when I am finished dealing with this bullshit." He called over his shoulder as he stalked toward his office. "This should only take a few minutes, I promise."

At nine Jeremy was still on the phone. By eleven, Kate was exhausted and stopped waiting for the phone call to end. She climbed into bed, alone.

## Chapter 40

TUESDAY MORNING, KATE ROLLED OVER and was pleasantly surprised to see Jeremy was beside her. He was on his phone, but when Kate roused, he said into the speaker, "I'll call you back." He clicked the end call button and looked at Kate. "I'm sorry about last night."

"What time did you get to bed?"

"Around one."

"That sounds miserable." Kate forced herself to sound cheery. "I got some awesome shots yesterday."

"I cannot wait to see them." He pushed a strand of hair behind her ear. "But first, I need to talk to you about something."

Kate felt her stomach churn. "What?"

"I have to do some traveling. There are things I committed myself to months ago. Contracts I must fulfill. Granting interviews, sitting on panels, maybe a few reshoots. I'll be in four cities in six days." He sounded exhausted just saying it.

"So, you'll be gone for even longer?" Irritation laced her voice.

"Kate, you know I'd rather be here with you, but this is my life."

"I thought it wasn't the life you wanted."

"What do you mean?"

There was an edge to her voice. "Do you remember what you told me in Slate, about why you came into the woods of West Virginia?"

Jeremy narrowed his eyes. "What does West Virginia have to do with this?"

"You said that you wanted to slow things down, not push yourself so hard." Kate threw her hands in the air. "Four cities in six days? Panels? Reshoots?"

"You don't understand," he said dismissively.

"What's so hard to understand? You're going back to the way things used to be, the way you said you hated. Have you forgotten everything you supposedly learned?" Her body was rigid, and her tone was barbed.

"You don't get it. I owe this to them."

"You owe this to whom?" Kate snapped back.

He stood from the bed. "To my fans! Without them, I'd be nobody. They made me who I am. I owe them everything."

"Bullshit! As one of your biggest fans, I can say with absolute authority: you don't owe them a damn thing!" She pressed her hands to her eyes and forced her voice into a calm tone. "They didn't make you who you are. YOU made you who you are. They may have made Jeremy Fulton, but that's not you."

Heat crept up Jeremy's neck. "What the hell does that mean? I am Jeremy Fulton!"

"No, you are Jeremy Post. You are the son of Margaret and Arthur Post." She locked Jeremy in a deliberate gaze. "You're the man who was so eager to get away from this rat race that you disappeared into the wilderness and almost died on the side of a mountain."

"You have no clue. What am I supposed to do? Look at the people who have given their hard-earned money so I can live my dream and just say bugger off, I'm sorry I don't have time for you?" He turned away and snorted. "You don't understand, you never could. You are a teacher for God's sake."

The statement hit Kate in the chest like a sledgehammer. She was used to having random citizens of her own country belittle her profession, but it was never somebody whom she cared about so deeply.

Jeremy turned to face her, but he wouldn't meet her gaze. His head hung with shame. "Kate, I'm sorry. I didn't mean…"

She swallowed back the lump forming in her throat and made her voice emotionless. "No, you're right. If I decided tomorrow to not teach, they'd replace me. My principal would hire a new teacher, and somebody else would teach algebra to a group of high schoolers. I don't have a publicist, manager, or cast mates depending on my performance. Nobody will miss their mortgage or not be able to send their kids to college if I leave my profession."

"I'm sorry. I'm an arse."

Kate raised her chin. "This isn't about me."

"It's not about me either." Jeremy sat on the bed and put his head in his hands. "If I'm scheduled to be somewhere, and I cancel, people lose money. I'm not talking publicists, managers, other actors. I'm talking about the vendor selling beer, the parking attendants, restaurants near the venue. They all lose money, and it'll be my fault. I let them down. They lose because of me."

Though his insensitive words still stung, Kate saw that behind the words was a wounded creature, a scared animal who had come out of the corner fighting. She'd had the misfortune of being the one who'd opened the cage door. She put her bruised ego aside. "That's a lot of responsibility on one set of shoulders."

"Don't do that. Don't be empathetic and sweet after I just acted like a world-class jackass."

She sat beside him. "Would it help if I said something bitchy?"

"No" He lay his head in her lap. "I'm going to miss you."

Kate's heart skipped a beat. She knew she missed him when she was spending time alone in his huge home, but it never occurred to her he missed her too. She brushed her knuckles along his cheek. "When do you have to leave?"

"The day after tomorrow, early in the morning."

She made her voice playful. "So, you can take me to the coast?"

"Anything you like." He kissed her lightly. "I'm all yours for the next thirty-six hours."

KATE TOOK FULL ADVANTAGE OF Jeremy's promise. By noon they were dressed and vagabonding across the Scottish countryside. Though she was still nervous about paparazzi or fans with cellphones, the desire to explore with Jeremy outweighed her fears.

Luckily, it ended up being a non-issue. Jeremy, who was famous for his thick, luscious hair and cute dimpled chin, now sported a full beard and shaved scalp. Hardly anybody gave him a second glance, and those who did paid no mind to Kate. She told herself perhaps being a plain Jane had its perks.

After their first evening of sightseeing, they sat in a dark corner of a cafe enjoying Cranachan, Kate's new favorite dessert. As Jeremy paid the tab, Kate walked up and down the cobblestone patio and watched the stars twinkle. Suddenly, she felt a tug on her shirttail and a soft voice ask, "Mummy?"

Kate spun around to see a round cherub face with chocolate ice cream smeared across his chin. Tears brimmed in the child's gray eyes as terror crossed his face. "You're not my mummy!" he whimpered.

Kate knelt, so that she was on eye level. "I'm not, but I'll help you find her. What's your name?"

Just as the boy began to answer, Kate heard a frantic voice behind her. "Brian! There you are!" A woman with mousy brown hair and exhausted eyes ran toward them. When she was within arm's length, she dropped to her knees and the boy leaped into her arms. "Don't you EVER do that again!" she half scolded; half cried.

The mother raised her eyes to meet Kate's, but then her brow wrinkled, and she cocked her head to the side. The boy turned to see what had grabbed his mother's attention. His eyes became saucer wide. "Mum!" he gasped. "That's Inspector Patrick Beth!"

Kate turned to see Jeremy standing behind her.

The boy piped up, "I told you he was real. You told me he was pretend!"

"No, honey, that's—"

The boy turned to Jeremy. "Are you here in secret, is that why you have a beard and no hair?"

Jeremy dropped to one knee and made a motion for the boy to come closer. Without waiting for permission from his mother, the boy sprinted toward Jeremy and jumped into his arms. They began to whisper in hushed tones.

The boy's ice cream smeared face lit up like a firefly. He bounced on the balls of his feet as Jeremy stood and loudly asked, "Think you can do that for me Deputy Inspector?"

"Yes, sir," the boy saluted then bounded back to his mom. Before she could even respond, the boy grabbed her hand and dragged her in the other direction. As they turned the corner, Kate could still hear the boy's excited chatter about spies and capturing bad guys.

Tears stung her eyes. In a previous life, she dreamed of watching her husband kneeling to share secrets and laugh with their children. Now she just chalked it up to another unfulfilled wish. As they walked to their hotel, the heaviness bore down upon her. It stayed with her as they changed into warmer clothes and headed to the flower garden with a bottle of wine. Jeremy pulled her onto a bench beside him. "Do you want to talk about it?"

Kate sighed heavily. "It was just watching you with the boy, it made me realize..." she paused. "That'll never be my life."

"What will never be your life?"

"Children," she exhaled.

He put his arm around her shoulders. "Can you not..."

Kate shook her head. "I had some issues when I was in my twenties. It's not a happy story." She shook her head as if trying to force the memory away. "I've made my peace with it, most of the time anyway." She forced herself to look at him. "How about you? Do you want children?"

"I was a dad." His face became as hard as granite. "Well, I was for about six months. Meghan was pregnant. Somehow we kept it hidden from the media." He laughed a laugh that teetered between pride and agony. "We were having a girl, a daddy's princess. Her name was Quin. I was so excited. I started buying pink stuff every chance I could. It all was online. God forbid a photographer was to see me in a store buying little pink booties." Tears filled his eyes. "Everything was wonderful for the first twenty-five weeks. Then one evening, I got home and found her sitting in the loo. There was blood everywhere. After she got home from the procedure, everything was different. She was different. Things weren't exactly good before, but she became cruel." He swallowed hard. "That's when she left me."

"I'm so sorry," Kate whispered.

"I told her we could try again, that the doctors said it was just a freak stroke of bad luck. I literally got on my knees and begged her to stay."

Kate swallowed hard, now she understood why he'd been so cold in the parsonage. He had begged one woman to stay, and she had ripped out his heart.

A tear rolled down his cheek and disappeared into his beard. "The worst thing is that she told me she was happy Quinn was dead because it was better she die than have me as a father."

Kate gasped. How in the world could one human being say that to another? The mere thought of how much pain that comment brought Jeremy made her own chest hurt. She took his hand. "My god, I am so sorry."

He shook his head, as if coming out of a trance. "You're only the second person to know that story. I told dad, and when he died, I thought nobody else would ever know. But there is something about you, Kate, something safe."


BEFORE EITHER WAS READY, Thursday morning reared its ugly head. They had coffee on the patio and when it was time; she kissed him goodbye.

Kate knew herself well enough to know that if she allowed the melancholy of missing Jeremy to set in, it'd take hold and fester into resentment. She grabbed her camera and began occupying her brain with a macro project she'd been planning.

When Jeremy's plane sat down in Cardiff, he called Kate and detailed how the moment he set foot on the plane Phil had bombarded him with a grueling schedule. She could hear the exhaustion and frustration in his words. Though she hated that he had left her all alone, there was no way she could resent him when he was clearly more miserable than she was. Late that night, when he finally made it back to his hotel room, he called again. They talked until both were too tired to speak.

Friday, Jeremy periodically sent selfies of himself with other actors, and Kate would reply with witty comments. During the day, her photography was enough to keep her mind occupied, but when she climbed into bed at night, the loneliness was impossible to ignore.

## Chapter 41

SATURDAY MORNING, KATE STARED at herself long and hard in the mirror. Dark bags under her eyes told the narrative of a night filled with nightmares and tears. "They were just dreams," she said to her reflection. "Nan and Penny are safe, they are fine."

It wasn't just the dreams that had taunted her. The Claudius-like Voice poured poison in her ear until the wee hours of the morning, "You're selfish for leaving Nan. You're a horrible daughter, a horrible friend. Wait until the tabloids start to dig into the past of the fat woman hanging out with Jeremy Fulton, all your dirty secrets will be revealed."

Kate had battled these demons long enough to know she could not do this on her own. She calculated the time change, and decided to call her psychiatrist in Leesburg. She unlocked her phone and saw that Jeremy had texted her:

*Kate. Being sent on location for a shoot. I may not have cell phone service. Should be home Tuesday, will text when I can.*

"Great," she grumbled. "Just what I need, more time alone." She scrolled through her contacts until she found the number of her doctor. Luckily, even though it was Saturday, she was able to talk to one of the physician assistants who she knew well. He offered to call something into the local pharmacy and gave her the advice she knew he'd give: Get busy and stay busy.

Kate hung up, grabbed her laptop, and obsessively planned out her days until Jeremy returned. Feeling better now that she had a plan, she picked up one of the credit cards Jeremy had left for her. A smile quickly spread across her face. It was a prepaid credit card with her name on it. On the back was a post-it-note with tidy, slanted handwriting, "I put 15,000 Euro on the card. Text me if you need more. Feel free to wander, but please don't get lost."

She shot off a quick text of appreciation and called the number for a cab. After a quick stop at the pharmacy, she directed the driver to the Glasgow Necropolis, a thirty-seven-acre cemetery that was the resting place for over fifty-thousand souls. Like in the US, she found an eerie peacefulness among the graves. She walked among the intricate monuments. There were full statues of men on horseback, intricately carved columns, and obliques that seemed to puncture the clouds. At the end of a winding pathway, she found a grave surrounded by weeping angels. The statues were so lifelike, she could swear they moved when she averted her eyes. Kate read the headstone, the deceased had been a doctor, but she could not make out any other information.

On Sunday she got busy straight away, uploading and editing the photos she had taken the day before. Around noon, she received a text from Jeremy: *Was able to find a spotty signal. Hope all is well. Reshoots are hell. I'll be home Tuesday.*

TUESDAY MORNING, AS SOON AS THE sun was up, Kate was out of bed. With every creak of the floorboard, every scratch of a tree limb on a window, her heart skipped a beat and her eyes darted toward the front door. Around noon, she received a text: *Things took longer, won't be home until late tonight. Don't wait up*

## Chapter 42

TUESDAY NIGHT, KATE CRIED AS SHE climbed into the empty bed. She awoke every hour to see if Jeremy had slipped in beside her, but his side of the bed remained empty. When the first rays of light streamed through the window, he still hadn't returned.

Irrational betrayal burned in her chest. He'd promised, and he lied. What had happened? Then, with a slight-of-hand slicker than any magician, fear replaced the anger. A million scenarios played in her mind, each more gruesome than the last. A plane crash, a distracted driver crossing the centerline, a drowsy chauffeur veering off a steep incline.

She grabbed her phone and punched in the security code. No texts, no calls. She dialed his number and heard a muted ringing come from downstairs.

*You and your overactive imagination*, she berated herself as she rushed down the stairs. She rounded the corner to the living room and saw Jeremy's head peeking above the top of the couch. She ran to where he was sitting and wrapped her arms around his neck. "I'm so glad you're home. I missed you so much!"

Jeremy didn't return the hug, in fact, he didn't move at all.

"Jeremy?" Kate stiffened. "Jeremy, what's wrong? Is everybody okay? Is Meredith okay? Did something happen on the set?"

He shook his head as if trying to clear a mental fog. "I'm just tired."

Kate looked at him carefully. Worry lines dug into his brow and his complexion was pale. There was something in his eyes that she couldn't identify, and it made her chest tighten. She crawled off his lap and onto the couch cushion beside him. "Why don't you go upstairs and lay down?"

He nodded. "You should come with me." Usually, that statement would make Kate's heart race, but now it made her blood run cold. She'd never heard him use this tone of voice; it sounded empty, emotionless, hollow.

She followed him up the stairs and into the bedroom. Jeremy sat on the side of the bed where he usually slept, the part of the bed that was still made. He put his head in his hands and remained silent.

Kate asked timidly, "Do you want to be left alone?"

He didn't look up. "You need to stay."

Kate's stomach felt like a cement mixer, sharp gravel churning and slicing her from the inside. She crossed to the bed and sat far enough away that no part of them was touching, but close enough he could reach out for her if he wanted.

"I need to tell you something." He took a ragged breath. "When I was in Dallas, I got a phone call from my ex-wife, Meghan."

Kate didn't reply.

"After she left here, after she left me, she spent several weeks in the hospital."

"Oh my God, is she all right?"

"It was a psychiatric hospital." Jeremy's voice was tired, like just saying the words drained him. "She said that the day she left she had to fight the urge to swerve into oncoming traffic. She hated herself, and she wanted to die. She made it to her mom's home, and her mom drove her to the psychiatric hospital." He finally took his head from his hands, but he refused to look at Kate. "She had to check in as a Jane Doe so nobody would know who she was, so the press wouldn't know."

Kate sat in silence, waiting for him to continue.

"Her doctors diagnosed her as having acute anxiety and bipolar disorder. She stayed for a few weeks, then saw the doctors and therapists outpatient. She's still seeing them. She may never stop seeing them."

The narrative was all too familiar to Kate. She swallowed hard. "I see."

"She doesn't want to come home or fix things. She said she's sorry, that it wasn't really her. She said she hates herself for all the pain that she caused me, but she doesn't want to be with me." A tear slid down Jeremy's cheek and disappeared into his beard. "She is actually with somebody else, some bloke she met in therapy. Her lawyers are drawing up the paperwork for a speedy divorce so that they can get married as soon as it is finalized."

Kate wanted to reach out to him, but her arms were glued to her sides. "Jeremy, I don't know what you want me to say."

"I don't know what I want you to say. It's unfair for me to even ask you to listen."

Kate looked at the ceiling in a failed attempt to keep the tears from flowing. It hurt so badly seeing Jeremy, a man she cared for so deeply, in pain. She wanted to reach out to comfort him. She wanted to run away and pretend none of this was happening. She wanted to scream at him, "How dare that bitch even call you!"

But no matter what she wanted, she knew there was only one thing she could do, even if it meant ripping out her own heart. She said the only three words she could get out before the tears came. "I'm going home."

Jeremy turned to look at her. His face was a mixture of confusion and horror. "You're what?"

"I can't stay, you need to work out your feelings about Meghan, and I can't be here for that."

Jeremy's face reddened. "I don't know what the bloody hell I have to work out. She has already moved on to somebody else." Tears spilled down his cheeks.

"I know."

Jeremy stood and paced across the room. "When I got down on my knees and begged her to stay, she said our Quin was better dead than to have me as a father."

Kate balled her hands into fists to keep from reaching out to him. "Nothing will ever be able to erase those words, but..." Kate exhaled heavily. "She was ill."

"What kind of illness makes you say such horrible things?" Jeremy roared.

Kate shrank back at his raised voice. "Mental illness," she whispered.

"That's just—"

"You still love her." Kate interrupted.

"What makes you think that?"

"Because we are having this conversation." Saying the words hurt Kate's heart.

"You know nothing!" he spat.

"Why did you fall in love with her in the first place?"

"Because she was kind, and sweet, and loving, she made me feel like I was the only man alive. But sometimes she was so angry. She was jealous of my costars, she accused me of cheating. It got so much worse when she got pregnant. I hardly knew her. Then when we lost Quin, she just turned hateful."

Kate mumbled to herself. "Classic bipolar."

"How do you know?"

Kate shook her head as she ignored the question. "I need to go home."

"So, you're just going to walk out on me too?" There was an angry edge to his voice that hurt almost as much as his words.

Kate's chin quivered. "I know you're upset. But I'm not going to fight with you."

Jeremy's shoulders sank with defeat. "You're right. That was unfair." He sat on the bed and buried his face in his hands. "But what about us? What about what we have? Are you just going to walk away from this?"

Kate let her tears fall freely. "We both knew this moment would come, that we would lose each other."

Jeremy started to protest, but Kate held up her hand to stop him. "You live here, in Scotland, I don't even live on the same continent. I've loved the past few days of being a tourist, but this could never be my life." She looked around the expansive bedroom. "I have no desire to move here, and I'd never ask you to move to America." She looked at him tenderly. "When this began, from the very first kiss, we both knew that this moment was coming."

"It doesn't have to come!"

"Are you willing to live in Virginia, to have to travel back and forth across the Atlantic between work and home?"

Jeremy was silent.

"You know it too; you just didn't want to admit it. It's why you didn't come to bed last night."

"I have breaks between shoots, you have a summer vacation. We can make it work."

"What happens in ten, twenty years? You're still traveling the world for shoots. I'm still in Virginia teaching. We see each other for a few days every three months. That isn't what I want in a life partner, and neither do you."

"What about love concurs all, love is all you need, all that shite Hollywood sells in those movies?"

"We both know that those tropes aren't true, but even if they were, what we have isn't love."

Jeremy looked like she had slapped him across the face. Her voice trembled as she continued, "You've only seen the best of me, and I've only seen the best of you. We haven't seen each other's dark side. The side we hide from only the most intimate people. Only after you have seen somebody at their very worst, the ugliest person they can be, and you STILL want to be with them. Then you can say you love them.

Only after the excitement wears off and daily routine becomes so boring it's unbearable, and you still want them by your side, then you can say it is love." She looked into his eyes. "What we have is amazing, it's passionate, it's the most powerful thing I've felt for a long, long time, but it's not love."

"You're wrong. I know you. It may not be love yet, but I know you."

Kate shook her head. "No, you don't. You know who I project myself to be."

"So, who the hell has been sleeping beside me for the past three weeks?"

"She's only the best part of me, not the whole me." Kate took a painful pause then continued, "I've told you so much, but even now, I keep part of myself hidden." She lowered her eyes in shame. "I used to be somebody ugly, somebody I was ashamed of being. I was mean, I was manipulative and controlling. I hurt a lot of good people. Part of the reason Nan and Penny are so important to me is because at my ugliest, when I hated myself and thought the world would be better off without me in it, they never wavered. I tried, I pushed them away, I hurt them, but they stayed loyal. You said you are a Marvel fan, are you familiar with the villain Killgrave?"

"He was one of my favorite villains, a master of mind control."

Kate nodded. "He could make his victims do things they didn't want to do. It was doubly vicious because his victims had the cognition to realize what they were doing, but they were unable to stop themselves. I remember one scene where he made a person commit suicide. You see him trying to resist, trying desperately to overpower that evil voice in his head, but he was helpless. He was a victim, not only of Killgrave, but of himself." Kate forced a sad smile. "When I would say and do things that hurt people whom I loved, it was like I was watching myself in the third person. I didn't want to do the things I was doing, but that villain in my head kept pushing me and pushing me. I'm ashamed of the person I was. I am ashamed of the things I did. I am ashamed of a lot."

"But that isn't who you are now."

Kate finally raised her eyes. "I know. I got help. I spent almost two weeks in a hospital after I chased an entire bottle of ibuprofen with a fifth of vodka. They diagnosed me as being bipolar."

"I don't understand. You are nothing like Meghan was."

"I'm nothing like her NOW, but I used to be exactly like her. I found great doctors, and I'm chemically balanced. The reason I insisted on stopping by my apartment was so I could get the medication that prevents me from becoming that villain again. The medicine that keeps Killgrave at bay." She took a deep breath. "I know exactly how Meghan hurt you because I hurt others in the same way."

Kate tried to make her voice lighter. "Do you remember when I asked you why you came to Riverside at the time that you came, that there had to be a reason?"

Jeremy nodded weakly.

Kate put her hand on his knee. "Maybe the reason I found you half-conscious on the side of a mountain was because I've battled the same demons as your ex-wife. I was the one person who could help you understand, help you heal."

He crossed his arms over his chest. "And now you are leaving, too." Kate could see the pain behind the thin veil of anger. "If you want me to beg you to stay, you're going to be disappointed."

"I would never want you to beg. What I am asking for is so much harder. I'm asking you to let me go." Kate shook her head. "I know you may not understand, but I know myself well enough to know I can't handle this type of isolation. I need to be around my family, I need to go home."

"And I need to be alone." He stormed from the room.

The moment the door closed, grief and pain slammed into Kate like a freight train. She wrapped her arms around her knees and sobbed. Her heart hurt so badly that she thought it would leap out of her chest and die in front of her. She sobbed until she had no more tears to cry. Finally, she dragged herself into the bathroom and looked in the mirror. Her eyes were swollen, her skin was red, her nose was still running. She leaned against the marble vanity and stared herself in the eye. "This is the right thing to do," she told herself. "It's the only thing you can do."

# Epilogue

## March 14, 2016

A GIRL WITH BUBBLEGUM PINK HAIR and a Hello Kitty t-shirt stood with her hands on her hips. "So, you won't let me do extra credit?"

Kate did her best to keep her voice calm. "I'll make a deal with you, Jenny. Why don't you do all the actual assignments from the quadratics unit, and then we can talk about extra credit."

The teen crinkled up her face like she had just smelled week old garbage. "That's like, eight homework assignments."

"Actually, nine."

Jenny set her jaw. "I'll think about it." She grabbed her backpack from her chair and stormed toward the door.

Kate pinched the bridge of her nose and wondered if she still had ibuprofen hidden in her desk. She was searching through the drawers when a petite woman wearing an orange cardigan appeared in the doorway. "That sounded like a fun conversation."

"Hey Debbie." Kate collapsed into her chair. "Can you believe, I had the audacity to suggest she try to earn the assigned credit before I give her EXTRA credit."

The woman's powder blue eyes grew wide with fake horror. "You monster!"

"That's what they call me, the Thorn amongst the roses."

Debbie laughed. "I don't even want to know what they call me."

"All the kids love you. You are everybody's favorite—" A melodic ringtone interrupted her thought. Kate held up one finger as she dug her phone out of her purse.

"Is it important?" Debbie asked.

Kate looked at the screen. It wasn't a number she recognized. "Nope," she said as she hit the silence button.

"Probably a telemarketer," Debbie said. "How was the rest of your—"

Kate's phone rang again. She looked at the screen, it was the same number. "Wonder who this is and why they want to reach me so badly."

"Perhaps you should answer it."

Kate shrugged and hit the talk icon. "Hello."

The caller was a man with a very distinct, British accent. "Ah, yes, is this Kate Thorn?"

Kate almost dropped her phone. "Why would you...what do you want?" She stammered.

"So, sorry, I should have introduced myself right away. This is William, Kate and I met this summer. Is this she?"

Kate's stomach turned to ice. She must have looked frightful because Debbie rushed to her side. "Is everything okay?"

Kate nodded weakly then said into the phone. "I remember meeting you."

"Kate, I don't quite know how to start this conversation—"

She cut him off. "Is it Jeremy, is he okay?"

Kate felt Debbie grab her shoulder. She was Kate's person at work, the only one who knew about her summer romance and trip to Scotland.

Will laughed. "Jeremy is fine. In fact, he asked me to do a favor for him. I'm doing a show at the Kennedy Center, and he asked that I deliver something to you. Would you be willing to meet me at my hotel?"

"At your hotel?" Kate gasped, and Debbie's grip on her shoulder tightened.

Will said, "I know this is going to sound a bit odd, but there is a car waiting for you in the parking lot, a black Lincoln. The driver will bring you here."

"Hold on a second, you want me to get in a car with a complete stranger and come to your hotel." Kate collapsed into her chair. "How do I know this isn't some elaborate scheme to kidnap me and lock me in some strange British dungeon?"

Will chuckled. "That would make for an intriguing drama." Then his voice lost all traces of playfulness. "Kate, I know this is an unorthodox request. I promise you, there is no malice. Jeremy is one of my dearest friends, he asked me to do this. Please, say you will come."

Kate swallowed hard. When she had returned from Scotland, she questioned every second if she'd made the right decision. Several nights she locked her phone in her car because she didn't trust herself to not dial Jeremy's number. She was finally to the point where she didn't cry herself to sleep, where she could turn on the TV without the fear of seeing his face. Now his best friend was calling, asking that she come to his hotel room, so he could deliver a message?

She just couldn't handle ripping open that wound. "Will, you are a good friend, and I appreciate what you are doing."

"Kate," his voice was high-pitched and desperate. "Please, I promised."

Her heart softened with sympathy. "Fine, I'll be downstairs in five minutes."

"Brilliant!" Will exhaled. "I'll ring the driver and say you'll be down shortly."

KATE LOWERED HERSELF ON THE IVORY sofa in the grand suite. The plush carpet, beige walls, and crisp furnishings gave the room a sophisticated look. It was perfectly complimented by the gorgeous man with chocolate brown eyes, high cheekbones, and a dimpled chin sitting across from her.

"Thank you for coming. It is nice to see you again," Will said.

Kate sat up straight. "I don't mean to be rude, but would you please tell me what this is about?"

"Yes, of course. Jeremy asked me to deliver a message to you—"

"Why couldn't he just tell me himself? I assume he still has my number."

Will shifted uncomfortably. "Actually, there is something he wanted me to show you." He reached under the coffee table that separated them and pulled out a large silver laptop. He opened the screen and typed rapidly on the keyboard.

"You brought me here to show me your computer?" Kate asked.

Will held his finger to his lips. "Just watch."

On the screen, the image of a woman in a red pants suit came into focus. Her auburn hair was pulled into a tight bun, accentuating her porcelain skin and heart shaped face. She gave a broad smile. "Hello, I am Coleen McCoy, and this is Britain Tonight."

Kate crinkled her brow. "Who is she?"

"I think she is similar to an American you watch named Barbra Walters."

"So, she is a talk show host of some sorts."

Will shrugged. "Of sorts."

Kate turned her attention back to the screen, the camera panned out to show Coleen was not alone. Sitting across from her was a man in blue jeans and a Ramones t-shirt. Kate broke out into a cold sweat, and tears filled her eyes. "Jeremy," she gasped. "Why are you doing this to me?"

Will reached across the table and took her hand. "It's not to bring you pain, I promise." He urged softly. "Just watch."

Kate forced herself to look at the screen. Coleen looked into the camera. "Tonight, I am here with international celebrity, and personal friend, Jeremy Fulton."

Jeremy shifted in his seat. "Thanks Coleen. It's lovely to be here."

"So, Jeremy, I just wanted to start by saying that you contacted me and asked to do this interview."

Jeremy smiled. "And you were gracious enough to oblige."

"You're one of my oldest friends in the business, as well as one of today's hottest celebrities. It would have been not only selfish, but also stupid to turn down an exclusive interview."

Jeremy's eyes twinkled. "I don't think you'll be disappointed."

Coleen leaned closer. "So, Jeremy, you're known as one of the hardest working men in the business. Can I assume that you came here tonight to talk about your next big project?"

"Actually, there is no next big project."

Coleen couldn't hide her surprise. "Really?"

He looked directly into the camera. "No, I came here to say something more important."

Kate's heart began to race. The intensity in his eyes made her feel as if she could touch him, like Jeremy, and not a computer screen, was sitting five feet in front of her. She gripped the couch cushion to prevent herself from reaching out for him.

"A year ago, I lost my father. Losing him broke me to my core. I had trouble sleeping, eating, even breathing hurt. The crushing pressure from the press, paparazzi, fame itself threatened to shatter me. So, I escaped. I flew to a remote location where nobody would know who I was and disappeared into the wilderness."

Coleen sat back in shock. "Where did you go?"

"I prefer not to say. However, when I was in this beautiful place, I was gravely injured. The locals took me in, treated my wounds, and cared for me like I was one of their own. I owe these people my life, literally. If not for them and the kindness they showed me, I would not be sitting here today."

Coleen leaned forward and touched Jeremy's knee. Kate could sense that she had forgotten cameras were rolling, true concern was evident in her face. "Why didn't you say something?"

Jeremy shook his head. "Because it took me a long time to process what had happened."

"And now?"

Jeremy gave a dry laugh. "You'd think a near death experience would be a wakeup call. That when I returned to my home, I would change my ways, amend my routine, focus on what was important. But within weeks of being back in Scotland, I had forgotten everything I swore I'd never forget. I went back to eighteen-hour days, red eye flights, wearing myself tissue thin. It amazes me how quickly I devolved back into the man I didn't want to be."

"That's why you wanted to do this interview, to talk about your personal revelations?"

Jeremy smiled and shook his head. "No, I want to announce my retirement."

Coleen let out a gasp. "What? You are the most popular actor in all of England if not the world?"

"Coleen, life is short, short and so very precious. I can no longer dish out myself to everybody and have nothing left for me. Life is too fleeting to not spend it with the people you love."

"I get that, but… but what do you say to your fans that love you?"

"What do I say to my fans?" Jeremy looked squarely into the camera. "I say thank you. Thank you for allowing some stupid bloke who can memorize a few lines to live his dream. Thank you for your emails, letters, and admiration." He ran his fingers through his hair. "But do not waste your love on me. Love is too precious a commodity to waste on some guy on the telly. Appreciate me, enjoy me, but I do not deserve your love. Love the person sitting on the couch next to you. Love your parents before it is too late. Love your kids with everything you have. And if you are lucky enough to fall in love with another human being, don't let them go."

Kate reached out and slammed the computer shut. She shot to her feet and turned on Will like a bobcat on a rabbit. "You sadistic bastard! Do you get some perverse sense of satisfaction from watching people have their hearts ripped out?"

Will cowered back against the cushions. "Kate, I swear, that is not what this is—"

"You have no idea how much it killed me to walk away from Jeremy in Scotland. How all I wanted to do was to melt into a puddle at his feet and beg him to choose me over his career. How many nights I have cried myself to sleep. Now you ambush me at my work, bring me to a hotel room so that you can watch me get my..." A sob escaped her mouth.

"Listen, there is something else I need to show you." He stood from the couch and sprinted toward the bedroom.

"Don't bother. I'm leaving!" She marched toward the exit and reached for the doorknob.

"Kate, please don't go."

Her hand stopped mid-reach. The voice that had just spoken did not belong to Will. It was a deep baritone with a Scottish accent.

She spun around to see Jeremy standing in the hallway. His messy dark locks had grown back, he was clean-shaven, and his eyes... those crystal blue eyes. The room began to spin. Kate leaned against the wall to keep herself from collapsing.

In four long strides, Jeremy was across the room. "Kate?"

He reached to embrace her, but she held up her hands. "Don't touch me."

Jeremy looked as if the words had slapped him across the face. "Okay. I won't touch you, but will you please listen?"

"Why?" She covered her face with her hands. "What can you possibly say?"

"Kate when you walked out —"

Her hands flew from her face, revealing an angry scowl. "I didn't walk out on you!" The accusation helped her find her voice. "I let you go, and it was one of the hardest things I have ever done."

Jeremy reached for her hand, and she didn't pull away. He placed her palm to his cheek. "I know. It was one of the most authentic and caring things anybody has ever done for me."

"Why are you here? I don't know if I can let you go again."

"Then don't."

She fought to keep her voice level. "Have you forgotten everything we discussed that day, about how we can never make our worlds combine? What about the fact that I don't want to quit teaching and move to Scotland? What about the fact that if you gave up acting for me, you'd resent me for the rest of your life?"

"Those things are still true," he said.

"I don't understand."

"I wanted you to see the interview so that you would know that I'm not giving anything up for you. I'm giving it up, for me. Kate, all of those lessons I supposedly learned in the cave, in Slate, in Riverside, the moment I was back in my world I forgot every single one. I jumped back into my old life, and I was as miserable as I was before. I don't want that life anymore. I want to be able to go to the café for a drink and not have it be a press conference. I want to sleep in my own bed for more than two nights in a row." He rubbed his thumb over her cheekbone. "I'm not giving it up for you. I'm walking away for me."

Kate pulled away slightly. "What about Meghan?"

Jeremy dropped his gaze. "You were right, part of me still loved her. Perhaps part of me always will, but what she and I had never was grounded in reality."

Kate scoffed. "What we had wasn't exactly grounded either. We were together for a very tumultuous, emotionally heightened time. That is not enough to base a..."

"Base what? Kate, I'm not asking you to marry me or to give up everything to return to Scotland with me. All I'm asking for is a chance."

"What are you going to do, pack up everything and move to Virginia to be my boyfriend?"

"No, I am going to rent a nice little villa on the Shenandoah River and spend the next year of my life writing. After decades of acting out somebody else's stories, I want to finally tell a story of my own. There is so much up here." He tapped his temple. "So much that I have wanted to say, but I never had the time to put it on paper. And the amazing thing is, I can write from anywhere. I can write in Scotland, I can write in Virginia, I can write in Slate if you want."

"You want to write?" Kate asked.

Jeremy nodded. "I didn't realize how badly I wanted to tell my own stories, but the words... they're inside me; they have to get out."

"What if you miss acting?"

"Then I will go back to it in moderation. It may again be a part of my life, but it never again will be my life." He took her hand. "When you left, you told me that what we had wasn't love. Only after the excitement wears off, and daily routine becomes so boring it's unbearable, and you still want them by your side, then you can say it's love. I can't give you any guarantees, but I can promise you that if I were ever to be content with a boring, day to day life, it would be with you." He pushed a piece of hair behind her ear. "I don't want to look back on this moment and wonder what might have been."

Kate felt her knees go weak. However, now instead of leaning back against the cold door jamb for support, she leaned forward, against Jeremy's chest. She pressed her cheek against his shirt and let the tears flow. "I missed you so much."

He wrapped his arms around her and pulled her closer. "You don't have to miss me anymore."

Made in the USA
Middletown, DE
29 July 2021